THE WHITON FAMILY
IN AMERICA

THE BRONZE TABLET MARKING THE DUAL GRAVE OF JOHN BLOXHAM AND JOHN WHITTON IN MAGDALEN CHAPEL, MERTON COLLEGE, OXFORD

From a drawing in the College Library

THE WHITON FAMILY

IN AMERICA

THE GENEALOGY

OF THE

DESCENDENTS OF THOMAS WHITON (1635)

COMPILED BY
AUGUSTUS SHERRILL WHITON
OF NEW YORK

WILDSIDE PRESS

EDITION OF 400 COPIES
Printed for Subscribers only

1 9 3 2

PRINTED IN U. S. A.

By E. E. DARROW, Printer, New London, Conn.

FOREWORD

THE Whiton Family Association is the outgrowth of meetings held by a group of cousins who had previously organized the Stephen and Abigail (Byles) Whiton Association. These gatherings developed an increasing interest in family history and genealogy and in the summer of 1925 other branches of the Whiton family were invited to meet with them at Westford, the ancestral home of the family in Connecticut. After a picnic luncheon and an interesting program, the desirability of forming a larger association to include descendants of Thomas Whiton of Hingham, Massachusetts, the first of the name in America, was discussed. Opinion was unanimously favorable and a committee was chosen to consider the subject and report at a meeting to be held the following year.

The Organization Committee consisted of Lucius E. Whiton of New London, Conn., William H. Hall of West Hartford, Conn., Miss Emily J. Chism and Miss Abigail D. Amidon of Westford, Conn., Frank Warren Whiton of Hartford, Conn., and Mrs. Julia B. (Chism) Gowdy of Hazardville, Conn. This committee later appointed a Genealogical Committee to gather data and prepare a mailing list of Whiton descendants. Members of the Genealogical Committee were Miss Emily J. Chism, Chairman; Miss Ellen J. Whiton of Waterbury, Conn., Miss Jennie E. Whiton of Hazardville, Conn., John M. Whiton of Plainfield, N. J. (since deceased), Dr. Walter H. Whiton of Neshanic Station, N. J., Glenville W. Whiton of Erie, Pa., Dr. Ernest A. Back of Washington, D. C., Frederick J. Whiton of New York City, Miss Flora E. Whiton of Los Angeles, Cal., and Mrs. Mary F. (Whiton) Shipman of New London, Conn.

The report of the Organization Committee was presented at a meeting of Whiton kindred held July 3, 1926, at Hartford, Conn., in a series of resolutions which were adopted, thus forming the Whiton Family Association, whose objects were to be the promotion of acquaintance and sociability among members of the family and the collection and preservation of genealogical data. Frank Warren Whiton was elected the first President with three Vice-Presidents, William H. Hall, Glenville W. Whiton, and Mrs. Julia B. Gowdy. Mrs. Mary F. W. Shipman was elected Secretary and Lucius E. Whiton was chosen Treasurer. The Genealogical Committee was continued. An Executive Committee, consisting of the officers and three additional members was elected to prepare By-laws for the Association and present them at the next meeting for which they were directed to make arrangements. The three members elected to this committee were Gilbert W. Amidon of Stafford Springs, Conn., Mrs. Anna L. (Chism) Dawley of Norwich and Miss Alice R. Gillette of Hartford.

September 1, 1928, the Whiton Association met in New London, Conn. At this meeting the By-laws were adopted. These fixed the name of The Whiton Family Association, with eligibility to all descendants of James and Mary (Beal) Whiton of Hingham, Massachusetts; re-stated the two objects previously given; named officers, and two standing committees—Executive and Genealogical; decided upon one meeting each year for the Association with a biennial election of officers. No annual dues were authorized, funds to meet the necessary expenses to be raised by voluntary contributions at the meetings or in some manner to be determined by the Executive Committee.

The work done by the Genealogical Committee revealed much interest in the preparation of a Whiton Genealogy. It also developed that A. Sherrill Whiton of New York City was already actively engaged in the compilation of such a volume. It was decided to cooperate in this work and that the Association sponsor the publication of the book when ready. To that end a Publication Committee was appointed with power to take such action as might be necessary. Lucius E. Whiton, Chairman; A. Sherrill Whiton and George F. Leary of Springfield, Mass., were the members of this committee. For business purposes the "Whiton Family Association, Inc.," was incorporated under the laws of the State of Connecticut January 4, 1929.

The proof sheets have been read carefully for typographical errors but some mistakes may be found and the Secretary requests notification if such instances are discovered. See also a further statement on page 202.

Without registration and payment of dues it is difficult to number the membership of the Association. The Secretary's mailing list now (1932) carries about 300 names but in many cases one name represents an entire family.

Present (1932) officers of the Association are: President, Dr. Walter H. Whiton of Neshanic Station, N. J.; Vice-Presidents, Mrs. Anna L. Dawley of Norwich, Conn., George F. Leary of Springfield, Mass., and Gilbert W. Amidon of Stafford Springs, Conn.; Secretary, Mrs. Mary F. W. Shipman of New London; Treasurer, Lucius E. Whiton of New London. Other members of the Executive Committee are William H. Hall of West Hartford, Conn., Miss Emily J. Chism of Westford, Conn., and Frank W. Whiton of Hartford. The Genealogical Committee is Miss Emily J. Chism of Westford, A. Sherrill Whiton and Louis C. Whiton of New York City, Dr. Ernest A. Back of Washington, D. C., and Mrs. Mary F. W. Shipman of New London.

M. F. W. S.

THE ENGLISH WHITON FAMILY

Some information obtained in England by John M. Whiton (270) of Plainfield, N. J.

A. D.

1085 **Roger Whiton, Allan deWhitting, Evereard deWhitting.** These are supposed to be father, son and grandson.

1157 **William deWhiton,** Knight of Yorkshire, Parish of Haverwood.

1195 **Hugo Whiting** of Dorset.

1207 **Magister Johanes Whiting.**

1217 **Alan deWhiting** of Yorkshire.

1279 **Sir Waterus de Wyton-Whitton,** Eng. Lord of Seaton & Merton.

1299 **Willis Whitingh,** Oxford.

1304 **Thomas & Katherine Whitton,** Meltonby & Grymethorpe, England.

1387 **Rev. John Whytton,** Merton Chaplain, Merton College. A bronze figure was found at Whitton tower and a bronze plate is in the Magdalen Chapel.

1405 **John de Whyton,** Sheriff of York, and **Henry Whyton,** principal of St. Mary's College, Oxford.

1435 Sir **Nichols Whiten, M.P.** Chosen Knight for Parliament from Devonshire. Learned in the law.

Roger Whitton of Kent. Married Mary Draycott.

John Whitton of Sarrott County Hertfordshire. Married Elizabeth Belson. Sons were Edmund, Owen, and John.

1490 **John Whitton,** Escheator in the County of Buckinghamshire.

Edmund Whitton, Sons, William and Thomas.

William Whitton, Nethercote. Married Catherine Arderne of Oxford. Sons, John, Robert, Edmund, Thomas and Henry.

1588 **Thomas Whiton,** Emigrated 1635.

CONTENTS

Title	Page
Foreword	7
English Whitons	8
Whiton Family	9
Whiton Arms	17
1st Generation	19
2d "	21
3d "	23
4th "	27
5th "	35
6th "	57
7th "	85
8th "	123
9th "	161
10th "	191
Publishers' Note	202
Cradle Roll	202
Cost of Publication	202
11th Generation	203
Amidon Family	205
Back Family	208
Chism Family	211
Ingersoll Family	213
Richards Family	215
Tuckerman Family	216
Records Not Placed	218
War Records	219, 220, 221, 222, 223
References	224
Index—Descendants	225
" —Collaterals	235
"Lost Tribes"	253
Blank Pages	259

ILLUSTRATIONS
Miscellaneous

		Page
Whitton Bronze Tablet, Oxford		4
Whitton Court		9
Hook Norton (Map)		15
Whiton Arms		16
A Family Tree		21
Old Ship Church		22
Hingham Tubs and Buckets		26
Whiton Homestead, Hingham, Mass.		27
Facsimile Signatures		27, 34, 41, 56
Tombstone Joseph Whiton	(10)	29
" Elijah Whiton	(28)	41
" General Joseph Whiton	(53)	59
" John and Mary Whiton	(55)	61
" Joseph Whiton	(60)	67
" Luther and Nancy Whiton	(105)	95
Old Cambridge Bridge		39
Piscataqua Bridge		66
Joseph Whiton House		67
Elijah " "		69
Old Center Church, Antrim, N. H.		106
Captain Joseph J. Whiting House		122
Stephen Whiton House		138
Ashbel " "		140
Whiton Memorial Library		174
Amidon Homestead		207
Chism "		212

ILLUSTRATIONS

Portraits

		Page
Joanna (Whiton) Walker		67
Israel and Dorothy Whiton	(63)	71
Edward Vernon Whiton	(103)	93
Rev. John M. and Abigail Whiton	(122)	107
Flavel Whiton	(123)	109
Chauncey Whiton	(125)	110
Rev. Samuel James Whiton		111
Frederick Whiton		115
Henry Kirke Whiton	(174)	131
Augustus Sherrill and Caroline Whiton	(178)	133
Stephen Whiton	(192)	139
Augustus Whiton	(195)	141
Sons of Heber and Marcia Whiton	(196-7-8-9-200-1)	143
David Erskine Whiton	(201)	145
James Morris Whiton	(206)	149
Col. John Chadwick Whiton	(212)	153
Starkes Whiton	(220)	155
Sylvester G. Whiton	(253)	173
Dr. Francis Henry Whiton	(259)	175
Tudor Whiton	(260)	177
Rev. James M. Whiton	(269)	182
John M. Whiton	(270)	183
Chauncey Gilbert Whiton	(278)	187
William E. Whiton	(281)	188
Royal Whiton	(285)	189
Henry Devereux Whiton	(298)	195

WHITTON COURT, Shropshire, England
(Four miles east of Ludlow.) Built 1550 - 1632

THE WHITON FAMILY

The collection of data included in the History of the Whiton family of New England is the result of the combined efforts of several widely separated individuals, who for several years worked independently in tracing their own ancestry, and eventually merged their records.

Several town histories were published during the middle and late Eighteenth Century (notably those of Hanover and Hingham, Mass.), which contained vital and other statistics of local descendants of James Whiton of Hingham. It is also recorded that a professional genealogist, as early as 1863, offered early records of the Whiton family to one of its members, but nothing definite resulted from this, as the individual to whom they were offered at that time was occupied with government work in connection with the Civil War.

In addition to the town histories, above mentioned, which included a considerable number of Whitons, individual families have had their names and statistics recorded in a large number of local town, church and graveyard records, particularly in Massachusetts, Connecticut and New York. Many of these records have been collected and republished by the better known historical, biographical and genealogical societies, and the author is particularly indebted to the Mayflower Society for what it has accomplished in this respect.

Several members of the Whiton family, including the author, while in England, have made investigations into the origin of the family in that country. The results, however, to date have not been quite as complete or definite as they might have been; but even with the information collected thus far it would appear that it would be abundantly profitable for some one to pass a few weeks in Buckinghamshire, Oxfordshire and Nottinghamshire to better verify the information already at hand, and to search for new facts of interest, particularly in connection with the political, religious and social life of our English ancestors.

The investigation of the lives of the individual members of the Whiton family shows that as a whole the family represents a fairly accurate cross-section of the development and history and early inhabitants of the English Colonies in New England. Members of the family have taken an active part in the political, religious and military life of their localities. The family has been well represented in all the wars in which the Colonies and the States have taken part, from the earliest Indian skirmishes to the World War of 1917-18. Its members have served in all the important peace-time pursuits. Shipping and navigation, agriculture, manufacturing, engineering, railroading, the arts, the educational field, the church, the legal profession, civil and political life, and philanthrophy have all been well represented.

Certain branches of the family have been imbued with the pioneering spirit, and in the early part of the Eighteenth Century were inspired with the enthusiasm and courage of the frontiersman, and moved westward to the then sparsely settled and unknown lands of central and western New York, Pennsylvania, Ohio, Illinois, Wisconsin, Minnesota, and finally Oregon, Washington and California.

The activities of the early settlers in New England were related to fishing, trading, navigation and kindred industries. The condition of the soil, and the lack of navigable rivers, which were so plentiful in the South, limited the growth of the agricultural industries and economically prevented a development of the plantation system of land exploitation. In many ways this was a blessing in disguise. Although wealth was brought to the early settlers through fur exportation, and the benevolent cod-fish, the real growth of New England has been due to its manufacturing industries, forced upon it by the poverty of the soil. The industries of the seacoast were soon overcrowded, and by the third generation we find the younger sons and daughters courageously marching inland to the fields and villages of western Massachusetts and Connecticut.

Without tracing the steps of any individual, it may be noted that the descendants of James Whiton seem to have divided themselves into three main groups: 1st: those who remained near Hingham; 2d: those who went to Connecticut, and 3d: those who went to western Massachusetts, and then moved to central and western New York, Pennsylvania, and Ohio—(the latter being then known as the Western Reserve), and to more distant points. Probably all the Whitons now residing in the western states are descendants of the group that went to Stockbridge and Lee, Massachusetts, from Ashford, Connecticut.

The greatest single group of Whitons are descendants of that strictly religious and enterprising man, Squire Elijah, of Ashford, Connecticut, who brought up fifteen children of his own, and, not satisfied with that, adopted five orphan boys, sons of his cousin, and brought them up to honorable manhood, and sent them on their way. Most of the western Whitons are descended from these five youths.

Frequently whole families, with their friends, moved with their household belongings, carried by teams of oxen, through roughly cut roads to western states, settling in small communities, establishing their churches and schools, and maintaining the traditions of their ancestors.

As was the custom in Colonial days, large families were the rule. The Whitons did their share in this respect, and although no one surpassed the record of Squire Elijah, a family of ten children was a common occurrence.

The population of the English Colonies in America increased from about 250,000 in 1649, to 17,000,000 inhabitants in 1840, of which about six per cent were foreign born, or had foreign born parents. From 1840 onward, the United States had successively the Irish, German, Jewish, Scandinavian and Mediterranean invasions. A total of 30,000,000 immigrants, or one-third of the population of the country in 1910, became resident in the United States; immigrants belonging principally to races whose religions, traditions and customs were either non-assimilable, or capable of slow assimilation. It would seem that the problem of the future is whether the families of the old traditions, the descendants of the early settlers of the United States, are going to remain in control of its destinies, or whether they are going to submit to the different standards of the newer element in our population. For these reasons, it is beneficial for us to study our ancestry, and from the early ideals strive to develop the character of our Nation according to the standards that have made it what it is.

It would seem that the Whiton family, small as it is, has done, not only its share, but more than its share in producing men and women of high calibre, of principle and of influence in their communities.

The great majority of the members of the Whiton family have had high moral standards with strong religious leanings. Most of them have been active members of some religious organization. Their connections have naturally been with the early independent churches of decentralized leadership, that were the rallying points of the Puritan thought.

The first Whitons who came to America undoubtedly made their momentous and courageous decision on account of the unbearable political and social conditions that existed in England during the reign of Charles the First. Although the emigration records state that they left England in conformity to the order and discipline of the Anglican Church, it is an accepted fact that a subterfuge was used in many cases to enable families to receive permission to emigrate to the New World; and as the emigration records differ from the Colonial records in many respects, it is reasonable to suppose that the former were in error as to the religious sentiments of the immigrants to Massachusetts. The Whitons were probably dissenters, as were most of the earlier voyagers to New England.

At any rate, the first Whitons to leave England must have been persons of ideals, who were vigorous both mentally and physically to be willing to run the risk of staking their future in a land so little known. They came of the yeomanry class,—the middle class of early English civil life,—half way between the nobility and the tillers of the soil. They were property owners in Oxfordshire and a family of liberal and independent thought, who asserted their rights and had the courage of their convictions.

The surname Whitton, or later Whiton, dates back to the earliest periods of recorded history in England. It is of Anglo-Saxon origin, and was derived from one of the several places that are called Whitton. It is of fairly common usage in England, and was undoubtedly adopted by several families as their surname as early as the Twelfth Century. The Anglo-Saxon form is *Hwit-tun,* meaning the "white farm" or "hamlet." *Hwita* was also an Anglo-Saxon word, meaning *Light* or *Fair,* and it is possible that the name means Hwita's farm or estate. It is interesting to note that the name is still pronounced as though the H was the first letter, even though this letter is now moved to the second place.

The name is found particularly in Buckinghamshire, Yorkshire, Lincolnshire, Staffordshire, Oxfordshire, Nottinghamshire, Shropshire and Norfolk. There is also a suburb to the west of London named Whitton. In Shropshire, about four miles east of Ludlow, is one of the most beautiful specimens of Elizabethan architecture in England, named Whitton Court. The existing building dates from the early Seventeenth Century; and records prove that this was preceded by an earlier building, dating from the Thirteenth Century, and was occupied by a family who derived their surname from their home.

There is another village named Whitton in Lincolnshire on the River Humber, opposite Hull, and not far from the towns of Bawtry and Scrooby, from which section the Mayflower emigrants left England for their short visit in Holland, before setting sail for the new land.

There are numerous early records of persons by the name of Whiton in the north of England. The town of Witun is mentioned in the Doomsday survey of Yorkshire. William de Whiton gave two "boucats" of land to Ravenswood Parish, and was known as the Knight of Yorkshire. He died in 1157. Sir Waterus de Wyton was Lord of the Townships of Seaton and Merton, Yorkshire. Agnes Whitton was prioress of St. Clements in the City of York. John Whytton, who died in 1387, was chaplain of Merton College, and a bronze figure of him was found in the grounds of the rectory of Whitton Tower, near the Round Tower. John de Whyton, who died in 1405, was sheriff of the City of York. Henry Whyten, who died in 1435, was principal of St. Mary Magdalen College, Oxford. Sir Nichols Whiten, M.P., was chosen Knight of Parliament from Devonshire. He was learned in the law and died in 1435.

The English home of the immediate ancestors of the original emigrant to this country has been fairly definitely traced. It is reasonable to suppose that he was at least from a family who lived in Oxfordshire, from which section of England came the great majority of the early settlers in this country.

The publication of this book has been made possible primarily through the organization in 1926 of the Whiton Family Association. It was due to this Association that the compiler has been able to collect the separate family records that have not heretofore been in print. The cost of publication was also guaranteed by members of the Association, and the author wishes to thank all those, who are too numerous to mention, who have contributed to the preparation of this work, and particularly Mr. Lucius E. Whiton of New London, Connecticut, Mr. Frank Warren Whiton of Hartford, Connecticut, Mr. George Francis Leary of Springfield, Massachusetts, Mr. Ernest Back of Washington, D. C., Miss Emily Chism of Westford, Connecticut, Mrs. John M. Whiton of Plainfield, N. J., Mr. Glenville W. Whiton of Erie, Pennsylvania, Mrs. Elva L. Whiton Parsons of Los Angeles, California, and also Mrs. Leander K. Shipman of New London, Connecticut, and Mr. Louis Claude Whiton of New York City, who have collaborated in the preparation of the book.

AUGUSTUS SHERRILL WHITON

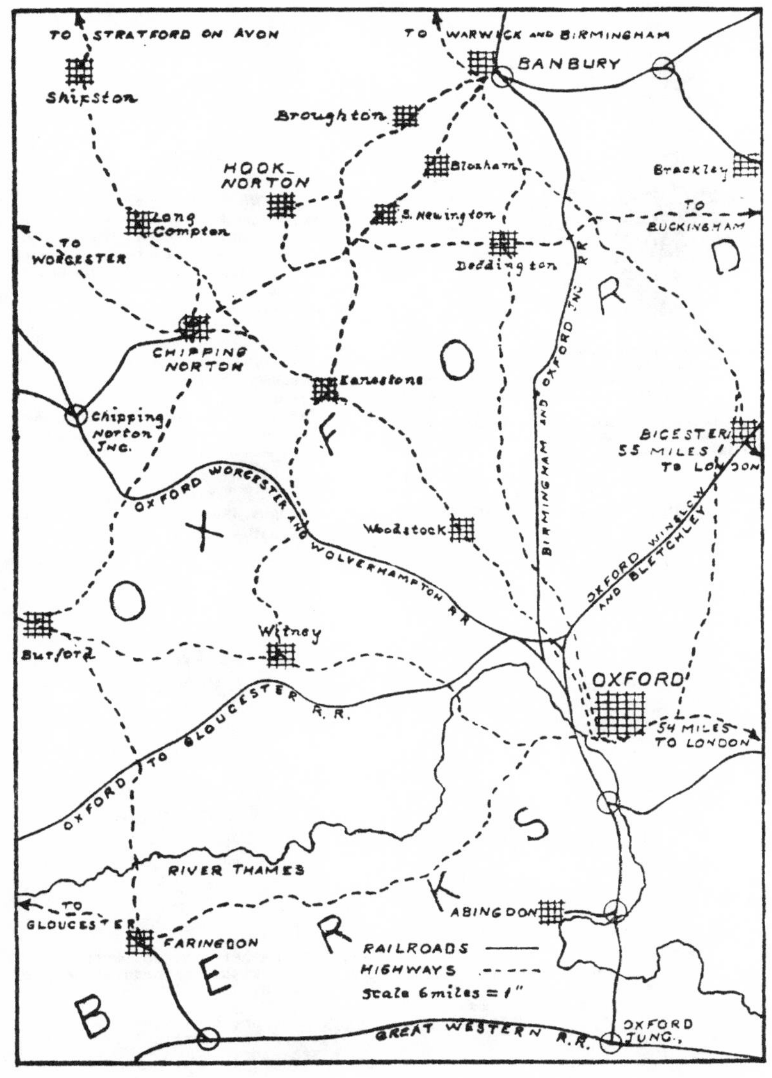

MAP OF "HOOK NORTON" AND ROADS FROM LONDON

WHITON, OR WHITING FAMILY.

Arms: Gyronny of four, az. and erm.; over all a Leopard's head, or; in chief 3 bezants.

Crest: A Lion rampant; beneath, a helmet, resting upon the shield.

WHITON, or WHITING, James, the ancestor of the families here recorded, appears in H'm., Mass., in 1647, Dec. 30th of which year, he m. Mary Beals. In his will, his name is spelled *Whiton*, and by a large number of families in H'm., it is still spelled in this way, though by others, it is spelled *Whiting*. The coat of arms handed down in the family, a copy of which is given above, agrees with that of the Whitings, as described by Burke, in his General Armory.

FIG. I
From Page 419—"Barry's History of Hanover"

THE WHITING FAMILY.

The Whitings in New England are descended from Rev. Samuel Whiting of Lynn, Mass. Cotton Mather says of him, he "drew his first breath at Boston, in Lincolnshire, November 20, A. D. 1597. His father, a person of good repute there, the eldest son among many brethren, an alderman, and sometime a mayor of the town, had three sons; the second of these was our Samuel, who had a learned education by his father bestowed upon him, first at Boston school, and then at the university of Cambridge.

By the kindness of Mr. Drake we give a cut of the arms; which are emblazoned; Party per saltire, azure and ermine, in the fesse point a leopard's face gold, in chief three besants. Crest, a lion's head erased.

FIG. II
From Pages 59 and 61—"The Heraldic Journal"—Vol. I, Boston 1865

WHITON.

THOMAS WHITON, of Hingham, Mass., 1635.

Arms—Gyronny of four azure and ermine, a leopard's head or, in chief three bezants.

Crest—A lion rampant.

FIG. III
From Page 83—"Matthew's American Armory and Blue Book"

WHITTON (Nethercott, co. Oxford) Ar. on a chev. within a bordure engr. sa. five plates.

WHITTON. Or, on a chev. sa. five plates. Crest--A ship in full sail, in a sea, ppr.

FIG. IV
From "Burke's General Armory" and "Fairbairn's Crests"—American Edition

THE WHITON ARMS

The Chairman of the Committee on Heraldry of The New England Historic Genealogical Society, in a prefatory note to its First Roll of Arms (1928—1 to 72), states that:

"The right to a Coat of Arms does not make a gentleman. But in the Seventeenth Century arms, as a rule, were borne by those who had risen into the gentry class. For example, every one of the fifty-nine Regicides who signed the King's death warrant also sealed it with his Seal of Arms. The Committee regards as of real importance the fact that a substantial number of our emigrant ancestors were of this same class, or sprang from gentle families. It throws much light on the character of the emigration as a whole, and helps to explain why men of the old stock have been able to contribute so much to civilization."

The introductory note to this First Roll states that:

"This Committee will now register all coats that come under one of the following heads:

"1—All coats that have been used time out of mind, regardless of whether or not they are registered at the College of Arms. This refers to coats that have been used by a family since the Middle Ages, and such coats are of course the blue-ribbon coats among those registered.

"2—Coats that have been granted or confirmed by the College of Arms.

"3—Coats that were brought over by an emigrant or first settler. The proof of such user establishes a *prima facie* case, but only a *prima facie* case; and the Committee reserves the right to disallow such a coat if hereafter proof be produced that the emigrant had no right to it. In registering such a coat, proof that the emigrant brought it over with him and used or claimed the coat is deemed sufficient. In each case what amounts to such proof is decided by the Committee."

In the Introductory to its Second Roll of Arms (July, 1932—73 to 162) the Committee states that:

"Occasionally somebody asks the Committee to register a coat, citing as authority for the right, books such as Crozier's 'General Armory,' Matthew's 'American Armory and Blue Book,' Bolton's 'American Armory,' and *The Magazine of American Genealogy*. Useful though they may be to show what Americans have used arms, these books contain so many coats that have been taken without right, that the Committee attaches no weight to them as authorities on the vital question of inheritance."

"The one hundred and sixty-two coats that have been registered are only a few of those that could properly be accepted on evidence already available. For many others the evidence is almost sufficient or is at least promising, and people are trying to bridge the gaps. Some undoubtedly will succeed. As time goes on, many an American will be surprised to find that he is entitled by inheritance to a good old Coat. The Committee hopes that the publication of its Rolls will arouse greater interest in the subject and lead to the registration of more and more Coats."

While some families claiming coats of arms in their genealogies may be disposed to question the right of the N. E. H. G. S. to assume authority in such matters, it is evident that its purpose is in the interest of accuracy, which all should concede to be important.

This (July, 1932) information led the Chairman of the Publication Committee to submit the picture of the James Whiton Arms (Fig. I, copied from Barry's History of Hanover) to the Committee on Heraldry, for comment, together with the information from Burke's General Armory about the Whitton (Nethercott co., Oxford) Arms and the statement by Mr. John M. Whiton about our English ancestors. The following quotations from the reply of the Committee Chairman are appended:

"The coat of arms in the photostat picture was borne to the best of my knowledge and belief by a family that spelled the name 'Whiting.' It is claimed by the descendants of the Rev. Samuel Whiting."

"Is it known that Thomas Whiton of Hingham was a son of William Whitton of Nethercott, Oxfordshire? Everything depends upon making a fairly good case to show that Thomas Whiton the emigrant did belong to the family in Nethercott which used the arms described by Burke. I trust that this will prove to be the case. I may remark that it is a good deal better Coat of Arms from an artistic point of view than that shown in your picture."

With the information about the Thomas Whiton ancestry obtained in England by Mr. John M. Whiton there would seem to be a presumption that the Whiton Family in America may claim, if they wish to do so, the Whitton (Nethercott) Arms as described by Burke, and shown in the drawing Fig. IV.

The delay in going to press has already been so great that it has not seemed advisable to wait an uncertain longer time required to obtain official confirming records from England and registration with the Committee on Heraldry of the New England Historic Genealogical Society. Such additional information, if and when obtained, will be furnished in the form of a supplement insert.

Comparing the drawings Figs. I, II, and III and the printed descriptions from Crozier and Matthews, it will be noticed that they are not identically similar. While all are azure and ermine with three roundels or bezants in chief, Figs. I and II have "Per Saltire" diagonal dividing lines, while the "Gyronny of Four" in Fig. III is shown by vertical and horizontal lines; i. e., the shield of Fig. III is "quartered." A leopard's face appears at the fess points of Figs. I and II; a leopard's head in profile at the fess point of Fig. III. The crests of Figs. I and III are lions rampant, while the crest of Fig. II is a lion's head erased.

L. E. W.

FIRST GENERATION

1 THOMAS, son of William Whiton and Catherine Ardene (or -derne), was one of six children. As stated above, he probably emigrated from Oxfordshire, as evidenced by the vital records in the parish register at Hook Norton in that Shire, and a letter of attorney issued by his son James (2) relating to property at that place. In Hotten's "List of Emigrants," appears the following, which would seem to differ from the last statement; greater credence, though, being given to the former statement:

> "In the Elizabeth & Ann, Roger Cooper, Master, bound to New England, the underwritten names are to be transported p. certificate from ye minister of Benendon* in Kent of their conformitie to ye order and discipline of ye Church of England, & yt they are no Subsedy Men. 12th, May 1635."

Among the names are Jeremy Whitton, aged 8, and "bro.wever" (meaning not clear) Thomas Whitton, aged 36 and Awdry Whitton, aged 45.

The first official notice in this country is taken from the Vital Records of Plymouth, Massachusetts, which state that Thomas Whiton and Wynyfride Harding were married November 22, 1639. Awdry Whiton disappears from the records and probably died shortly after her arrival. The names in the emigration records were frequently misspelled, and the ages given, inaccurate. The Jeremy (Jamie) is undoubtedly James (2), who later settled in Hingham.

Thomas settled in Old Plymouth in 1637, where he was granted seven acres of land, and his name appears as a Proprietor in 1638. This would indicate that he was a man of character and influence, as land was only given to men of that type, and the proprietors had the power of confirming all grants or purchases from the Indians. On account of fear of Indian raids, these grants were small in size and contiguous. In 1644 he bought of Edward Edwards a house and two

*Benendon is a parish in the Hundred of Rolvenden in the Lathe of Scray.

acres of land for nine pounds, two shillings and six pence. He died in 1664.*

It does not appear that there were any children by his marriage to Wynyfride; and in 1643, they adopted Sarah Hopkins, aged six years, "Until she should become twenty," agreeing "to be a father and mother to her, to instruct her in sewing, and to find meat, drink, apparel and lodging." If she married before she was twenty Thomas was to be paid for the remaining time as shall be judged just by two "indifferent" persons. It is conjectured that Sarah was a sister or niece of Oceanus Hopkins, who was born at sea on the Mayflower. In 1649 they adopted Jeremiah Smith, aged four years.

Wynyfride was evidently a woman of spirit and determination, for when in 1653 she was accused by one John Barnes of "telling lies," she promptly haled him before a magistrate and compelled a retraction. She died in 1660.*

Son:

JAMES (2).

*Vital Records and Town Records of Plymouth. Pioneers of Mass. p. 495.

SECOND GENERATION

2 JAMES, son of Thomas (1) was born in Hook Norton, near Banbury, Oxfordshire, England, where he was baptized in 1624, as appears by the parish register of that place.

After arriving in America, he lived with his father in Plymouth, Mass., until twenty-one years of age, when he moved with others to effect a settlement at Lancaster, Mass., where he signed the covenant entered into by the original settlers.* Two years later he moved to Hingham, Mass. The early name of Hingham was Bare Cove, so called because it was bare or open to the tide. Later, it was called Over The River, and subsequently Liberty Plain, and South Hingham. Here James settled and married Mary, daughter of John and Nazareth (Hobart) Beal in 1647, she being then 25 years of age.† On October 6, 1647, he gave a Letter of Attorney to Richard Betscomb of Hingham to collect a legacy of property in Hook Norton from the estate of Thomas Whiton.‡ He took the oath of freeman in 1660. In 1676 his home was burned by the Indians, led by Chief Philip of the Pokanoket Tribe, to meet the attacks of whom the men residents of Hingham were impressed into service.§ He served as Town Constable, in Hingham, an office at that time of dignity and importance.† He was a farmer and possessed of considerable real estate, for the records show him to have been one of the largest taxpayers in Hingham. He also owned land in Scituate, Abington, Hanover and other places and died at Hingham April 26, 1710. He was prominent in securing the erection of the Old Ship Church in Hingham, which is still standing, and to the building fund of which he donated fifty pounds, a large sum in those days. He died April 26, 1710, and his wife in 1696. Both are buried in Hingham.*
Children:

JAMES, born April 10, 1649, died November 11, 1650.

*Hist. Lancaster. Public Records, Lancaster.
†Vol. III, Hist. Hing., p. 288.
‡Geneol. of New England, Vol. IV, p. 172.
§Hobart's Diary.

JAMES (3).
MATTHEW (4).
JOHN, baptized December 1755, and died in infancy.
DAVID and JONATHAN, twins born February 22, 1658, died young.
ENOCH (5).
THOMAS (6).
MARY, born April 29, 1664, married (1st) Isaac Wilder; (2d) Baruch Jordan, and (3d) Thomas Sayer. No children lived to maturity.

THE OLD SHIP CHURCH

THIRD GENERATION

3 JAMES, son of James (2), was baptized August 13, 1651. (Some records give July 15, 1651.) He married Abigail, daughter of Giles and Hannah (Dunham) Rickard,* who was born in 1655 and died in Hingham May 4, 1740.†‡ James resided near his father's home at Liberty Plain, South Hingham. He was a farmer, and also had a cooperage business, making what was known as Hingham Tubs. He was said to have been an industrious man, quiet, unobtrusive and well respected, and served in King Philip's War. With his children began the first migration; some of them removing to Plympton, Hanover and other adjacent towns, and others to Connecticut. He died February 20, 1725.†

Children:

JAMES (7).

HANNAH, born July 4, 1678, married July 8, 1706, John King, of Plympton, and had three children: Hannah, John, who married Hannah Pierce April 20, 1750, and Eleazer.

JOHN (8).

ABIGAIL, born September 5, 1683, and died December 10, 1695.

SAMUEL (9).

JOSEPH (10).

JUDITH, born May 6, 1679, married (1st) December 13, 1712, James White, and (2d) December 22, 1737, Jonathan Farrow.

REBECCA, born December 6, 1691, and died young.

BENJAMIN (11).

SOLOMON (12).

*Savage, Vol. III, p. 540.
†Hist. Hing., Vol. III, p. 289. Hist. Hanover, p. 420.
‡Annals of Plympton, Davis. p. 213.

4 MATTHEW, son of James (2), was baptized October 30, 1653, and married Deborah, daughter of Edmund and Ann Pitts, widow of Daniel Howard, who was born in Hingham November 6, 1651, and died there September 19, 1729. In the Hingham Records, Matthew spelled his name Whyton. He was a large landholder, and engaged in the business of coopering,

manufacturing "Hingham Buckets," then well known throughout the settled part of the state, and died July 22, 1725.* In the Records of Hingham, under the date of February 7, 1709, appears the following (spelling as in the original):

> "Whereas we underwritten have heard that there are scandolous reports of the Widow Mahitable Warren of Plymouth, we knowing that she was brought up in this place, and in her younger time had been a person of great affliction before she was married, and hath lived in this towne divers years in her widowhood, and we never have had any thoughts or sispition nor have never heard that any amonst us have had the least sispition that she was ever guilty of the sin of being a witch of anything that may occation such a sispition of her.
>
> Hingham, Feb. 10, 1709
>
> I having had knowledge these eleven years of the above named Mahitable Warren and being her phisition doe know that she has been a woman of great affliction by reason of many distempers of body but never heard nor had thought that ever she was guilty of any such thing as above named but contrarywise did & doe believe God gave her a sanctified improvement of his afflictive hand to her. (signed) Nathaniel Hall, Ann Hall, Matthew Whiton, Deborah Whiton, Enoch Whiton and fifty-eight other witnesses."

Children:

MARY, born September 25, 1678, married James Whiton, Jr. (7) December 26, 1704.

JOHN (13).

DAVID (14).

MATTHEW (15).

ELIZABETH, born March 31, 1685, married Hezekiah Tower January 13, 1704.

SUSANNA, born November 14, 1686, died 9, or 22, August, 1750, unmarried.

LYDIA, born April 2, 1693, married Samuel Tower.

ISAAC (16).

*Hist. Hing., Vol. III, p. 421. Hist. Hanover, p. 289.

A "FAMILY TREE"
Owned by Mrs. Starkes Whiton (220)

5 ENOCH, son of James (2), was born March 8, 1659, and married Mary, daughter of Stephen and Elizabeth (Hawkes) Lincoln, January 11, 1687, who was born December 27, 1662, and died October 2, 1716. He was called Sergeant Enoch, and lived in Hingham and was a "trader." He signed the statement about witchcraft set forth in (4) together with his brother Matthew. His estate was appraised at one thousand and twenty-one pounds.*

Children:

SARAH, born October 27, 1687, married Caleb Marsh December 19, 1711.

MARY, born September 21, 1690, died May 28, 1692.

MARY, born November 1, 1692, married December 2, 1714, Jedediah Beal and died September 24, 1736.

BETHIA, born January 20, 1695, married Jedediah Lincoln January 2, or 9, 1717. Their grandson was Levi Lincoln, Attorney General of the United States, and their great-grandson was Levi Lincoln, Governor of Massachusetts.

ABIGAIL, born September 8, 1697, married David Waters March 10, 1720.

ENOCH (17).

MARGARET, born January 28, 1702, married John Collamore of Scituate, Mass., April 27, 1732.

*Hist. Hing., Vol. III, p. 290. Hist. Hanover, p. 421.

6 THOMAS, son of James (2), was born May 18, 1662, and baptized June 16, 1662, and married January 26, 1690, Joanna May, widow of Francis Garnett, and daughter of Samuel May of Roxbury, Mass. He was a farmer and cooper, and owned a large tract of cedar swamp in Abington, Mass., from which large trees were cut and split into clapboards for the Boston market. He was killed by the fall of a tree September 17, 1708.*

Children:

JOANNA, born January 27, 1691, married Jonathan Farrow October 27, 1714, died April 11, 1737.

JAEL, born February 12, 1693, married Peter Hobart December 31, 1715, died September 4, 1775.

*Hist. Hing., Vol. III, p. 290. Hist. Hanover, p. 422.

LEAH, born April 4, 1695, married Benjamin Farrow December 14, 1715.
THOMAS (18).
JONATHAN (19).
RACHEL, born July 12, 1700, married Samuel Richard October 19, 1721, who was born May 21, 1696, and died August 18, 1796. She died January 30, 1792.
ELEAZER (20).

HINGHAM TUBS AND BUCKETS
Sketched from a collection in the "Old Ordinary" at Hingham

WHITON HOMESTEAD, HINGHAM, MASS.
Portions built in 1680, probably by Matthew (4). Owned and occupied by ancestors of Mrs. Alice Whiton Foster (p. 152) who now lives there. One of the oldest houses in Hingham.

---

11 Benjamin Whiton

14 Dan'l Whiton

17 Enoch Whiton

FACSIMILE SIGNATURES—4th Generation
From Barry's History of Hanover

FOURTH GENERATION

7 JAMES, son of James (3), was born in Hingham, February 17, 1676, and married Mary, daughter of Matthew and Deborah (Pitts) Whiton (4), in Hingham on December 26, 1704; who was born September 25, 1678. He lost an arm in King Philip's War, during which his house was burned.*

The family removed to Plympton, Mass., soon after 1708, and subsequently to Middletown, Conn., where he died March 13, 1760.*

Children:

BATHSHEBA, born March 16, 1705.
ELISHA (21).
JOB, born September 17, 1708.
MARY, or MARCY, born September 2, 1710, and married Abraham Jackson in 1741, and died in 1744.
JAMES (22).
MATTHEW (23).
SUSANNAH, born September 24, 1716.
JAEL, born September 12, 1718, married Isaac Thayer March 28, 1753.
NATHAN (24).
CORNELIUS, born May 3, 1723.

*Hist. Hing., Vol. III, p. 290. Vital Records Plympton.

8 JOHN, son of James (3), was born in Hingham, April 5, 1681, married Bethiah Crocker, and removed with his brother to Plympton, Mass.*

Children:

AZARIAH (25).
ALICE, born February 28, 1713, and married Ellis Doten July 27, 1742.
JEDIDAH, born February 8, 1715, married Elisha Whiton.
ZACCHEUS, born May 1, 1716.
ALPHEUS, born March 10, 1718.
BETHIAH, born August 16, 1720, married September 28, 1744, Abraham Jackson.
JOHN, born February 27, 1722, married Martha Tilson of Plympton, February 19, 1746, who died December 5, 1748. They had one child, Sarah, born August 8, 1748, and died October 16, 1748.
THOMAS, born May 27, 1724, and died December 25, 1725.

*Vital Records. Plymouth.

9 SAMUEL, son of James (3), was born in Hingham, November 12, 1685, and married Margaret, daughter of Samuel and Silence (Damon) Tower, at Hingham, March 11, 1712, who was born in Hingham, March 18, 1687, and died April 3, 1738. He married (2d) Mrs. Elizabeth Garnet, widow of Charles Williams, and daughter of James and Elizabeth (Ward) Garnet, who was born in Hingham, September 25, 1693, and died May 24, 1747; and (3d) Rebecca Garnet, widow of John Garnet. He was known as "King Whiton," and was a large landowner and a farmer.*

Children:

MARGARET, born in 1712, and married (1st) Obadiah Gross January 8, 1739, and (2d) Amasa Turner November 6, 1754.

SAMUEL (26).

DANIEL, born and died October 13, 1714.

MOSES, born December 2, 1715, and died August 8, 1717.

DESIRE, born April 6, 1717, and died young.

HANNAH, born December 7, 1718, married Samuel Curtis November 14, 1739, and died October 26, 1789.

KEZIAH, born June 4, 1720, and married Stephen Dunbar December 13, 1739.

DANIEL (27).

ABIGAIL, born in 1724, and married Hezekiah Stodder of Scituate, Mass., November 22, 1743.

*Hist. Hing., Vol. III, p. 290. Hist. Hanover, p. 422.

10 JOSEPH, son of James (3), was born in Hingham, March 23, 1687, and married (1st) Martha, daughter of Samuel and Silence (Damon) Tower, December 10, 1713, who was born in Hingham July 20, 1693, and died in Rehoboth, Mass., September 19, 1719; and (2d) Rebecca, daughter of Benjamin and Elizabeth Wilson, of Rehoboth.* He was a farmer and cooper, and served as town constable of Hingham. About 1718 he removed to Palmer's River, now Rehoboth, Mass., where he carried on his business as cooper for about ten years.† In 1726 he removed to Ashford, Conn., where he bought one hundred acres of land and where he died in 1777. He was buried in the cemetery in Westford,

TOMBSTONE OF JOSEPH WHITON (10)
Westford Hill, Conn.

Conn., in the establishment of which he was one of a committee of three.‡ In 1727 he, his wife and his son Elijah, were received as members of the Congregational Church in Ashford, from which they were dismissed in 1768. At that time there was trouble in the church. A new minister had been called. At his ordination he was asked: "Do you believe that when a child is born into the world he brings enough sin to damn him forever?" On his replying, "No," ordination was refused and many left the church. Among these were Joseph and his son Elijah, from whose grandson these facts were obtained. In 1769 Rebecca Wilson Whiton, his second wife, was dismissed from the same church to the new church in Westford, and their graves are in the Westford Cemetery. At that time the town of Ashford was about nine miles square and included Eastford and Westford. The History of Hingham describes him as a conscientious, unobtrusive and hard-working man. He must have thought very much of his second wife, for in his will he provided that if she married again she should in addition to her share of his estate have £100 additional.

Children by Martha Tower:

ELIJAH (28).

ABIGAIL, born April 20, 1716, and married Peter Barnes of Hopkinton, Mass.

MARTHA, born September 4, 1718.

Children by Rebecca Wilson:

JOSEPH, born June 23, 1722, at Rehoboth.

REBECCA, born March 7, 1725, at Rehoboth, married William Goffe, October 18, 1747, and had eleven children.

ELIZABETH, born in Ashford August 22, 1729, married John Cummings of Stafford, Conn. Had a son Joseph and other children.

HULDAH, born in Ashford July 29, 1733, and married June 2, 1754, Nathan Bullock of Rehoboth, Mass., then settled in Nine Pastures, N. Y. He was said to have been a Revolutionary soldier and to have been captured by the British.

JAMES (29).

WILSON, born August 4, 1740, went "west" to Onondaga

County, N. Y., and changed the spelling of his name to Whiting.

ALICE, born December 17, 1742, married December 8, 1768, Ransom Curtis, removed to Willington, Conn., and had children: Joseph, William, Jason, Alice, and Asa. (Curtis Genealogy.)

*Town Records of Rehoboth at Hartford.
†Hist. Hing., Vol. III, p. 291.
‡Hist. Windham County.

11 BENJAMIN, son of James (3), was born in Hingham, December 21, 1693. On April 19, 1716, he married Sarah, daughter of Benjamin and Deborah (Garnet) Tower. She was born in Hingham, December 18, 1689. Her grandfather was one of seven men chosen to "manage the prudential affairs of Hingham." Benjamin lived and died January 22, 1783, in Hingham at, or near, what was known as Queen Anne's Corner.*

Children:

BENJAMIN (30).
THOMAS (31).
WILLIAM (32).
JACOB, born August 10, 1723, resided at Plainfield, Mass., and married Ann Gibb of Scituate, and had daughter who married Caleb Beal of Plainfield, Mass.
NATHANIEL, born and died 1725.
SARAH, born January 15, 1727.
ABEL, born May 7, 1733.
LEMUEL (33).

*Hist. Hing., Vol. III, p. 291. Hist. Hanover, p. 422.

12 SOLOMON, son of James (3), was born in Hingham June 10, 1695. He married Jael, daughter of Joseph and Christiana (Garnet) Dunbar, October 19, 1721, who was born November 27, 1698, and died in 1772. The Dunbars were Scotch and emigrated to Hingham about 1650. Solomon was a blacksmith and lived and died in Hingham.*

Children:

JAEL, born July 3, 1722.
SOLOMON (34).
RUTH, born September 22, 1726.
DEBORAH, born October 7, 1728.

MERCY, born September 22, 1730, married July 10, 1760, Elisha Howard.

THANKFUL, born October 26, 1732, married November 21, 1751, Simeon Bonney.

SILENCE, born November 22, 1734, married February 5, 1761, Timothy Tilson.

COMFORT (35).

MELIA, born November 5, 1739, married James Chubbuck March 9, 1767.

REBECCA, born November 27, 1741.

*Hist. Hing., Vol. III, p. 291. Hist. Hanover, p. 423.

13 JOHN, son of Matthew (4), was born in Hingham January 10, 1680, and married February 3, 1704, Mary, daughter of Ibrook and Margaret (Hardin) Tower. She was born in Hingham, August 16, 1677.* He was a private, in Capt. Theophilus Cushing's 2d Foot Company of Hingham, according to a muster roll dated September 15, 1755, now in the possession of the Society of Colonial Wars, New York City. His children, all born in Hingham, were:

JOHN, born November 7, 1704, drowned November 15, 1725.

DEBORAH, born March 3, 1706, married Solomon Bates of Scituate, May 1, 1731, removed to Chesterfield, Mass.

MARGARET, born February 3, 1708, married (1st) John Collomore of Scituate, April 27, 1732, and (2d) Peter Lincoln, September 23, 1737. She died August 12, 1771.

JOSHUA, born April 14, 1710. He, according to the muster roll (supra), was a private in the same company with his father. He died February 6, 1792.

ANN, born June 16, 1711, died unmarried September 13, 1789.

LYDIA, born March 26, 1714, and died October 19, 1732, or 1734.

MARY, born 1716, married Hosea Garnet November 15, 1736.

*Hist. Hing., Vol. III, p. 292. Hist. Hanover, p. 423.

14 DAVID, son of Matthew (4), was born in Hingham June 5, 1681. He married Elizabeth, daughter of Peter and Sarah (Lasell) Ripley, March 10, 1716. She was born in Hingham, March 26, 1694. He was Constable of Hingham and resided at Liberty Plain, South Hingham. The History of Hanover speaks of him as "up-

right and industrious and one who enjoyed the confidence and respect of his townsmen."*

Children:

DAVID (36).

ELIZABETH, born January 29, 1719, married Jeremiah Sprague, Jr., December 19, 1739, and died July, 1800.

SARAH, born August 10, 1720, married Jonothan Hersey November 19, 1741, and died January 28, 1794.

PETER (37).

SUSANNA, born August 21, 1726, married Ephraim Wilder December 29, 1748.

ABIJAH (38).

LYDIA, born June 9, 1729, married (1st) Elisha Beal May 19, 1752, and (2d) Stephen Lincoln October 28, 1762, and died May 7, 1778.

MARY, born May 20, 1734.

*Hist. Hing., Vol. III, p. 292. Hist. Hanover, p. 423.

15 MATTHEW, son of Matthew (4), was born November 28, 1682. According to the History of Hingham he removed to Pembroke, Mass.

Children:

MATTHEW, born in 1718, married Mary ———, and died January 8, 1811, in Pembroke (Vital Statistics). His children were: John, born December 19, 1747, Matthew, born May 11, 1751, and Ruby, born October 20, 1752.

16 ISAAC, son of Matthew (4), was born in Hingham March 25, 1695, and married Lydia, daughter of Stephen and Sarah (Warren) Garnet, March 17, 1720. She was born in Hingham January 22, 1695, and died January 26, 1756. His occupation was that of a weaver. He died in 1756. His children, born in Hingham, were:

ISAAC (39).

STEPHEN (40).

LYDIA, born November 27, 1724, died March 30, 1728.

DEBORAH, born January 1, 1727, died January 24, 1756.

LYDIA, born February 23, 1729, died May 6, 1729.

ABRAHAM (41).

JACOB (42).

ISRAEL, born August 19, 1734, died February, 1756.

LYDIA, born May 14, 1738, died January 26, 1756.

17 ENOCH, son of Enoch (5), was born September 25, 1699, in Hingham. He married Leah, daughter of Benjamin Stetson, of Scituate, November 16, 1732, who died in Hingham, March 22, 1751. He was a farmer and selectman of Hingham for seven years, and resided at Liberty Plain, South Hingham. He left a will dated February 8, 1772, leaving several houses and land to his son. His children, all born in Hingham, were:

ENOCH (43).

LEAH, born June 19, 1735, married Ebenezer Simmons of Scituate.

ELIJAH (44).

MARY, born July 15, 1739, died young.

GRACE, born March 22, 1741, married Stephen Stodder of Cohasset, December, 1774.

ELIAS (45).

*Hist. Hing., Vol. III, p. 292. Hist. Hanover, p. 424.

18 THOMAS, son of Thomas (6), was born February 10, 1698, and married February 21, 1718. He was a soldier in the Foot Company in Hanover, Plymouth County, under Colonel Ezekiel Turner, Captain Stetson, on May 9, 1750, as appears by an original muster roll on file with the Society of Colonial Wars, New York Chapter. Child:

THOMAS, born 1719. No other records have been found.*

*Vital Records. Plymouth.

19 JONATHAN, son of Thomas (6), was born March 5, 1703, in Hingham, and married Hannah, daughter of Joshua and Hannah (Hatch) Dunbar, July 13, 1732, who was born in Hingham December 12, 1703, and died June 19, 1751. His occupation was that of a "House-Wright," and he resided at Liberty Plain, South Hingham.*

Children:

HANNAH, born October 14, 1733, married (1st) Moses Leavitt November 29, 1767, and (2d) Benjamin Barnes, Sr., June 7, 1789; and died October 8, 1823.

JONATHAN (46).

ELISHA (47).

*History Hanover, p. 424.

20 ELEAZER, son of Thomas (6), was born November 15, 1706, and married Sarah, daughter of Jedediah and Mary (Whiton)-(5) Beal, March 6, 1746, at Abington, Mass., where he resided and built, first a log cabin and later a frame house, which is still standing. He was a cooper and died January 17, 1795. She died September 9, 1789.*

Children:

JOTHAM (48).

THOMAS, born September 10, 1753, married Jane Smith, and died January 1, 1826.

BARZILLAI (49).

*History Hanover, p. 424.

---

27 Samuel Whiton

30 Beniamin Whiten

31 Thomas Whiten

32 Willeam Whiton

49 Barzillae Whiting

FACSIMILE SIGNATURES—5th GENERATION
From Barry's History of Hanover

FIFTH GENERATION

21 ELISHA, son of James (7), was born November 7, 1706, in Hingham, and married Joanna, daughter of John Dunham in 1728, and removed to Plympton, Mass., and later to Middletown, Conn.

Children:

ELISHA (50).

JOANNA, born 1731, married November 16, 1749, Edward Doten.

ALPHEUS, born in 1733, married Ruth Grafton of Plymouth, November 5, 1753.

AZARIAH, married Rebecca, daughter of Elnathan and Rebecca (Churchill) Holmes, a widow.

MERCY, married Ebenezer Doten June 12, 1750.*

*Anc. Landmarks of Plymouth, p. 285.

22 JAMES, son of James (7), was born at Plympton, Mass., December 17, 1712, and married Molly, daughter of Samuel and Elizabeth (Shaw) Lucas, January 19, 1743, in the 1st Congregational Church of Plymouth. She was born in Plymouth in 1723. Samuel Lucas was a son of Captain Benoni Lucas who was born in Plymouth October 3, 1659, and is listed as a Mayflower Descendant in Vol. IV of Mayf. Desc'ts, p. 112. His wife Elizabeth was the daughter of Lieutenant Jonathan Shaw, who was born in Plymouth in 1663, and died there January 18, 1728. Her grandfather came over in the Mayflower (see Vol. III Mayf. Desc'ts, p. 91, also Vol. III ibid, p. 204, also Vol. V ibid, p. 207). John, father of Jonathan Shaw, is said to have served in King Philip's War, in which he was killed. James Whiton moved to Chatham (now East Hampton), Conn., where, with his wife, he was buried, dying August 29, 1768. His wife was on May 8, 1769, appointed "guardian of Thomas and Joseph Witon, minor sons of Mr. James Witon." The inscription on his tombstone is: "A man faithful in all the relations of life." Their children, James, Joseph, Thomas, Ebenezer and John were brought up by their father's cousin, Squire Elijah Whiton (28) of Westford, together with the fifteen children of his

own.* James is said to have been a seafaring man, trading with the West Indies.

In the official records of Middletown, he spelled his name Witon. His estate was administered upon by his widow, and divided among his children. His personal property was inventoried April 3, 1769, at £428 and from the assets named it would appear that he kept a general store.† He also owned considerable real estate, located on the east side of the Connecticut River, among which was the house in which he resided, with eight acres of land which he purchased February 28, 1756, for £750.†

Children:

JAMES (51).

SAMUEL, born in 1748 and died October 16, 1762.

ELIZABETH, died July 6, 1751, young.

RUTH, died young.

THOMAS (52).

ELIZABETH, born March, 1758, and died May 25, 1759.

JOSEPH (53).

EBENEZER (54).

JOHN (55).

*Vital Records of Plymouth. Ancient Landmarks of Plymouth. Tombstones at Chatham, Conn., and notes and records kept by the mother of Jerome Whiton Norris of Lexington, Mich., who knew personally all the older persons in the record, except James and Molly Whiton themselves. Also Town Records of Ashford in Hartford.

†Probate Records and Records of Deeds, Middletown, Conn.

23 MATTHEW, son of James (7), was born March 4, 1714, married Sarah Thayer February 7, 1758, who after his death married Samuel Palmer. Although an elderly man, according to the Mass. Revolutionary Records, he marched on the Lexington Alarm April 19, 1775, as a private in Captain Elijah Cushing's Company of Militia, from Pembroke to Marshfield. He died April 26, 1776.*

Children:

WILLIAM, born September 6, 1759, married Maletiah ——, and had a son, James, born April 29, 1786, in Plympton.

JAMES, born May 16, 1762.

ISAAC, baptized February 24, 1765.

ANNA, baptized April 1, 1770.

MOLLY.

SAMUEL.

THOMAS, born July 22, 1772, "lived in a number of towns," and died in Halifax, Mass., December 28, 1836.*

*Hist. Hing., Vol. III, p. 292.

24 NATHAN, son of James (7), was born January 13, 1721, and married June 21, 1750, Phoebe Spicer, in the 1st Congregational Church in Chatham, Conn., and died early in 1776. In the official records his name is spelled Witon. Upon his death Daniel Bidwell was appointed guardian of his son Daniel, and Daniel Shephard, Jr., guardian of his son Samuel.

Children:

MARY, born December 9, 1751, married William Manley of Windsor, Conn., May 3, 1774, in 1st Congregational Church of Chatham (now Portland), Conn. (Vol. IV, p. 96 of Conn. Marriages.)

PHOEBE, born October 2, 1753.

NATHAN, born October 17, 1755. According to Mass. Revolutionary Rolls he served as a private in Capt. Raymond de Ginscard's Co., Col. Turner's Regiment, raised in defense of Rhode Island, from July 20, 1781, to November 27, 1781. Roll sworn to in Boston.

ELIJAH, born February 21, 1758.

SARAH, born April 23, 1760, married July 12, 1787, Nathaniel Roberts, Jr., of Middletown.

ESTHER, born April 22, 1762, and married September 18, 1785, Elijah Atwood of East Haddam, Conn.

DANIEL, born March 16, 1764.

DESIRE, baptized April 23, 1766.

SAMUEL, born December 3, 1768.

JACOB, born December 27, 1770.

*Official records of Middletown, Conn.

25 AZARIAH, son of John (8), was born August 9, 1711, and married Elizabeth Barrows in Plympton, Mass., June 10, 1736. She died June 22, 1744, and he married (2d) Rebeccah, widow of Elnathan Holmes, and daugh-

ter of John and Desire Churchill, in Plymouth on September 10, 1745, who was born in 1713. She died September 5, 1751. He then married (3d) Elizabeth, daughter of Ephraim and Elizabeth (Brewster) Bradford, July 12, 1753, in Kingston, who was born in 1717.

Children by Elizabeth Barrows, born in Plympton:

PHOEBE, born March 16, 1737, married Simeon Bradford December 11, 1759.

ELIZABETH, born September 28, 1739, died December 11, 1739.

BETHEA, born March 29, 1741, died July 12, 1741.

RUTH, born August 10, 1743, died August 28, 1744.

Children by Rebeccah, born in Plympton:

HANNAH, born October 13, 1746, married Israel Dunham December 13, 1764.

THOMAS, born March 17, 1748.

PRISCILLA, born January 1, 1750.

EBENEZER, born August 2, 1751, died September 23, 1751.

Children by Elizabeth Bradford, born in Plympton:

JOHN, born August 6, 1754. According to Mass. Revolutionary Rolls he was a private in Capt. Bridgham's Co., which marched on Lexington Alarm April 19, 1775, to Marshfield; served twelve days. Also in same Co. from May 3, 1775, to August 1, 1775. Also received government uniform at camp at Roxbury November 11, 1775. Also worked as armorer in Col. Wm. Burbeck's Regiment several months in 1782.

EPHRAIM and PATIENCE, twins, born January 21, 1757.

ELIZABETH, born October 6, 1759.

PATIENCE, married John Chamberlain February 19, 1778.*

*Hist. Hing., Vol. III, p. 293. Vital Rec. Plympton.

26 SAMUEL, son of Samuel (9), spelled his name Whiting, born Hingham, March 8, 1713, married Mary Wing of Hanover. She died in Hingham, August 24, 1795. He was Constable at Hingham from 1747 to 1753, and resided at Liberty Plain, South Hingham.* He served as a private in 2d Foot Company of Soldiers under Capt. Theophilus Cushing of Hingham.† In his will he provided liberally for his wife and children.

Children born in Hingham:

JOANNA, born July 26, 1734, married October 30, 1755, Enoch Whiton, Jr. (43).

MARY, born June 17, 1736, married April 9, 1754, Lemuel Whiton (33).

MARGARET, born August 4, 1738, married David Prouty November 27, 1777.

THANKFUL, born September 13, 1740, married Obadiah Gross.

SAMUEL, born August 22, 1742, died March 18, 1752.

JUDITH, born September 21, 1744, married April 19, 1764, Job Loring.

*Hist. Hing., Vol. III, p. 293. Hist. Hanover, p. 424.

†Original Muster Roll in possession of N. Y. Chapter, Society of Colonial Wars.

27 DANIEL, son of Samuel (9), born in Hingham November 15, 1722, married Jael Damon who died August 1, 1812. He was a constable of Hingham in 1750 and resided at Liberty Plain, and afterwards removed to Connecticut. He was a man of mechanical ability, having superintended the erection of the old Cambridge Bridge.* He served as a private in the 2d Foot Com-

OLD CAMBRIDGE BRIDGE

From a Sketch in "A Tour to the Eastern States in the year 1797" by Robert Gilmor of Baltimore

pany, Capt. Theophilus Cushing, according to original muster roll dated September 15, 1755, now in possession of Society of Colonial Wars, New York Chapter.

Children, all born in Hingham*:

DANIEL (56).
ZACHARIAH (57).
AMASA (58).
MARTHA, born July 14, 1752 (see 83).
ZENAS (59).
HOSEA, born 1757. Hist. Hingham states that he was in active service during the Revolutionary War and died upon an expedition to Canada. Mass. Rev. Rolls state that he was a private in Capt. Jotham Loring's Co., Col. John Greatoris's Regiment, from April 17, 1775, to August 1, 1775. Also in Capt. Chas. Cushing's Co., 36th Regiment, according to return dated Camp at Fort 2, October 5, 1776, announcing his death September 8, 1776.

*Hist. Hing., Vol. III, p. 293. Hist. Hanover, p. 425.

28 ELIJAH, son of Joseph (10), was born in Hingham July 7, 1714, and married in Ashford, Conn., December 11-16, 1741, Priscilla, daughter of Joseph and Priscilla (Moore) Russ. She was born in 1716, and died July 19, 1756. On November 23, 1758, he married Hannah Crocker‡, of Willington, Conn., who died in 1809. He died August 20, 1784, and is buried at Westford Hill, Conn. When four years old he moved with his father to Palmer River, now Rehoboth, Mass., and later to Seekonk, and afterwards to Ashford, Conn. He accumulated a comfortable estate as a farmer, cooper and wheelwright. He was a man of exemplary piety; and states in one of his letters that he remembered each one of his children by name in prayer three times a day. At one time he was brought up before the church as having been intoxicated, but he defended himself with so much ability that he was acquitted. Upon the death of his cousin James (22) he assumed the care of his five orphan children, viz: James, Thomas, Joseph, Ebenezer and John. When the new church was built in 1768 he was assigned pew No. 1, and made Church Treasurer. On December 14, 1769, Ashford held a town meeting and appointed a committee, of which he was a member "to correspond with other committees in the County and elsewhere to encourage and help forward

TOMBSTONE OF ELIJAH WHITON (28)
Westford Hill, Conn.

manufactures and a Spirit of Industry in this government." In 1777-8-9 he was appointed by the General Assembly as Justice for Windham County. He served in the State Legislature and was in early life one of the Town schoolmasters.* The Department of Archives in the Connecticut State Library at Hartford certifies as

Dated at Ashford 25th June 1775

Elijah Whiton }
Benj.a Sumner } Justices of Peace

This facsimile signature, from a document in the Connecticut State Library, shows that Elijah Whiton was Justice of Peace in 1775

to his services as Justice (53-b) and acting as moderator at Ashford (11-12).†

Children by Priscilla Russ:

SYBIL, born 1742, died February 18, 1823, buried in Willington, Conn.

ABIGAIL, born in 1744, married Hezekiah Eldredge and had eight children: Abiel, Hezekiah, Elijah, Sybil, Abigail, Micah, Hosea and Stephen. She died in 1786.

JOSEPH (60).

ELIJAH (61).

PRISCILLA, born in 1749, married Rev. Nicholas Dudley of Vermont, and had two children, both of whom died young.

STEPHEN (62).

ABRAHAM, born in 1753 and died October 5, 1754.

ISRAEL (63); also, infant, born and died July, 1756.

Children by Hannah Crocker:

MARTHA, born July 8, 1759, and died January 17, 1775.

JUDITH, born July 8, 1759, and married August 28, 1783, Abijah Smith in Ashford. They had two children born in Ashford: Martha, called Patty, and Abijah. In 1793 they removed to North Randolph, Vt., and had six other children: Judith, Polly, Stephen, Elijah W., Hannah, and William H. Abijah, Sr. served in the Revolutionary War, and Abijah, Jr., in the War of 1812, according to family records.

HANNAH, born May 2, 1761, married Samuel Stowell of Willington, May 17, 1787, and moved to Oswego County, N. Y., dying there in 1833. Their children were: (a) Eunice, born March 16, 1788, and married November 26, 1812, Jason Smith; (b) Elijah, born December 27, 1789, married December 2, 1814, Selinda Williams; (c) Samuel, born July 26, 1791; (d) Florella, born July 24, 1793; (e) Apphia, born November 12, 1798; (f) Florella, born September 29, 1802.

BOAZ (64)

RUTH, born December 24, 1762, married Benjamin Collins of Lockport, N. Y., and died in 1854.

SARAH. (See Appendix F.)

ELEAZER, born August 7, 1766, and died March 1, 1778.

TOWER, born February 2, 1768. He graduated from Dartmouth College in 1796 and was one of the first instructors at Phillips Academy, Andover, Mass. He afterward lived at Richford, N. Y., where, after a long practice as a physician and an influential life in the community, he died in 1850. He married, had a son, Walter, who died before 1855, and a daughter, Betsey Ann, who inherited her father's farm and married James Wattles. They had five children: (a) Mason, who died very young; (b) Walter Tower, who died in 1929, in Neligh, Neb.; (c) Gurdon Wallace, born in 1855, and died January 31, 1932, in Los Angeles, Cal.; (d) Chauncey Lathrop, and (e) Caroline Swender, both of whom live in Los Angeles.

AMY. (See Appendix B.)

*Town Records of Ashford in Hartford.

†Conn. Men in Revolution, and State Records.

‡Hannah Crocker was a Mayflower descendant—See footnote, page 56.

29 JAMES, son of Joseph (10), was born in Ashford, Conn., August 4, 1736, and married Mehitable, daughter of Samuel and Mercy (Richardson) Blancher. He spelled his name Whiting, and was a soldier in the Revolutionary War from Ashford, as appears by Sick Bill 156 in the archives of the State Library in Hartford. Later in life he removed to Onondaga, N. Y.*

Children:

SAMUEL (65).

WILSON (66).

DELIVERANCE, born February 20, 1763.

MARY or MARAH, born February 11, 1765.

MERCY, born April 8, 1767.

MEHITABLE, born May 4, 1769.

REBECCA, born November 9, 1771, and married November 29, 1792, Benjamin Chaffee. (See Chaffee Genealogy.)

*Town Records of Rehoboth at Hartford.

30 BENJAMIN, son of Benjamin (11), was born December 28, 1716, and spelled his name Whiten. He married (1st) Sarah, daughter of Amos and Ruth (Garnett) Berry, who was born in Hingham January 6, 1720, and died February 18, 1780; and (2d) Jemima, widow of Samuel Stodder, and daughter of Richard and Esther Cobb, who was born in Hingham June 7, 1724, and died December 3, 1808. He resided near Accord Pond, South Hingham, and died December 5, 1808. His children were all born in Hingham.*

Children:

BENJAMIN (67).

ABEL, born and died in 1743.

EZEKIEL (68).

JOSEPH, baptized November 1, 1748. He was a soldier in Capt. Martin's Co., Col. William's Regiment, in 1777 (Mass. Rev. Rolls), and according to History of Hingham was killed before Fort Ticonderoga.

ABIGAIL, baptized September 1751.

ABEL (69).

NATHANIEL, baptized July, 1763, and married November 30, 1790, Lydia, daughter of David and Ann (Loring) Gardner, who was born July 27, 1763. Their children were: Lydia, who married ——— Harrington; Mary, Nathaniel, who married ——— Adams; Sarah and Abigail W.

*Hist. Hing., Vol. III, p. 293. Hist. Hanover, p. 425.

31 THOMAS, son of Benjamin (11), was born December 29, 1718, and spelled his name Whiten. He married Lydia Pratt of Weymouth, Mass., who died November 7, 1802. He settled in Hanover and was an enterprising farmer, and died there September 23, 1793.* He served as a private in Captain Josiah Soper's Company, North Company of Militia, from Hanover, on the Lexington Alarm.†

Children:

THOMAS (70).

LYDIA, born May 22, 1745, and died November 8, 1801.

OZIAS, born July 20, 1746, and married (1st) ——— Vinal and (2d) ——— Fadden. His children were: Lucy, Lillas, Ozias, and Jacob. He was a private in Capt. Edward Cobb's Co., Major Eliphalet Cary's Regiment, which marched from Abington to Tiverton, R. I., on an alarm July 30, 1780, and he was also a member of the Committee of Safety for Hanover.†

LUCY, born January 27, 1748, and died November 28, 1749.

SARAH, born November 16, 1749, and died June 11, 1826.

JAMES (71).

PRISCILLA, born March 14, 1757, married Noah Beal of Abington, Mass., and died in 1819.

CELIA, born June 8, 1759.

CALEB (72).

ELIAS (73).

ASA (74).

*Hist. Hanover, p. 425.
†Mass. Rev. Rolls.

32 WILLIAM, son of Benjamin (11), born March 28, 1721. He married Mary Ramsdell in 1748, and lived in Hanover,* and was a private in Captain Ezekial Tanner's Company on May 9, 1750, according to original Muster Roll in possession of Society of Colonial Wars, New York Chapter.

Children:

WILLIAM, born and died in 1751.

ABEL, born October 12, 1752, and married Priscilla Peakes February 19, 1784, who was born in 1762, and died January 10, 1851. He died January 24, 1821, without issue.

MARY, born March 21, 1755, married Isaac Turner, Jr., and died in 1795.

AVIS, born May 14, 1760, and died October 12, 1793.

BETTY, born May 4, 1758, and married April 12, 1789, Asa Whiting.

WILLIAM (75).

GRACE, born July 8, 1764, and married Luther Turner.

HOMER, born August 24, 1761, married (1st) Anna Studley May 8, 1785. She died August 24, 1789. (2d) Tryphena Beal, who died October 31, 1851. Their children were: Homer, baptized September 24, 1786, who married Hannah White and removed to Vermont, and Anna, born in 1788, and died in 1793.

TRYPHENA, baptized October 21, 1792, and married Zadoc Beal May 22, 1816.

*Hist. Hanover, p. 426.

33 LEMUEL, son of Benjamin (11), was born August 7, 1729, and married Mary, daughter of Samuel Whiting (26), in Hingham April 9, 1754, who was born in 1731, and died June 12, 1826.* He served as a private in Captain Caleb Richard's Company, Colonel Timothy Walker's Regiment, July 13, 1776, to August 1, 1776, and also from November 1, 1776, for one month.† He resided in Whiting Street, Hanover.

Children:

MARY, born April 18, 1755, and died unmarried June 21, 1849.

SAMUEL, born June 4, 1757, married Elizabeth Gardner September 6, 1778. He served as a private in Capt. Noah M. Littlefield's Co., as per abstract for wages for two months, billeting at Wells and Arundel for defense of the seacoast, September 16, 1775, and in same company, enlisting for six months July 10, 1776.†

THANKFUL, born February 19, 1759, married James Whiting.

LUCINDA, born March 8, 1761, and died July 19, 1771.

MARGARET, born November 18, 1763.

BEULAH, born March 17, 1766.

LEMUEL, born and died 1772.

LEMUEL, born November 5, 1773.

LUCINDA, born December 14, 1776.

PEREZ, born September 18, 1778, at Hanover.

BUCHSA, born April 9, 1782.

*Hist. Hanover, p. 426.
†Mass. Rev. Rolls.

34 SOLOMON, son of Solomon (12), was born in Hingham December 5, 1724, and married August 12, 1746, Mary, daughter of Caleb Campbell. She died October 15, 1793. He resided on South Pleasant Street in Hingham, and was a blacksmith.* He served as a private in the 2d Foot Company, Captain Theophilus Cushing of Hingham, on September 15, 1755.† Also in Captain Enoch Whiton's Company, Colonel Benjamin Lincoln's Regiment, on the Lexington Alarm, April 19, 1775, and in the same Company from March 11, 1776, to March 29, 1776, to guard the shore. Also as a private in Lieu-

tenant Jabez Wilder's Company, Colonel Lothrop's Regiment, assembled at Hull, February 25, 1778.‡

Children:

ASA, born February 25, 1747.

SOLOMON, born August 10, 1751. According to Mass. Rev. Rolls he was a member of Stephen Cushing's Co. of Hingham on alarm list in 1776.

JOSEPH (76).

PELEG, born November, 1758. According to Hist. Hing. he was a member of Gazee's Artillery Co. in Revolutionary War.

JAEL, born 1761 and married October 31, 1784, Thomas Berry, Jr.

MARY.

RUTH.

BETSY, who died in Hingham unmarried.

*Hist. Hing., Vol. III, p. 294. Hist. Hanover, p. 426.
†Muster Roll filed with Society Colonial Wars, New York Chapter.
‡Mass. Rev. Rolls.

35 COMFORT, son of Solomon (12), was born September 15, 1736, married Grace Fadden and settled in Dorchester, Mass.* He was a private in Captain Asahel Smith's Company of Militia, Colonel Lemuel Robinson's Regiment, which marched on the Lexington Alarm, April 19, 1775.†

Children:

JOANNA, born April 27, 1759.

NATHANIEL, born January 28, 1761, died young.

PHILIP, born January 28, 1761.

MARY, born December 1, 1762.

RUTH, born December 6, 1764.

REBECCA, born March 6, 1767, married Peter Billings Canton December 2, 1784.

NATHANIEL, born December 24, 1768.

ABIGAIL, born March 1, 1771.

LEMUEL, born 1773.

GRACE, born July, 1775.

COMFORT, born March, 1777.

*Hist. Hanover, p. 427.
†Mass. Rev. Rolls.

36 DAVID, son of David (14), was born in Hingham April 12, 1717. He married Mary, daughter of Nathaniel and Judith Gilbert, October 29, 1739. She was born January, 1716, and died November 10, 1799. He was a yeoman and resided near Bull Pond, Hingham Center. He died October 12, 1751.* His children were all born in Hingham.

Children:

ELIZABETH, born July 20, 1740, married Elijah Lewis April 14, 1762, and died February 21, 1815.

ELIJAH (77).

EZRA (78).

SARAH, born December 5, 1745, and died October 5, 1751.

DAVID, born January 31, 1748, and died September 15, 1767.

MOSES, born April 8, 1750, and died October 11, 1751.

MOSES (79).

*Hist. Hing., Vol. III, p. 294. Hist. Hanover, p. 427.

37 PETER, son of David (14), was born in Hingham October 21, 1722. He married Anna, daughter of Thomas and Ann (Eels) Wilder, July 4, 1746. She was born in Hingham September 18, 1723. He died October 23, 1751.* His children were born in Hingham.

Children:

RACHEL, born January 23, 1747.

ANNA, born November 25, 1748.

*Hist. Hing., Vol. III, p. 294.

38 ABIJAH, son of David (14), was born in April, 1729, and married (1st) Mary Gardner, and (2d) Miriam, daughter of Robert and Sarah (Dunbar) Gardner, on August 13, 1767. She was born in Hingham August 3, 1739. He was a constable in Chesterfield.* He served as a private in Captain Enoch Whiton's Company, Colonel Benj. Lincoln's Regiment, which assembled April 19, 1775, and served three days. Also a corporal in Captain Jotham Loring's Company, Colonel John Greatoris's Regiment, enlisted April 27, 1775; served three

and a half months. Also a sergeant in Captain Cushing's Company, 36th Regiment. Also private in Captain Cushing's Company, Colonel Solomon Lovell's Regiment, to guard the shore between March 11 and 29, 1776.†

Children by Mary Gardner:

PETER, born April 23, 1754. Hist. Hingham says he was a soldier in the Revolutionary War.
ABIJAH (80).
LUCY, born October 4, 1760.
LUTHER, born June 21, 1764.
MARY or MOLLY, born October 22, 1765.

Children by Miriam Gardner:

DAVID (81).
ELIZABETH, born August 17, 1771.
PEGGY, born December 17, 1772.
LUCINDA, born June 8, 1768.

*Hist. Hing., Vol. III, p. 294. Hist. Hanover, p. 427.
†Mass. Rev. Rolls.

39 ISAAC, son of Isaac (16), was born in Hingham January 7, 1721. He married (1st) January 7, 1746, Rachel Taylor, who died April 10, 1746, and (2d) Sarah Sears on November 27, 1746, born in 1727 and died September 15, 1804. His occupation was a cooper and he resided on Main Street, Hingham.* He was a private in Captain Pyam Cushing's Company, and served four days, and in Captain Seth Stower's Company, Colonel Josiah Whitney's Regiment, and served June 1, 1776, to November 30, 1776.† Also a private in 2d Foot Company, Captain Theophilus Cushing of Hingham.‡ His name also appears as a private in Captain Fisher's Company, which served 22 days and marched to Hull October 4, 1782.† Children born in Hingham:

DEBORAH, died January 24, 1756.
LYDIA, died January 26, 1756.
ISRAEL, died February 15, 1756.

*Hist. Hing., Vol. III, p. 295.
†Mass. Rev. Rolls.
‡Original Muster Rolls in possession of Soc. Col. Wars, N. Y. Chapter.

40 STEPHEN, son of Isaac (16), was born in Hingham October 13, 1722, and married (1st) Mercy, daughter of Caleb Campbell, and (2d) Sarah, daughter of Jeremiah and Sarah (Macvarlo) Stodder, on December 20, 1775. She was born in Hingham June 25, 1739, and died September 30, 1823. He was by occupation a cooper and resided on Main Street, Hingham, and died January 14, 1812.* His name appears as a private on muster roll dated September 15, 1755, of 2d Foot Company, Captain Theophilus Cushing, of Hingham;† also as a private in Captain Seth Stower's Company, Colonel Josiah Whitney, from May 27, 1776, to December 31, 1776, for defense of seacoast at Hull.

Children by Mercy Campbell, born in Hingham:

DEBORAH, born February 5, 1756.
ISRAEL (82).
SARAH, born November 8, 1759.

Children by Sarah Stodder, born in Hingham:

ISAAC, born October 21, 1778. His name appears on an original muster roll of Capt. Laban Hersey's Co. of Foot soldiers, 1805, on file with Hingham Hist. Society. Also on another roll, there filed, as a private in Capt. John Fearing's Co. of Foot soldiers, 1809-10. He died February 1, 1856.
DANIEL, born July, 1781, died June 8, 1857.

*Hist. Hing., Vol. III, p. 295. Hist. Hanover, p. 427.
†Original Muster Roll in possession of Soc. Col. Wars, N. Y. Chapter.
‡Mass. Rev. Rolls.

41 ABRAHAM, son of Isaac (16), was born in Hingham March 18, 1730. He married Mary, daughter of Hezekiah and Sarah (Garnet) Ripley, on February 21, 1751.* He was, on September 15, 1755, a private in 2d Foot Company, Captain Theophilus Cushing.† Also a corporal in Captain Pyam Cushing's Company, Colonel Solomon Lovell's Regiment, which assembled for four days, March 4, 1776, at Dorchester. Also same Company and Regiment from March 11 to March 29, 1776, and at Hull in June, 1776.‡

Children, born in Hingham:

MARY, born October 8, 1752, married Loring Tomson January 28, 1782.§

ABRAHAM, born February 12, 1755, married Abigail Wood August 25, 1775.§

LYDIA, born October 8, 1758, married Sherabeth Corthell.

REBECCA, born July 12, 1762.

*Hist. Hing., Vol. III, p. 295.
†Original Muster Rolls in possession of Soc. Col. Wars, N. Y. Chapter.
‡Mass. Rev. Rolls.
§Vital Rec., Halifax, Mass.

42 JACOB, son of Isaac (16), was born in Hingham February 7, 1732, and married Bette (Elizabeth), daughter of Nathaniel and Susanna (Worrick) Marble, November 10, 1756. She was born in Hingham April 20, 1736. He was by occupation a cooper and resided on Main Street, Hingham.* He was a private in Captain Abraham Brown's Company, Colonel Josiah Whitney's Regiment, and served from November 1 to December 1, 1776; roll dated at Hull. Also a private in Captain Seth Stower's Company; served thirteen days, between December 1, 1776, and December 31, 1776, at Hull. Also a private in Captain James Lincoln's (Independent) Company, stationed at Hingham for defense of the seacoast, May 22, 1776.† He also served as a private in Hanover under Captain Ezekial Turner in the Indian War Roll, dated September 15, 1755.‡ He died April 14, 1816.

Children, born in Hingham:

JACOB, born September 10, 1757.

1798, and had a son, David, whose daughter, Helen, married Starkes Whiton (220).

BETSY, born August 23, 1759, married Josiah Sprague March 4, 1785.

LABAN, born November 18, 1761, died at sea.

SUSA, born March 2, 1764, married her brother-in-law Josiah Sprague (widower) December 14, 1794.

CHLOE, born in 1768, married (1st) Elijah Fearing November 9, 1788, and (2) Seth Lincoln (widower) on December 21, 1818.

LYDIA, born in 1772, married Benjamin Thomas August 19, 1798.

DEBORAH, born in 1775, married Amos Sprague October 2, 1796.

REUBEN, died unmarried.

*Hist. Hing., Vol. III, p. 295. Hist. Hanover, p. 427.
†Mass. Rev. Rolls.
‡Original Muster Rolls in possession of Soc. Col. Wars, N. Y. Chapter.

43 ENOCH, son of Enoch (17), was born in Hingham August 29, 1733, and married October 30, 1755, Joanna, daughter of Samuel and Mary (Wing) Whiton (26). She was born in Hingham July 26, 1734. He was by occupation a cooper and farmer.* He served as a private in Captain Pyam Cushing's Company, assembled in April, 1776, to guard the shore, also on two different occasions in June, 1776, at Hull.† He was also a captain of a company in Colonel Benjamin Lincoln's Regiment, assembled April 19, 1775.† Also his name appears in an "alarm list" of Captain Cushing's Company of Hingham in 1755.‡ His bravery is mentioned in Thatcher's Military Journal, and he is said to have commanded a company at the Surrender of Burgoyne at Saratoga, October 17, 1777. He died June 21, 1778.§

Children, born in Hingham:

JOANNA, born October 6, 1757, married June 11, 1787, Thomas Chubbuck, Jr., and died January 22, 1850.

CHLOE, born in 1759, married August 23, 1789, Samuel Gardner, a widower.

BETHIA, born in 1761, married October 8, 1780, David Loring.

ENOCH (83).

LEAH, born March 8, 1765, married John Abbott of Newark, N. J.

LAURENA, born March 4, 1767, married November 11, 1805, David Parks of Lincoln, Mass.

POLLY or DOLLY, born March 5, 1769, married Lewis Squire of Newark, N. J.

PHOEBE, born April 12, 1771, married January 11, 1798, Daniel Whiting of North Brookfield, Mass. (107).

*Hist. Hing., Vol. III, p. 295. Hist. Hanover, p. 428.
†Mass. Rev. Rolls.
‡Original Muster Rolls in possession of Soc. Col. Wars, N. Y. Chapter.
§Tombstone in Liberty Plain, Mass., Graveyard.

44 ELIJAH, son of Enoch (17), was born in Hingham June 8, 1737. He married July 13, 1764, Mary, daughter of Theophilus and Mary (Hersey) Wilder. She was baptized July 4, 1742. He was by occupation a farmer, and was a constable in Hingham in 1774, and resided on Main Street, South Hingham.* He was a private in Captain Theophilus Cushing's 2d Foot Company on September 15, 1755.† He was a sergeant in Captain Peter Cushing's Company, Colonel Solomon Lovell's Regiment, which assembled at Hull, March 11, 1776, to guard the shore.‡ He died June 15, 1797.

Children:

MARY, born October 7, 1764, married May 7, 1786, Enoch Dunbar.

PERSIS, born September 21, 1766, married June 1, 1794, Jacob Sprague.

ELIJAH (84).

ELIZABETH, born August 7, 1769.

TAMSEN, born October 2, 1771, married December 7, 1794, Charles Simmons of Scituate, Mass.

CHARLOTTE, born February 24, 1774, married November 26, 1803, Nathaniel Bump of Quincy.

MERIEL, born July 3, 1776, married November 23, 1800, George B. Lapham of Medford, Mass.

ISAIAH, born November 7, 1778, died unmarried September 5, 1820.

BLOSSOM (85).

WALTER, born November 28, 1783. Was a major in the War of 1812, killed that year in the Battle of Bridgewater.*

*Hist. Hing., Vol. III, p. 296. Hist. Hanover, p. 428.
†Muster Roll, filed with Soc. Col. Wars, N. Y. Chapter.
‡Mass. Rev. Rolls.

45 ELIAS, son of Enoch (17), was born in Hingham June 10, 1743, and married June 22, 1769, Sarah, daughter of Zacheus and Sarah (Hersey) Blossom, who was born in June, 1749, and died May 16, 1817. He was a farmer, a town constable in 1775, and a selectman in 1776, and he died of smallpox at Dorchester, Mass., in 1778.* He served as a sergeant in Captain Enoch Whiton's Company, assembled on the Lexington Alarm, and as a lieutenant in Captain Charles Cushing's Com-

pany in "ye 36th Reg't of foot in ye Continental Army encamped in Fort No. 2"; also as a lieutenant in Captain Pyam Cushing's Company under General Thomas at Dorchester Heights. Also as a captain in Colonel Lyman's Regiment.†

Children:

ELIAS (86).

SARAH, born October 18, 1771, married (1st) Henry Cushing December 28, 1791, and (2d) Seth Cushing, a widower, November 30, 1815.

PRISCILLA, born December 21, 1773, married December 28, 1801, Josiah Lane, Jr.

PATTY, born and died in September, 1775.

PATTY, or MARTHA, born October 10, 1776, and married December 25, 1818, Thomas Fearing, Jr.

MARGARET, born October, 1778, and married February 10, 1799, ——— Dimick of Scituate.

*Hist. Hing., Vol. III, p. 296. Hist. Hanover, p. 428.
†Mass. Rev. Rolls.

46 JONATHAN, son of Jonathan (19), was born March 9, 1735, and married (1st) Rhoda, daughter of Joseph Rose, and (2d) ——— Gardner.* He was a private in 2d Foot Company, Captain Theophilus Cushing, of Hingham on September 15, 1755.† Also a private in Captain Enoch Whiton's Company, Colonel Benjamin Lincoln's Regiment, which assembled April 19, 1775, and served three days. Also a private in Captain Pyam Cushing's Company, Colonel Solomon Lowell's Regiment, assembled at Dorchester, March 4, 1776.‡ He died May 1, 1814. His children, born in Hingham were:

JONATHAN, born September 23, 1757.

MELZAR, died at sea.

RHODA, married Thomas Steel October 21, 1810.

JOSHUA.

*Hist. Hing., Vol. III, p. 297.
†Original Muster Rolls in possession of Soc. Col. Wars, N. Y. Chapter.
‡Mass. Rev. Rolls.

47 ELISHA, son of Jonathan (19), was born in Hingham November 3, 1737, and married January 10, 1760, Jael, daughter of Samuel and Martha (Groce) Dunbar. She

was baptized in Hingham May 28, 1738, and died September 21, 1832. His occupation was that of a butcher; he resided on Gardiner Street, Hingham, where his childred were born.* He was a private in 2d Foot Company, Captain Theophilus Cushing's Company, 2d Foot Soldiers, on September 15, 1755.† He was a private in Captain Joseph Baxter's Co., General Lovell's Brigade, enlisting August 5, 1776. Also in Captain Pyam Cushing's (3d) Company of 2d Parish, Hingham, Colonel Solomon Lovell's Regiment, April 4, 1776, also March 11, 1776, to March 29, 1776. Also in Captain Wilder's Company, Colonel Nicholas Dike's Regiment, from February 3, 1776, to March 1, 1776, credited to Hingham. Also in Captain Silas Wild's Company, Colonel Brook's Regiment, guarding troops of the convention at Cambridge, Mass., from November 12, 1777, to April 3, 1778.‡ He died February 8, 1819.

Children:

ELISHA, born October 27, 1760, married Chloe Wilder September 12, 1782. His daughter Tamar, born in 1783, married February 24, 1805, William Perry of Andover, Mass.

HANNAH, born September 21, 1762, married May 16, 1784, Elijah Lewis, and died September 20, 1789.

GRACE, born June 2, 1765, died unmarried in Boston.

RACHEL, born August 23, 1767, died unmarried in Boston May 13, 1803.

EMMA, born February 8, 1770, married Martin Hersey of Gilbert, Mass.

CALEB, born May 7, 1772, and died July 4, 1773.

TAMAR, born and died February, 1775.

CALEB, born in 1777. Removed to Vermont and had one child.

*Hist. Hing., Vol. III, p. 297.
†Original Muster Rolls in possession of Soc. Col. Wars, N. Y. Chapter.
‡Mass. Rev. Rolls.

48 JOTHAM, son of Eleazer (20), was born December 18, 1746, and married Susanna, daughter of Ephraim and Susanna (Whiton) (14) Wilder, January 1, 1771. She died January 24, 1828. His occupation was that of a

blacksmith and he resided in East Abington.* He was a private in Captain William Reed's Company, Colonel John Bailey's Regiment of Minute Men, who marched on the alarm of Lexington, April 19, 1775; served one week and five days. Also a private in Captain Edward Cobb's Company, Major Eliphalet Cary's Regiment, from July 30, 1780, to August 9, 1780, marching from Abington to Tiverton, R. I., on an alarm.† He died May 24, 1828.

Children:

SUSANNA, born in 1771, died in 1773.

SUSANNA, born March 9, 1774, married Bela Cushing in 1803, and died August 27, 1818.

MARY, born October 9, 1775, married Jos. Turner in 1796 and died in 1800.

SARAH, born March 6, 1778, married Melzar Beal of Abington July 15, 1797, and died January 31, 1850.

LYDIA, born January 14, 1780, married Jared Shaw of Abington in 1802, and died December 15, 1819.

LUCY, born April 10, 1782, married Jos. Benner of Abington in 1803, and died July 3, 1836.

JERUSHA, born August 12, 1785, married Wm. Wheeler of Quincy in 1806, and died June 5, 1810.

MERIEL, born July 24, 1787, married Samuel Colson of Abington in 1812, and died March 29, 1834.

EPHRAIM (87).

EMMA, born September 3, 1793, in Abington.

*Hist. Hanover, p. 429.
†Mass. Rev. Rolls.

49 BARZILLAI, son of Eleazer (20), was born March 5, 1757, and married Abigail, daughter of Jedediah and Hannah Beal, of Hingham, who was born May 28, 1760, died April 24, 1844.* He served as a private in Captain Edward Cobb's Company, Major Eliphalet Cary's Regiment, marched July 30, 1780, from Abington to Tiverton, R. I., on an alarm, serving ten days. Also on December 9, 1776, to Bristol, R. I., from Abington, on an alarm.†

Children:

ABIGAIL, married Isaac Turner of Hingham, and died October 14, 1845.

ELEAZER (88).

ITHAMAR (89).

JOANNA, born February 28, 1791.

MARILLA, born in 1799, and died January 25, 1802.

*Hist. Hanover, p. 429.
†Mass. Rev. Rolls.

HANNAH CROCKER—See 28, page 42.

In August, 1932, after pages were made up, and just before printing, the chairman of the Publication Committee received the following information showing the Mayflower descent of Hannah Crocker, second wife of Squire Elijah Whiton of Westford, Conn.

John and Elizabeth Tilley, their daughter Elizabeth, and her husband, John Howland, came over on the Mayflower.

Their daughter, Hope Howland, married John Chipman
Their daughter, Ruth Chipman, married Eleazor Crocker
Their son, Eleazor Crocker, married Judith Sanders
Their daughter, Hannah Crocker, married Elijah Whiton

---

58 Amasa Whiton

70 Thomas Whiting

72 Caleb Whiting

75 William Whiting

79 Moses Whiton

FACSIMILE SIGNATURES—6th GENERATION
From Barry's History of Hanover

SIXTH GENERATION

50 ELISHA, son of Elisha (21), born in 1729 in Plympton, Mass., married (1st) Betsy Holmes and (2d) Mary Harding, widow of John Howard, February 10, 1774, in Pembroke, Mass.*

Children:

LEVI (90).
JOSEPH (91).
NATHAN (92).
EPHRAIM (93).
BENJAMIN (94).
JOSIAH, moved to Ohio.
MARY, married Josiah Morton.
JOSIE.

All of the above, children of Betsy, assumed the name of Whiting.

ABRAHAM (95).
AMOS (96).
MELZAR (97).

The last three, children of Mary, assumed the name of Whitten.

*Anc. Landmarks of Plymouth, p. 284.

51 JAMES, son of James (22), was born in Chatham, Conn., December 18, 1757, and married (1st) Sarah, daughter of Joseph and Kezia Loomis, on December 12, 1776, who was born at Windsor, Conn., April 13, 1759, and died May 29, 1781; and (2d) Abigail, daughter of John C. Seward, on February 17, 1782, who died June 13, 1863. He joined the church at Wintonbury, Conn., December 28, 1777, on which day his son James was baptized. He owned much valuable real estate in Lenox, Lee and Granville, Mass.* He served as a private in Captain Benjamin Clark's Company, Connecticut Militia, in the Revolutionary War,† and died at Lee, March 18, 1823.*

Children:

JAMES (98).
POLLY, born June 30, 1779, in Granville, Mass., married June 22, 1806, John Hubbard, Jr.
JOHN MANDLEY (99).

FLAVEL, born June 24, 1783, and died in June, 1816, in New York.
SAMUEL, born August 1, 1785.
EPAPHRODITUS, born May 13, 1787, married Sibel Melissa Whitmore, and died June 19, 1822.
SHERMAN, born April 4, 1790, and died February, 1817.
SARAH, born November 26, 1792, married September 18, 1816, Moses Strong.
PERSIS, born January 22, 1795.
SOPHIA, born March 15, 1799, married May 14, 1824, Dr. Reuben Nims.
TERZA, born October 31, 1802, married Cyreno Berk.

*Official Records. Lee, Mass.
†Conn. Rev. Rolls, p. 134.

52 THOMAS, son of James (22), was born in Chatham, Conn., March 3, 1756, and died April 29, 1829. He married Lucy Flint, who was born September 2, 1757, and died October 14, 1833.* He enlisted in the Revolutionary War at Ashford, Conn., in December, 1775, and served in Captain John Keyes's Company, Colonel John Durkee's Connecticut Regiment, and was in the battles at Harlem.† He also stated that he was "in the cannonading at Cambridge and the battles of Bergen Point and Paulus Hook, New York."‡ He is said to have been in Colonel Waterbury's 10th Connecticut Regiment.† He was granted a pension under the Act of 1818, at which time he was living at Eaton, Madison County, N. Y.‡

Children:
Daughter, born in 1792.
THOMAS (100).

*Family Records.
†Conn. Rev. Rolls., p. 644.
‡Rev. Pension Rolls, Claim S. 44049.

53 JOSEPH, son of James (22), was born in Chatham, Conn., November 9, 1759, and married October 17, 1793, in Lee, Mass., Amanda Garfield, who was born in 1775 and died January 15, 1847. Orphaned in boyhood, Joseph and his four brothers were brought up by their father's cousin, Elijah Whiton of Ashford.

TOMBSTONE OF GEN. JOSEPH WHITON (53)
In Fairmount Cemetery, Lee, Mass.

He first enlisted in the Revolutionary War in August, 1776, in Captain Simeon Smith's Company, Colonel Experience Storrs's Connecticut Regiment: in August, 1777, in Captain Isaac Stone's Company, Colonel Jonathan Lattimer's Connecticut Regiment, and was in battles preceding the surrender of Burgoyne: he enlisted again in April, 1780, and was acting steward in Captain Bottome's Company, Colonel Levi Wells's Connecticut Regiment.* He is also said to have been Adjutant of the 2d Battalion in General Waterbury's Regiment, Major Elijah Humphrey, in defense of New Haven, enlisting April 24, 1781. In 1776 he received pay as a wounded soldier,† and was later granted a pension.‡ About 1784 he went to Berkshire County, Massachusetts, where he taught school for a time and then settled in Lee, where he entered the mercantile business. He became a prominent citizen, serving as a Justice of the Peace and as a member of the Legislature. He also served in the War of 1812, and was appointed a General.§ He died in Lee, Mass., August 16, 1828. A tract of land in the Western Reserve, now Amherst, Ohio, was granted him for his Revolutionary service: there some of his descendants are now living.

Children:

SAMANTHA, born August 30, 1794, married in 1810, her cousin Ebenezer (105), and lived in Elyria, Ohio, and died in 1878.

HARRIET, born March 9, 1796, married ——— Freeman, lived in Rochester, N. Y., and died in 1872.

AMANDA, born October 10, 1797, married February 24, 1819, Henry Church, lived in Rochester, N. Y., and had four children: Joseph, Helen, Frances, and Catherine. The last married Giles H. Gray and had a daughter, Frances H. Gray.

JOSEPH LUCAS (101).

DANIEL GARFIELD (102).

EDWARD VERNON (103).

ELIZA, born April 16, 1807, and died in 1885. She married in 1835, Hiram Guthrie Daniel, who was born in 1816 and died in 1893. They had two children: Mary Garfield, born in 1845, who married George Wyatt Plantz of Pomeroy, Ohio, October 11, 1870, who was born in Pomeroy September 27, 1843, in which city he was cashier of the First City Bank, and died April 7, 1914, leaving a son, Wyatt Garfield, who was born in Pomeroy, November 24, 1873, succeeded his father as cashier of the First City Bank, and resides at 314 Main Street, Pomeroy, Ohio. The second child was Catherine Whiton, born in 1836, and married William Perry Rathburn, who was born in 1822, and died in 1884. She died in 1910, leaving a daughter, Anna Grace, who married Clarence C. Nottingham, who died in 1928. She resides at 603 Pine Street, Chattanooga, Tenn.

CATHERINE, born March 8, 1810, and married Hiram Howe, had a daughter, Agnes, who died young.

AGNES, born August 12, 1813, married February 1, 1838, Lorenzo D. Brown, and died in Lee, Mass., in 1874. They had several children who died young, and a daughter, Agnes, who married Doctor Clifford C. Holcomb.

*Rev. Pension Records, Claim W. 14145. Conn. Men in the Rev.
†Conn. Rev. Sick Bills, p. 156.
‡Draper's Pensions, p. 599.
§Family Records.

54 EBENEZER, son of James (22), was born in 1762, and married (1st) Caroline ———, and (2d) Rosannah ———. There were several conveyances of realty to him recorded in Pittsfield, between the years 1782 and 1792. Upon his death in 1828, Joseph Whiton was appointed guardian of his children, and Joseph and John Whiton, his administrators.* His tombstone is in Stockbridge, Mass. He served as a private in Captain Matthew Chamber's Company, Lieutenant Colonel Calvin Smith's (6th) Regiment, from August 22, 1782, to December 31, 1784; also in the same regiment under Captain Manning, from June 6, 1777, to January 9, 1778. Also in Captain Hill's Company, Colonel Samuel McClellan's Regiment, from July 1, 1778, to March 1, 1779.†

Children:

EBENEZER (104).

CAROLINE, born December 6, 1786.

LYDIA, married a Rossiter and joined the Congregational Church in Stockbridge in 1813.

*Probate Records in Pittsfield, Mass.
†Mass. Rev. Rolls.

TOMBSTONES OF JOHN and MARY WHITON (55)
Ithaca City Cemetery, Ithaca, N. Y.

55 JOHN, son of James (22), was born September 11, 1763, and married in Wintonbury, Conn., September 27, 1784, Mary, daughter of Joel and Mary (Evans) Griswold, who was a descendant of Edward, David and Joel Griswold, who served in the Colonial Wars. She was one of eight children and was baptized December 2, 1764. The family moved to Great Barrington, and then about the year 1789 to Stockbridge, Mass., where they united in 1791 with the First Congregational Church, in which he was a deacon from 1817 to 1819. About 1812 he built a house in Stockbridge, which is still standing, having for many years been used as a rectory of the Episcopal Church, and is now occupied by a sister of a former rector. It was enlarged and modernized some years ago by the architectural firm of McKim, Meade and White, who endeavored to retain as much of the original character as possible. There are several conveyances of realty to him recorded in Pittsfield between 1772 and 1824. He was a skilled cabinet maker, and engaged in that business both in Stockbridge and in Ithaca, N. Y., to which place he removed and where he died March 24, 1827.

Children:

WARREN, born July 25, 1785.

MARY. (See Appendix D.)

SAMUEL, born September 24, 1788, and died October 31, 1788.

LUTHER (105).

CLARISSA, born December 26, 1791, and married in 1814, Augustus Sherrill, "a lawyer who has borne many honors," and died in 1854. Their child was Mary, born in Stockbridge, July 31, 1815, and married Hezekiah Seymour in Ithaca, N. Y., February 8, 1836, who was born in Westmoreland, Oneida Co., N. Y., June 24, 1811, and died in Piermont, N. Y., July 29, 1885. Their children were: (a) Augustus Sherrill, born November 30, 1836, who married Nannie O. Barton at Clinton, N. Y., October 22, 1863. He was appointed a U. S. District Judge and resided at Newbern, N. C., where he died February 19, 1897. Their children were: (1) Nellie, born September 17, 1865, at Clinton, N. Y., who married William Welsh of Marshfield, Manchester, England, August 7, 1887, having two children:

William Talcott, born May 17, 1888, and Augustus Seymour, born November 17, 1891; (2) John Barton, born July 4, 1873, at Clinton, and (3) Minnie Thomas, born March 17, 1877, dying March 10, 1878. (b) Louise, born November 22, 1838, married Elihu R. Houghton at Piermont, N. Y., December 30, 1856. They had five children: (1) Mary, born April 10, 1858, at Piermont; (2) Clara, known as Daisy, born June 11, 1861, at Piermont, and married Joseph Hutchinson at Amherst, Mass., July 2, 1885, and died at Newbern, N. C., June 8, 1887; (3) E. Russell, born March 26, 1864, at Piermont, and married Louise Phillips, October 7, 1891. Their children were: Seymour Phillips, born May 7, 1893, in Havre, France; Augustus Sherrill, born in New York City, January 15, 1898, and Margaret, born October 16, 1898, on Staten Island, New York City; (4) Augustus Seymour, born January 3, 1866, at Piermont, and married Carolyn LaBarr Squire, November 12, 1896; (5) Matthew Henry, born October 10, 1878, at Piermont, and married Lucile W. Haplinger at Newcastle, Kentucky, June 1, 1898. (c) Sarah, born September 7, 1840, and married September 7, 1859, Matthew H. Houghton, a brother of Elihu R. (supra). Their children were: (1) Hezekiah Seymour, born April 7, 1862, at Piermont, and married Sadie Preston January 5, 1885. They had three children: Florence born June 28, 1889; Helene, born June 8, 1891, and Henry Seymour, born January 3, 1896; (2) Clarence Sherrill, born April 28, 1864, at Piermont, and married Suzanne Clark of Louisville, Ky., December 18, 1895. He was a United States Commissioner in the Southern District of New York, where he died; and (3) Robert Serviten, born May 28, 1874, at Monmouth Beach, N. J., and died August 16, 1875. (d) Clara, born February 20, 1843, and married A. B. Dennison of Newbern at Norwood, N. J., January 13, 1869. They had four children: (1) Louise Seymour, born at Newbern December 15, 1869; (2) Mary Sherrill, born at Newbern, N. C., May, 1873, and died in June, 1876; (3) Amy, born at Monmouth Beach, N. J., and died August, 1875, and (4) Augustus Seymour, born at Newbern October 8, 1878. (e) Amelia, born January 27, 1845. (f) Henry Cook, born February 27, 1847, and (g) Mary, born May 3, 1850.

SOPHIA, born March 13, 1794, and died October 10, 1795.

JOHN, born February 13, 1796, and graduated at Williams College (1818) and Andover Theological Seminary. He was a trustee of Williams College from 1833 to 1838, and preached at Union, N. Y., Salem, N. Y., Enfield, Mass.,

Amherst, Mass., and Stockbridge, Mass. In 1825 he married Eunice Wright, by whom he had a son Henry. He removed finally to Wolcott, N. Y., where he died November 25, 1868.

JULIA, born July 15, 1799, and married Henry Leonard at Ithaca, N. Y., November 13, 1821. One child was born, Caroline, on May 27, 1823, who married Thedosius Judd, May 27, 1841, at Ithaca, and moved to Elmira in 1852. Her other child, Anna May, was born May 13, 1856, in Elmira, N. Y., and married May 9, 1877, John Hathorn, by whom she had a son Judd Whiton, born January 9, 1887.

GEORGE (106).

56 DANIEL, son of Daniel (27), was born in Hingham, October 30, 1745, and married April 7, 1767, Desire, daughter of Hezekiah and Abigail (Whiton) (9) Stodder, of Scituate, Mass., who was born in Scituate November 16, 1745, and died in Hingham February 28, 1820. He was a farmer and resided on Whiting Street, Hingham, where his children were born.* He served as a private in Captain Pyam Cushing's Company, Colonel Solomon Lovell's Regiment, assembled to guard the shore, March 4, 1776; and in the same company assembled at Dorchester and at Hull, Mass., in June, 1776.† He died about 1822.

Children:

MARTHA, born November 29, 1768, and married Enoch Whiton (82) September 14, 1786.

MEHITABLE, born April 23, and died young.

DANIEL (107).

GALEN (108).

SYLVANUS (109).

HOSEA, born June 24, 1778.

MEHITABLE, born January 23, 1781, and married Elias Whiton (86) July 1, 1804.

JOSIAH (110).

ABIGAIL, born March 1, 1788, and died December, 1795.

*Hist. Hing., Vol. III, p. 297. Hist. Hanover, p. 429.
†Mass. Rev. Rolls.

57 ZACHARIAH, son of Daniel (27), was born in Hingham December 19, 1747. He married Keziah, daughter of Theophilus and Mary (Hersey) Wilder,

December 12, 1770. She was born in Hingham in 1747 and died in 1834. By occupation a carpenter, he served as constable in 1774, and resided at Liberty Plain, Hingham.* He served as sergeant in Captain Pyam's Company, Colonel Solomon Lovell's Regiment, from March 4 to 8, 1776, and from November 14 to 29, 1776; also as 2d Sergeant in Captain Lincoln's Company, Colonel Lovell's Regiment, from December 14 to 18, 1776. Also as 2d Lieutenant in Joseph Baxter's Company, Colonel Macintosh's Regiment, detached from militia for expedition to Rhode Island. Also in Captain Elias Whiton's Company, Colonel Symms's Regiment, March 9, 1777, to June 9, 1777. Also 1st Lieutenant in Captain Jabez Wilder's Company, 2d Regiment, Suffolk County Militia, March 10, 1779.† He is also mentioned with credit in Thatcher's Military History. His children were born in Hingham and he died May 15, 1814.

Children:

PRUDENCE, born 1771, married November 29, 1789, Enoch Lovell of Weymouth, Mass.

CHARLES, born 1773, married November 19, 1795, Lois, daughter of Laban and Persis (Wilder) Stodder.

THEOPHILUS (111).

SUSA, born 1777, married December 29, 1796, Stephen Gardner the 3d.

SYBIL, born October 27, 1780, died unmarried August 13, 1861.

HOSEA (112).

POLLY, born April 27, 1784, married September 25, 1806, Joel Seymour.

MARTHA, born 1787, married November 28, 1811, Jotham Shaw of Weymouth.

PRISCILLA, born 1788, married November 26, 1812, Justin Rogers.

*Hist. Hing., Vol. III, p. 297. Hist. Hanover, p. 430.
†Mass. Rev. Rolls.

58 AMASA, son of Daniel (27), born in Hingham August 24, 1749, and married Lydia, daughter of Dr. Joseph Jacobs, of Scituate. She was born there May 30, 1743. He was a farmer and resided on Main Street, Hingham, where his children were born. He served as Constable in 1776.* He was a private in Captain Enoch Whiton's

Company,* Colonel Benjamin Lincoln's Regiment, assembled on the Lexington Alarm April 19, 1775. Also in Captain Pyam Cushing's Company, Colonel Solomon Lovell's Regiment, assembled at Dorchester March 4, 1776, to guard the shore, and also at Hull in June, 1776.† He died November 5, 1818.

Children:

DAVIS (113).

PEREZ (114).

JAEL, born March 18, 1777, married October 19, 1799, Harris Turner of Scituate.

JOSEPH JACOB (115).

LYDIA, born October 25, 1780, married June 15, 1807, Nathaniel Bump of Middleborough, Mass.

ABIGAIL, born September 30, 1783, married February 3, 1807, Alexander Vining of Abington, Mass.

EUNICE, born June 14, 1786, married February 1, 1807, Nehemiah Ripley, Jr.

*Hist. Hing., Vol. III, p. 298. Hist. Hanover, p. 430.
†Mass. Rev. Rolls.

59 ZENAS, son of Daniel (27), was born in Hingham October 1, 1754, and wrote his name Whiting. He married (1st) Sarah Loring, who died in 1779, and (2d) Leah, daughter of Thomas and Bethia (Smith) Loring, of Hingham, who was born December 4, 1754;* (3d) Phebe Raymond, a widow. He is said to have served on the armed brig Hazard in 1776.* He was also a private in Captain Pyam Cushing's Company, Colonel Benjamin Lincoln's Regiment, assembled at Dorchester to guard the shore March 4, 1776, and also at Hull in June, 1776.† He moved to Norwich, Conn., and in 1794 advertised for workmen to assist him in building a bridge over the Piscataqua River at Portsmouth, N. H. The *Norwich Packet* of January 8, 1795, in a news article, described this as the "most elegant bridge in North America. It is viewed as one of the greatest pieces of mechanical genius done in America; one hundred piers from 20 to 25 feet in length, from 10 to 25 tons of timber in a pier." The same paper on March 17, 1796, tells us that "a model of an arch bridge, on an

entirely new construction, has been completed by the celebrated architect, Captain Zenas Whiting, of this City, and was sent off on Saturday last for Newport to be embarked on a ship bound for Petersburg in Russia. Thus we see the great Tyrant of the north condescending to become dependent for mechanical invention on the genius of the New Hemisphere. The bridge which the Empress has it in contemplation to build is to be erected over the River Neva, which divides the City of

THE PISCATAQUA BRIDGE

From a Sketch in "A Tour to the Eastern States in the year 1797" by Robert Gilmor of Baltimore

Petersburg, and is to be a single arch of eight hundred feet in length."‡

Child, by Sarah:

SARAH, born in Hingham March 3, 1779, and married Peakes Groce.

Children, by Leah:

ZENAS LORING, born July 3, 1780.
HARRIET, born August 3, 1782.
SOPHIA, born in 1784, married Captain Shuball Bronson, and died in New Haven, Conn., November 9, 1868. Their son George, born in 1812, died January 19, 1830.
FRANCIS.
LEAH, baptized in 1792.
DANIEL, baptized in 1792.

*Hist. Hing., Vol. III, p. 298.
†Mass. Rev. Rolls.
‡Old Houses of the Ancient Town of Norwich, p. 274.

HOMESTEAD AT WESTFORD HILL, CONN.
Built about 1800 by Joseph Whiton (60)

TOMBSTONE OF JOSEPH WHITON (60)
Westford Hill, Conn.

JOANNA (WHITON) WALKER
Daughter of Joseph (60)

60 JOSEPH, son of Elijah (28), was born at Ashford, Conn., in 1745, and married there October 4, 1770, Joanna, daughter of David and Martha (Walker) Chaffee, who was born January 3, 1750, and died August 11, 1820. He combined the trades of carpentry and coopering with farming. The house built by him in 1800 has always been owned and occupied by members of the family, and is now (1932) the home of Miss Ellen L. Whiton. He was a member of the Ashford, Conn., Committee on Supplies during the Revolutionary War.* When the new church at Westford was organized he was one of the first signers of the church covenant February 15, 1768. An old record calls him a "very pious and worthy man." He died at Westford June 6, 1817.

Children:

PRISCILLA, married May 21, 1823, Asa Royce of Willington, Conn.

MARTHA, born January 25, 1774, died January 25, 1847.

STEPHEN (116).

JOSEPH (117).

ELIJAH (118).

DAVID, born March 25, 1780, married December 10, 1805, Mary, daughter of Nathaniel and Jerusha Hodgkins of Hampton, Conn., who was born February 11, 1785, and died February 5, 1843. Their son, John H., was born September 4, 1806, and died May 11, 1826, and their son Warren was born May 10, 1810, and died 1811.

HEBER (119).

JOANNA, born May 10, 1784, married January 24, 1804, Timothy Walker, who was born May 19, 1781, and died September 15, 1855. She died November 22, 1870. Their children were: (1) John Milton, born May 2, 1804, and married Caroline Ashley of Hampton, Conn., and had a son, Philo; (2) Lyman, born November 5, 1805, and died September 30, 1828; (3) Harvey, born February 22, 1808, married Julia Ann White, and died March 4, 1860. Their children were: Laura W., Josephine, and Frederick H.; (4) Levi, born March 11, 1810, and married Ludisa Sabastian, who was born December 27, 1831, and died November 21, 1911. Their children are (aa) Harvey S., born August 31, 1851, married Maggie E. Hart December 9, 1874, and died July 29, 1922; (bb) Mary Belle, born July 8, 1853, married August 18, 1874, Curtis L. Spicer and died December 7, 1928; (cc) Frank, born November 21, 1856, married October 15, 1885, Mollie A. Fulmer; (dd) John, born October 15, 1858, and died January 1, 1873; (ee) Daniel, born April 13, 1863, and (ff) Annie, born March 9, 1868, who married May 22, 1889, John W. Kelley. They had three children: Walker, born January 24, 1890, and served in France in Company C, 8th Field Signal Battalion, and now resides in Wallace, Neb.; Herbert, born April 13, 1894, was a Sergeant in Company B, 529th Engineers, in the World War and resides in Kansas City, Mo., and D ——— L———, born October 25, 1897, and is the President of the Union Savings and Loan Association of Kansas City, Mo.; (5) Minerva, born July 12, 1812, married Willard Fuller of Willington, Conn.; (6) Hartley, born December 22, 1814, married Josephine Reed of Union, Conn., and died in July, 1887. Their children are Judge Hartley Reed Walker of Orange, Mass., and Harriet J., who married Frederick H. Moore of Worcester, Mass.; (7) Paulina, born January 27, 1817, and died 1819; (8) Timothy, born September 28, 1819; (9) Milo, born October 25, 1821; (10) Celia, born September 15, 1823, and died June 2, 1856.

SARAH, born February 26, 1785, married Ezekiel Chapman, who was born in 1785 and died May 16, 1873. She died October 25, 1847. Their children died young.

ABNER (120).

*Conn. Rev. Records.

61 ELIJAH, son of Elijah (28), was born in Ashford, Conn., in 1747 or 1748, and married January 3, 1771, Anna, daughter of Obadiah and Anna (Watkins) Brown, also of Ashford, who was born September 14, 1750. They settled in Tolland where their children were born and where he died May 5, 1804. He is buried in the South Cemetery there.* In the Revolutionary War he was a member of Captain Willes's Company, Douglas's Regiment and is mentioned in "Private Clothing Account" and as a soldier at Tolland in 1776.† June 29, 1778, he enlisted for three months as a sergeant in Captain Robinson's Company, Colonel Roger Eno's Regiment, in service on the Hudson;‡ in May, 1780, he was ensign in First Company of the Train Band, 22d Regiment.§ He was a pensioner and received

ELIJAH WHITON'S (61) HOUSE (The Brick House), Westford Hill, Conn.

a Bounty Land Warrant for his service. In May, 1781, the Connecticut Legislature appointed him Surveyor for Hartford County.§

Children:

MATILDA, born May 29, 1772.
MARTHA, born February 29, 1775.
ANNA, born April 6, 1778.
VODICEA, born August 9, 1780.
HANNAH, born January 26, 1783.
ELIJAH (121).
SYBIL, born February 8, 1788, died February 28, 1790.
MARIA, born October 16, 1790, married Jason Smith and lived in Randolph, Vt., where a daughter, Julianna Matilda, was born April 6, 1812. She married, in Hampton, Conn., June 1, 1836, Ephraim Keep of Monson, Mass., and had children: Elvira, Marcus, Jason S., and Julia. The last was born February 26, 1849, and married August 4, 1875, Daniel Green Hitchcock of Warren, Mass.

*Town Records, Tolland.
†Sick Bills, p. 152.
‡Conn. Men in the Rev.
§Official Public Records of Conn., Vol. III.

62 STEPHEN, son of Elijah (28), was born in Ashford, Conn., August 2, 1752, and killed with his father-in-law, in the Wyoming Indian Massacre, in Pennsylvania, July 3, 1778. He married Eunice, daughter of Anderson and Susannah Dana, who was born June 10, 1758, and who fled on foot, back to Ashford, a distance of 300 miles, where their daughter was born.

Child:

EUNICE DANA, born September 12, 1778, and married Hezekiah Parsons, who was born March 25, 1777, and died April 9, 1845. Their children were: Calvin, born in Parsons, Pa., April 2, 1815, and died January 1, 1900; he married Ann Pasco and had children: Oliver A., born 1837, died 1920, who married Martha ———; Louisa A., born May 4, 1840, married Clarence P. Kidder May 4, 1864, and died January 28, 1927. Louisa A. had children: Calvin P., born March 17, 1865, died 1912, married Emma E. Nichols, born at West Pittston, Pa., August 27, 1864, died at Wilkesbarre, Pa., June 4, 1923; Mary Louise, born in Wilkesbarre, April 27, 1868, resides at Forty Fort, Pa.; Clarence L., born November 15, 1874, married Ada Wilkie and resides at Wilkesbarre, Pa.

63 ISRAEL, son of Elijah (28), was born in Ashford, Conn., September 3, 1754, and married October 26, 1784, Dorothy, daughter of Samuel and Azubah (How) Crosby of Shrewsbury, Mass., who was born August 26, 1760, and died October 7, 1826. By his own efforts he acquired an education, studying first for the ministry but later turning to medicine. When news came of the battle of Lexington he, with others of his family,* joined the Connecticut troops and marched to Boston. He is said to have been an aide to General Putnam at the battle of Bunker Hill. He went with the army to New York and was in the engagements at Long Island, Harlem and White Plains; he was a surgeon in the Regiment of Colonel Knowlton. At the expiration of his term of service he located in Winchendon, Mass., and entered upon the practice of his profession. At the time of Shay's Rebellion in 1786/7 Israel Whiton was a loyal supporter of the government and opposed the movement. A party of insurgents attacked his home and threatened him with a bayonet; an old soldier, he successfully defended himself with a long-handled shovel. His wife siezed her sleeping child and fled to the woods; that child became the Rev. Dr. Whiton (122). A practicing physician for forty-two years he became eminent in his profession; at one time he maintained a medical school. He was a deacon in the church, a magistrate, represented his town in the Legislature and in 1808 he was chairman of a committee to petition the President of the United States to suspend the embargo as a whole or in part. In 1812 he was chairman of a committee to memorialize the President to the effect that the town beleived the war to be unnecessary. It is said that later, smallpox having broken out in the army, he volunteered to serve in a smallpox hospital near Mystic, Conn. In 1811 he bought 240 acres of land, including an outlet on Monomonauk Lake. He died May 19, 1819, and his epitaph says of him: "A member of the Christian Church, a friend of the Gospel and a lover of good

ISRAEL WHITON (63)

DOROTHY, WIFE OF ISRAEL WHITON

men." On his tombstone in Winchendon appears the following:

"Reader, who e'er thou art attend,
And as these earth-born glories end,
I once had hopes, fears, joys and pains,
And now cold clay's all that remains.
I've paid the debt to Nature due,
Relentless death says so must ycu."

At the centennial celebration of the town of Winchendon, Mass., a hymn was sung, one verse of which read:

"Our father's God, to Thee we raise
Our hearts in songs of grateful praise.
For all the mercies Thou hast shown,
E'er while a hundred years have flown.
The wild woods waved o'er all the waste,
The streams flowed by in useless haste;
In swift pursuit the fierce wolf ran,
The stealthy savage marked his man."

A footnote adds that this refers to an incident in the life of Dr. Whiton.

Children:

JOHN MILTON (122).

DOLLY, born April 6, 1788, died unmarried October 7, 1812.

ISRAEL, born May 30, 1791, died unmarried March 17, 1815.

OTIS CROSBY, born September 27, 1794, married Polly Gibbs Jewett, who died November 25, 1824. He was a clergyman, settled in Canterbury, Conn., and later in Yarmouth, Me.*

Tradition says that several of the sons and foster-sons of Squire Elijah Whiton were active at the battle of Bunker Hill.

*Family Records.

†Hist. Winchendon, pp. 4, 72, 115, 250, 420 and 423.

64 BOAZ, son of Elijah (28), was born December 25, 1762. He married January 31, 1788, Tryphena, daughter of Peter and Abigail (Hill) Eastman. She was born October 2, 1765, and died in Westford, Conn., December 30, 1831. Her father is said to have served in the Revolutionary War. Boaz was a man of exemplary piety, and very highly respected. He died January 22, 1852.

Children:

ABIGAIL, born September 30, 1789, married September 27, 1821, George Dunworth, and had a daughter, Matilda, born in 1822, and died in 1830. Abigail died July 27, 1855.
HANNAH, born October 29, 1790, and died April 12, 1880.
FLAVEL (123).
ELEAZER, born September 9, 1795, married January 17, 1832, Lucretia Searles, and died May 3, 1858.
HORACE (124).
MATILDA, born April 19, 1800, and died March 25, 1830.
ROSWELL, born May 18, 1803, and died May 3, 1892.
CHAUNCEY (125).

*Town Records in Hartford.

65 SAMUEL, son of James (29), date of birth unknown. He was said to have been a sergeant in the Revolutionary War, and to have been killed while scouting at Horse's Neck, N. Y.

66 WILSON, son of James (29), was born April 9, 1759, married November 20, 1783, Mary, daughter of John and Tabitha (Hall) Hanks, who was born November 12, 1764, in Mansfield, Conn., and died in Westford, Conn., August 22, 1809. After her death he, with his nine children, moved to Onondaga County, N. Y.*

Children:

TABITHA, born July 17, 1784.
PERSIS, born May 20, 1786.
SAMUEL, born April 2, 1788.
JARED, born September 26, 1790.
MEHITABLE, born November 11, 1792.
JAMES, born February 6, 1795.
PHILENA, born April 12, 1797.
ANNA, born March 1, 1802, and married Dr. Tower Whiton Crain.
JOHN, born October 16, 1803.

*Town Records of Ashford in Hartford.

67 BENJAMIN, son of Benjamin (30), was baptized in Hingham November 29, 1741, and married Joanna, daughter of John and Joanna (Farrow) Gardner, September 22, 1766, who was born in Hingham February

28, 1744, and died April 15, 1807. He was a farmer and resided near Accord Pond, South Hingham.* He was a private in Colonel David Cushing's Regiment on March 4, 1778. He also had served under Major Thos. Lathrop at Hull on February 27, 1778. He also served as a private in Captain Enoch Whiton's Company, Colonel Benjamin Lincoln's Regiment, on the Lexington Alarm April 19, 1775. Also in Captain Pyam Cushing's Company, Colonel Solomon Lovell's Regiment, at Dorchester March 4, 1776, also March 11, 1776, and March 29, 1776, and twice in June, 1776, assembled at Hull. Also in Captain Herman Lincoln's Company, Colonel Lovell's Regiment, on the march to Hull, December 14, 1776†

The History of Hingham says that he was a man of great mechanical ingenuity and industry. His children were all born in Hingham.

Children:

JOANNA, born January 11, 1768, died July 1782.
ASENATH, born April 10, 1770, died February 11, 1840.
BENJAMIN (126).
JOSEPH (127).
ARCHELAUS (128).
LUTHER (129).

*Hist. Hingham, Vol. III, p. 298. Hist .Hanover, p. 430.
†Mass. Rev. Rolls.

68 EZEKIEL, son of Benjamin (30), was born in Hingham May 4, 1745, and married (1st) Olive, daughter of Hezekiah and Abigail (Whiton)-(9) Stodder, of Scituate, Mass., who was born April 21, 1751, and (2d) Molly, daughter of Thomas and Mary Beal. She was born in Hingham May 1, 1763, and died in November, 1826. He was a farmer and resided on Main Street, Hingham.* He served as a private in Captain Clift's Company, Colonel Josiah Whitney's Regiment, that marched to Rhode Island July 29 to September 13, 1778.† Children all born in Hingham.

Children by Olive:

SARAH, married Asa Souther of Cohasset, November 29, 1795.

LOIS, married Joseph Hill, Jr. of Abington, April 10, 1802.
OLIVE, married Peleg Dunbar February 15, 1805.
ABIGAIL, probably married John Black of Plymouth.
JUDITH, married (1st) Quincy Gardner and (2d) Nicholas Daniels January 12, 1833. She died in Hingham April 15, 1834.

Children by Mary:

EZEKIEL, born in 1804, was a mariner and died in Hingham January 25, 1875.

*Hist. Hingham, Vol. III, p. 299. Hist. Hanover, p. 431.
†Mass. Rev. Rolls.

69 ABEL, son of Benjamin (30), was baptized in Hingham, April, 1759, and married Grace Magneau, widow of Samuel Stoddard, January 9, 1779, and removed to Worcester, Mass., where he died.* He was a private in Capt. Enoch Whiton's Co., Col. Benj. Lincoln's Reg., on the Lexington Alarm April 19, 1775, and served three days. Also in Capt. Cushing's Co., Col. John Greatoris's Reg., as by muster roll dated August 1, 1775. He also served three months beginning April 27, 1775. He was also a private in Capt. Elias Whiton's Co., Col. Symm's Reg., for three months from March 9, 1778. Also in Capt. Jos. Baxter's Co., Col. Macenmoth's Reg., Gen. Lovell's Brigade, August 5, 1778, to September 14, 1778, in Rhode Island.†

Children:

ABEL, born December 4, 1779, lived in Blandford, Mass.
SARAH, born March 19, 1782.
AMOS, born July 1788, married Hannah Keith Bridge and had a son Sidney, and other children.
EZEKIEL, born May 7, 1790.
AMBROSE.
LABAN.
ANDREW, married Lucy Briggs and lived in Waltham, Mass.
SAMUEL, born August 1785, removed to New York, and had a son James W.

*Hist. Hanover, p. 431.
†Mass. Rev. Rolls.

70 THOMAS, son of Thomas (31), sometimes signed his name Thomas Whiting, was born June 3, 1743. He married Rachael Peakes November 15, 1770, and was a

selectman in Hanover in 1780-2 and in 1789.* He served as a private in Capt. Wm. Reed's Co., Col. John Bailey's Regiment of minute men on April 19, 1776.† He died in Hanover December 13, 1805.

Children:

WILLIAM P. (130).
RACHEL, born October 14, 1773, died May 7, 1849.
THOMAS (131).
CHARLES, baptized June 27, 1784.
OLIVE, baptized July 22, 1787, married Pyam Damon June 15, 1814.
MARTIN, baptized July 22, 1792, died young.

*Hist. Hanover, p. 431.
†Mass. Rev. Rolls.

71 JAMES, son of Thomas (31), was born July 26, 1751, and married Thankful, daughter of Lemuel and Mary (Whiting) (26) Whiting (33). She was born February 19, 1759, and died August 3, 1832.* He was a private in Captain Soper's Company, which marched on the Lexington Alarm April 19, 1775; also in same company which marched to Bristol and Providence, R. I., December 10, 1776.†

Children:

THANKFUL, born November 6, 1781, died February 1, 1793.
REBECCA, born May 28, 1784, died August 13, 1786.
JAMES, born December 5, 1789, married Ann Brooks.
MARY, born May 8, 1786, married Uriah Lawrence.
HORATIO (132).
THANKFUL, born December 1, 1794, died unmarried.
RUFUS, born August 7, 1797, died December 24, 1799.
REBECCA, born September 28, 1800, married Zadoc Beal November 20, 1837.

*Hist. Hanover, p. 432.
†Mass. Rev. Rolls.

72 CALEB, son of Thomas (31), born August 9, 1761, married Susa Marne April 23, 1785. She died November 25, 1842. He lived in Hanover and died May 20, 1848.

Children:

CALEB, born 1788, died 1792.
LUCY, born January 17, 1791, died June 15, 1840.

SUSA G., born December 26, 1793, died October 11, 1794.

CALEB, born March 21, 1795, married (1st) Mary Whiting (75) June 9, 1823. She died September 2, 1850, and (2d) Anne, daughter of Gideon Studley, May 11, 1852, by whom he had a daughter, Mary W.

SAGE, born April 20, 1797, married Davis Nichols of Cohasset, November 28, 1817.

EZRA (133).

JARED, born March 15, 1804, married Desire Loring of Hingham, 1838.

LYDIA P., born September 26, 1806, married ——— Briggs, and died September 28, 1849.

*Hist. Hanover, p. 431. Hist. Hing., Vol. III, p. 300.

73 ELIAS, son of Thomas (31), was born February 8, 1753, and married Deborah Jackson, who was born in 1757, and died May 20, 1818. He died in Hanover May 20, 1790.* He was a sergeant on the Lexington Alarm in Captain Enoch Whiton's Company, Colonel Benjamin Lincoln's Regiment, serving three days. Also ensign in Captain Jotham Loring's Company, General Heath's Regiment, stationed at Hingham May 28, 1775. Also a lieutenant in Captain Cushing's Company, 36th Regiment, according to return dated October 5, 1775. Also a lieutenant in Captain Pyam Cushing's Company, assembled at Dorchester April 4, 1776. Also in the same company between March 11 and 29, 1776, assembled to guard the shore.†

Children:

RUTH, born January 30, 1779.

JUSTUS, born September 14, 1780, married Abigail Wilder of Hingham, was a farmer in Hanover, and had no children.

BENJAMIN, born April 23, 1782, and removed to Maine.

SARAH, born August 27, 1784, died April 4, 1804.

AMOS, born August 9, 1786.

EDMUND, born and died 1788.

ELIAS, born 1789, died 1793.

*Hist. Hanover, p. 432.
†Mass. Rev. Rolls.

74 ASA, son of Thomas (31), born April 2, 1755. He married (1st) Deborah Dweller April 3, 1786, who died January 8, 1787, and (2d) Betty Whiting (32) April 12, 1789. He lived in Hanover and moved to Lunenburg, where he died.* He was a private in Captain Joseph Soper's Company (North Company of Militia for Hanover), marching to Marshfield on the Lexington Alarm. He also served under the direction of the field officers of 2d Plymouth Company, and was also a private in Captain Soper's Company, Colonel John Cushing's Regiment, marching to Bristol, R. I., December 8 and 10, 1776.

Children:

ASA, born 1790, died 1793.
ELIJAH, born August 22, 1792, died in 1842 unmarried.
DEBORAH, born December 10, 1794, married Nathan Beal of Abington, died December 17, 1821, leaving a son, Nathan.
ASA, born October 14, 1797, moved to Lunenburg.
BETTY, baptized October 23, 1803, married ——— Battles and removed to Fitchburg, Mass.

***Hist. Hanover, p. 433.**
†Mass. Rev. Rolls.

75 WILLIAM WHITING, son of William (32), was born May 23, 1762, and married Betsy Clapp of Scituate, Mass. He was a selectman in Hanover in 1803 and died March 19, 1825.*

Children:

AVIS, born March 17, 1803, married G. W. Turner October 22, 1829.
MARY, born January 30, 1805, married Caleb Whiting (32) June 9, 1823, and died September 2, 1850.
SYLVANUS (134).
WILLIAM (135).

***Hist. Hanover, p. 433.**

76 JOSEPH, son of Solomon (34), was born April 19, 1754. He married Abigail, daughter of Isaac Alden, in 1778, and moved to Bridgewater, Mass.* He served in Captain John Alden's Company at Pepperellborough, according to a receipt dated April 17, 1776. Also as a

private in Captain Amasa Soper's Company, Colonel Thomas Marshall's Regiment, from July 13, 1776, to August 1, 1776, and from November 1, 1776, to December 1, 1776.†

Child:

ASA (136).

*Hist. Hanover, p. 426.
†Mass. Rev. Rolls.

77 ELIJAH, son of David (36), was born in Hingham February 5, 1741, and married Lydia, daughter of Peter and Margaret (Whiton) (13) Lincoln. She was born in Hingham July 7, 1741, and died March 23, 1827. He was a farmer and resided at Hingham Center.* He was a private in Captain Pyam Cushing's Company, Colonel Solomon Lovell's Regiment, assembled at Dorchester March 4, 1776, served four days; and also in the same company, assembled to guard the shore, serving from March 11, 1776, to March 29, 1776. Also in the same company assembled at Hull on two different occasions in June, 1776.† He died March 16, 1814.

Children:

LYDIA, born October 29, 1768, married January 30, 1798, John Chadwick of Boston.
ELIJAH, born March 29, 1770, died July 11, 1778.
PEGGY, born December 17, 1771, died July 9, 1773.
BELA, born May 31, 1776, died July 7, 1777.
OLIVE, born December 3, 1777, married ——— Felch of Boylston.
ELIJAH (137).
BELA, born June 4, 1783, moved "south," married and died there.

*Hist. Hanover, p. 434. Hist. Hing., Vol. III, p. 299.
†Mass. Rev. Rolls.

78 EZRA, son of David (36), was born in Hingham December 21, 1743, and married Martha, daughter of Moses and Mary (Burr) Lincoln. She was born in Hingham February 11, 1746, and surviving him, married (2d) Moses Whiton (79). He resided in Hingham

Center and died October 25, 1773.* He was a private in Captain Enoch Whiton's Company, Colonel Benjamin Lincoln's Regiment, which assembled on the Lexington Alarm, serving three days.†

Child:

EZRA (138).

*Hist. Hing., Vol. III, p. 299. Hist. Hanover, p. 434.
†Mass. Rev. Rolls.

79 MOSES, son of David (36), was born in Hingham, March 3, 1752, and married Mrs. Martha (Lincoln) Whiton, a widow of Ezra (78), in 1774, who was born in Hingham February 11, 1746, and died November 13, 1812. His occupation was that of a "Trader," and he lived at Hingham Center. He also served as a constable. He was said to be a man of excellent character and much respected.* He served as a private in Captain Peter Cushing's Company, Colonel Solomon Lovell's Regiment, assembled at Hingham to guard the shore March 15, 1776; also at Hull, June 14, 1776, and June 23, 1776. He was also named in return of men drafted, who served on an expedition to Rhode Island until January 1, 1779.†

Children:

DAVID (139).
WILSON (140).
MARY, born August 26, 1780, married November 28, 1799, Peter Sprague.
SARAH, born January 11, 1783, married Judge Abel Cushing June 16, 1811, and died at Dorchester January 27, 1862.
MOSES (141).
STARKES (142).

*Hist. Hing., Vol. III, p. 299. Hist. Hanover, p. 435.
†Mass. Rev. Rolls.

80 ABIJAH, son of Abijah (38), was born October 11, 1756, and married Deborah Bates. He owned valuable real estate, one conveyance on April 12, 1779, recorded in the Hampden County, Mass. Registry of Deeds, names the consideration as 1,400 pounds. His will is

recorded in Northampton, Mass. He died at Grafton, New York, in 1801.

Children:

JAEL, married Joshua Littlefield of Chesterfield, Mass., and had children: Abijah, Joshua, William, Hiram and Caroline.

DESIRE, married Elias Ford, and had children: Horace, William and Elizabeth.

DEBORAH, married Alpheus Ford, and had children: Daniel, Alpheus, Emily, Ira and Mary.

ABIJAH (143).

RHODA, married David McComber.

HULDAH, married Adam Whittenback.

LUCINDA, married William Keane.

MARY.

ANNA.

CHLOE.

81 DAVID, son of Abijah (38), was born in Hingham November 10, 1769, and married in January, 1795, Rachel Randall of Hatfield, who, from tradition, was descended through her mother from Robert Bruce of Scotland. He was a man of executive ability and was often moderator of town meetings at Plainfield, Mass., and died September 9, 1849.

Children:

MARY, born November 28, 1796.

FIDELIA, born December 27, 1799.

BETSY, born December 22, 1801, married Dana Shaw.

DAVID RANDALL (144).

THEODORE, born March 26, 1805.

HARRIET, born May 18, 1807, married Freeman Shaw August 28, 1828, and died June 5, 1888.

CLARISSA, born January 21, 1910, married ——— Hamlin and died October 13, 1847.

RACHEL, born October 9, 1811, and married Royal B. Hibbard of Burre, N. Y., May 27, 1835.

WILLIAM CHANDLER, born February 10, 1813, and married Lucretia Shaw October 30, 1836. Child: William Augustus born 1838 and died 1840.

LEWIS E., born March 7, 1815, married Diantha Shaw and settled in Saratoga, N. Y.

MARY, born June 10, 1818, married James Joy and died April 12, 1888.

FIDELIA, born September 23, 1824, married James Warner and died August 11, 1887.

82 ISRAEL, son of Stephen (40), was born in Hingham September 20, 1758,* and married January 14, 1781, Hannah, daughter of Adam and Deborah (Cowen) Stowell, who was born January 9, 1761, and died August 12, 1827. He enlisted for three years in Colonel Jackson's Regiment in 1778, also in Captain Daniel Fisher's Company, Major Job Cushing's Regiment, in 1782, at Hull. He was also a private in Captain Charles Cushing's Company in January, 1776, which after the evacuation of Boston marched to New York, embarking there for Albany, arriving there April 25, 1776, and on May 21st, reaching Montreal. He enlisted in 1777 in Captain Brown's Company, Colonel Jackson's Regiment. Also served for relief of Newport in July, 1780, under Captain Theophilus Wilder, Colonel Thayer's Regiment.† He died August 2, 1840.

Children:

ISRAEL, married Rebecca Cleverly, died without issue November 6, 1825.
CAMPBELL (148).
HANNAH, born 1787, died 1788.
ISAIAH (145).
ROYAL (146).
JOB STOWELL (147).
HANNAH STOWELL, born January 30, 1799, married Lyman Barnes, November 20, 1823, and died January 6, 1881.

*Hist. Hing., Vol. III, p. 299. Hist. Hanover, p. 435.
†Genealogy Mass. by Wm. Richard Cutter, Vol. III, p. 1613. Also Mass. Rev. Rolls.

83 ENOCH, son of Enoch (43), was born in Hingham December 27, 1763, and married September 14, 1786, Martha, daughter of Daniel and Desire (Stoddar) Whiton (27), who was born in Hingham November 29, 1768, and died April 3, 1848. He was a farmer and resided at Liberty Plain, South Hingham, and died December 30, 1811.*

Children:

DESIRE, born April 15, 1787, married June 9, 1811, Jairus Mann of Hanover.

ENOCH, born August 11, 1789, died May 11, 1790.

ENOCH, born August 8, 1791, died June 1, 1792.

JOANNA, born May 30, 1793, married Edward Humphrey January 18, 1818.

MARTHA, born February 27, 1795, died unmarried August, 1853.

SAMUEL, born April 7, 1797, removed to Charlestown, Mass.

MARY WING, born April 5, 1799, married Jonathan Pratt of Weymouth, Mass., November 17, 1823, and died May 4, 1885.

ENOCH, born October 12, 1801, married Sarah, daughter of John Collomore of Scituate. Had children: Sarah, and Mary, who married Henry W. Clark of Boston. Enoch died in 1838.

BERTHA, born July 27, 1803.

CHRISTOPHER, born December 8, 1806, removed to Nashua, N. H.

LEAH STETSON, born March 21, 1808, married Cushing Barnes December 16, 1830, and died April 20, 1841.

*Hist. Hing., Vol. III, p. 300. Hist. Hanover, p. 436.

84 ELIJAH, son of Elijah (44), was born about 1768, and married Charity, daughter of Job and Judith (Whiton) (26) Loring, May 20, 1798. She was born in Hingham, September 10, 1772. He was a carpenter and farmer and resided at Liberty Plain, South Hingham, and died in March, 1837.*

Children:

ELIJAH (149).

LORING (150).

LAVINIA, born February 2, 1804, married Jacob Tirrell of Weymouth, and died September 12, 1880.

ELIZABETH, born 1806, died unmarried May 9, 1883.

CHARLOTTE, born 1808, and died 1813.

ALVAN, born September 23, 1811, and died unmarried at Taunton, July 11, 1882.

*Hist. Hing., Vol. III, p. 300. Hist. Hanover, p. 436.

85 BLOSSOM, son of Elijah (44), was born in Hingham April 30, 1781, married Sarah Lincoln and lived in Charlestown, Mass. He was one of the charter members

of the Bunker Hill Monument Association, and died in Charlestown, Mass., April 20, 1842.*

Children:

BLOSSOM.
JAMES (151).
ALBERT, went to California in 1849.
WALTER.
HENRY.
SARAH.
MARY, married Mark Warren.
LINCOLN B. (152).

*Hist. Hanover, p. 436.

86 ELIAS, son of Elias (45), was born December 18, 1761, and married Mehitable, daughter of Daniel Whiton or Whiting (56), July 1, 1804, who was born January 23, 1781. He died in Brookfield, Mass.

Children:

ELIAS, a mariner, died off the coast of Africa.
FRANKLIN, removed to Ohio.
NYMPHAS.
EDWARD, removed to North Brookfield.
SARAH, married ——— Bailey of Worcester, Mass.
MEHITABLE, married Edward Humphrey of Charlestown, Mass.
ABIGAIL, died unmarried.
DESIRE.

87 EPHRAIM, son of Jotham (48), was born September 26, 1790, and married Mehitable Hobart of Abington, Mass., in 1810. He lived in Abington, and was a merchant in Boston, and died April 14, 1842.*

Children:

EPHRAIM (153).
GEORGE L., born March 24, 1813, married Maria Peterson of Duxbury, Mass., and had a daughter, Susan M., born July 4, 1835.
ALDEN, born May 9, 1816, married Sophronia Huntington of Connecticut; had daughters: Amelia S. and Lydia.
HENRY, born February 23, 1819, married Almedia Watson and removed to Duxbury.
POLLY, born November 15, 1821, and married John W. Estes of Hanover.

PETER W., born December 3, 1825, and died October 1, 1847.
LYDIA, born December 3, 1825, and married Benjamin H. Bowker of Hanover.
MERIEL, born September 25, 1835.

*Hist. Hanover, p. 437.

88 ELEAZER, son of Barzillai (49), was born September 28, 1782, and married (1st) Reverence Nash of Abington, in 1810, who died February 19, 1816, and (2d) Nancy Hobart on November 18, 1821. He resided in East Abington.*

Children:

CLARISSA, born January 27, 1811, married Vincent Blanchard of North Abington.
ELBRIDGE, born August 1, 1822, was a surveyor and civil engineer in Illinois.
LEONARD (154).
JACOB, born December 28, 1825, and resided at Milford.
MARILLA, born May 26, 1828, married Joseph W. Davis of Abington and had sons: Willard W. and George H.
ROWENA, born 1831, and died 1832.
ROXANA, born July 13, 1833.
JOANNA E., born January 3, 1838.

*Hist. Hanover, p. 437.

89 ITHAMAR, son of Barzillai (49), was born in 1786, married Abigail, daughter of Charles and Abigail (Gill) Mann, resided in East Abington, and died July 31, 1820.*

Children:

LYDIA G., born December 28, 1811, married Gideon B. Phillips.
ABIGAIL, born April 24, 1813, married John H. Marsh of Worcester.
STEPHEN (155).
ROWENA, born May 11, 1814, died æt. 3 years.

*Hist. Hanover, p. 437.

SEVENTH GENERATION

90 LEVI, son of Elisha (50), spelled his name Whiting, and married (1st) Ruth, daughter of John and Rebecca (Holmes) Finney, in 1784, who was born in 1757, and (2d) Mary Barton in 1812. He had one son Levi, who married Deborah Morton.* He was a private in Captain Samuel Whiting's (2d Company) of Massachusetts, from May 8 to October 30, 1775.†

*Anc. Landmarks of Plymouth, p. 284.
†Mass. Rev. Rolls.

91 JOSEPH, son of Elisha (50), spelled his name Whiting, and married (1st) Sarah Morton, in 1789, and (2d) Polly, daughter of Ichabod and Zilpha (Thayer) Morton.*

Children by Sarah:

ABIGAIL, born in 1790, and married Rufus Gibbs.
JOSEPH, born in 1792, and married Betsy, daughter of Ichabod and Sarah (Churchill) Morton.
HENRY (156).

Children by Polly:

SARAH, born in 1804, and married Joseph Phillips of Duxbury, Mass.
ELEANOR, born in 1806.
JAMES HARVEY, born in 1809.
ELISHA (157).
GEORGE (158).

*Anc. Landmarks of Plymouth, p. 284.

92 NATHAN, son of Elisha (50), spelled his name Whiting, and married (1st) Rebecca, daughter of Isaac and Mary (Lanman) Doten, in 1795, who was born in 1762, and (2d) Betsy, widow of Abraham Howland, and daughter of William and Elizabeth (Sherman) Finney, in 1817.* He was a private in Captain John Douglas's Company (Massachusetts), from July 12, 1775, to December 10, 1775.†

Children:

NATHAN (159).
ELIZABETH DOTEN, born in 1798, and married Seth Finney.
OLIVE, born in 1800.

REBECCA, born in 1803, and married Henry Morton.
ADONIRAM, born in 1805, and married (1st) Lucy F. Ingalls, and (2d) Sarah W. Manter.
STEPHEN, born in 1807.
LEVI, born in 1808, and married Betsy Hueston.
STEPHEN, born in 1810.
HANNAH, born in 1810, and married Abner Burgess.

*Anc. Landmarks of Plymouth, p. 284.
†Mass. Rev. Rolls.

93 EPHRAIM, son of Elisha (50), spelled his name Whiting, and married Elizabeth, daughter of Ephraim and Elizabeth (Kempton) Bartlett, in 1795.*

Children:

EPHRAIM, married Patience Everson.
BENJAMIN, married Phebe R. Flemmons.

*Anc. Landmarks of Plymouth, p. 284.

94 BENJAMIN, son of Elisha (50), spelled his name Whiting, and married Martha, daughter of Ezra and Susanna (Warren) Harlow.*

Children:

BENJAMIN (160).
ELLIS, married Hannah C. Nickerson.
JOHN.
JOSIAH.
MARTHA, married Ephraim F. Churchill.
NANCY, married Rufus Sampson.

*Anc. Landmarks of Plymouth, p. 284.

95 ABRAHAM, son of Elisha (50), spelled his name Whitten, married Sally, daughter of Rufus Robbins, and resided in Kingston, Mass.*

Children:

ABRAHAM (161).
SALLY, married Joseph Wright.
POLLY, married Thaddeus Washburn of Kingston.
CHARLES (162).

*Anc. Landmarks of Plymouth, p. 284.

96 AMOS, son of Elisha (50), spelled his name Whitten, and married Priscilla, daughter of Barnaby and Pris-

cilla (Marshall) Holmes, in 1803,* and died in Alfred, Me., about 1824.

Children:†

SAMUEL MARSHALL, married Harriet, daughter of Nathaniel and Mary (Bartlett) Bartlett. Had children: Abbie, married Leonidas C. Jewett; Cora, married John B. Wilson, Jr.; Alice, married Albert T. Harlow; Harriet E., married Josiah Russell Drew; Samuel A., married Nellie Ellis, and Joseph B.

AMOS (163).

PRISCILLA, married Joseph Murdock of Wareham, Mass.

LUCIA ANN, married ——— Stetson of Kingston.

Other children as by family records: Nathan, Matthew and Isaac.

*Anc. Landmarks of Plymouth, p. 284.
†Probable children shown in *.

97 MELZAR, son of Elisha (50), spelled his name Whitten, resided in Kingston, Mass., and married (1st) Wealthea, daughter of Joshua and Mary (Chandler) Delano, in 1805, who was born in 1785, and (2d) Deborah Caswell.

Child:

MELZAR, married Susan, daughter of Benjamin and Susannah (Holmes) Delano.*

*Anc. Landmarks of Plymouth, p. 284.

98 JAMES, son of James (51), was born October 8, 1777, at Wintonbury, Conn., and married Deborah, daughter of Nathaniel, Jr., and Bertha (Smith) Webb Bassett, of Lenox, Mass., December 18, 1800, who was born in Lenox August 18, 1782, and died in Elizabeth, N. J., December 15, 1876. He was known as Captain James, and died in Wethersfield, Conn., December 12, 1850.* Family tradition is that he left home at the age of fourteen, owing to a disagreement with his stepmother, and went to live with his uncle Joseph Whiton, at Lee. He established a large paper manufacturing business, and was a member of the Massachusetts Legislature and of the Committee to revise the State laws.

Children:

MILO JAMES (164).

LYMAN (165).

SARAH LOOMIS, born July 9, 1803, in Lee, and married August 20, 1810, George Stillman, Jr.

EVALINE, born December 12, 1806, married October 22, 1826, Benjamin Starbuck, and died November 29, 1891. The *Troy Times* of November 30, 1891, said of her: "She was a gifted lady, and noted for her mental strength. She was a passenger on the Steamer Swallow, which went down on the Hudson River, near Athens in 1845. By her bravery Mrs. Starbuck saved many lives at the time, remaining in the cabin to give aid to those who were helpless." She had seven children: (a) William, born in Troy, N. Y., in 1833, married Nellie Wilbur, and had a son Theodore Wilbur, born October 8, 1859, who married Bertha Grant, June 20, 1888. Their children were: Theodore W., born April 1, 1889; William H., born February 12, 1891; Grant N., born October 18, 1892, and Dorothy Edyth, born May 18, 1900. (b) James; (c) Sarah; (d) Julia, born in Troy February 23, 1836, married James Thomas Palmer of Troy and had a daughter, May, born in Troy, who married Thomas Fowler in Troy November 30, 1888, by whom she had a daughter, Lois Anita, born in Green Bay, Wis., May 3, 1897, and resides at 4232 Alden Drive, Minneapolis, Minn.; Julia died in Troy October 23, 1927. (e) Alice; (f) Minnie; (g) Walter, who died in Troy November 29, 1872.

MARY ANN, born January 7, 1809, married (1st) June 12, 1830, Henry Collins, by whom she had a daughter, Susan, and (2d) Robert B. Thompson, by whom she had the following children: Helen, born May 26, 1850, who married Ebenezer B. Price September 7, 1870; Carolyn Sherman, born July 1, 1852, who married Ferdinand P. Pepin March 31, 1875; Anne May, born April 9, 1854, who married (1st) Daniel Wheeden, and (2d) Charles G. Brown.

JOHN BASSETT, born July 13, 1811, and died July 18, 1852.

CATHERINE DELIA, born July 29, 1813, and married Thomas Perkins.

NANCY MARIA, born November 21, 1815, and married Edward Sherman.

HENRY, born June 8, 1817, and died October 14, 1818.

LORETTA, born February 2, 1819, and married (1st) Oakley Bartlett, and (2d) Townsend Wickes.

FRANCES JEANETTE, born January 11, 1821, and married Rufus Platt.

*Vital Records, Lee. Probate Records, Pittsfield, Mass.

99 JOHN MANDLEY, son of James (51), was born in Lee, Mass., March 11, 1781, and married (1st) January 20, 1808, Sally Couch, who died May 5, 1814, æ. 29; and (2d) December 7, 1815, Sally Bradley, who was born October 6, 1793, and died June 2, 1867. He moved to Huntington, Lorain County, Ohio, where he died August 6, 1833.

Children:

WILLIAM LOOMIS (166).

SHERMAN, born March 5, 1819, and died at Huntington, in infancy.

SALLY COUCH, born March 7, 1820, and married William June March 7, 1838, and died at Huntington, February 16, 1840. They had one son, Edwin Mandley, born June 11, 1839, and died in Greenwich, Ohio, June 10, 1929.

HIRAM B. (167).

MARY S., born February 13, 1824, and married William June October 7, 1840, and died at Huntington, April 17, 1888. He was born May 22, 1807, and died in September, 1889, and resided at Huntington, a farmer and pioneer. Their children, all born in Huntington, were: (a) Lyman, born December 29, 1845; (b) Louisa Eugenia, born November 27, 1847, and married October 7, 1872, Myron Luther son of David and Cynthia (Kingsley) Brown, who was born in Potsdam, N. Y., November 7, 1846. They reside at 312 William Street, Huron, Erie County, Ohio, and had the following children: (1) Perry, born in Strongsville, Ohio, May 22, 1876; (2) Earel Whiton, born in Huntington, March 13, 1878; (3) Nelson W., born in Emerson, Gratiot County, Michigan, June 8, 1881, and (4) Pearl Sophia, born in Emerson January 10, 1895, and married ——— Wasmund; (c) Henry O., born November 5, 1849; (d) John W., born June 8, 1852, and (e) Milo James, born March 21, 1855, and had two daughters, Pearl and Dawn, and (f) William D., born December 26, 1859.

JOSIAH B. (168).

JAMES F. (169).

JOHN M. (170).

JANE ANN, born January 21, 1833, married, March 6, 1862, John C. McLain, and died in Grand Rapids, O., July 12, 1919. Their children were: Lewis Whiton, born May 31, 1864, died April 20, 1883, and Herman F., born September 26, 1871, married June 25, 1898, Della M. Weaver, and has three children, Lewis Dale, Edna Belle and Grace Ann.

100 THOMAS, son of Thomas (52), was born in the Catskills, N. Y., April 11, 1793, and married Mabel, daughter of Samuel and Mindwell North, who was born near the Connecticut border and died in Wiscoy, N. Y., May 10, 1870. He was a farmer and, from family records, a captain in the War of 1812; and died at Wiscoy, December 7, 1862.

Children:

SAMANTHA, born February 28, 1819.
ENOCH F., born October 5, 1820, married Harriet Wilkenson and died May 29, 1863.
LUCY ANN, born February 19, 1822, married Dr. Charles Ackley, and died October 27, 1836.
ARTEMUS, born September 4, 1823, and died August 21, 1824.
HENRY, born September 4, 1823, and died April 25, 1873.
LAURA J., born July 21, 1827, and died February 20, 1829.
ALPHA (171).
CHARLES (172).

101 JOSEPH LUCAS, son of Joseph (53), was born in Lee, Mass., July 14, 1799, and married Lavina Wright, who was born February 16, 1807, and died at Amherst, Ohio, April 8, 1874. That he was a man of the highest character is evidenced by the following extract from an obituary, published in a local newspaper at the time of his death:

> "It is with unfeigned diffidence we attempt to speak of this truly great and good man. Having chosen the plain and inconspicuous occupation of a farmer, an avocation to which the labors of his life were mainly devoted, his great abilities were shaded from public view by the retirement of his rural retreat, and were best known to his immediate neighbors and the friends who sought his counsel and opportunities to draw instruction from his ample stores of knowledge and wisdom. Had he selected for the exercise of the great natural powers with which his Creator endowed him the broad theatre of statesmanship, for which his abilities so eminently qualified him, his death would have been the signal of National mourning, and the stainless purity of his character, his sterling integrity, which no ambitious motives, no induce-

ments of personal gain could swerve, would have served as a luminous example in this epoch of National calamity and political degeneracy to point the young and aspiring throughout the entire country to the true and only path that leads to a cloudless and unsullied renown. It is impossible that such a man as Judge Whiton, with those clear and deep convictions that spring from mature reflection and ample knowledge, should entertain other than the most fixed and earnest opinions upon all subjects in which he was interested or had made the subject of examination. Such was the character of his political convictions. His infant ear almost caught the dying echoes of the Revolution. He lived in the living presence of the Fathers of the Republic. The vigor of his manhood was wrought up to enthusiasm by the conflicts of those intellectual giants, Webster, Clay, Calhoun, Wright and Benton. He deeply and earnestly studied the great problems of free government that engaged the highest faculties of those powerful minds. His admiration for the free, unostentatious government of the earlier days of the Republic ripened into patriotic zeal for its perpetuation in its pristine purity. His close attention to history led him to apprehend that this admirable system might be overthrown by the gradual and stealthy approaches of the machinery and methods of oppression. To the last day of his life he carefully weighed the changing phases in our political phenomena, and was greatly exercised by hopes and fears in regard to the future of his Country. In his political associations he was a Democrat, and gave the last days of his active labors, and the almost hallowed aspirations of his fading life, to the re-establishment of the principles of that party. Though he received no special legal education, he was seven years an Associate Justice of the Court of Common Pleas. He represented his County in the Legislature, and for twelve years filled the office of Justice of the Peace. In every position, the man dignified the office, not the office the man. His knowledge of the nature and character of mankind was ample. So accurate was his analysis of cause and effect in the affairs of State, that his predictions of future results from present policy was almost prophetic. He was a constant student, and in daily communion with the best authors and greatest intellects of the past and present. His death is a public loss, and the vacancy he has left in the community will not soon be filled."

Children:

AGNES LAVINA, born in 1825 and died in Amherst, Ohio, in 1863. She married Henry Allen, by whom she had a daughter, who married Bryant O'Bannon, and resides at 1818 Park Drive, Charlotte, N. C.

CATHERINE, married M. W. Axtell, and died in San Francisco in 1918, leaving a daughter Agnes May, who married H. J. Moule; had children, M. Axtell, and Richard H., and resides at 610 Melville Avenue, Palo Alto, California.

JOSEPH LUCAS (173).

102 DANIEL GARFIELD, son of Joseph (53), was born in Lee, Mass., March 20, 1801, and married March 4, 1825, Anna Foote of Lee, who died in Milwaukee, Wis., in March, 1886. He was a storekeeper and, later in life, a district judge, and died in Janesville, Wis., in 1865.

Children:

HENRY KIRKE (174).

ELLEN, married (1st) William King, and (2d) Robert C. Spencer of Milwaukee, who died in 1886.

ANNA ELIZA, married George Chapman, who died in 1857.

103 EDWARD VERNON, son of Joseph (53), was born June 2, 1805, and married Amoret, daughter of Horatio and Maria (Hinkley) Dimock, who was born in Batavia, N. Y., in 1823, and died in Janesville, Wis., in 1902. The following is from an obituary notice in a local paper:

"The worst fears of the friends of Judge Whiton have been realized. He died at his residence in the City yesterday noon. This event, though not unexpected, will touch a vibrating chord in the public mind. For many years his name has been a familiar word in every household in the state, and by all classes his talents respected, while in his integrity the most implicit confidence has been reposed. His death makes a vacancy in the public service that will not easily be filled, and his immediate friends have suffered a loss that will

EDWARD VERNON WHITON (103)

> never be supplied. Without a stain upon his reputation, he leaves the legacy of a name all will cherish, and the remembrance of private and public virtues affording alike an example and a solace in the bereavement all have sustained. He emigrated to Janesville in the year 1837. He soon occupied among the earlier settlers of the Territory the prominent position to which he was entitled by his ability and learning. He repeatedly occupied seats in both Houses of the Territorial Legislature, and was a leading and influential member of the convention which formed the present Constitution of the State. Immediately upon the admission of Wisconsin into the Union, and the adoption of a Judicial system, he was elected Judge of this (the 1st) Circuit, and ex-officio member of the Supreme Court, which position he held until the organization of a separate Supreme Court. From that time he has continued to be Chief Justice of the State. Before Mr. Whiton was elected to the Bench, he had sustained for several years at the Bar and in the Legislature a reputation second to none in Wisconsin. He was distinguished for the clearness of his mind, the calmness of his judgment, and above all for his inflexible integrity. Upon the Bench these qualities, combined with unquestioned impartiality, made him in the best sense of the term a popular Judge."

He died in 1859.

Child:

EDWARD VERNON (175).

104 EBENEZER, son of Ebenezer (54), was born March 13, 1788, and married August 20, 1810, Samantha, daughter of Joseph Whiton (53). He was for many years Registrar of Deeds for Lorain County, Ohio, and died in Elyria, Ohio, August 31, 1834, and is interred in Stockbridge, Mass., as appears by his tombstone in the cemetery at that place.

Children:

JOSEPH SEWARD (176).
EMILY, born March 1, 1811, and married Henry Murray.
AMANDA.

FRANCIS E., born at Lee, Mass., September 30, 1814, and married Edna Ingraham, who died in 1880, leaving a daughter Edna F. (Bessie). He was at first a manufacturer of wagons, and removing to Winona, Ohio, became sheriff, and subsequently City Judge. He died June 10, 1888.

FRANCES, born in 1815 and died in 1816.

MARIA A., born September 3, 1818, and married Harvey Bush, and died at Sparta, Wis., in 1866, leaving a daughter Emily, who married Theodore Powers, and died in Grand Rapids, Mich., leaving two children, Bert, and William; also a daughter Alice, who married A. E. Bleekman and had four children: Bet, Ruth, who resides at Lacross, Wis., Arthur, who died in Colorado, and Clara, who resides in Superior, Wis.

JENNIE, died young.

CAROLINE WARNER, married in 1858 Samuel Smith Beman and had children: (a) Louise, married James Drumond Marston; (b) Katherine, married Darwin Dudley Olds; (c) Nathan S.

105 LUTHER, son of John (55), was born at Great Barrington, Mass., November 26, 1789, and married there May 13, 1813, Nancy, probably daughter of Frederick Cooper of Sheffield, who, upon the death of her parents, became the adopted daughter of General John Whiting of Great Barrington. She was born September 10, 1791, and died in Ithaca February 19, 1879.* Luther was a cabinet maker, and in association with his brother George was engaged for many years in the manufacture of fine furniture at Ithaca, N. Y., to which town he moved about the year 1827, having for about ten years previously lived in Binghamton, N. Y. He was a member of the Methodist Church, and died September 5, 1832, in Ithaca, where both he and his wife are interred. It is stated by those who remember his wife, that she was a woman of high mental attainments.

Children:

MARY SOPHIA, born at Great Barrington, August 31, 1814, and died at Ithaca, unmarried, April 17, 1881.

JOHN LEWIS (177).

JULIA EMMELINE, born in Binghamton, August 7, 1818, and died at Ithaca, unmarried, June 9, 1878.

TOMBSTONES OF LUTHER and NANCY WHITON (105)
Ithaca City Cemetery, Ithaca, N. Y.

AUGUSTUS SHERRILL (178).
WILLIAM HENRY (179).
FRERERIC L. (180).
ALBERT G. (181).
CAROLINE E. (See Appendix D.)

*Early Conn. Marriages, Vol. I, p. 18.

106 GEORGE, son of John (55), was born April 20, 1801, in Stockbridge, Mass., and married February 24, 1824, in New Hartford, Oneida County, N. Y., Sylvia, daughter of Rufus and Cynthia (Marsh) Northway, who was born March 9, 1807, and died April 6, 1891. He was a cabinet maker, and resided in Ithaca, N. Y., and died November 25, 1877.

Children:

RUFUS HENRY (182).
CYNTHIA MARSH, born August 31, 1826, and died November, 1920.
GEORGE EGBERT, born February 21, 1831, and died August 30, 1832.
SUSAN MARY, born September 18, 1837, and died January 13, 1863.
CATHERINE LOUISE, born July 29, 1840, and died July 14, 1924.

107 DANIEL, son of Daniel (56), spelled his name Whiting, was born April 23, 1772, and married Phoebe, daughter of Captain Enoch Whiton (43), January 11, 1798, who was born April 12, 1773, and died February 23, 1861. He settled in North Brookfield in 1810, and died February 14, 1850. On the fiftieth anniversary of his marriage the following poem was read:

Our Father God, before Thee now
Together we, Thy children bow,
And joyful willing song of praise
From lip and heart to Thee we raise.

We're gathered in the cherished spot,
Where Thou in wisdom cast the lot
Of parents, who before Thee stand
With children, these a filial band.

Back half a century; rolling years
This night; with love and hopes and fears
Their bridal vows, they made in youth,—
Since kept with holy faith and truth.

Through life's bright prime; through wiser days,
Together toiled their blended ways,
And now age smiles, they kiss the rod,
And patient wait their call to God.

Now sons and daughters come to bless
Their kind parental faithfulness,
And children's children, join and sing,—
While orphan hearts thanksgiving bring.

Departed ones, who shared this love
Raise holier songs in homes above,
Help us, Oh God, to join their song
And in Thy praise their strains prolong.*

Children:

ABIGAIL, born December 11, 1798, and died April 10, 1815.

ELIZA, born May 22, 1802, married Parker Johnson of North Brookfield, Mass.

LEWIS, born June 10, 1803, married and had children: Caroline, Rebecca, Phoebe and Frances.

NELSON, born June 15, 1804, married Catherine, daughter of Samuel Gardner, of Hingham, and had one son, Gardner, who died, aged eleven.

DANIEL, born June 6, 1806.

LYMAN, born April 28, 1817, and was a minister at Reading, Mass.

*Hist. Hanover, p. 437.

108 GALEN, son of Daniel (56), was born February 1, 1774, and married Rachel Prouty of Scituate September 11, 1796, settled in Brookfield, Mass., and died December 31, 1847.

Children:

GALEN, born December 11, 1797, and died in the West.

LEONARD, born April 26, 1799, and settled in Illinois.

ANDREW, born February 28, 1801.

CHARLES, born May 1, 1802, and settled in Illinois.

LOUISE, born July 5, 1803.

WILLIAM P., born October 24, 1805.

DAVID, born January 18, 1809.

RACHEL, born January 7, 1810, and married Jeremiah Deming.

109 SYLVANUS, son of Daniel (56), was born December 7, 1775, and married Hannah, daughter of Laban and Persis (Wilder) Stodder, or Stoddard, February 26, 1800, who was born in Hingham December 6, 1778, and died there February 27, 1865. They resided at Liberty Plain, South Hingham.* He was a private in Captain Joseph Whiton's Company of Hingham Militia, organized to repel an invasion by British marines June 11 and 12, 1814.†

Children:

SYLVANUS (183).

HANNAH, married Charles Gardner and had son, Charles.

NATHAN, married Temperance Bicknell, and had children: Temperance, Susan and George.

NAHUM, married Meribel Orcutt, lived in East Weymouth, Mass., and had children: Mary A. and Anna L.

SILAS, married (1st) Mary Dyer of Braintree, Mass., and (2d) Anne Newcomb; children: Mary L., Susan and Emma J.

LYDIA, married Charles Whiton (112) April 1, 1837.

MARY, married James Matthewson of Weymouth.

*Hist. Hing. Vol. III, p. 300. Hist. Hanover, p. 438.
†Mass. Men in War of 1812.

110 JOSIAH, son of Daniel (56), was born November 29, 1784, married Meriel Prouty, and settled in Brookfield, Mass. He was a farmer and real estate operator, and died February 17, 1845.

Children:

JULIA A., born September 23, 1810, married Leonard Stoddard.

OSBORN, born February 11, 1812.

ELIZABETH, born February 7, 1813, marrried Daniel D. Hunter.

JOSIAH, born June 5, 1815.

MERIEL, born June 6, 1817, and died September 3, 1837.

ABIGAIL, born April 26, 1819, married Erastus Horton and died June 17, 1848.

JACOB, born July 18, 1822.
MARTHA L., born October 25, 1823, married J. F. Hebard, and died September 2, 1872.
MARY B., born March 27, 1825, married H. Brigham, and died January 4, 1873.

111 THEOPHILUS, son of Zachariah (57), was born March 30, 1775, and married Hannah Collamore of Scituate, who died September 25, 1824. He was a private in Captain Joseph Whiton's Company of Militia, formed to repel an invasion by British marines from the ships lying off Cohasset, June 11 and 12, 1814. He died May 4, 1831.*†

Children:

HANNAH C., born December 14, 1798, married David Cushing of East Abington, and had children: William S., Davis, Brainard, Urban W., Sarah C., Andrew J., Fanny W. and Henry J.
SUSANNA, born December 21, 1800, married Silas Ripley in 1821 and died February 15, 1830.
THEOPHILUS W., born December 7, 1802, married Mary Paine and had children: Nancy, born and died in 1833, and Leonard who died in 1840.
ZENAS L. (184).
MARIA, born July 28, 1807, married Peter W. Beal of Abington.
GILMAN (185).
PIAM C. (186).
EDWIN, born July 19, 1813, married Mary Battles, and died without issue in 1851.
HIRAM, born January 28, 1818, and died February 6, 1823.

*Hist. Hanover, p. 439.
†Mass. Men in War of 1812.

112 HOSEA, son of Zachariah (57), was born in Hingham September 11, 1782, and married (1st) Anna, daughter of Laban and Persis (Wilder) Stodder, or Stoddard, November 11, 1804, who was born in Hingham October 14, 1781, and died June 16, 1844, and (2d) Mrs. Alice (Turner) Tisdale of Stoughton, Mass., April 7, 1845, who died September 12, 1869. He was a farmer, resided at Liberty Plain, South Hingham, and served in Captain Joseph Whiton's Company of Militia, formed

to repel an invasion of British marines at Cohasset June 11 and 12, 1814. He died September 19, 1869.*†

Children:

HOSEA (187).

ANN, born March 6, 1808, married Spencer Shaw, April 1, 1831.

CHARLES, born March 30, 1811, married March 1, 1829, Lydia, daughter of Sylvanus Whiton (109), and resided at Weymouth.

JANE, born May 6, 1813, and married Charles Shaw.

PERSIS, born January 2, 1815, and married John Haynes of Scituate, April 27, 1834.

RUTH, born May 10, 1817, and married John W. Penniman February 6, 1837.

HARRIET, born June 27, 1819, married Dexter Walcott January 8, 1843.

DEXTER, born June 5, 1821, married ——— Tisdale October 20, 1847, and died January 10, 1869.

ALICE REED, born June 6, 1846, and married Nathan Goodrich of Hanover.

*Hist. Hing., Vol. III, p. 301. Hist. Hanover, p. 439.
†Mass. Men in War of 1812.

113 DAVIS, son of Amasa (58), was born in Hingham August 20, 1773, and married Abigail Bowker of Scituate, who was born in 1772 and died in Hingham October 10, 1833. He kept an inn at Liberty Plain, South Hingham, and died April 12, 1833.*

Children:

MARY COLLIER, born June 17, 1797, and married Leonard Cushing January 1, 1821.

ABIGAIL BOWKER, born January 4, 1799, married James W. Swift, and died in Boston, April 9, 1885.

DAVIS, born February 2, 1801, was First Officer of the brig Globe of Boston, and died at sea.

*Hist. Hing., Vol. III, p. 301.

114 PEREZ, son of Amasa (58), was born in Hingham April 3, 1775, and married (1st) Mary Bowker of Scituate, who died April 7, 1823; and (2) Sarah Simmons of Duxbury. He was a carpenter and resided at Liberty Plain, South Hingham, and died August 15, 1860.

Children all by Mary:

PEREZ S., born October 19, 1800, married Lucy Jacobs and removed to New York.

MARY, born February 6, 1802, and married December 26, 1825, Rev. Calvin Gardner.

ADELINE, born February 2, 1804, and married April 16, 1826, Edward Jacobs of Scituate.

CAROLINE, born February 2, 1804, and married February 2, 1823, Laban Jacobs.

GEORGE, born March 1, 1806, and died April 7, 1823.

CHARLES (188).

ALBERT (189).

WINSLOW LEWIS, born April 1, 1813, and married Ann E. Ripley April 16, 1835, and removed to either New York or Newark, N. J.

BENJAMIN SHURTLEFF (190).

DAVIS JACOB, born November 15, 1816, and moved to Chicago.

JULIA ANN BOWKER, born February 7, 1820, and married William Brown of Abington.

*Hist. Hing., Vol. III, p. 301. Hist. Hanover, p. 440.

115 JOSEPH JACOB, son of Amasa (58), signed his name Whiting, was born in Hingham December 29, 1778, and married (1st) Ann Eliza Crane, who was born in 1790 and died July 25, 1812; and (2d) Catherine Bowker of Scituate, who was born December 20, 1786, and died July 17, 1871. He was a mechanical engineer, engaged in business in Boston, and resided at Liberty Plain, South Hingham.* A sketch of his house, built on the site of his father's house, appears at foot of page 122.

Child by Ann:

ANN ELIZA, born March 6, 1811, died March 24, 1812.

Children by Catherine:

JOSEPH JACOB, born in Boston June 25, 1818, and was a member of the firm of Whiting, Kehoe and Galloupe, wholesale clothiers.

AMASA (191).

CATHERINE, born January 19, 1824, and died December 9, 1926.

*Hist. Hing., Vol. III, p. 302. Hist. Hanover, p. 440.

116 STEPHEN, son of Joseph (60), was born in Westford, Conn., June 30, 1775, and married March 27, 1806,

Juliana, daughter of Jonathan and Jerusha (Welch) Martin, of Westford, who was born February 2, 1783, and died December 29, 1851. He died October 20, 1829.*

Children:

MARY, born February 10, 1807, married Sylvester Gilbert Farnham at Westford, March 1, 1827, and had three children: (a) Sylvester Gilbert, born in East Hartford, Conn., April 11, 1828, married Sarah Ann Smith and was a merchant in Hartford, and died in Brooklyn, N. Y., December 11, 1884. Their children were: John Reed, born in Hartford, July 7, 1854, and died in New York November 2, 1905; Alice, born February 16, 1859, in Hartford, and resides now in 59 Whiting Lane, West Hartford, and is well known as a landscape painter; (b) Mary, married Franklin Woodruff; (c) Frank, who resided in Brooklyn, N. Y.

STEPHEN (192).

MARVIN, died young.

ASHBEL, born July 10, 1813, died March 25, 1814.

ASHBEL (193).

*Town Records of Westford in Hartford.

117 JOSEPH, son of Joseph (60), was born in Westford, Conn., September 24, 1776, and married Betsey, daughter of Joseph and Lucy (Houghton) Otis, who was born in Norwich, Conn., July 10, 1777, and died November 10, 1828.

Children:

BETSY, born May 15, 1803, married October 24, 1825, Francis Whitmore of Westford, and had two sons, Joseph and Harvey. She died August 5, 1840.

LUCRETIA, born August 20, 1804, married November 5, 1837, Seth Walker of Westford, Conn.

LUCY, born August 6, 1806, married March 17, 1834, Edwin Hall, and had three children: William Albert, who died young; Henry James, who died in 1862, and William Henry, who became Superintendent of Schools of West Hartford. He is an Ex-President of the Whiton Family Association. She died May 14, 1884.

JOANNA, born April 2, 1808, married November 25, 1830, Aaron Flint, and died September 9, 1844. Their children were: John L. of Monson, Mass., who had a son Frederick; Harriet, married Frederick Warfield and had five children: Alice, Julia, John, George, and Charles.

OTIS, born January 20, 1810, married October 14, 1833, Sophia Simonds of Chaplin. He died October 29, 1850, without issue. He had an adopted daughter, Mary Cutler Hough, who, by act of General Assembly in 1848, changed her name to Mary Cutler Hough Whiton.

CHESTER (194).

MARCIA, born August 22, 1814, married Hiram Newton, December 29, 1833, resided at Brookfield, Mass., and had four children: Hiram Otis; Caroline, who married Russell Lombard; Mary, who married Charles Blackmer, and Edwin Hall who married Jennie Blackmer, and had a son, Frederick Hall Newton, who is a professor at Phillips Academy, Andover, Mass. Hiram Otis (supra) was born in Brookfield, Mass., July 31, 1835, and married Mary Simmonds in Rome, New York, February 2, 1867, and died December 19, 1929, at Utica, N. Y. Their children are: Carrie, born July 1, 1869, who married R. W. Dodge; Nellie, born October 29, 1871, married D. M. Walsh; Frank, born January 13, 1875, and George, born March 8, 1877.

118 ELIJAH, son of Joseph (60), was born in Westford April 3, 1778, and married Matilda, daughter of Simeon and Anna (Byles) Smith, in Westford November 25, 1802, who was born there in 1781 and died August 10, 1861. He was a manufacturer of bricks, and built a brick house for himself, which still stands. He died September 17, 1854.*

Children:

SOPHRONIA, born March 6, 1803, and married April 10, 1823, Stephen Saunders, and had children: Delia, Sophronia and Stephen, the last dying in infancy.

SIMEON (194*a*).

AUGUSTUS (195).

MATILDA W., born February 15, 1810, married May 8, 1833, Nathan B. Huntington, and removed to Groveland, Ill.

MARIA, born March 13, 1812, and married January 4, 1837, Reuben Green, and had one child, Greeley, who resided in Wethersfield, Conn.

HENRY, born October 29, 1817, married Jerusha H. Fuller January 25, 1837, and died April 21, 1839. His widow later married Ashbel Whiton (193).

HARRIET, born February 26, 1826, and married June 14, 1850, William H. Storrs, and had four children: (a) William Henry, born December 1, 1854, who married (1st)

Marian Ruthven, December 20, 1877, and (2d) Alice Matthews on June 7, 1904, and died December 2, 1913; (b) Alice Mary, born March 14, 1858, and died March 8, 1863; (c) Arthur Hovey, born October 12, 1862, who married Jane Scranton Fuller, June 2, 1886, and died September 22, 1919; their children were: (1) Janet, born July 24, 1887, who married Gregory Barrett Littell November 25, 1920, and has a daughter Elizabeth, (2) William J., born August 24, 1889, and died January 13, 1890, (3) Elizabeth Scranton, born April 16, 1891, and died December 16, 1921; (d) Harriet Grace, born June 7, 1865, married Charles S. Weston September 2, 1891, at Scranton, Penn., and resides there at 624 Monroe Street.

ELIJAH and CALISTA, died in infancy.

*Stiles Ancient Windsor, and Town Records of Ashford in Hartford.

119 HEBER, son of Joseph (60), was born at Westford, Conn., February 11, 1782, and married May 5, 1808, Marcia, daughter of Ebenezer and Elizabeth (Leavens) Gay, who was born in November, 1784, and died June 13, 1848. He settled in Stafford, Conn., and lived for many years on a farm on what is called Cooper Lane, where he divided his time between coopering and farming. He is buried on West Stafford Hill. After his death his widow removed to Monson, Mass., where she married Spencer Keep. She was a woman of deep piety, and some of her letters now in existence show her devotion to the best interests of her family. She is buried in Monson.

Children:

LUCIUS HEBER (196).

JULIUS ROYAL (197).

EBENEZER GAY (198).

JOSEPH LEANDER (199).

EDWARD FRANKLIN (200).

HANNAH CADY, born August 18, 1821, and married November 10, 1844, Penuel Eddy of Stockbridge, Mass., who was born March 7, 1816, and was a member of Company D, 25th Regiment Connecticut Volunteers in the Civil War, and died June 25, 1873. Their children were (a) Elizabeth Leavens, born January 19, 1847, married Ralph Brown and died October 15, 1921; (b) Minnie Frances, born February 1, 1858, and died March 8, 1931, at New London, Conn.; (c) Idella Hannah, born at Stafford, Conn., August 7, 1860, married William F. Damas, August 15, 1893, and resides at 231 Crystal Avenue, New London; (d) Lillie May, born at Stafford, March 16, 1865, and also resides at 231 Crystal Avenue, New London.

DAVID ERSKINE (201).

120 ABNER, son of Joseph (60), born August 17, 1788, married in 1814, Amy, daughter of Abner and Judith (Walker) Chaffee, resided at Willington, Conn., and died at Westford, Conn., January 20, 1854. His wife was born August 7, 1791, and died in October, 1849. He served in the War of 1812, and was Sergeant under Commander Charles Abel, August 23, to October 19, 1814.

Children:

ISRAEL, born February 25, 1815, married and moved west.

GEORGE (202).

CHARLOTTE, born April 22, 1818, married November 26, 1838, Haley Webster of Woodstock. No children.

JUDITH AMELIA, born June 19, 1821, married November 20, 1848, Philo Ledoyt of Stafford, Conn., and moved west with Israel.

FRANCIS (203).

MARILLA, born in Willington, Conn., June 18, 1828, married Alfred Lee November 10, 1850, and died November 25, 1883. They had three children: (a) Harriet, born July 19, 1852, married George A. Rounds at Mansfield, Conn., April 29, 1871, who died February 14, 1927. They had two children, Una, born April 10, 1873, and married ——— Blakely; and Mabel, born in Willington, August 15, 1875, and married Frank J., son of Junius and Anna (Watrous) Burr, at Willington, December 26, 1903, to whom a daughter, Doris, was born December 26, 1904; (b) Albert, born February 1, 1854, who married Sarah Pitkin December 15, 1874, and had six children: (1) Blanche Caroline, born November 12, 1875, who married ——— Webster; (2) William A., born October 5, 1877; (3) Edith, born December 1, 1879, and married ——— Daggart; (4) Esther Pitkin, born September 20, 1882; (5) Harriet, born October 6, 1884, and married ——— Pitkin, and (6) Grace, born January 11, 1891, and married ——— Frazier; (c) Caroline, born September 2, 1855, married Lee Burdick, who died in April, 1929, leaving two daughters: Minnie and Ethel, the latter married ——— Parkhurst and lives at Three Rivers, Mass.

MARY ELIZABETH, born April 10, 1831, married May 4, 1851, Benjamin Dwight Lillibridge.

ABNER, born July 16, 1833, married at Rochester, Minn., in 1869, Samantha, daughter of John and Anna Bell. He died in September, 1889, at Anatone, Wash. Children: (a) Herman Abner, born February 2, 1871, at Rochester, Minn., married, at Anatone, January 23, 1893, Mahala Margerette Bushell and has children: (1) Ralph Abner, born February 10, 1894, and married Pearl Misner; (2) Rena, born February 17, 1895, and married Walter Dixon; (3) Lloyd Garland, born September 4, 1898, and married Ethel Jones; (4) Nora, born July 14, 1903, and married Curtis M. Wormell, and (5) Lorne Herman, born May 25, 1910, and married Mildred Simpson. (b) Charles Washington; (c) Ida, married ——— Sangster; (d) Effie, married ——— Fountain; (e) Rose, married ——— Dorfler.

JOHN, born July 10, 1835. He enlisted as a private in Company B, of the 12th Regiment, Connecticut Volunteers, in 1861, was promoted to a corporal November 1, 1862, wounded June 10, 1863, at Port Hudson, La.; promoted to Sergeant August 1, 1863; captured October 19, 1864, was a prisoner in Salisbury Prison, Maryland, paroled February 28, 1865, and discharged April 24, 1865. He purchased a ranch in Washington Territory, where he died unmarried February 15, 1898.

AMY ANN, born April 23, 1837, married ——— Morse; no children.

*Town Records of Ashford in Hartford.
†Conn. Civil War Records.

121 ELIJAH, son of Elijah (61), was born July 5, 1785, and married March 23, 1808, Keziah, daughter of Captain Ammi Paulk (a soldier in the Revolutionary War) and Esther (Chapman) Paulk. They lived in Tolland, Conn., where he died July 31, 1827; his widow died in 1875, aged 89 years; they are buried in the South Cemetery.* He served as a corporal in Colonel Isaac Phelps's Regiment from September 8, 1814, to October 25, 1814.†

Children:

AMMI, born April 3, 1809, died July 7, 1833, in Harrisonburg, Miss.

MARIA, born May 19, 1811, married January 2, 1833, Dearborn Mathews of North Coventry, Conn., and died August 6, 1837.

ELIJAH, born March 6, 1813, married and went west; was killed by Indians.

LUTHER, born January 20, 1816; went west.

CALVIN (204).

STEPHEN (205).

MARCIA, born May 14, 1822, died February 11, 1824.

ERASTUS, born May 18, 1824, died October 16, 1846.

*Early History of Tolland. Loren P. Tolland.
†Conn. Men in the Rev. War and in War of 1812.

122 JOHN MILTON, son of Israel (63), was born in Winchendon, Mass., August 1, 1785, fitted for college at Ipswich Academy, and entered Dartmouth College in 1801, leaving in 1804 for Yale College, from which he graduated in 1805. On October 18, 1808, he married Abigail, daughter of James and Elizabeth (Hubbard) Morris, of South Farms, Conn. He studied for the ministry and retained the charge at the Congregational Church at Antrim, N. H., for forty years. In his late life he removed to Bennington, N. H., dying there September 27, 1856. His widow died April 12, 1865. The degree of Doctor of Divinity was conferred upon him by Princeton College. Of a calm judicial temperament, sound judgment, and a man of peace, he is said to have had a passion for righteousness and justice, for which he boldly fought. It was not by brilliant rhetoric or splendor of style, but by broad-minded views and loyalty to truth that he gained his leadership, not only about Antrim, but in all matters affecting the people of the entire state. His wife, Abigail Morris, traced her descent back to Thomas Morris, who emigrated by the ship Hester, and settled in Roxbury, Mass., in 1637.

Children:

JAMES MORRIS (206).

ELIZABETH DOROTHY, born March 7, 1811, married Rev. Josiah Ballard October 1, 1835, and lived in Carlisle, Mass.

THE OLD CENTER CHURCH, ANTRIM, N. H.
Built in 1826, during the pastorate of
Dr. John M. Whiton (122)

John M. Whiton

A. M. Whiton

He was born April 14, 1806, and died December 12, 1863; two children surviving him (A) Edward, born April 19, 1837, and died October 27, 1916; and married (1st) Lauretta Sophia Thayer Yates, September 24, 1859, who was born February 8, 1835, and died July 9, 1883, and (2d) Katherine Agnes McConnellogue, September 4, 1884, who was born November 11, 18—, and died in March, 1917. Their children were: (1) Herbert Edward, born August 21, 1863, and died August 11, 1864, (2) Clarence Eugene, born October 9, 1866, and died February 7, 1867, (3) Ettie Elizabeth, born August 8, 1869, and married Eddy B. Swett, M.D., June 2, 1892, who was born November 3, 1867, and resides at Grasmere, N. H. Their children were: (a) Lauretta Lucy, born January 1, 1895, married Merrill G. Sumner December 2, 1916; (b) Donald Benjamin, born February 12, 1897, married August 14, 1926, Carolyn McQueston, and has a son Douglas McQ., born August 4, 1929; (c) Dorothy Ballard, born November 4, 1899, married Webster Little Simons September 1, 1921, and has four children: Virginius B., born June 5, 1922; Ada Elizabeth, born May 6, 1923; Webster Little, born November 12, 1925, and Duncan Foster, born November 25, 1929, (d) Margaret Agnes, born December 12, 1902, married Bert F. Anderson January 8, 1927, (e) Mary Elizabeth born February 19, 1906; (f) Douglas Stephen, born January 4, 1910, and died July 24, 1929, and (g) Barbara Louise, born July 17, 1912; (4) Agnes Anna, born August 30, 1870, and died October 15, 1870. (B) Kate, married Emory Smith. Their children (1) Katherine; (2) Bertha, married, and had three children, and (3) Walton.

HELEN D. (See Appendix E.)

ABIGAIL, born May 31, 1817, married in 1840, Charles P. Whittemore of Boston, later of Bennington, N. H.; no living children.

MARY CHRYSTIE, born February 20, 1819, married in 1841, George Duncan, and after his death, 1857, John Taylor, and lived in Bennington, N. H., and in Antrim, N. H. By her first husband she had a daughter, Kate, who married in Charlestown, Mass., September 11, 1877, Edward Sargent Paine, who was born in South Amesbury, Mass., May 3, 1851, was a wholesale paper merchant in Boston, and died in Kansas City, Mo., March 17, 1891. Their children were: (1) Marian D., born September 5, 1878, married Dr. Charles W. Stevens, and resides at 1 West 68th Street, New York City; (2) Elizabeth, married Frederick Collins, and had two daughters, Barbara and Marjorie, and (3) Horace Whiton, born in Hyde Park, Mass., December 9, 1885, and married Madeline Florence, daughter of George Edward and May (Lincoln) Harding, in New York City September 23, 1914. He graduated from Phillips Andover Academy in 1902, and from Harvard University in 1906, and resides in Westport, Conn., where he is engaged in real estate development. He is a member of the Westport County, the Fairfield County Hunt, and of the Knickerbocker Whist (N. Y.) Clubs. They have two sons, Whiton, born November 9, 1916, and Malcomb, born May 28, 1920.

JOHN MILTON, born March 7, 1821, married (1st) in 1844 Fidelia Wilson of Nelson, N. H.., and (2d) Mary Jane Hartshorn of Norwich, Conn. His five children by his first wife were: (a) Charles Albin, born June 25, 1845; (b) John M., born June 4, 1848, who had a son Morris, who married Nora Gulliford, by whom he had four children: John, William, Charles and Mary Emily; (c) Helen, born January 9, 1852, married Edward B. Woodworth and had two children, John and Helen; (d) Frank Henry, born May 26, 1854; (e) Mary Fidelia, born July 10, 1859. John Milton had two children by his second marriage: (a) George Morris, born December 4, 1863, who died young, and (b) Abbie Morris, born June 13, 1866, who married Willys Duer Thompson by whom she had two children: (1) Raymond, who died in 1918, and (2) Willys Duer, Jr., who married Frances Heath and has three children: Virginia, Frances and Willys Duer, 3d. John Milton died in 1884.

123 FLAVEL, son of Boaz (64), was born at Westford, Conn., January 16, 1793, and married May 12, 1819, Mary, daughter of John and Charity McKnight, who was born in Ellington, Conn., May 23, 1792, and died June 30, 1860. He spent the active years of his life in Ellington, where his name was identified with whatever was good and right in church and society. "Of him might truly be said, 'a perfect and upright man, one who feared God and eschewed evil.' Honest and upright in his private business transactions, so in those of more public nature, above reproach. He filled many places of public trust with honor. As a leader in school, ecclesiastical and political affairs, his rule seemed to be 'in word, or deed to do all to the glory of God.' His

FLAVEL WHITON (123)

influence will not cease to be felt, and eternity alone will disclose the blessed results of such a life."* In 1849 he was elected senator from the 20th Senatorial District. He was a soldier in the War of 1812, in Colonel Samuel Hough's Regiment, from June 29, 1814, to August 31, 1814.† He died at Vernon Center, Conn., April 12, 1874.

Children:

MARY, born May 13, 1820, married Henry R. Russell of Arcadia, Mo., February 22, 1843, removed to Wisconsin and died October 31, 1849.

JANE ROSETTA, born April 2, 1822, married Albert Keeney April 15, 1841.

FLAVIA RODELIA, born November 25, 1825, died April 14, 1897.

ABIGAIL, born September 28, 1827, married Charles N. Pitkin May 15, 1854, and died May 24, 1856. He died April 16, 1877. They had one son, Charles Whiton, who was born March 18, 1856, married Emma Dart May 2, 1877, and has one son, Alfred N., born August 15, 1881. He resides at Talcottville, Conn.

FLAVELINE, born November 6, 1832; died January 19, 1853.

FLAVEL, born November 6, 1832, died December 22, 1842.

ESTHER E., married (1st) Edwin Birge by whom she had a daughter Lucy Maria, who married Eben Henry Stocker of Hartford, who was born August 3, 1845, and died in Hartford August 27, 1916; and (2d) Francis Woodworth, son of Judge Woodworth, by whom she had a son Flavel Whiton, born at South Windsor, Conn., January 22, 1851, and married October 15, 1874, Martha Susan, daughter of Gideon W. and Mary (Pursell) Hart of Hartford, who died in 1930. They have two daughters, Mrs. William J. Mandigo, of Madison, Conn., and Helen Van Rensselaer, born at Hartford, October 3, 1889, who married M. C. Andrews and lives at The Ridges, Willimantic, Conn. Esther E. (supra) died in Hartford in 1900, and is buried in South Windsor, under the name of Birge.

*From an obituary in a local paper. The other records are from a family Bible in the possession of Charles W. Pitkin.

†Conn. Men in War of 1812.

124 HORACE, son of Boaz (64), was born in Westford, Conn., November 24, 1797, and married Mary Ann, daughter of William and Sophia (Converse) Brett, at

Willington, Conn., March 27, 1838, who was born there December 16, 1807, and died at Westford February 4, 1898. He was a farmer and cooper, and died at Westford February 13, 1871.

Children:

MARY MATILDA, born in Westford July 18, 1839, and died in East Woodstock, Conn., September 18, 1920. She married B. Monroe Robbins in Ashford, Conn., who died there January 25, 1927. They had two daughters: (1) Mary Gertrude, born January 19, 1862, and married Wilbur Towne of Woodstock, Conn., who died in Willimantic January 10, 1927, leaving a daughter May Agnes, born May 7, 1884, who married Frederick Copeland of Willimantic, and died January 3, 1927, leaving four children: Philip, May, Alice, and Robert. The other daughter of Mary Matilda was Martha, born July 18, 1869, and married Frank Olin Chaffee of East Woodstock, Conn., and died September 18, 1920, leaving a son Herman R., who resides in Quinebaug, Conn.

ELLEN LUCRETIA, born in Westford, Conn., April 15, 1844, and resides in the old homestead there unmarried.

HARRIET TRYPHENA, born in Westford, January 17, 1847, married Charles W. Brett, and died in North Woodstock December 19, 1900, leaving a son Samuel, who died in Woodstock in 1914, leaving no children surviving.

125 CHAUNCEY, son of Boaz (64), was born in Westford, Conn., May 20, 1805, and married Lucinda, daughter of Samuel and Amy (Whiton)-(28) Moore, at Westford March 26, 1833, who was born at Union, Conn., September 30, 1804, and died at Westford August 8, 1882. He was a farmer, and for many years a deacon in the Westford Hill Congregational Church, and died October 6, 1886.

Children:

CHAUNCEY NEWTON, born April 18, 1835, and died January 16, 1847.

ANNE LUCINDA. (See Appendix C.)

SAMUEL JAMES, born September 11, 1839. After a course in the New Britain Normal School, he decided to go as a missionary to West Africa, where his mother's sister, Hannah Moore, was then stationed. He married (1st) Lydia Danforth, a fellow missionary in Africa. Two years later she

CHAUNCEY WHITON (125)

REV. SAMUEL JAMES WHITON
Son of Chauncey Whiton (125)

died, with her infant son. He then returned home and went to Fortress Monroe, where he taught the freedmen for a time, and later he removed to Iowa, where he married (2d) Emily Pitkin. He died in 1871 of illness contracted in Africa. He is the author of the book, "Glimpses of West Africa."

JULIA ELIZA, born April 6, 1845, and died September 5, 1845.

126 BENJAMIN, son of Benjamin (67), was born January 22, 1773, and married Lydia, daughter of Richard and Monica (Marsh) Stoddard, December 10, 1797, and resided at Hingham.*

Children:

JARED, born May 26, 1798, and died in December, 1817.

RICHARD, born April 19, 1800, married Mary Stoddard; no children.

LYDIA, born January 3, 1803.

MARIA, born December 7, 1804, married Freeman House of Hingham.

JOANNA, born March, 1807, married Freeman French December 28, 1826.

JOEL, born May, 1809, married Eunice Ide of Seekonk, lived at Abington and had a son Benjamin, who died young, and a daughter Eunia.

PAMELA, born October 6, 1814, married Benjamin Mann of Hanover.

JARED, born March 31, 1819.

ELIZABETH, born October, 1821, married James M. Burrell of Hingham.

*Hist. Hing., Vol. III, p. 298.

127 JOSEPH, son of Benjamin (67), was born in Hingham January 9, 1777, and married Lucy, daughter of William and Rebecca (Wilder) Barrell, of Scituate. She died there November 4, 1859. He was a farmer and died in Hingham February 14, 1857.*

Children:

JOSEPH MERRILL, born June 6, 1813.

LUCY BARRELL, born January 17, 1815, married Albert G. Mann, October 19, 1834. She died January 3, 1837.

RUTH, born January 26, 1818, and died February 10, 1839.

SALOME, born November 30, 1813, married George Lincoln November 13, 1857.

*Hist. Hing., Vol. III, p. 302.

128 ARCHELAUS, son of Benjamin (67), was born in Hingham September 30, 1778. He married May 4, 1799, Elizabeth, daughter of David and Elizabeth Gardner. She died October 26, 1802. He enlisted in 1812 on the frigate Constitution to go to the Great Lakes, and this was the last heard of him.*

Daughter:

ELIZABETH, born January 24, 1801, married January 30, 1838, Eleazer Chubbuck, and died May 10, 1878.

*Hist. Hing., Vol. III, p. 302.

129 LUTHER, son of Benjamin (67), was born in Hingham March 16, or 26, 1781. He married (1st) Cynthia E. Stetson, who died May 29, 1818, and (2d) Lois, daughter of Jeremiah and Lois (Stodder) Gardner, who was born in Hingham September 20, 1778. He resided at Liberty Plain, South Hingham, and died July 7, 1842.*

Children by Cynthia:

CYNTHIA STETSON, born March 21, 1818, married February 6, 1844, Benjamin White of Duxbury.

SOPHIA STETSON, born March 21, 1818, marrried March 22, 1840, Abner Loring.

Twin sisters, they died aged 64, April 16th and 17th, 1882.

*Hist. Hing., Vol. III, p. 302.

130 WILLIAM P., son of Thomas (70), spelled his name Whiting. He was born April 28, 1771, and married Sally Waters of Randolph. He was a lawyer in Boston.

Children:

MARY W., married Levi H. Marsh.

SARAH A., died æt. 25.

EPHRAIM W., had two children. He was lost at sea.

ELLA S.

131 THOMAS, son of Thomas (70), was born August 16, 1776; spelled his name Whiting; married Hannah Mann June 8, 1797, and lived in Hanover. He died in 1806.

Children:

MARCIA, born May, 1798.
JAIRUS, moved to New York.
OREN (207).
LEWIS.
HANNAH M., married Elisha Faxon.

132 HORATIO, son of James (71), was born November 2, 1791, and married (1st) Ruth Lovell, who died April 26, 1839, and (2d) Lucy Lane.

Children:

LUCY, born August 15, 1828, died in 1848.
FLORA, born April 24, 1830.
MARCIA.
ALDEN.

133 EZRA, son of Caleb (72), was born May 8, 1772, married Sally Curtis, and lived in Hanover, where he died October 3, 1831.

Children:

EZRA, born September 9, 1823, removed to Cohasset.
JOSHUA S., born December 6, 1825, married Betsy B. Dwelley June 20, 1847. Had one daughter Elmira L., born August 10, 1850.
LUCIUS C., born March 20, 1828, and removed to California.
EDWIN, born August 22, 1831, and died in 1835.
JARED (208).
LYDIA P., born September 26, 1806, married Briggs Freeman of Abington, and died September 28, 1849.

134 SYLVANUS, son of William Whiting (75), was born February 9, 1808, married Lucy Bates November 20, 1828, and lived in Hanover.

Children:

SYLVANUS, born November 24, 1829, married Sarah J. Torrey January 14, 1852.
BETSY C., born October 7, 1831.
NATHAN, born July 12, 1833.
LUCY M., born July 5, 1835.
LAURA A., born July 28, 1837.
ADELAIDE, born February 10, 1840.
THOMAS H. B., born January 10, 1842.

GEORGE D., born March 18, 1845.
MARY R.
ELMER, born February 8, 1849.

135 WILLIAM, son of William Whiting (75), was born February 5, 1811, married Cynthia Curtis November 20, 1831. Was a selectman and farmer in Hanover.

Children:

TRIPHENA, born December 13, 1832.
CYNTHIA, born September 14, 1834.
WILLIAM, born May 19, 1836.
SIMEON, born July 16, 1838, died March 4, 1839.
BETSY, born May 18, 1840.
MARY, born April, 1847.
WALTER, born March 6, 1850.

136 ASA, son of Joseph (76), married Anna Thistle and settled in Salem.

Child:

ASA ALLEN, who married Mary Millet Nichols of Plymouth and lived there. Children: (a) George A., born in 1838, and married Sarah Elizabeth, daughter of Francis J. Goddard; (b) Annie, born in 1840, and married Charles O. Churchill of Plymouth; (c) Lucy, born in 1843, and married William A. Tarbell; (d) John, married Mary Winsor, and (e) Sarah, married William A. Monroe.

137 ELIJAH, son of Elijah (77), was born in Hingham, December 29, 1779. He married (1st) Susan, daughter of Jairus and Susanna (Lincoln) Beal, on December 18, 1808, who was born in Hingham February 18, 1787, and died August 1, 1812; and (2d) Mary, daughter of Frederick and Tabitha (Whitmarsh) Lincoln, of Weymouth, who was born November 5, 1787, and died at Hingham September 10, 1859. He was a packet-master, resided in Hingham, and died June 19, 1841.*

Child by Susan:

SUSAN LINCOLN, born December 27, 1809, married Ebenezer Pratt of Boston, June 20, 1839, and died December 15, 1846.

FREDERICK WHITON
Son of Elijah (137)

Children by Mary:

ELIJAH LINCOLN (209).

BELA HERNDON (210).

FREDERICK, born May 14, 1818, married August 31, 1845, Sarah H. Waters. Was a member of the House of Representatives, and died in Boston January 4, 1862; child, Susan L.

MARY LINCOLN, born April 19, 1820, married Sidney Sprague September 15, 1844.

LUCY, born October 9, 1822, married May 28, 1848, Luther Sprague.

ERASTUS (211).

JOHN CHADWICK (212).

*Hist. Hing., Vol. III, pp. 303 and 307. Hist. Hanover, p. 441.

138 EZRA, son of Ezra (78), was born in Hingham May 8, 1772, and married Emma, daughter of Thomas and Sarah (Lane) Jones, who was born there December 29, 1774, and died March 8, 1850. He was a packet-master and farmer and resided in Hingham. He died March 9, 1850.*

Children:

EZRA J., born April 5, 1797, resided in Boston, and died August 30, 1858; two sons survived him, Lewis C. and Ezra J. (probably 272).

EMMA, born April 17, 1800; married November 17, 1882, Benjamin Andrews of Hingham.

EBEN, born September 18, 1802, married (1st) Esther C. Richardson, and (2d) Mary A. Howe, who died in Somerville, Mass., March 24, 1888. He died in Boston December 11, 1879.

BELA, born October 18, 1804; married Martha L. Whitney, and had a son George H., born in 1829 and died in 1830.

MARTHA, born September 16, 1807; married Asa A. Wiggan of Boston November 22, 1835.

SUSAN CUSHING, born September 8, 1810, married December 14, 1834, Zadoc Hersey.

THOMAS LOWELL, born December 1, 1812, died March 1, 1913.

THOMAS LOWELL (213).

PETER LANE (214).

HANNAH RICHMOND, born August 17, 1818, and married Bela H. Whiton (210) February 2, 1844.

*Hist. Hing., Vol. III, pp. 303 and 308.

139 DAVID, son of Moses (79), was born in Hingham April 23, 1775, and married January 16, 1803, Nabby, daughter of Thomas and Lydia (Ripley) Fearing. She was born in Hingham February 20, 1781, and died August 14, 1843. He was a flour and grain merchant, and died in Hingham August 14, 1843.*

Children:

MERIEL, born December 3, 1803, died October 28, 1884.

NABBY FEARING, born September 6, 1805, married April 12, 1832, Morris Fearing.

MARY RIPLEY, born September 28, 1806, and died January 2, 1808.

DAVID, born October 29, 1809, married (1st) Lucy P. Dorr of Boston, who died September 4, 1843; (2d) Ellen D. Kelleran of Portland, Me., who died in Hingham August 3, 1886. He was a merchant in Boston, a member of the firm of Whiton, Train & Co. He died June 23, 1889; left no children.

WILLIAM (215).

HARRIET, born January 9, 1814.

LYDIA RIPLEY, born February 11, 1816, died unmarried September 29, 1886.

THOMAS FEARING (216).

*Hist. Hing., Vol. III, p. 303. Hist. Hanover, p. 441.

140 WILSON, son of Moses (79), was born in Hingham September 26, 1777, and married Chloe, daughter of Jeremiah and Jane (Tirrell) White, of Weymouth October 21, 1804. She died March 24, 1853. He was a packet-master and commission merchant and resided in Hingham Center. He died December 27, 1854.*

Children:

WILSON, born February 1, 1805, died unmarried July, 1873.

JANE TIRRELL, born March 31, 1807, and died August 27, 1869.

THOMAS J., born March 7, 1809, removed to Bangor, Me., and died in 1869.

JOHN P. (217).

HENRY (218).

ADELINE, born September 16, 1816, died January 12, 1898.

ELIZABETH, born March 2, 1820.

SARAH C., born April 5, 1822, and died September 29, 1823.

*Hist. Hing., Vol. III, p. 304. Hist. Hanover, p. 442.

141 MOSES, son of Moses (79), was born in Hingham June 26, 1785. He married Ann, daughter of Demerick and Polly (Stodder) Stodder, January 7, 1810. She was born in Cohasset November 7, 1790, and died in Hingham October 16, 1851. He was a master-mariner, and later in the grain and flour commission business. He died in Hingham October 26, 1862.*

Children:

MOSES LINCOLN (219).
MARY ANN, born June 8, 1816, married John W. Peirce, February 11, 1841.
STARKES, born September 21, 1825, died October 10, 1828.
STARKES (220).

*Hist. Hing., Vol. III, p. 304. Hist. Hanover, p. 442.

142 STARKES, son of Moses (79), was born June 26, 1785. He married Hannah, daughter of Captain Benjamin Dyer, a merchant in Weymouth.* Starkes was a member of Captain Laban Hersey's Company of Foot Soldiers in 1805. Also a member of Captain John Fearing's Company of Foot Soldiers in 1804.†

Children:

JOSEPH, of Cambridge.
LYDIA, married John P. Lovell.
BENJAMIN, died unmarried.
LUCINDA.
HANNAH, married ——— Reed and resided in Bangor, Me.

*Hist. Hanover, p. 442.
†Original Muster Rolls in possession of Hingham Historical Society.

143 ABIJAH, son of Abijah (80), was born March 7, 1787, and married Rachel Remington. He moved from Chesterfield, Mass., to Pierpont, Ashtabula County, Ohio, about 1812, and from there to Springfield Township, Erie County, Penn., in 1820, taking up a grant of a hundred and sixty-five acres of land on the Ridge Road. They traveled from Massachusetts in an ox cart to a country as yet rough and unsettled. To the back of the cart was tied their cow, to provide milk for their infant son, Madison, then a little over a year old. The story is told by his children that their father, hearing that a

boat load of pigs had arrived at Connaut Harbor, drove with a neighbor fifteen miles from Pierpont to purchase them. They had great difficulty in driving the pigs back, and while awaiting the return of his neighbor with teams and wagons, he corralled the pigs and spent the entire night fighting off an attack of wolves. The property in Erie County remained in the family until 1905. While constructing a barn he was injured, and was lame during the latter years of his life. He died July 7, 1849.

Children:

MADISON (221).

WILLIAM, died in Sandusky, Ohio, suffocated by charcoal fumes.

LOUISE, married and settled in Springfield Township, Penn.

LUCY, married and settled in the same township.

EDWIN, born June 8, 1826, resided at his father's homestead until his death January 13, 1888, and being short and stocky was known as "Short Ed."

EDWARD (222).

144 DAVID RANDALL, son of David (81), was born February 6, 1803, and married Harriet Parker of Belchertown, Mass., in September, 1833.

Children:

DAVID BRUCE, born August 15, 1834.

THEODORE P., born January 28, 1836.

145 ISAIAH, son of Israel (82), was born in Hingham October 8, 1789, and married November 5, 1810, Martha, daughter of Gorham and Susanna (Gorham) Easterbrook, of Boston. She died in Hingham November 21, 1857.* He was captain of a packet-boat, resided in Hingham and died April 2, 1871.

Children:

MARTHA DAVIS, born September 18, 1811, married September 25, 1835, Josiah Gorham of Nantucket.

ISAIAH GORHAM (223).

CHARLES EASTERBROOK, born February 22, 1816, married (1st) Susanna, daughter of Martin Hobart, December 1,

1839, and (2d) Georgiana Cole on December 5, 1883. He resided at Quincy, Mass., and died September 6, 1889.

SUSAN ALLEN, born May 24, 1817, married Thomas D. Blossom May 9, 1837.

DEBORAH KIMBALL, born May 19, 1820, and married Samuel Bronsdon June 1, 1843.

ALBERT, born December 9, 1823, and died September 6, 1824.

ANNA EASTERBROOK, born June 13, 1825, married Isaac B. Damon January 17, 1846.

EMILY E., born October 11, 1827, married Moses Cross January 17, 1848.

ALBERT (224).

OLIVE MARBLE, born May 4, 1832, married Edwin Wilder.

WILLIAM STOWELL (225).

*Hist. Hing., Vol. III, pp. 304 and 309.

146 ROYAL, son of Israel (82), was born in Hingham February 22, 1792, and married Esther Cleverly of Quincy July 3, 1811. She was born in 1787 and died April 19, 1867. He was a trader and resided in Hingham, dying August 18, 1877.*

Children:

ELIZABETH DEVINA, born April 9, 1812, married Dr. Larkin Turner of Boston April 3, 1843. She died December 20, 1879.

HANNAH STOWELL, born April 25, 1814, married Captain James Beal November 29, 1838, and died March 24, 1878.

CATHERINE CUSHING, born 1816, and died in 1818.

CATHERINE CUSHING, born 1818, and died July 18, 1838.

ROYAL (226).

HIRAM, born March 27, 1823, married (1st) Lydia, daughter of Captain Hawkes Loring, who died June 25, 1847; and (2d) Abigail, daughter of Amasa Hyland, who died August 15, 1882. Hiram died November 19, 1857, leaving Sarah Augusta, born April 15, 1847.

JAMES, born 1825, and died 1826.

HENRY JACKSON, born 1826 and was killed by a railroad accident October 24, 1848.

REBECCA CLEVERLY, born 1830 and died 1832.

*Hist. Hing., Vol. III, p. 305.

147 JOB STOWELL, son of Israel (82), was born in Hingham January 23, 1797, and married Lucy, daughter of Jacob and Lydia (Dunham) Farren, February 22,

1821. She was born at East Haven, Conn., February 3, 1802, and died in Hingham December 14, 1884. He was a master-mariner, resided at Hingham, and died February 8, 1875. He served in the Navy in the War of 1812.*

Children:

LUCY, born September 26, 1822, married Walton V. Mead.
LYDIA ALMIRA, born December 26, 1824, married James W. Vose December 25, 1841, and died June 8, 1845.
JOSIAH WILDER, born December 24, 1827, and died October 15, 1846.
MEHITABLE SISER, born December 11, 1829.
LYMAN BARNES (227).

*Hist. Hing., Vol. III, pp. 305 and 309.

148 CAMPBELL, son of Israel (82), known also as Kimball, was born February 19, 1784, and married Desire Jordan. He resided in Boston and died December 5, 1851.

Children:

HENRY.
KIMBALL.
HARRIET, married ——— Smith.
LYDIA A., married ——— Watson.
MARY A.
ALMIRA, married ——— Leavens.
ELLEN.
GEORGE.

149 ELIJAH, son of Elijah (84), was born in Hingham March 6, 1799, and married (1st) Lydia, daughter of Crocker and Deborah (Jacob) Wilder, September 18, 1822, who was born in Hingham January 24, 1801, and died December 4, 1864; (2d) Mary, daughter of Samuel and Mary (Saunders) Stodder, of Scituate, who was born April 23, 1812.* He was a manufacturer of wooden ware at Groton, Mass., and later at Hingham, where he resided. The History of Hanover, p. 436, says of him, "A man of rare mechanical ability and the inventor of various machines, several of which have been patented and have been found highly useful. He was active in political life and was a man of great energy

of character, perservering in whatever he undertook, and carrying it on to a successful issue." He died February 10, 1871.

Children:

CHARLES (228).

GEORGE, born at Groton October 12, 1828, and died at Hingham September 5, 1863.

*Hist. Hing., Vol. III, p. 305.

150 LORING, son of Elijah (84), was born October 29, 1801.

Children:

GEORGE, was one of the Community of Shakers at Harvard, Mass.

STEPHEN, was a mariner, and was drowned in 1852 on a voyage to Smyrna.

CAROLINE.

LAVINIA, born February 2, 1804, and married Jacob Tirrell.

ELIZABETH, born in 1806.

CHARLOTTE, born in 1808, and died in 1813.

ALVAN, born September 23, 1811.

151 JAMES, son of Blossom (85), was born in Boston, December 23, 1811, and married June 17, 1847, Sally Bryant, who was born in Scituate December 3, 1817. He died at Charlestown, Mass., August 13, 1874.

Child:

EDWARD EVERETT (229).

152 LINCOLN B., son of Blossom (85), was born at Charlestown, Mass., March 4, 1808, and married Susan, daughter of Samuel F. Echem, who was born in Boston, April 21, 1814, and died in Somerville, Mass. He was a ship-joiner, connected with the U. S. Navy Yard in Boston.

Children:

LORING LIVINGSTON (230).

RUSSELL J., born February 12, 1836, and married Lizzie Watson, March 4, 1886.

EMILY A., born May 21, 1846.

GEORGE F. (231).

153 EPHRAIM, son of Ephraim (87), was born in Boston, March 16, 1811, and married Sarah Morton of Duxbury, Mass.

Children:

HELEN E.
ADELAIDE L.
WALTER B.

154 LEONARD, son of Eleazer (88), was born May 8, 1824, married Elizabeth Hobart of Dorchester, and lived in Abington.

Children:

HARRIET E., born July 23, 1847.
LEONARD A., born January, 1849.
HENRY, born 1850.

155 STEPHEN, son of Ithamar (89), was born April 13, 1819, married (1st) Mary Prouty, who died April 10, 1844, and (2d) Judith A. Baker. He lived in East Abington, Mass.

Children:

STEPHEN W., born 1843, and died 1844.
SIMEON D., born June 15, 1847.
HERBERT J., born August 6, 1849.

HOUSE OF CAPTAIN JOSEPH J. WHITING (115)
From Barry's History of Hanover

EIGHTH GENERATION

156 HENRY, son of Joseph (91), spelled his name Whiting, and married Grace, daughter of Ellis and Grace (Symmes) Holmes, and was a large landholder in Plymouth.*

Children:

HENRY, born 1816, married Nancy, daughter of William Burgess, and died in 1876.
WINSLOW, born 1820, and married Abby Holmes.
PELHAM, born 1823 and married Sophia Straffin.

*Anc. Landmarks of Plymouth, p. 285.

157 ELISHA, son of Joseph (91), spelled his name Whiting, was born in 1811, and married Almira Holmes.*

Children:

CAROLINE.
AUGUSTA, married William F. Speare.
MARY.
ELLEN, married Winslow Holmes.
ABBY.
IOWA.
ELISHA.
JOSEPH, married Laura, daughter of John T. Hall.
FANNY, married William H. Moore of New York.

*Anc. Landmarks of Plymouth, p. 284.

158 GEORGE, son of Joseph (91), spelled his name Whiting, and married Betsey Holmes.*

Children:

EMMA, married William H. Clark.
GEORGIANA.

*Anc. Landmarks of Plymouth, p. 285.

159 NATHAN, son of Nathan (92), spelled his name Whiting, was born in 1797, and married Experience (Polly), daughter of Clark and Mary (Wetherel) Finney. He resided in Plymouth, Mass.*

Children:

POLLY, born in 1818.
JOHN, born in 1822.
NATHAN, born in 1823.

ALBERT, born in 1828.
EDWARD, born in 1830.
LYDIA, born in 1835.
HARRIET, born in 1837.
ADONIRAM, born in 1840.
LEAVITT, born in 1842.

*Anc. Landmarks of Plymouth, p. 284.

160 BENJAMIN, son of Benjamin (94), spelled his name Whiting, married Susan L., daughter of Robert and Sarah (Leach) Finney.*

Children:

BENJAMIN, married Lucy Hammond.
JOSIAH, married Lydia C. White of Weymouth.

*Anc. Landmarks of Plymouth, p. 284.

161 ABRAHAM, son of Abraham (95), spelled his name Whitten, married Lucia H., daughter of Peter and Sally (Harlow) Holmes, and was a large property holder in Plymouth.*

Children:

FRANCIS L., married the widow of Augustus P. Cady.
HORACE C., married Jane E., daughter of William Stephens.
ORRIN B., married Abby Cushing.

*Anc. Landmarks of Plymouth, p. 284.

162 CHARLES, son of Abraham (95), spelled his name Whitten, and married Mary Rickard, daughter of Nathan and Ruth (Cobb) Holmes.*

Children:

CHARLES, married (1st) Lydia N. Bradford, (2d) Anne Sears, and (3d) Charlotte Irving.
LEWIS HOLMES, married Emmeline, daughter of Robert Hutchinson.
ABRAHAM, married Ruth W. Sears.
RUFUS ROBBINS, married the widow Pauline (Wheeler) Wellington.
ELISHA COBB.
EDWARD W., married Laura Dorman.

*Anc. Landmarks of Plymouth, p. 284.

163 AMOS, son of Amos (96), spelled his name Whitten, was born in Alfred, Me., in May, 1818, and married Frances Lodenia, daughter of Nelson and Adaline (Stannard) Benjamin at Barcelona, N. Y., in 1846. He died in Roxbury, Mass., in May, 1887.

Children:

CHESTER H., born in 1847 and died in 1910.
EDGAR BENJAMIN (232).
CHARLES N., born in 1855, and died in 1927.
WILLIAM MELVILLE, born February 23, 1862.

164 MILO JAMES, son of James (98), was born in Lee, Mass., November 21, 1805, and married (1st) Sophia Tuttle at Lee, July 23, 1826, who was born September 15, 1807, and died April 4, 1845, at Broadalbin, N. Y.; married (2d) Mary E. Clute, born March 19, 1820, died August 26, 1867, at Troy, N. Y.; married (3d) Julia Lawrence (a sister of Commodore Lawrence of Lake Erie fame). He studied medicine and after practicing for several years entered the ministry. He died at Fishkill, N. Y., December 15, 1867.

Children, by Sophia:

HENRY BENJAMIN (233).

JAMES CLINTON, born July 20, 1830, died November 11, 1852.

GEORGE LESLIE, born September 15, 1833, at Amsterdam, N. Y., and died in Toronto, Canada, July 11, 1921. He married (1st) in 1855, at Elmira, N. Y., Robie Delphine Parmenter, and had two children: Julia Francis, born December 12, 1861, died in 1926; and Emily, born January 31, 1870, who married ——— Smith and resides at 69 Highland Parkway, Rochester, N. Y. His wife died March 17, 1879, and he married (2d) in 1882, Mary Elizabeth Elton. They had three children: (a) Leslie S., died in infancy; (b) George Eby, born August 27, 1885, who married and has four children, Leslie V., Marjorie, Grace and Elizabeth, and lives at 1811 Peer Street, Niagara Falls, Ont.; (c) Dorothy Elton, born August 10, 1887, who married L. Joslyn Rogers, a professor in the University of Toronto. They reside at 112 Garfield Avenue, Toronto, and have a son, Joslyn Whiton.

JULIA FRANCES, born December 7, 1838, died July 11, 1855.

MILO JAMES, died in infancy.

Child, by Mary:

CHARLES CHAMBERS, born October 29, 1846, married December 14, 1869, Isabella Knickerbocker and had two children, Hamson Sweet, died September 29, 1875, and Mary.

165 LYMAN, son of James (98) was born July 31, 1801, and married Nancy Emmeline Couch, September 23, 1823.*

Children:

SARAH ANTOINETTE, born July 19, 1824.
JULIAN, born May 17, 1826.
LUCY EMMELINE, born October 13, 1829.
MARY JANE, born September 26, 1831.
NATHANIEL STARBUCK, born June 26, 1833.
HENRY LYMAN, born May 1, 1835.

*Vital Records, Lee, Mass.

166 WILLIAM LOOMIS, son of John Mandley (99), was born at Lee, Mass., December 17, 1816, married September 17, 1838, Marietta Bradley, and died at Wellington, Ohio, September 2, 1898. He adopted his wife's niece, Mary Jane Bradley, who was born October 17, 1862, and who inherited his farm. She married March 16, 1898, J. T. Rathwell and had three children, Margaret, Robert T. and Isabel.

Children:

GEORGE W., born October 10, 1840, served in the Civil War and died February 18, 1862, in the Army Hospital, Platt City, Md.
CHARLES M. (234a).

167 HIRAM BRADLEY, son of John Mandley (99), was born at Lee, Mass., February 27, 1822, and married Sally Roice October 15, 1844, and died May 13, 1892, at Lyons, Fulton County, Ohio.

Children:

ALMIRA, born at Huntington, Ohio, July 4, 1845, married July 26, 1865, Henry Corkendale. Moved West.
JOHN EDGAR, born at Huntington, Ohio, February 15, 1847, died May 24, 1865.
HEZEKIAH J. (235).
GEORGE (236).

168 JOSIAH BARTHOLOMEW, son of John Mandley (99), was born at Lee, Mass., April 17, 1826, and married at Canaan, N. Y., October 23, 1848, Ellen McCarty, who was born in Ireland, December 24, 1829, and died April 18, 1903, at Ithaca, Mich., where he died April 6, 1911.

Children:

MARY JANE, born September 27, 1852, died December 31, 1852.

FRANK J. (236a).

ADELAIDE M., born February 28, 1857, died March 27, 1861.

WALTER SCOTT, born January 31, 1859, died April 2, 1861.

GEORGE EDWIN (236b).

IDA MAY, born October 12, 1866, married at Emerson, Mich., September 29, 1887, John H. Gray, who was born April 10, 1854, and died April 29, 1931. Their children: a son, born and died in 1888; Ethel, born April 25, 1894, married March 6, 1922, Norman Buchanan and had a daughter, Ida May, born and died in February, 1930; they live at 3728 Tuxedo Avenue, Detroit, Mich.; Ruth Gertrude, born March 27, 1908.

WALTER GRANT (236c).

169 JAMES FLAVEL, son of John Mandley (99), was born at Lee, Mass., March 22, 1828, married (1st) February 21, 1853, Electa Ann Bingham, who was born July 5, 1836, and died May 4, 1871; married (2d), May 13, 1873, Louisa Hixon. He died June 3, 1892, at Wakeman, Ohio.

Children:

MANDLEY BINGHAM, born at White House, Ohio, December 4, 1853, married December 16, 1873, Susannah Craig, and had two sons, John M., born August 27, 1875, died December 24, 1877, and Fred M., born 1878, died 1882.

JAY, born at Eldora, Ia., September 1, 1858, and died at Ithaca, Mich., June 6, 1880.

CORA ELECTA, born at Eldora, October 18, 1867, married May 26, 1886, Edward R. Austin, and had four children: Mary Electa, born February 14, 1887, married June 24, 1909, Harry Miller Rainey, and has three sons, Harry A., Rowland K., and Roger F.; Gertrude Agnes, born October 22, 1893, married July 30, 1923, James Elwood Fletcher, and has a son, James A.; Mandley Whiton, born April 13,

1903, married July 3, 1927, Almira Rees, and has a daughter, Janet Ann; and Clarence Julius (twin with Mandley W.), born April 13, 1903, married April 29, 1924, Agnes Claffe, and has a daughter, Clarice A.

170 JOHN MANDLEY, son of John Mandley (99), was born April 25, 1830, at Lee, Mass., and married Sarah M., daughter of ——— and Lucy (Coalter) Kimmel, who was born in Montclair, Ohio, January 1, 1835, and died at Wakeman, Ohio, October 21, 1918. He was a merchant and died at Wakeman June 10, 1916.

Children:

ELVA LUELLA, born in Brighton, Lorain County, Ohio, February 27, 1862, and married George A., son of Charles C. and Elmira (Arnet) Parsons, at Wakeman, Ohio, June 12, 1888, who was born at Townsend, Huron County, Ohio, January 6, 1859, and died at Wakeman June 29, 1927. Their children were: (a) Frank Whiton, born January 7, 1891, (b) Ruth Luella, born June 29, 1893, and married Joseph Harris June 12, 1926; both reside with their mother at 5425 Ash Street, Los Angeles, Cal.

WILL W., born at Brighton, Ohio, May 27, 1863, and married (1st) Gertrude L. Humphrey, September 20, 1888, in Wakeman, Ohio, who was born September 21, 1864, and died in Wakeman May 11, 1904, and (2d) Julia E., daughter of John G. and Elizabeth D. (Miller) Sherman, at Wakeman, on June 14, 1905. He is a merchant and resides at Wakeman, Ohio, and at 1017 3d Street, North, St. Petersburg, Fla.

171 ALPHA, son of Thomas (100), was born at Portageville, N. Y., August 21, 1829, and married Mary Jane, daughter of Solomon and Phoebe Mason, who was born at Bridgeport, Vt., May 27, 1832, and died at Lockport, N. Y., July 29, 1916. He was Superintendent of Construction at Reynold's Basin, N. Y., and served in the Civil War as First Lieutenant of Company E of the 8th New York Cavalry, and died at Reynold's Basin, April 26, 1906.

Children:

ALPHA MASON (234).

INEZ, born at Reynold's Basin, October 16, 1863, and married there January 6, 1909, John Dickie Gammack, who was born at Craig Head, Stricken, Scotland, March 23, 1865, and was the son of Williamson and Isabella (Dickie) Gammack. They reside at Lockport, N. Y., and have a daughter, Olive May, born at Gasport, N. Y., October 9, 1909, who married, September 5, 1928, Alton Dumpelberger of Lockport, N. Y.

172 CHARLES, son of Thomas (100), was born January 21, 1831, at Eaton, Madison County, N. Y., and married Phoebe Emmeline, daughter of Marvin and Phoebe Ann (Dunbar) Briggs who was born at Independence, N. Y., February 26, 1845. He was from 1856 to 1865 a miner in California, and died at Wiscoy, N. Y., September 4, 1909. His widow died September 30, 1930.

Children:

NELLIE, born at Wiscoy, January 8, 1868, and lives at Portageville.

CASSIUS, born March 20, 1869, and lives at Portageville, N. Y.

CARRIE ETTIE, born November 9, 1870, and married Eugene Munger, and lives at Castile, Wyoming County, N. Y.

HATTIE EMMERETTA, born April 21, 1874, married Lewis A. Pfaff, and lives at Portageville.

173 JOSEPH LUCAS, son of Joseph Lucas (101), was born in Amherst, Ohio, March 28, 1848, and married Annetta Josephine, daughter of Daniel and Susanna (Spooner) Gawn, on June 24, 1874, who was born in Lorain, Ohio, May 22, 1853. He is a farmer, residing at Amherst.

Children:

JOSEPH EDWARD, born September 16, 1875, at Amherst, and married Elsie Schubert and resides at Elyria, Ohio; has a daughter, Lillian M.

CURTIS WARREN, born June 21, 1877, married (1st) Emma Axt, and (2d) Lydia Grubb, and resides at Lorain, Ohio.

EDITH LAVINA, born July 14, 1879, and resides at 845 Buchtel Avenue, Akron, Ohio.

AGNES LILLIAN, born January 3, 1883, married Hezzleton E., son of George E. and Anna (Farnum) Simmons, at Amherst, July 29, 1909, and resides at 331 Beechwood Drive, Akron, Ohio. She graduated from Buchtel College, receiving the degree of Ph.B. in 1906. Their children are:

George H., born in LeRoy, Ohio, July 7, 1910; Catherine Whiton, born in Akron January 13, 1912; Mary Agnes, born in Akron June 24, 1916; Ruth Lavina, born March 1, 1924, and died May 27, 1924; and Priscilla J., born July 5, 1925.

ARTHUR LUCAS, born November 10, 1890, at Akron, married Frieda Kappely and resides at Amherst on the farm which his great-grandfather (53) received for his service in the Revolution. He has two sons, Joseph Lucas and Norman Curtis.

174 HENRY KIRKE, son of Daniel Garfield (102), was born at Chillicothe, Ohio, and married (1st) Mary Florence, daughter of Caleb B. and Elizabeth (Hunter) Phinney, in September, 1855, who died February 7, 1864, and (2d) Louise Lauder at Janesville, Wis., in June, 1867, who was born December 20, 1841, and died in Chicago December 26, 1906. He was educated at Marietta College, and was valedictorian of his class when he graduated in 1848. He was a lawyer in Chicago, where he died July 14, 1886.

Child by Mary:

ARTHUR LEE (238).

Children by Louise:

LAUDER KIRKE, born June 11, 1868, and died in Chicago August 14, 1916.

VERNON CONGER, born November 9, 1870, and died in Chicago May 15, 1891.

LOUISE, born October 11, 1875, and resides at 603 Pine Street, Chattanooga, Tenn.

WALTER STARR (239).

175 EDWARD VERNON, son of Edward Vernon (103), was born in Janesville, Wis., November 1, 1853, and married August 9, 1876, Mary, daughter of Volney and Catherine (Holmes) Atwood, who was born October 13, 1855. He died in Janesville March 19, 1900.

Children:

EDWARD VERNON (240).

LUCRETIA ATWOOD, born in 1881.

HENRY KIRKE WHITON (174)

AMORET T., born in 1883, married October 23, 1913, Hugh Emery McCoy.

VICTOR ATWOOD, born December 22, 1885.

176 JOSEPH SEWARD, son of Ebenezer (104), was born at Elyria, Ohio, September 1, 1824, and married Nancy Elizabeth Cosgrove, in March, 1861, who died January 21, 1869, at Winona, Minn. An obituary notice in a local newspaper, at the time of his death, April 11, 1893, stated that he went to Cleveland, Ohio, and worked on *The Herald* of that city, and lived after that in Madison, Wis., St. Louis, Mo., New York, and finally moved to St. Charles, Minn., where he edited and published *The Union*. He was a man of pronounced opinions in regard to both politics and religion. In politics he was a stalwart among stalwart Republicans. In religion he was a firm and ardent Liberalist or Free-Thinker.

Children:

MARIE REBECCA, born at Winona March 18, 1862, married Charles E. Miller of Athens, Oregon, and had children: Hazel, who married Orwin Otterson of Orting, Wash.; and Katy, who married J. D. Marston, who was killed in the Ashtabula Bridge disaster in 1876.

JOSEPH EBEN (237).

177 JOHN LEWIS, son of Luther (105), was born in Binghamton, N. Y., October 29, 1816, and married in Ithaca, N. Y., April 26, 1838, Keziah, daughter of Abram and Emma Byington, who was born June 16, 1817, and died in Ithaca February 13, 1879. John Lewis received his education in the public schools of Ithaca, and then learned the baker's trade and the baking business. While still a young man he established his own bakery, which he conducted in connection with a grocery business and a confectionery store. He was regarded by his associates as a man possessed of sound judgment, keen discernment, and pronounced initiative. He was one of the founders of the Ithaca Savings Bank in 1863, and from 1883 until his death was its president. He

was one of the founders of the Incorporated Schools of Ithaca in 1874, and in 1875 became a member of the school board. He was a trustee of the Village of Ithaca, first elected in 1849. In 1862 he was elected a supervisor of the town, and in 1868 became an incorporator of the waterworks. In 1881 he purchased a fine brick mansion on South Aurora Street, where he died March 13, 1896. An obituary in the *Ithaca Journal* said of him:

> "To the needy he was a liberal giver, as hundreds of poor people in the City can testify, and his acts were always performed without ostentation. In his domestic relations he was generous and loving. In his habits and manners he was exceedingly plain. He was greatly respected by all who knew him. He had an abhorence of deceit in every form, and for honesty and fair dealing he had no superior. As a mark of respect every store in the City closed during the hour of his funeral."

Children:

ALMIRA, born September 24, 1839, married Charles Rowland October 5, 1887, who was born August 23, 1839. She died December 24, 1903.

EMMELINE J., born October 16, 1841, married Charles M. Williams September 22, 1864, and died in Ithaca in 1911. He died in 1900.

HENRY CLAY, born November 13, 1843, and died July 20, 1856.

LOUISE B., born January 16, 1846, and died February 3, 1865.

ADDIE KEZIAH, born November 13, 1848, and died unmarried in Ithaca July 13, 1929.

178 AUGUSTUS SHERRILL, son of Luther (105), was born in Binghamton, N. Y., December 25, 1820, and married at Ramapo, N. Y., March 18, 1843, Caroline, daughter of Thomas and Elizabeth (Dater) Ward, one of thirteen children. He was educated at the Ithaca Academy, and became a Civil Engineer. In 1841-5 he was first assistant to Silas Seymour, who constructed the branch of the Erie Railroad from Goshen to Piermont on the Hudson, the first railroad outlet to the West from New York. After practicing his profession

CAROLINE and AUGUSTUS SHERRILL WHITON (178)

for several years in Kentucky, Ohio, and New York, he became the General Superintendent of the Erie Railroad. In 1853 he became chief engineer of a Kentucky railroad, and later one in Virginia. Removing to New York City he entered the steel and iron rail business and was the agent for several English firms. He was for many years an elder of the Collegiate Reformed (Dutch) Church of New York City, and lived an active Christian life. Personally he was a man of high principle and kindly bearing. He died in New York City February 7, 1898, and his wife died January 31, 1905. Both are interred in Greenwood Cemetery, Brooklyn, N. Y. The following is taken from an obituary notice published in the *Christian Intelligencer:*

> "The pastor of one of the New York City churches has written us in a recent letter, 'Many a time in recent years as I have reviewed my own life and recalled those whose character has inspired me, the picture of Mr. Whiton has been recalled to my mind. His balance of judgment was so true, his sympathy so constant, that as I think of him over the space of almost a score of years his likeness is very near the ideal of Christian manhood.' "

Children:

JULIA, born February 11, 1844, married Robert Forsyth Little February 11, 1869, who also was born February 11, 1844. She died June 18, 1916. They had three children: (a) Carrie Whiton, born December 6, 1869, and died July 24, 1877; (b) Robert Forsyth, born May 14, 1874, married Janet Heath June 7, 1905, and died at Garden City, Long Island, July 23, 1923. Their children were: Janet, born October 1, 1908, married Arthur Cherouny May 25, 1930, in Paris, France, and Robert Forsyth, born May 8, 1917; and (c) Julia Whiton, born May 21, 1876, and married E. Ross Faulkner, M.D., in 1910, and resides at 570 Park Avenue, New York City.

ELIZABETH, born May 9, 1846, and died in New York City October 19, 1878.

AUGUSTUS WARD (241).

ALBERT C., born June 29, 1860, and died February 22, 1861.

LOUIS CLAUDE (242).

179 WILLIAM HENRY, son of Luther (105), was born in Binghamton, N. Y., April 3, 1823, and married at Piermont, Rockland County, N. Y., October 2, 1845, Sarah Pierson, daughter of Eleazer and Sarah (Pierson) Lord, of Piermont, who died June 13, 1903. They moved to Ohio, and thence to Kentucky, Tennessee, and other mid-western states, where he was engaged in the construction of railroads. From 1862 to 1865 he was in charge of the Headquarters Offices of the U. S. Military Railway Department at Washington, D. C. After the war they returned to their home in Piermont. He died October 17, 1908.

Children:

ELIZABETH PIERSON, born March 11, 1847, married May 11, 1869, Jerome B. Stillson, and died April 26, 1875. They had a son, Henry Whiton, born in 1875 and died young. He died December 26, 1880.

EDWARD NATHAN (243).

JULIA CAROLINE, born March 16, 1853, married Oscar Gunkel in Piermont September 15, 1886, and died at Jackson Heights, Long Island in 1927.

FLORENCE, born June 28, 1859, and died September 4, 1860.

SALLIE CRAIG, born July 6, 1862, married Edward Henry Harris at Piermont June 21, 1882, and died at Glen Cove, Long Island, N. Y., in 1928. They had three children: Agnes Freneau, born March 17, 1883, and married Archibald McLintock; Ruth Lord, born September 11, 1885, and married (1st) Ralph C. Law, by whom she had a daughter, Mildred, born February 17, 1910, and (2d) Russell T. Nixon, and Gwendolen, born March 10, 1895, at Piermont, and married Henry D. Whiton (298) and resides at Glen Cove, Long Island.

WILLIAM HENRY, born April 5, 1864, died August 31, 1865.

ANTOINETTE, born June 19, 1868, died September 29, 1868.

DEVEREUX, born June 19, 1868, died December 25, 1869.

MARY LORD, born October 30, 1870, died August 7, 1871.

180 FREDERIC LUTHER, son of Luther (105), was born in Ithaca, N. Y., July 4, 1826, and married in November, 1853, at Great Barrington, Mass., Ellen Smith, daughter of Jeffrey and Ann Smith, formerly of Brooklyn, N. Y., who was born April 24, 1835, and

died December 12, 1866. He started business as a clerk for his brother John, in Ithaca, and removing to New York became associated with his cousin George R. Ives in the woolen business. In 1857 he formed the partnership of Masury and Whiton, manufacturers and dealers in white lead and paints. He died at Aiken, South Carolina, February 25, 1870.

Children:

FREDERIC A., born October 28, 1854, and died April 19, 1856.

FREDERIC JEFFREY (244).

MARY JEWETT, born November 21, 1858, and resides at the Hotel Willard, New York City.

LILLIE CROCKER, born March 4, 1864, and married James Weston, son of James S. and Juliet (Weston) Myers, on June 13, 1888. He was Adjutant General of the State of New York at the time of his death on April 29, 1929. She died April 23, 1930.

181 ALBERT G., son of Luther (105), was born August 11, 1828, at Ithaca, N. Y., and married in Trinity Church, New York City, May 12, 1863, Laura Vaughn, daughter of William Caldwell and Eliza (Hawkins) Templeton, who was born September 10, 1836, and died March 7, 1904. He studied Civil Engineering at Union College, N. Y., and started his professional career as an axeman in a surveying party of the Ohio Coal and Iron Co. Later he was Division Engineer on the Maysville and Lexington Railroad of Kentucky. His wife, born in Virginia, was strongly sympathetic to the Confederate cause during the Civil War. He later engaged in the banking business in New York City. He died in Georgetown, D. C., March 2, 1864.

Children:

ALBERTA, born June 28, 1864, and married Peter S. Roller March 27, 1889, who died December 11, 1914. They had three children: (a) Laura Antoinette, born January 22, 1893, who married Alfred Evans in November, 1912, resides at Mt. Jackson, Va., and has five children: (1) Julia Whiton, (2) Alberta Antoinette, (3) Bertie Roller, (4) Alfred Roland, (5) Leila Ann; (b) Alberta Whiton, born March 26, 1895, and married (1st) Guymond McD. Stacks

June 18, 1918, who died September 16, 1923, and (2d) John Wilmerton Dawley June 16, 1924, by whom she had one son, John Wilmerton, born May 11, 1925, and resides at Roland Park, Baltimore, Md.; (c) Leonidas T., born April 13, 1897, and died December 11, 1900.

182 RUFUS HENRY, son of George (106), was born August 21, 1826, at Ithaca, N. Y., and married Matilda, daughter of James L. Husted, October 12, 1856, at Jerseyville, Ill., and removed to Champaign, Ill. He was a manufacturer of furniture and a farmer, and died at Perry, Iowa, in July, 1911.

Children:

GEORGE JACKSON (245).

CHARLES LYMAN (246).

ARTHUR SYLVESTER (247).

JULIA MARSH, born March 24, 1868, married Edward Parr, and resides at Great Bend, Kan. They have three children: Burnham E., born October 16, 1893; Rufus H., born December 11, 1896; Arthur D., born June 18, 1899, and Cynthia Grace, born January 4, 1901, and died February 6, 1901.

183 SYLVANUS, son of Sylvanus (109), was born in Hingham in May, 1801, and married Sybil, daughter of Stephen and Susa (Whiton) Gardner, who was born in Hingham April 12, 1802, and died November 18, 1873. He was a stone mason, resided in Hingham and died March 15, 1872.*

Children:

ADELINE, died æt. four years.

ADELINE OSBORN, married ——— Barry of East Weymouth.

*Hist. Hing., Vol. III, p. 306.

184 ZENAS L., son of Theophilus (111), was born October 3, 1804, and married Mary Lane of Abington in 1825.

Children:

HIRAM L., born November, 1825.

MARY A., born September 6, 1827, and married Andrew Rogers of Hanover.

EDWIN W., born December 9, 1820.

ALBERT L., born and died in 1834.
HARRY L.
EMILY L.
ALBERT F.
JOSEPHINE M.
WILLIAM L., born January 26, 1849.

185 GILMAN C., son of Theophilus (111), was born February 16, 1809, and married Diantha Stoddard of Abington. He was a constable and lived in Hanover.

Children:

DIANTHA S., born September 27, 1830.
MARY W., born August 22, 1831.
NATHAN G., born April 15, 1833.
HANNAH M., born June 10, 1835, died September 27, 1852.
LORANUS W., born October, 1836, and died July, 1837.
ANSON V., born August, 1838.
LUSANNE, born April 14, 1842.

186 PIAM C., son of Theophilus (111), was born June 27, 1811, and married Sarah D. Brown September 15, 1831, and died August 12, 1845.

Children:

PIAM W., born 1832, and died 1833.
EDWIN W., born December 2, 1833.
ANGELINE S., born August 9, 1836.
PIAM A., born April, 1838.
LEROY M., born February 28, 1843.

187 HOSEA, son of Hosea (112), was born in Hingham January 12, 1806, and married (1st) Bethia Curtis, who died July 13, 1831, and (2d) Maria Ann Hawes of Weymouth November 20, 1831, who died in September, 1841, and (3d) Mary E. Stone, June 10, 1843, who died September 12, 1883. He was a manufacturer of shoes, resided at Hingham, and died April 12, 1883.*

Children:

GEORGE BRAINARD, born October 19, 1828, and married Mary Damon.
ALFRED B. (248).

FLORINDA C., born October 22, 1839, married Charles A. Gardiner April 5, 1857.

*Hist. Hing., Vol. III, p. 306.

188 CHARLES, son of Perez (114), was born in Boston May 29, 1808, and married in Hingham October 17, 1830, Anna C., daughter of Ezekiel and Anna (Cushing) Fearing, who was born at Hingham January 2, 1812, and died at Abington January 17, 1888. He resided at Hingham, was a manufacturer of edged tools, and died November 16, 1887.*

Children:

CHARLES DAVIS, born March 19, 1831, and died June 30, 1848.

CATHERINE BOWKER, born June 5, 1834, and married Dexter Groce.

GEORGE FRANCIS, born October 5, 1840.

*Hist. Hing., Vol. III, p. 306.

189 ALBERT, son of Perez (114), was born in Boston February 23, 1810, and married October 24, 1832, Sarah G., daughter of Ezekiel and Anna (Cushing) Fearing, who was born in Hingham March 26, 1814. He was a contractor and builder and resided in Hingham.*

Children:

ALBERT TURNER, born in Charlestown September 30, 1833, married Harriet E. Warren July 15, 1856, by whom he had a daughter Helen G. They resided in Boston.

GEORGE FRANKLIN, born in Hingham May 17, 1837, and died September 29, 1840.

SARAH HENRIETTA, born in Boston March 21, 1849, and married Alexander H. Caryl, Jr., of Groton, on October 20, 1870.

GEORGE, born in Hingham May 6, 1857, married Erminia W. Jacobs on November 10, 1881, and who died January 5, 1884. He was a wholesale clothier at Boston.

*Hist. Hing., Vol. III, p. 306.

190 BENJAMIN SHURLEFF, son of Perez (114), was born March 22, 1815, and married Olive, daughter of Ezekiel and Anna (Cushing) Fearing, of Hingham, who died in 1849. He resided at Abington.

STEPHEN WHITON'S HOUSE (192)
Westford Hill, Conn.

**STEPHEN WHITON (192) at left; Henry Storrs, a friend, at right
Westford Hill, Conn.**

Children:

WEBSTER, born September 27, 1840.
SHURLEFF.
OLIVE A.

191 AMASA, son of Joseph Jacob (115), was born in Hingham October 15, 1821, and married Hannah L., daughter of Ezekiel and Anna (Cushing) Fearing, October 27, 1844, who was born in Hingham April 1, 1825. He resided at South Hingham and died October 2, 1883.*

Children:

MARY LINCOLN, born June 21, 1845, and married July 30, 1868, Byron Groce.
AMASA (249).
ADA BOWKER, born September 14, 1853, and married September 14, 1876, Cyrus V. Bacon.

*Hist. Hing., Vol. III, pp. 307 and 310.

192 STEPHEN, son of Stephen (116), was born in Ashford, Conn., December 10, 1809, married (1st) October 29, 1839, Laura, daughter of Moses and Betsey White, who was born in 1818 and died from burns July 23, 1844; (2d) Abigail, daughter of Elisha Byles, April 14, 1845, who was born November 1, 1816, and died in Ashford April 21, 1872, and (3d) Eliza Burnham (Jones) November 28, 1872, who died January 2, 1897, leaving several children by a former husband. He was a school teacher, book dealer and at one time a member of the State Legislature, and died at Ashford January 27, 1901.

Children:

ANDREW (250).
ELISHA BYLES (251).
EDWIN MARTIN (252).
JULIA SOPHIA. (See Appendix A.)
SARAH. (See Appendix C.)

193 ASHBEL, son of Stephen (116), was born in Westford, Conn., May 1, 1815, and married (1st) Jerusha, daughter of John and Jerusha (Hodgkins) Fuller, and widow of Henry Whiton (118), in 1840, who was born

at Hampton, Conn., August 23, 1815, and died at Westford June 24, 1881, and (2d) Phoebe Foy, widow of Ebenezer Smith. He was a farmer and died in Westford April 9, 1902.

Children:

ASHBEL HENRY, born in 1844, died in 1852.
SYLVESTER GILBERT (253).
JOHN FULLER (254).
MARY, born in 1852, and died in 1858.
ANNE, born in 1854, and died in 1858.

194 CHESTER, son of Joseph (117), was born in Westford, Conn., March 22, 1812, and married Philura, daughter of Codington and Sylvia (Maine) Brown, who was born March 22, 1818, and died in 1902. He was was a builder and resided in Mansfield, Conn.

Children:

OLIVER OTIS, born August 8, 1833, and died in Three Rivers, Mass., July 30, 1836.

EDWIN DWIGHT, born August 16, 1835, and married Angeline McCracken in Coventry, Conn.

HARRIET AUGUSTA, born October 1, 1839, and resides in Mansfield Center, Conn.

CHARLES M., born November 16, 1841, and is now deceased.

ALBERT FRANKLIN (255).

HARLAN EUGENE (256).

FRANCIS HENRY (257).

ELIZA ROSEBELLA, born February 9, 1851, and died February 25, 1851.

ARMINIUS WESLEY (258).

ELIZABETH ANGELINA, born July 6, 1855, married November 26, 1874, Otto Hiram Bennett who died March 23, 1916. They had four children: (a) Forrest Clayton, born July 27, 1875, married October 14, 1918, Elizabeth (Thistle) Smith and resides at No. 140 Blydenburg Avenue, New London, Conn.; (b) Minnie Almira, born April 7, 1878, who married August 10, 1905, Philip Henry Sheridan and lives at No. 21 Colman Street, New London; (c) Clarence Otis, born July 22, 1880, who married September 28, 1899, Bessie A. Turner, had two children, Roland Allen and Claire, and died August 10, 1905; (d) Cora May, born October 22, 1886, who married June 25, 1902, Benjamin Lawrence Rasie, has one son, Lawrence Bennett, and lives

ASHBEL WHITON'S HOUSE (193)

AUGUSTUS WHITON (195)

at R. F. D. No. 1, Gales Ferry, Conn. She died March 7, 1916.

OLIN EVERETT (259).

194*a* SIMEON, son of Elijah (118), was born in Westford April 13, 1804, and married April 18, 1832, Cordelia, daughter of James and Lovicia (Swetland) Bidwell of Windsor, who was born January 24, 1807, and died October 8, 1853. He was a farmer and lived in Bloomfield.

Children:

MARY, married Charles Fuller.

HARRIET, married John Hill.

HENRY, married and had two sons; lived in Philadelphia, Pa.

LESTER (259*a*).

PORTER (259*b*).

WILBUR, served in the Civil War and died in a Soldiers' Home at Bangor, Maine.

195 AUGUSTUS, son of Elijah (118), was born in Westford, Conn., August 5, 1807, and married Harriet, daughter of William and Eunice (Dart) Foster, at South Windsor, Conn., May 1, 1834. He owned the Whiton Wagon Works, at Bloomfield, Conn., and was a staunch abolitionist and active in educational, church and temperance work. He died in July, 1885.

Children:

TUDOR (260).

EMILY, born in 1837, and died August 30, 1896.

ELLEN J., born at South Windsor June 15, 1839; was educated at Mt. Holyoke College, and resides at 337 Lincoln Street, Waterbury, being active in Women's Clubs, Girls' Clubs, The King's Daughters and church work. Prior to 1900 she taught for twenty-five years in the Waterbury public schools. Former pupils say that they felt in her teaching an influence that was of more value for them in life, both educationally and ethically, than any other influence exerted in the community.

CHRISTIANA, born 1844, married in 1865, Imri A. Spencer and had two children: Antoinette W., born April 11, 1868, and died July 26, 1871; and Alice W., born February 16, 1871, married Davis Rich, and has two children. They reside at 340 South Fifth Street, St. Petersburg, Fla.

196 LUCIUS HEBER, son of Heber (119), was born February 26, 1809, and married March 20, 1836, Almeda A., daughter of Captain Solva and Esther (Blodgett) Converse,* who was born April 3, 1813, and died February 15, 1893, at Stafford Springs, Conn. He died November 7, 1856.

Children:

ADELINE FRANCES, born July 9, 1837, married Edward Nelson Washburn, and had seven children: Blanche, William, Eugene, Jennie and Mary, all of whom died in infancy; Florence Bell, who was born February 22, 1875, and resides at 25 Fisk Avenue, Stafford Springs; and Myrnie Almeda, born in Staffordville, Conn., January 9, 1873, and married Ernest K., son of Ephraim K. and Augusta (Field) Taft, at Stafford Springs, September 25, 1901, and resides at 25 Fisk Avenue, Stafford Springs.

ANDREW, born December 30, 1838, and married (1st) on July 1, 1862, Ruth E. Waldo of Tolland, Conn., who was born June 13, 1837, and died November 26, 1894; and (2d) Hannah Allen, May 20, 1896, who was born April 22, 1840, and died June 9, 1929. He died August 10, 1914.

HANNAH, born September 10, 1845, and married October 19, 1871, James M., son of John K. Lord, who was born June 18, 1837, and died in 1915. They had one child, Kate Imogene, born April 1, 1882, and died August 12, 1923. Hannah died August 4, 1907.

ESTHER, born August 24, 1848, and married November 23, 1870, Albert C., son of Calvin W. and Louise A. (Presby) Eaton, who was born December 17, 1848. They had three children: Lucius F., born January 12, 1876, married Esther Tuttle, and died March 20, 1929, leaving a daughter, Esther Lou; Alberta Louise, born August 20, 1878, and died August 25, 1927; and Ivy Gertrude, born August 8, 1887.

*The Converse Family by Charles Allen Converse, pp. 256 and 505.

197 JULIUS ROYAL, son of Heber (119), was born at West Stafford, Conn., October 4, 1810, and married (1st) Nancy Cooley, January 23, 1833, who was born April 23, 1810, and died August 30, 1840; and (2d) Eliza, daughter of Moses and Marcia (Lillibridge) Chandler, June 12, 1844, who was born at Woodstock,

(196) (197) (198)

(199) (200) (201)

SONS OF HEBER (119) and MARCIA GAY WHITON

Conn., January 1, 1826, and died at New London, Conn., May 16, 1883. He died January 2, 1882.

Children by Nancy:

HENRY (261).

JULIA, born August 14, 1840, and married at Stafford, Conn., Parley S. Anderson, January 1, 1862, who was born December 30, 1828, and died January 17, 1898. They had seven children: (1) Henry; (2) Harriet Melina, born August 17, 1864, married John P. Rand, and had a son, Frank Prentice, and died May 6, 1892; (3) Mabelle Louise, born July 15, 1867, and married Frederick F. Bugbee September 18, 1906, at Pittsfield, Mass., and resides at 156 Clinton Street, Watertown, N. Y.; (4) Idella May, born October 10, 1869, and married Charles F. Smith November 14, 1899, at Monson, Mass., and died May 6, 1921. They had three children: Maxfield M., born August 25, 1900, who married Gladys Elderkin, and had a daughter, Elizabeth, born August 23, 1927; Mabelle A., born July 7, 1903, and Douglas, born January 30, 1906. Idella (supra) died May 6, 1892. (5) Mary Eliza, born July 8, 1874, and married Eugene R. Cooke May 11, 1897, at Monson, Mass., and resides at 1302 8th Avenue, Arcadia, Cal.; (6) Bert Parley, born July 25, 1878, and married Anna E. Erlandson, June 6, 1906, at Barre, Mass., and had a daughter, Helen Eugenia, born March 8, 1907, at Barre, and resides at Monson, Mass.; (7) Martha King, born June 28, 1882, at Monson, and married Howard Davis May 14, 1908, at Monson, and resides at 75 Davis Street, Danbury, Conn. She is a popular author of short stories under the name of Martha King Davis, and has one child, Virginia Anderson Davis, born in Danbury March 19, 1910.

Child by Eliza:

MERRILL (263).

198 EBENEZER GAY, son of Heber (119), was born October 5, 1813, at West Stafford, Conn., and married October 31, 1836, Thankful Yeomans of Willington, Conn., who was born May 14, 1814, and died November 15, 1896. He died June 9, 1890. No children.

199 JOSEPH LEANDER, son of Heber (119), was born at West Stafford, Conn., April 11, 1816, and married Ann Sarepta Anderson, who was born October 8, 1824, and died December 19, 1915. He died at Monson, Mass., February 14, 1875.

Children:

ISABEL, born April 2, 1845, and married Luther A. Abbe August 28, 1863, and died January 27, 1917.

NELSON (263).

ARTHUR, born February 11, 1856, and died December 7, 1872.

200 EDWARD FRANKLIN, son of Heber (119), was born at Stafford, Conn., August 29, 1818, and married Aurelia Lydia, daughter of Luther and Araminta (Harrington) Eaton, at West Stafford May 26, 1843, who was born at Stafford August 13, 1819, and died January 14, 1897. He was postmaster at Stafford for twenty-four years, and died February 16, 1893.

Children:

MARCIA GAY, born November 5, 1845, and died September 9, 1902.

NETTIE MELISSA, born November 24, 1853, and died July 18, 1916.

EDNA AURELIA, born October 21, 1861, and resides at 231 Crystal Avenue, New London, Conn.

201 DAVID ERSKINE, son of Heber (119), was born at West Stafford, Conn., October 15, 1825, and married at Stafford Springs, November 13, 1856, Asenath, daughter of James and Achsah (Howe) Francis, who was born June 12, 1833, and died September 25, 1902. His father and grandfathers were coopers; the choice of a wood-working trade was a natural selection. As a boy of fourteen he was "bound out" until twenty-one years of age to learn the carpenter's trade. He spent laborious hours in the pit helping to saw by hand the boards then used for builder's finish. Naturally he became interested in power. Before the age of twenty-one he purchased his time by extra work and became a millwright, helping to build large wooden water-

DAVID ERSKINE WHITON (201)

wheels, flumes, etc., at the water-power developments at Willimantic, Conn., and at Colchester, Conn., where one of the early rubber industries was located. He worked for a time as a pattern-maker in a machine shop and foundry in Hartford, where he was a fellow employee with several young men who afterwards established important machine tool industries. While in Hartford he was an evening student in drawing and other classes in the old Wadsworth Atheneum. He started in business for himself in West Stafford in 1856, building a dam and developing a small water-power machine shop, and began making iron turbine water wheels. He soon gave his attention to the manufacture of centering machines and lathe chucks, upon which patents had been obtained. He was a skilled mechanic and inventor and his business of manufacturing special machines and chucks from his own patents was successful. Thirty years later the business was incorporated as The D. E. Whiton Machine Company, and removed to New London, Conn., where he also established his residence. An enthusiastic Republican from the first organization of the party, he held various town offices and was twice a member from Stafford in the Legislature. He was a member of the Methodist Episcopal Church, which he generously supported and served in official capacity both at Stafford Springs and New London. He died at New London September 11, 1904.

Children:

ROSELLA LENETTE, born at West Stafford, November 2, 1860, and died February 15, 1865.

LUCIUS ERSKINE (264).

MARY FRANCIS, born at West Stafford, July 21, 1867, and married April 23, 1890, at New London, Leander Kenney Shipman, M.D., son of Joseph A. and Abby Jane (Kenney) Shipman, who was born June 25, 1853. They reside at 160 Hempstead Street, New London. She is interested in church, charitable and patriotic work and is a member of the Society of Mayflower Descendants, the National Society of Daughters of Founders and Patriots of America

(2) Leora E., born March 14, 1886, and died April 19, 1900; (3) Edna F., born June 29, 1884, and married Max S. Reager and resides at 37 River Street, Springfield, Mass.; (4) Milton W., born August 18, 1892, at Southampton, Mass., married Idella Thoyse, and has five children: Idella M., Ruth C., Lillian M., Walter W., and Carl C. Harriet Bombard (supra) resides at 54 Beacon Avenue, Holyoke, Mass., with her son, Milton W.

FLORA DAISY, born February 25, 1874, and married Isaac Seelye, son of Enoch and Rachel (Barnum) Knapp at Tolland, December 31, 1912. They reside at 625 South Painter Avenue, Whittier, Cal., and have a son, Frederick Whiton, born in Danbury Conn., March 19, 1915.

205 STEPHEN, son of Elijah (121), was born in Tolland, Conn., March 19, 1820, and married Juliana V. Ward, November 30, 1848, and died in Holyoke, Mass., February 17, 1876, and is buried in Tolland.

Children:

ELIZABETH JULIA, born in Tolland September 11, 1855, and married William B. Gero November 26, 1877, at Holyoke, died in Hartford, July 7, 1922, and is buried in Holyoke. Their children were: (a) Raymond Whiton, born in Rome, N. Y., May 26, 1878, and married Winona Dean September 18, 1899. They had two children: (1) Robert Melbourne, born in Holyoke September 18, 1901, and (2) Marshall Dean, born in Holyoke December 6, 1908, and reside at 331 Pleasant Street, Holyoke, Mass. (b) Irving Ward, born in Holyoke, April 1, 1883, married Anna Gauthier, and had three children: (1) Robert Irving, born in Jamaica Plains, Mass., March 6, 1917; (2) Roland Edmund, born in Hartford October 31, 1920; and (3) Paul William, born in Hartford June 1, 1922, and resides at 26 Brown Street, Hartford, Conn. (c) Karl William, born in Holyoke April 9, 1887, and married Eva Loraine Glen October 22, 1912. They had two children: (1) Pauline May, born in East Liverpool, Ohio, November 14, 1915, and (2) Doane Russell, born in Pittsburgh, Penn., August 6, 1919, and reside at 1330 St. Clair Avenue, East Liverpool, Ohio. (d) Stephen Wilmont, born in Holyoke July 29, 1892, died August 14, 1892, and is buried in Tolland.

NELLIE K., born in Tolland December 20, 1858, married Adolph G. Foote in Rome, N. Y., and died in Holyoke January 15, 1902, where she is buried.

JAMES MORRIS WHITON (206)

206 JAMES MORRIS, son of John Milton (122), was born in Antrim, N. H., November 8, 1809. In 1832 he married Mary Elizabeth, daughter of Ebenezer and Mary (Bass) Knowlton. Her mother, Margaret Bass, is a descendant of John Alden and Priscilla Mullin of Mayflower emigrants, through her father Moses Bass, grandfather Moses Bass, his father Joseph Bass, his father John Bass, who married Ruth Alden, daughter of John and Priscilla. He studied at the academy of his grandfather, James Morris, at Litchfield, Conn. In 1825, at the age of sixteen, he became a clerk in a store in Boston. In 1831 he organized the firm of Whiton and March in Boston, agents and dealers in cotton and woolen goods. In 1837 he was elected a member of the Boston City Council, and in 1839-40 a member of the Massachusetts Legislature. He was the author of a monograph on Post Office Reform, also one on Railways and their Management. In 1855 he received the degree of M.A. from Yale University. The life of James Morris, although he was not a minister, but a merchant, was inspired by the high sense of honor and independence which he thought a clergyman should possess. He was independent in politics, adopting as his guiding principle: "I stand alone, I would not give my free thought for a throne." In answer to a letter from his son James, in which his son refers to what seemed to him to be the voice of duty, calling him to be a minister, he wrote on the 12th of November, 1850, with other extended advice: "To be a minister, comfortably settled over a comfortable people, with a nice comfortable church, with a comfortable salary, with no ideas of what mankind are doing save what comes through some comfortable conservative religious newspaper, that is not only behind the age, but behind all ages, with no charities save those doled out through a few comfortable safe societies, that once a month take their collections by appointment, with no thought save to get through the world with ease, without rapping the knuckles of anybody who happens to be rich

and 'respectable'; rather than see you such a minister, I would have you a hewer of wood or a drawer of water." He died, honored by all his friends and business associates, March 22, 1857.

Children:

JAMES MORRIS (269).

MARY ELIZABETH, born September 19, 1836, married Charles F. Washburn of Worcester, Mass., October 10, 1855, and had children: Charles G., deceased; James M. W., deceased; Philip B., deceased; Miriam, died February 14, 1930; Robert M.; Rev. Dr. Henry B. of Cambridge, Mass.; Reginald and Rev. Arthur of Providence, R. I.

CHARLOTTE GROSVENOR, born in East Boston September 27, 1839, and married the Rev. Wolcott Calkins of Corning, N. Y., on June 6, 1860. Their children were: (1) Mary Whiton, born in Hartford, Conn., March 30, 1863, and died February 26, 1930, at Newton, Mass. She was for many years professor of Philosophy and Psychology at Wellesley College; (2) Maud, born October 9, 1864, and died March 28, 1883; (3) Leighton, born in Buffalo, N. Y., March 12, 1868, married Nella B. Whiton and resides in Plainfield, N. J. He is a lawyer in New York City; (4) Raymond, born in Buffalo, August 10, 1869, married Emily B. Lathrop and resides at Cambridge, Mass. He is pastor of the First Congregational Church of Cambridge, Mass.; (5) Grosvenor, born in Buffalo July 17, 1875, married Patty Phillips and resides at Newton, Mass., and is a lawyer with offices in Boston, Mass.

LUCY WELLINGTON, born March 27, 1842, and died February 18, 1847.

JOHN MILTON (270).

MIRIAM BLAGDON, born December 12, 1848, and married Henry B. Opdyke of New York City September 24, 1868. She died in 1902, leaving three children: Henry B., Agnes and Howard.

GRACE RICHARDS, born November 10, 1853, and married the Rev. Washington Choate of Essex, Mass. She died in 1908, leaving five children: three died in infancy, Miriam F., who married Newton B. Hobart of the Taft School, Watertown, Conn., and Helen A., who is a professor of Botany at Smith College.

207 OREN, son of Thomas (131), adopted the name of Whiting, and married (1st) Sarah C. Faxon, who died February 20, 1827, and (2d) Mary Jones, daughter

of Simeon Jones, in May, 1831. He resided in Hanover and died there October 16, 1867.

Children:

LEWIS, born January 24, 1833, married Mary B. Wood, and died at Conaut, Fla., in December, 1899.
OREN T., born August 28, 1834, married Lucy J. Hatch, and died in Hanover November 26, 1918.
LUCIUS A. (271).
ABEL H., born in 1841 and died in 1842.
ABEL H., born in July, 1843, and died in 1863.
ALBERT, born March 24, 1846, and died October 12, 1859.
JOHN B., born March 24, 1849.

208 JARED, son of Ezra (133), was born April 15, 1804, lived in Hanover, and married Desire, daughter of Job and Desire (Clapp) Loring, of Hingham in January, 1838.

Children:

CALEB L., born January 4, 1838.
JARED, born August 15, 1842.

209 ELIJAH LINCOLN, son of Elijah (137), was born in Hingham January 15, 1814, and married Rachel C., daughter of Asa and Charlotte (Lincoln) Lincoln, who was born in Hingham October 30, 1811. He was a merchant in hats, boots and shoes and died in Hingham December 12, 1881.

Children:

DEXTER BRIGHAM, born February 26, 1842, and died unmarried April 24, 1880.
CHARLOTTE LINCOLN, born in 1844, and died February 27, 1854.
MARY LINCOLN, born August 6, 1848.

210 BELA H., son of Elijah (137), was born in Hingham February 14, 1816, and married (1st) February 22, 1844, Hannah R., daughter of Ezra (138) and Emma (Jones) Whiton, who was born in Hingham October 17, 1818, and died January 11, 1860, and (2d) March 27, 1870, Mary C., daughter of Stephen and Maria (Lincoln) Hersey, who was born in Hingham April 8,

1836, and died May 28, 1905. He was a carriage maker and lived in Hingham where he died November 1, 1898.

Children by Hannah:

FRANCES HOWES, born January 30, 1846, married February 21, 1871, Edwin Clapp of Weymouth, and died August 25, 1928.

ELEANOR RICHMOND, born January 24, 1848, and died August 29, 1853.

ALICE LINCOLN, born October 1, 1854, and on April 11, 1878, married Stetson, son of Zabud and Nancy (Miller) Foster at Hingham Center, where they now reside. Children: Frances R., born July 22, 1879; Hannah W., born October 19, 1881, and died April 30, 1884; Lewis W., born August 17, 1886, and married Bertha Copethorn; Mayone L., born August 24, 1889, and Helen M., born October 20, 1893, and married Alfred Jacobs.

WALLACE (273).

BELA HERNDON, born and died in September, 1857.

Children by Mary:

HENRY EDSON HERSEY (273a).

ELIJAH (273b).

211 ERASTUS, son of Elijah (137), was born January 11, 1826, in Hingham, and married Priscilla, daughter of John and Priscilla (Bourne) Burr, who was born in Hingham December 12, 1828, and died in Melrose, Mass., in November, 1903. He was the town constable in Hingham for many years, and died February 28, 1889.

Children:

ERASTUS, born April 25, 1855, married Mary F., daughter of Gardner M. Jones, and had a daughter, Mildred, born February 21, 1885. He died in Somerville, Mass.

HELEN, born February 20, 1858, and died in Hingham May 19, 1884.

MARY ALICE, born April 22, 1862, and died in Hingham May 21, 1864.

ANNA LINCOLN, born January 11, 1864, and married John A. Ackley of Roxbury, Mass., in 1913, and died February 10, 1926.

PRISCILLA, born April 6, 1867. She is a teacher in Dorchester High School, and has been President of the Boston Teach-

COL. JOHN CHADWICK WHITON (212)

ers' Club. She has traveled extensively, and resides at 497 Talbot Avenue, Dorchester, Mass.

FREDERIC (274).

212 JOHN CHADWICK, son of Elijah (137), was born in Hingham August 21, 1828, and married Ann Maria, daughter of Jairus and Hannah (Waters) Sprague, at Hingham October 19, 1862, who was born in Hingham, December 3, 1835, and died in Boston May 25, 1913. He was the Superintendent of Deer Island Institutions and Master of the House of Correction in South Boston. In the Civil War he served at Fort Warren as Captain of Company A, 2d Battalion, Massachusetts Volunteers, and later as Lieutenant Colonel of the 43d Massachusetts Volunteers, being mustered out in 1863. In the winter of 1863 he was Supervisor of Recruiting for Plymouth County, and was appointed (Brevet) Colonel of the 58th Regiment of Volunteers, with which regiment he served until mustered out in July, 1865. He died in Boston January 2, 1905.

Children:

HENRY CHADWICK, born August 1, 1864, and died in 1865.

MARIAN C., born in Boston March 7, 1868, and resides at 175 Dartmouth Street, Boston, and is a musician.

213 THOMAS LOWELL, son of Ezra (138), was born in Hingham December 28, 1813, and married Elizabeth B. Loring April 4, 1844. He removed in late life to Newton, Mass. His children were born in Hingham. He died at Watertown, Mass., February 15, 1889.

Children:

ELIZABETH LORING, born December 18, 1847, and died April 22, 1861.

EZRA THOMAS, born April 8, 1850, married at West Dedham, Mass., June 9, 1885, Charlotte M. Scott of Wisconset, Me.

214 PETER LANE, son of Ezra (138), was born in Hingham May 1, 1816, and married December 27, 1846, Sarah A. P. Densmore of Northboro, Mass., who was born in Boston February 8, 1828. He was by occupation

a "Trader," also Deputy Inspector of Fish. He resided at Hingham, and had a child, George Henry, born March 20, 1848, who died at West Newton April 22, 1863.

215 WILLIAM, son of David (139), was born in Hingham November 3, 1811, and married Abigail, daughter of Nehemiah and Eunice (Whiting) Ripley, January 31, 1839, who was born in Hingham August 12, 1814, and died August 25, 1863. He was a ship chandler, and also Treasurer of the Hingham Cordage Co., and resided in Hingham, dying there July 29, 1876.

Children:

ABBY HARRIET, born January 20, 1840, died in infancy.

WILLIAM FRANKLIN, born March 30, 1842, died young.

CHARLES FEARING (275).

LUCY DORR, born October 20, 1846, married John O. Baker, Jr., of Brooklyn, N. Y., October 2, 1871.

ABBY R. RIPLEY, born August 25, 1848, and married Charles C. Melcher January 9, 1878.

LAURA, born March 23, 1851.

FANNIE, born March 23, 1851, and died July 6, 1883.

DAVID, born March 24, 1854, and died August 5, 1855.

216 THOMAS FEARING, son of David (139), was born in Hingham April 14, 1821, and married Hannah S., daughter of David and Hannah (Souther) Lincoln, who was born in Hingham January 24, 1830. He was a merchant in Boston, and resided in Hingham, where he died June 6, 1872.

Son:

MORRIS FEARING, born April 12, 1855, and married in Boston, October 20, 1887, Sarah Julia, daughter of Ephraim Seabrook and Eliza Yonge (Waring) Mikell, who was born at Charleston, S. C., May 21, 1857, and died in Hingham November 15, 1913. He is a merchant in Boston, and also President of the Hingham Institution for Savings, and of the Derby Academy, and Treasurer of the Hingham Public Library and of the Hingham Water Co.

HON. STARKES WHITON (220)

217 JOHN P., son of Wilson (140), was born June 13, 1811, and married (1st) Maria E. Orne of Cambridge on February 5, 1838, who died May 5, 1844, and (2d) Lydia B. Bancroft of Danvers June, 1846. He was a merchant in Boston.

Children:

JOHN W.
CHARLES H.
MARIA L.

218 HENRY, son of Wilson (140), was born in Hingham August 14, 1813. He married Emily, daughter of Reuben Farrington, at Dedham, who was born there July 11, 1822, and died in Boston September 9, 1878. He was a carriage manufacturer and died in Boston March 14, 1867.

Children:

HENRY LEWIS, born in Boston March 21, 1859, and died July 28, 1887.
LIZZIE L., born in Boston June 3, 1856, and died August 12, 1888.
ANNIE WILSON, born December 16, 1861, and died November 12, 1879.
EDWARD WINSLOW (276).

219 MOSES LINCOLN, son of Moses (141), was born May 1, 1814, and married Sophia P. ——— and resided in Somerville, Mass.

Child:

HARRY F. (277).

220 STARKES, son of Moses (141), was born in Hingham April 11, 1829. He married Helen, daughter of David and Adaline (Sprague) Thomas, December 13, 1870. She was born in Boston June 3, 1841. Her father was a grandson of Jacob (42) and Elizabeth (Marble) Whiton. Starkes was the Treasurer of the Boston and Hingham Steamboat Co., and a State Senator for 1880-1. In 1885 he was Chairman of the Boston Board of Gas Commissioners, and from 1887 to 1903, was State

Commissioner of Savings Banks. He died February 12, 1904.

Children:

CHAUNCEY GILBERT (278).
DAVID THOMAS (279).
HERBERT STARKES (280).

221 MADISON, son of Abijah (143), was born in Chesterfield, Mass., March 1, 1811. He married Parmilla, daughter of Josiah and Sarah (Pelton) Clark, at West Springfield, Penn. Her father was said to have been in the War of 1812, having enlisted at Woodstock, Vt. Madison was a farmer, and lived first at West Springfield, Penn., and later removed to Kingsville, Ohio, where he died June 20, 1874.

Children:

MADISON MUNROE, born February 9, 1839, and died in Alabama November 16, 1898 with no descendants.

SARAH JANE, born June 27, 1840, married Joseph Colby of Galva, Kan., where she died in 1908.

WILLIAM, born at West Springfield July 19, 1842, married Katherine Van Wagenen, and died in Kingsfield, Ohio.

ANTOINETTE, born in West Springfield December 27, 1846, married Leander White and died in Galva, Kan., in 1908.

EMILY, born in West Springfield, September 12, 1848, married Nathan Whitney and died in West Charleston, Va., in 1908.

ABIJAH, born in West Springfield September 10, 1852, and died at Kingsfield, Ohio, in 1858.

RACHEL, born in West Springfield June 21, 1844, married Henry Jonathan, son of Jonathan and Jane (Gleazen) Gillette, and lived at 26 Atwood Street, Hartford, Conn. Their children are: (1) Lena, born at Kingsfield, Ohio, September 30, 1867, and married the Rev. John Luther Kilborn, and died July 4, 1931, at Brooklyn, N. Y.; (2) Mary Parmilla, born September 20, 1869; (3) Rev. Dr. Edwin Carlton, born in Kingsfield July 13, 1871, married Jennie M. Gardner and resides at Jacksonville, Fla.; (4) Frank Whiton, born at South Windsor, Conn., March 31, 1875, married Nellie Burritt, and resides at Wethersfield, Conn; (5) Alice R., born at Hartford, Conn., September 16, 1885. She died June 23, 1931.

222 EDWARD, son of Abijah (143), was born June 8, 1826, on the Whiton homestead in Springfield Township, Erie County, Penn. He married Theresa, daughter of Jehial D. and Tirza (Woodworth) Dewey, August 7, 1852. They settled in the South Ridge, where he spent the remainder of his life. In 1861 he was licensed to preach in the Methodist Church, and in 1872 was ordained deacon at Akron, Ohio, by Bishop S. M. Merrill. As a preacher he was earnest, poetical, and original. He took an active interest in the local debating society, and was respected by all who knew him. He died of neurasthenia April 19, 1890.

Children:

ELLEN, born May 29, 1854, married Calvin Johnson and died without children March 31, 1914.

WILLIAM E. (281).

MARIETTA, born September 2, 1858, married Joseph, son of Benjamin and Betsy Johnson, a farmer, January 16, 1878, and resides at Girard, Penn. Their children are: Theresa, Merrill, Nellie, Stanley and Howard. Stanley was born at Conneaut, Ohio, September 22, 1892, and married Bertha May, daughter of Clarence and Anna R. Sanders at Conneaut November 24, 1918, and his children are: Clarence Joseph, born September 29, 1920, and Stanley W., born December 14, 1923. They reside at 287 Sandusky Street, Conneaut.

BELLE, born July 6, 1860, and married Horace Thayer, a farmer. They had three children: Edward, Eugene, and Beryl. She died at West Springfield, Penn., March 6, 1915.

CHARLES H. (282).

223 ISAIAH GORHAM, son of Isaiah (145), was born in Hingham May 5, 1813, and married (1st) Mary W. Lincoln November 13, 1836, and (2d) Mrs. Susan M. (Lincoln) Nash December 25, 1866, and resided at Quincy, Mass. He kept a store and was a prominent mason. He died October 17, 1886.

Children:

MARY LINCOLN, born in 1837, married Andrew Jackson Bates.

MARTHA GORHAM, born July 24, 1840, and married (1st)

born December 16, 1856. He died at Greenwood, Mass., October 28, 1906.

Children:

ARTHUR ELBERT (287).

CHARLES EDWARD (288).

EVERETT BRYANT, born April 11, 1876, married Christina Crosby, and resides at 22 Summer Street, Wakefield, Mass.

LAURA ERNESTINE, born December 25, 1880, is a graduate nurse and resides at 115 Crescent Street, West Quincy, Mass.

230 LORING LIVINGSTON, son of Lincoln B. (152), was born at Charlestown, Mass., September 3, 1830, and married January 2, 1859, at Somerville, Mass., Anna Elizabeth (Morse) Martin, who was born at Sutton, Mass., May 16, 1836, and died at Somerville November 20, 1904. He was a manufacturer of piano hammers. He served in the Civil War and was the last survivor of the "Housatonic," which was blown up in Charleston, S. C., Harbor, and died June 12, 1921.

Children:

EDWARD HUMPHREY (289).

CHARLES B., born November 5, 1872, died in 1873.

231 GEORGE F., son of Lincoln B. (152), was born at Charlestown, Mass., September 3, 1850. He is a leather merchant, and resides on Walnut Road, Winterhill, Mass. He is unmarried.

NINTH GENERATION

232 EDGAR BENJAMIN, son of Amos (163), spelled his name Whitten, was born at Barcelona, N. Y., August 19, 1849, and married Mary Agnes, daughter of John and Naomi (Slocomb) Gates, at East Boston December 10, 1874, who was born at Gates Mountain, Nova Scotia, July 30, 1854; his only child was:

Son:

ROSCOE BENJAMIN (290).

233 HENRY BENJAMIN, son of Milo James (164), was born at Lee, Mass., September 24, 1827. He was a graduate of Albany Medical College and served as a surgeon with the 2d and the 60th New York Volunteers during the Civil War. He was the curator of the Albany Medical College until his death. He married Hannah, daughter of Isaac T. and Maria (Alexander) Grant, in Troy, N. Y., June 11, 1855, who was born at Schaghticoke, N. Y., in 1832, and died at Adama, N. Y., in 1904. She was a member of the Daughters of the American Revolution. He died in Troy May 2, 1885.

Children:

JAMES CLINTON, born in 1856, and died in Troy in 1876.
ALICE MARIA, born in 1858.
WALTER LESLIE, born in 1860.
HENRY GRANT (291).
SOPHIA TUTTLE, born in 1872, and died in Troy in 1875.

234 ALPHA MASON, son of Alpha (171), was born at Royalton, N. Y., June 15, 1857, and married Julia, daughter of Benjamin and Sarah (Bean) Child, at South Byron, N. Y., February 14, 1888, who was born there August 21, 1858, and died at Batavia, N. Y., March 9, 1917. He was a physician and surgeon and died on the Indian Reservation at Devil's Lake, N. D., February 10, 1919.

Children:

JULIET, born at South Byron, N. Y., November 9, 1888, and graduated at Mount Holyoke College (A.B.) in 1911. During the World War she served as a canteen worker with the Y. M. C. A. in 1918-19, with the 6th Division of the A. E. F. at Vitry-en-Montagne, France, and at Pommern, Germany, and the following year with the Army of Occupation at Coblenz, Germany. She is a teacher of English at the Brearley School, New York City, and resides at 360 East 50th Street, New York City. She has written a number of poems, which were published in the leading magazines, the following appearing in Scribner's Magazine, from which it is reprinted, by permission:

SHIPS IN THE FOG

I hear them through dark streets along the town,
Reverberating mournfully, these slow
Black ships that sail up all the seas and down,
That come like shadows and like shadows go.
I hear them through the walls of every dream
Like wraiths that beckon, whom I cannot follow,
Voices of mist and fog and dark that seem
To echo and re-echo, hollow, hollow.
Some warm still night when stars and planets sleep,
When fickle suns to other worlds have gone,
I hope that I shall find, on a far deep,
A ship at anchor waiting, tall and lone,
To take me from a world of time well-lost,
To high adventurous days, wind-swept, wave-tossed.

ALPHA RAY (292).

234a CHARLES M., son of William Loomis (166), was born at Wellington, Ohio, November 30, 1849, married October 19, 1871, Emma E. Standard.

Children:

BELLE, born and died in 1874.
CHARLES L. (292a).
ROY, born and died in 1877.

235 HEZEKIAH J., son of Hiram B. (167), was born at Huntington, Ohio, July 4, 1849, married (1st) June 29, 1879, Elizabeth A. Brockway; married (2d) April 15, 1891, Clara E. Cotton. He died April 12, 1916.

Children by Elizabeth:

ALVIN GEORGE, born February 19, 1880, married December 22, 1915, Carrie Snyder, and had daughter, Doris Evelyn, born July 18, 1918.

VIDA PEARL, born November 4, 1881, married November 10, 1900, Albert Osgood, and had two children, Beth Irene, born February 8, 1903, and Alberta Helen Osgood, born July 13, 1913, married June 13, 1930, Francis Eldredge, and has daughter Gerry Dean, born May 13, 1931. Beth married Marvin King, and had four children, Albert Hugh, Ivan E., Robert M., and Phyllis Jean.

Children by Clara:

JOHN MANDLEY, born at Lyons, Ohio, January 14, 1893, married June 22, 1917, Opal Hopkins. No children.

IDA McKINLEY, born November 20, 1897, married December 31, 1919, Arthur Bevelheimer; children: Ruth Irene, born September 14, 1921, Lois Martha, born August 30, 1926, and Esther Marie, born October 14, 1930.

HARLEY BERT (293).

236 GEORGE, son of Hiram B. (167), was born at Brighton, Ohio, August 19, 1858, and married Mary Stuck, October 19, 1882. He died at Lyons, Ohio, February 1, 1912.

Child:

EDITH MAY, born February 23, 1884, and married Bert Kahle, September 1, 1903. They have two children, Freida May, born June 10, 1904, and Letha Vivian, born July 15, 1916.

236a FRANK J., son of Josiah B. (168), was born at Huntington, Ohio, March 2, 1855, and married at Ithaca, Mich., December 31, 1881, Elizabeth J. Wolfe, who was born February 2, 1867, and died September 17, 1928, at Clovis, California. He died there May 11, 1918.

Children:

MAUD M., born September 20, 1882, married (1st) April 23, 1900, James Hart, who died May 26, 1923, and had two children, Marie, born February 9, 1901, and James B., born May 13, 1902; (2d) June 30, 1927, J. C. Carter.

HARRY J., born January 14, 1887, married Kate Anderson October 17, 1907, and lives at Clovis, Cal. His children are Frank Earl, born December 7, 1907, died May 21, 1920; Edna May, born January 23, 1909, married April 24, 1927,

Robert Henry Rogers, and has children, Robert H., Jr., and Peggy Marie.

MINNIE B., born December 18, 1888, married March 10, 1913, Galon B. Alderman, and lives at Clovis, Cal. Their children: Bruce, born and died in November, 1919; Galon Robert, born January 9, 1921; Ida Leona, born February 4, 1922; Dortha Mae, born August 13, 1923, and Harry Lenous, born June 18, 1927.

FRANK E., born April 28, 1893, married (1st) December 8, 1913, Ida L. Lathrop, and had a son, Vernon E., born October 8, 1914; married (2d) February 11, 1916, Eloise Chadwick.

RAY A., born November 20, 1895.

WILLIAM J., born March 29, 1897, married July 4, 1916, Mary Devine. Their children are William E., born November 14, 1916, died July 23, 1918; Wilma Nell, born August 25, 1919; Eleanor May, born March 26, 1922, and John Edward, born October 17, 1925.

RUTH E., born May 26, 1900, married July 30, 1920, Cecil Dunham; has two children, Eileen and Merle; resides at Ventura, Cal.

ELLEN L., born October 31, 1902, married November, 1920, Alva Maze; has two children, Virgil Clark and Betty Louise. They live at Long Beach, Cal.

236b GEORGE EDWIN, son of Josiah B. (168), was born in Damascus Township, Henry County, Ohio, March 3, 1863, and married at Greenville, Mich., November 5, 1885, Ella M. Carpenter. He died September 21, 1892.

Children:

ARTHUR EMERSON (293a).

MABELLE GEORGIE, born July 11, 1892, and married August 27, 1921, Earl Henry Spencer, who died October 26, 1929. She lives at Berkeley, Cal.

236c WALTER GRANT, son of Josiah B. (168), was born at Huntington, Ohio, July 31, 1869, married (1st) February 28, 1894, Mrs. Ella M. (Carpenter) Whiton, and (2d) November, 1915, Frances M. Miller. He died at Stryker, Ohio, in 1919.

Children:

JOSIAH B., born at Ithaca, Mich., March 8, 1898, married in 1918, Beaulah Godfrey, and has three children, Geraldine

Ellen, born July 4, 1921; Ella Jean, born July 4, 1921, and Bonnie Bell, born September 21, 1923.

LOIS ELLEN, born November 23, 1903, married February 9, 1922, Cecil E. McConkey; has two children, Jack C., born April 4, 1923, and Phyllis Elaine, born December 4, 1924.

FLORENCE ELLA, born March 27, 1910.

237 JOSEPH EBEN, son of Joseph Seward (176), was born at Winona, Mich., January 11, 1864, and married Sylvia Myrtle, daughter of Robert and Maria Elizabeth Cosgrove, at Winona October 1, 1891, who was born August 28, 1865, and died February 6, 1928. He is a publisher and resides at 419 East 47th Street, Portland, Oregon.

Child:

MILDRED, born in Winona May 31, 1893.

238 ARTHUR LEE, son of Henry Kirke (174), was born at Lee, Mass., July 9, 1856, and married (1st) Martha Belle Shafer on February 12, 1879, who died September 28, 1910, and (2d) Mrs. Ida E. (McCoy) Spielman on August 13, 1913. He is a retired farmer and resides at Webster City, Iowa.

Children:

MARY FLORENCE, born June 9, 1881, married Samuel Young in 1923.

CORA PHINNEY, born August 13, 1886.

ANNA LOUISE, born July 28, 1894, married Ralph Crose in 1912.

JOSIE BELLE, born in October, 1896, and died May 12, 1908.

239 WALTER STARR, son of Henry Kirke (174), was born in Chicago July 28, 1869, and married (1st) Alice L., daughter of John G. and Emma (Ekman) Nelson, at Everett, Wash., November 14, 1900, and (2d) Blanche G., daughter of John C. and Emma (Morrow) Wagner, September 12, 1914. He is a lawyer and resides at 1929 Hennepin Avenue, Minneapolis, Minn.

Children:

MARY, born September 5, 1901, and died April 28, 1906.

JOHN STARR (294).

240 EDWARD VERNON, son of Edward Vernon (175), was born at Janesville, Wis., in 1878, and married in Aberdeen, S. D., Valois, daughter of George Henry and Mary Louise (Beach) Sult, who was born at Vinton, Iowa, in 1892. He is a saleman and resides at 4937 Newton Avenue, South Minneapolis, Minn.

Children:

MARY LOUISE, born June 28, 1915.
MARJORIE ANN, born January 30, 1918.

241 AUGUSTUS WARD, son of Augustus Sherrill (178), was born in Newburgh, N. Y., December 13, 1850, and married Jennie Madeline, daughter of Jesse and Cornelia (Newcomb) Paulmier, in Jersey City on October 15, 1872. He graduated at Columbia University in 1871, and was a member of the Delta Kappa Epsilon Fraternity. He was a member of the firm of Tyng and Whiton, dealers in railway supplies. He died at Augusta, Ga., April 8, 1875, from illness contracted on his wedding trip in Europe. His widow subsequently married Robert Watson Stuart of New York.

Child:

JESSE PAULMIER (295).

242 LOUIS CLAUDE, son of Augustus Sherrill (178), was born in Jersey City, N. J., December 29, 1857, and resides in New York City. He married Harriet Louise, daughter of Charles and Angeline (Redman) Bell, on June 10, 1884, in New York City. She was born March 3, 1865, in New York City, where she died February 14, 1923, and is interred in Greenwood Cemetery, Brooklyn. An obituary notice published in a Norwich, Connecticut, paper, in which city she was well known states:

> "She was an ideal wife, mother, sister, and daughter, devoted, considerate, and always just, and loved by all her friends."

He was graduated first honor man and Valedictorian from New York University in 1878, from which he received the degree of M.A. in 1880. He graduated from the Law School of Columbia University and was admitted to the Bar of the State of New York in 1880, since which time he has practiced law in New York City. He was active in the Republican party and in civic reform, and was a member of the Bar Association, Sons of the Revolution, Society of Colonial Wars, and the Phi Beta Kappa Fraternity. He is the President of the Alumni Association of New York University, and resides at 1 West 30th Street, New York City.

Children:

ANGELINE BELL, born December 13, 1885, in New York City, and married (1st) Hanbury Watkins April 24, 1905, by whom she had a son, Armitage, who was born December 20, 1906, in Newport, N. Y., graduated from Yale College (Ph.B) in 1928, and on June 16, 1928, married Mary White, daughter of Charles E. and Ethel (Moses) Merrill, at Huntington, Long Island, and resides at 61 East 96th Street, New York City. Angeline married (2d) on October 1, 1914, Hartley Cortlandt Davis. They reside at 210 Madison Avenue, and at Oyster Bay, Long Island.

AUGUSTUS SHERILL (296).

LOUIS CLAUDE (297).

243 EDWARD NATHAN, son of William Henry (179), was born at Coal Grove, Ohio, September 12, 1848, and married Mary, daughter of John H. and Antoinette (Kelsey) Devereux, at Cleveland, Ohio, September 15, 1869, who died in April, 1914. He resided at Cleveland, and later at Piermont, N. Y., where he died November 12, 1907.

Children:

HENRY DEVEREUX (298).

ANTOINETTE LORD, born in Cleveland, Ohio, April 25, 1872, married Arthur Hobart Lockett, and has one daughter, Mary, born at Montclair, N. J., June 23, 1903, and married in Quogue, Long Island, June 8, 1929, Charles F. Kenzle. They reside at 983 Park Avenue, New York City, and at Quogue, Long Island.

JOHN L. (299).

244 FREDERIC JEFFREY, son of Frederic Luther (180), was born in Brooklyn, N. Y., September 26, 1857, and on May 21, 1929, in New York City, married Christina (Kitty), daughter of Edward G. and Sarah M. (Lane) Williams, and widow of Edward H. Cobb of Bay City, Mich. He was educated at the Ithaca, N. Y., Academy, and at Cornell University, where he graduated in 1880 with the degree of B.A., and was admitted to the New York Bar in 1883. He was the secretary and treasurer of the Ithaca Trust Company in 1891-96, when he removed to New York City and entered the real estate business. He is a director of the Ithaca Trust Company, Rockland Cemetery Improvement Company, and a member of the Cornelian Council, the Kappa Alpha Fraternity, the County Lawyers Association of New York City, the Columbia Yacht Club, the Megantic Fish and Game Corporation, and of the Anglers Club of New York, and resides at The Dacota, 1 West 72d Street, New York City.

245 GEORGE JACKSON, son of Rufus H. (182), was born August 16, 1857, at Champaign, Ill., and married December 25, 1875, at Covington, Ind., Annie C. Foster, and died May 5, 1900, at Norwood, Mo. His widow resides at Mahomet, Ill.

Children:

CYNTHIA MABEL, born December 16, 1879, married January 15, 1902, Charles Fay Wilson. Their children are: Louisa M., born October 30, 1905; Fay Pleasant, born February 15, 1909; Eunice Marsh, born March 19, 1912, and Charlotte Elizabeth.

FRANCES SYLVIA, born January 15, 1881.

NELLIE IRENE, born April 20, 1883.

PEARL M., born April 19, 1884.

FANNY LOUISE, born July 24, 1886.

GEORGE RUFUS, born August 12, 1889, and died in 1902.

EUNICE JULIA, born October 5, 1890.

ELIZABETH, born August 29, 1895.

246 CHARLES LYMAN, son of Rufus H. (182), was born July 29, 1859, at Champaign, Ill., and married (1st) Ella Jackson, and (2d) Viola Frost Parr, and resides in Forest City, Iowa.

Children:

EDWARD RUFUS, born November 14, 1891, died April 18, 1915.

JULIA MAY, born January 25, 1893, married September 7, 1922, Mountford S. Stokely, and resides at Des Moines, Iowa. Their children are: Mountford S., Jr., born July 18, 1924; David Allen, born May 6, 1926, and Richard Whiton, born August 14, 1928.

ETHEL GRACE, born August 13, 1894.

LYMAN CHARLES, born March 21, 1897. A farmer, living at Forest City, Iowa.

BESSIE MABEL, born May 6, 1900, married (1st) Alva Winterton and had a daughter, Shirley Alice, born May 23, 1926; married (2d) Roy McMullen. Children, Altha L., born April 30, 1929; Frances E., born April 3, 1930. They reside at Rockwell, Iowa.

ARTHUR PARR, born September 28, 1901, died October 15, 1908.

WINNIE BELLE, born June 20, 1903, married in 1923, Clifford Lackore, and lives at Forest City, Iowa. Their children are La Voune A., born October 27, 1923; Donald E., born October 13, 1925, and Veoune, born September 27, 1928.

ALTHA VIOLET, born April 3, 1907, married Lester Buland, and lives at Forest City, Iowa. Children: Bonnie Ruth, born July 29, 1926; Wayne, born July 4, 1928, and Robert A., born January 26, 1930.

247 ARTHUR SYLVESTER, son of Rufus H. (182), was born April 10, 1862, at Jerseyville, Ill., and married November 27, 1895, at Perry, Iowa, Grace Darling, daughter of Russell Gillette and Mary E. White, and resides at Perry, Iowa.

Children:

RUSSELL RUFUS (300).

GEORGE HUSTED (301).

MARY DOROTHY, born January 13, 1904, and married Merle Leroy Bryant.

248 ALFRED B., son of Hosea (187), was born in Hingham June 27, 1832, and married Martha, daughter of Charles and Hannah (Whiting) Gardner, who was born in Hingham in 1832 and died August 20, 1865. He was a manufacturer of shoes, and died in Hingham August 7, 1872.

Child:

A daughter, born October 9, 1854, who married George B. Gardner August 11, 1874.

249 AMASA J., son of Amasa (191), was born in Hingham April 2, 1849, and married September 10, 1871, Mary W., daughter of Andrew and Lucy (Hersey) Cushing. He resided at South Hingham.

Children:

MARY CUSHING, born June 29, 1873.
AMASA.
MARIA J., born October 9, 1879.
ANSON, born and died October 9, 1879.

250 ANDREW, son of Stephen (192), was born in East Hartford, Conn., May 2, 1846. He married in Buckland, Conn., September 21, 1870, Ann Jane McAllister who was born July 4, 1849, and died in East Hartford February 5, 1919. He removed to Westford, Conn., and later removed to Hartford and was connected with the Police Department in Hartford for twenty-three years. He made several inventions in electrical work, including the first telephone switch-board, and died in Hartford May 8, 1919.

Children:

FRANK WARREN (302).

CLARA ABIGAIL, born in Hartford December 28, 1873, married Selden Watson, son of Watson and Carrie Hayes, of Granby, Conn., December 26, 1901, in Hartford. One son, Chester S., was born and died in November, 1905.

MARY FARNHAM, born November 4, 1878, married Henry M. Barnard of Rocky Hill, Conn., at Hartford, April 25, 1905. She was during the World War Chairman of the Woman's Committee on Liberty Loans and War Savings Stamps. She is a life member of the Connecticut Congress of Parents and Teachers and a writer on the staff of the Hartford Courant. Their children are: Helen Cyr, born July 24, 1908, married February 8, 1930, Frederick W. Griswold, Jr.; Jane W., born July 5, 1912; and Robert Selden, born October 30, 1913. She resides at 143 Main Street, Rocky Hill, Conn.

LUCY CORNELIA, born January 17, 1884, is a teacher in a Hartford school and resides at 14 Stanley Street, East Hartford.

251 ELISHA BYLES, son of Stephen (192), was born at Westford, Conn., February 23, 1852, and married Etta Bessie, daughter of Alfred and Almira (Dean) Chaffee, at Westford February 13, 1877, who was born there July 23, 1858. He died at Worcester, Mass., May 3, 1917, and she subsequently married Horace A. Nichols October 6, 1921, and resides at 58 Paine Street, Worcester, Mass.

Children:

BERTHA JULIA, born January 3, 1880, at Stafford, Conn., married Willis E., son of William P. and Ellen (Converse) Cary at Worcester, September 4, 1907, and resides at 5 Chesterfield Road, Worcester, Mass.

IDA ISABEL, born December 31, 1882, married Frederick J. Roberts and resides at 58 Paine Street, Worcester.

WALTER THAYER (303).

252 EDWIN MARTIN, son of Stephen (192), was born at Westford, Conn., September 29, 1853, and married Laura E., daughter of David L. and Lydia (Chamberlain) Duncklee, at Manchester, Conn., February 8, 1877, who was born March 3, 1860. He died at Hampden, Mass., January 10, 1925.

Children:

ALICE, born July 9, 1880, married George W., son of Charles H. Stevens, October 11, 1904, and resides at 94 Prospect Street, Stafford Springs, Conn. She has been active in social clubs. They have one son, Charles H. Stevens, born in Springfield, Mass., January 13, 1909.

ADDIE, born March 11, 1883, married at Terryville October 9, 1907, Alfred H., son of Emil and Frederika Mathes.

She is a teacher, having graduated from the Willimantic State Normal School, and lives at Terryville, Conn.

253 SYLVESTER GILBERT, son of Ashbel (193), was born in Westford, Conn., August 8, 1846, and married (1st) Mary Virginia, daughter of Chester Steele Kasson, in Brooklyn, November 12, 1867, who was born in Brooklyn August 7, 1847, and died April 21, 1878; and (2d) Isabel Taylor, daughter of George Raymond and Mary (Hale) Atwater, in Brooklyn, June 10, 1880, who was born there May 17, 1847, and died March 1, 1890, and whose father, George Atwater, is descended from David Atwater, one of the founders of the New Haven Colony, and Mary Hale, his wife, descended from Samuel Hale of Hartford, residing there in 1639, and dying at Glastonbury, Conn., in 1693; and (3d) Ella French Skidmore on March 10, 1892, who was born in Brooklyn February 24, 1867. In 1868 he formed the partnership of Nash & Whiton. In 1895 he organized the Worcester Salt Co., of which he was president until his death. He was also vice-president of the Merchants Exchange National Bank. He was a director of the Preferred Accident Insurance Co., the Union Typewriter Co., the West Virginia Pulp & Paper Co., and the Patka Mining Co. He died in Brooklyn April 10, 1910.

Children by Mary Kasson:

LAURA EDNA, born in Brooklyn January 25, 1868, and married Frank Merrill and resides at Neshanic Station, N. J. Their son, John Franklin Merrill, was born January 5, 1894, at Brooklyn, N. Y., studied at the New York Military Academy, Stevens Institute, The University of Wisconsin and Columbia Unversity which he left in March, 1917, to enlist in the war. He had ground training at Ithaca, N. Y., and went to France in September, 1917. He joined the 28th Aero Squadron, First Pursuit Wing, Third Pursuit Group, First Army Air Service, about September 1, 1918. He participated, as First Lieutenant, in a number of flights, became Patrol Leader September 29th and led several flights. His Patrol Squadron was attacked by a superior enemy force on October 4, 1918. Lieutenant Merrill became detached from Patrol and his fate remained uncertain until

SYLVESTER G. WHITON (253)

report came that his body had been found by our advancing troops. He is now buried in the Meuse-Argonne American Cemetery Romagne-sous-Montfaucon (Meuse) France.

MABEL, born in Brooklyn November 7, 1872, and married William, son of Ardon K. and Mary B. Powell, in Brooklyn June 30, 1898. Their son, Whiton Powell, born at Silver Springs, N. Y., September 21, 1903, married Jeannette Gardiner at Fredonia, N. Y., September 3, 1927, and has two children, Jeannette Alice, born April 28, 1929, at Fountain Hill, Pa., and Gardiner Whiton, born June 4, 1931, at Ithaca, N. Y. The degrees of A.B., 1924, M.S., 1925, Ph.D., 1929, have all been given him by Cornell University where he is professor of Business Management in the College of Agriculture. His residence is at 115 Irving Place, Ithaca, N. Y.

ALICE, born in Brooklyn November 10, 1874, married Walter Dean, son of John M. and Maria Louise (Carrique) Ferres, who was born in New York City December 28, 1871. They reside at 78 Sunset Avenue, Ridgewood, N. J., and have a son, Walter D., born in Brooklyn January 1, 1899, who married Maurine Beals and resides at 201 Linwood Avenue, Ridgewood, N. J., and has two children: Walter D., born December 25, 1925, and Laura Ann, born May 23, 1927.

Children by Isabel Atwater:

HELEN ATWATER, born in Brooklyn June 22, 1888, married John D. Page and died in Honolulu December 25, 1921.

WALTER H. (304).

Children by Ella Skidmore:

MILDRED, born in Brooklyn June 10, 1893, married (1st) Eugene Ellery March 15, 1915; a daughter, Phyllis, was born June 3, 1916; and (2d) Richard Williams in May, 1920.

SYLVESTER G. (305).

CHARLES S. (306).

254 JOHN FULLER, son of Ashbel (193), was born at Westford, Conn., June 28, 1848, and married December 22, 1870, Minah Isabel Slade of Ashford. In 1880 he moved West and engaged in farming and stock-raising in Missouri and Kansas. He later located at Bassett, Nebraska, where he built a hotel which he managed

until his death April 11, 1906. His wife died August 17, 1899.

Children:

FLORENCE EUGENIA, born September 12, 1871, married George Sewell and lives at Norfolk, Neb.

SYLVESTER GILBERT, born January 28, 1873, died July 19, 1912.

CHARLOTTE BELLE, born August 16, 1876, married Charles Brady.

255 ALBERT FRANKLIN, son of Chester (194), was born December 9, 1842, and married Belle Janet, daughter of Jeremiah S. and Nancy (Morgan) Latham, of Willimantic, Conn. He was a wagon manufacturer at Mansfield, Conn., and died there August 10, 1885.

Children:

ALBERT ERNEST (306a).

CHARLES ALONZO, born at Mansfield September 29, 1869.

MABEL JANET, born March 21, 1884, and married Joseph Depeau at Mansfield.

256 HARLAN EUGENE, son of Chester (194), was born at Mansfield, Conn., October 27, 1846, and married Harriet Alida, daughter of John and Harriet (Clark) Williams, at Willimantic, Conn., May 1, 1870, and is a spool-turner, residing at Mansfield, Conn.

Children:

ANNIE LAURIE, born at Mansfield and married Herbert Griffin Chappell at Mansfield August 17, 1887, and resides at Mansfield Center, Conn. He was the son of Samuel and Eliza (Wrightmeyer) Chappell. Their children are: Herbert Eugene, born December 25, 1910, and died December 28, 1910; Reginald Herbert Whiton, born April 6, 1912 at Willimantic.

BERTHA E., born May 7, 1873, and married Wilbert F. Jacobs of Willimantic.

ALICE P., born January 29, 1876, married Frank Snow of Willimantic and died at Ashford January 19, 1902.

RUBY W., born May 18, 1879, married Howard M. Downing, and lives at 1941 Garfias Drive, Pasadena, Cal.

LOUISE V., born in Mansfield January 10, 1881, and married Frank W. Hoxie of Manchester, Conn.

WHITON MEMORIAL LIBRARY
Manchester, Conn.

THE READING ROOM

DR. FRANCIS HENRY WHITON (257)

RUTH E., born January 25, 1885, at Mansfield, married (1st) Ernest McIntire, and (2d) Alonzo E. Hankinson, and lives at Newark, Ohio. Her daughter, Mrs. Raymond Hanna, lives at Willimantic, Conn.

MILDRED A., born in Mansfield July 18, 1892, married Arthur King of Massachusetts and died October 31, 1919.

ELMER E., born in Willimantic June 20, 1893, married Olive Cady and resides at Willimantic, Conn.

257 FRANCIS HENRY, son of Chester (194), was born at Mansfield, Conn., May 16, 1846, and married May 17, 1876, Mary Elizabeth, daughter of George and Mary A. (Sweetland) Loomis, of Portsmouth, N. H., who died in 1929. He was for years an active and successful physician in Manchester, Conn., where he died May 21, 1921, bequeathing a substantial fortune for the establishment of a Whiton Memorial Library at Manchester.

258 ARMINIUS WESLEY, son of Chester (194), was born in Willimantic, Conn., June 1, 1853, and married Elizabeth Ann, daughter of Daniel K. and Lucinda (Phillips) Sweet, June 21, 1874, who was born April 25, 1853, and died January 11, 1924. He is a retired merchant and resides at Willimantic.

Children:

LILLIAN ELIZABETH, born March 23, 1875, and married Benjamin P., son of Henry and Warty Phillips, at Willimantic July 10, 1928, and resides at 79 Maple Avenue, Willimantic.

ARTHUR WESLEY (307).

EDITH, born in Mansfield, Mass., August 15, 1878, married John Baldwin in 1897 in Willimantic, and resides at 84 Irvington Avenue, Waterbury, Conn. A son, Raymond John, was born April 2, 1898, and married Dorothy Morgan in Waterbury April 2, 1921; resides in Willimantic and has two children: Barbara M., born January 1, 1922, in Waterbury, and Eleanor M., born July 4, 1923, in Willimantic.

259 OLIN EVERETT, son of Chester (194), was born at Willimantic, Conn., July 29, 1858, and married Sarah Ellen, daughter of Isaac and Elizabeth (Corbit) Mason,

at South Coventry, Conn., on June 10, 1884. He is a farmer and resides at Mansfield, Conn.

259*a* LESTER, son of Simeon (194*a*), born in Bloomfield and married June 22, 1850, Harriet Ellen, daughter of Elihu and Tryphena (Roberts) Latimer. He was First Lieutenant in Company D, 22d Regiment, Connecticut Volunteers in the Civil War. His business was that of a carriage-maker and he resided in West Hartford.

Children:

FRANK H., born October 7, 1855; he died at Hartford in 1928.

CHARLES L., born April 9, 1858, and died in July, 1858.

EDWARD L., born October 15, 1867, and married in 1889, Gertrude Drew. He lived at Johnson City, Tenn., where he died in 1929.

ARTHUR H., born May 12, 1869, and married Bessie Lane. They had a daughter, Grace Isabel, who married William Leining of Durham, Conn., and has five children: Edith Caroline, William, Jr., Herbert Kenneth, Irvin Lane and Paul.

259*b* PORTER, son of Simeon (194*a*), born October 12, 1841, married Elizabeth Deming, who was born in 1834 and died June 3, 1891. He was a corporal in Company D, 22d Regiment, Connecticut Volunteers. He was a contractor and builder and resided at Hartford, Conn., where he died December 7, 1894.

Children:

MARY ELIZABETH, married Ezra Bates; had two children, James, who died young, and Jane, who married Burges Fisher, of Hartford.

ELIZABETH CORDELIA, married Louis F. K. Whitman of Hartford. They both died in 1930, leaving two children: Theodore and Tirzah.

ELLA MATILDA, married Emil C. Wander and had a daughter, Mabel, who married Charles M. Gregory of Hartford.

ANTOINETTE JERUSHA, married Hayden R. Lathrop of Hartford and now resides at Hamburg, Conn. They have four children: Elizabeth L., married Frederick White and resides at Hamilton, Ont.; Eleanor L., married Cushman Sears of Hartford: she is a portrait artist and lives at

TUDOR WHITON (260)

Hamburg; Berenice C., married Max Brevillier of Hamilton, Ont.; Robert Hayden, who lives in New York.

ROBERT PORTER, born at Hartford, January 14, 1872, married Annie Sutherland and resides in New York. They have a son, Porter.

260 TUDOR, son of Augustus (195), was born at East Windsor (Wapping) Conn., March 24, 1835, and married Ellen Augusta, daughter of Harrison J. and Sarah (Blakeslee) Barnard, at Bloomfield, Conn., May 18, 1859, who was born at North Bloomfield (formerly part of Simsbury), Conn., January 31, 1836, and died there June 7, 1918. He was by occupation a wagon manufacturer. He was a member of the Board of Assessors and also a selectman for a number of years at Bloomfield, and served in Company D, 22d Connecticut Infantry, in the Civil War. He died in Bloomfield July 19, 1929.

Children:

HARRIET ELLEN, born 1860 and died in 1878.

ALICE ALENA, born in 1864, married in 1883, Walter D. Wyckoff. Children: Isabel, born in 1885; Grace, born in 1887, died in 1887; Dayton T., born in 1888; Edith M., born in 1889, died 1889. Dayton married in 1923, Madeline Brady.

JENNIE BARNARD, born May 16, 1868, married Marshall T. Bradley. Children: Tudor W., born at Bloomfield, Conn., July 16, 1896, married at Fall River, Mass., July 5, 1924, Jessie, daughter of John H. and Jessie L. Hunter, who was born September 1, 1901. He resides at 819 Bay River Avenue, Gardner, Mass., and is secretary of Trade Organization, and has one son, Tudor W. Bradley, born January 4, 1927. Marshall J., born in 1898, died in 1925, and Donald H., born in 1907.

HENRY A. (308).

BESSIE AND GRACE, born and died in 1879.

261 HENRY, son of Julius Royal (197), was born at West Stafford, Conn., March 14, 1834, and married (1st) Miranda Pomeroy, who was born September 19, 1837, and died October 29, 1858, and (2d) Hattie E., daughter of Norman and Mary (Pomeroy) Buck, who was

born September 7, 1834, and who died at Pasadena, Cal., in 1896/7. He served in the Civil War as Corporal in Company D, 25th Regiment Connecticut Volunteers. He died at New London, Conn., November 2, 1888.

Children:

JULIA, born January, 1862, and died August 2, 1862.
ALBERT, born March, 1865, and died September 26, 1865.
FLORA ESTELLE, born August 11, 1867, and resides at 2405 Ninth Avenue, Los Angeles, Cal.

262 MERRILL, son of Julius Royal (197), was born at West Stafford, Conn., June 15, 1851, and married Emma Chapman September 25, 1872, who was born in Newport, R. I., January 26, 1853. She was the daughter of Harlow B. and Nancy (Ford) Chapman. They lived at 539 Atlanta Street, Pasadena, Cal., where she died June 21, 1930, and where he died February 29, 1932.

Children:

LILLIAN EVA, born April 12, 1876, in West Stafford, Conn., and is a teacher at Long Beach, Cal., where she resides.
ETHEL CORA, born August 10, 1881, in West Stafford, Conn., and resides in Pasadena, Cal.

263 NELSON, son of Joseph Leander (199), was born at West Stafford, Conn., June 14, 1843, and married September 11, 1865, Adeline, daughter of William and Catherine (Wildish) Prickett, of Hazardville, where she was born March 4, 1840. He served in the Civil War in 1861 as a private in Company C, 1st Regiment, Connecticut Volunteers, and in 1862 and later as a member of Company I, 16th Regiment, Connecticut Volunteers. He was wounded at the battle of Antietam and in April, 1864, he was captured by the enemy and confined a prisoner of war in Andersonville for six months from which severe experience he never fully recovered. He died October 15, 1904, in Palmer, Mass.

Children:

LENA BELLE, born August 7, 1867, married December 21, 1887, Ernest C. Buddington of Somersville, Conn., and died September 24, 1920. She had four children: Roy Whiton, born May 21, 1889; Ruth Sarah, born April 6, 1896; Lena Adeline, born July 31, 1900; Leon Daniel, born December 9, 1902, and died aged three months.

ERNEST LEANDER (309).

FORREST NELSON, born August 10, 1881, and married March 17, 1928, Helen Lee. They reside at Belchertown, Mass.

264 LUCIUS ERSKINE, son of David Erskine (201), was born at West Stafford, Conn., December 25, 1862, and married at Lowell, Mass., October 12, 1887, Viola Emma, daughter of George and Joanna (Dellehunt) King, who was born May 5, 1867, and died July 9, 1907. He graduated in 1881 from Wilbraham Academy, Wilbraham, Mass., and became associated with his father in the manufacture of machinery. Since 1886 he has lived in New London, Conn. He is the inventor and patentee of special machinery, and improvements in Centering Machines, Lathe Chucks, Gear Cutting Machines and Steam Turbines which his firm manufactures. He is President and Treasurer of The D. E. Whiton Machine Company, a Trustee of The Savings Bank of New London, a Director and Vice-President of The Union Bank and Trust Company. He published in New London during 1904, *"The Weekly Binnacle,"* but was forced to give it up because of other responsibilities. He was Representative from New London in the 1907, 1909 and 1911 legislative sessions, a member and chairman of the Committee on Banks. He was active in the movement to create the Connecticut Public Utilities Commission. He actively urged, and was always beaten through non-concurrent action in the Senate, the policy of limiting Connecticut corporations to the issue of but one class of capital stock. He was Senator from the 18th District in the session of 1915, and chairman of the Committee on Railroads. For eight years he was a city councilor and the first Mayor of New London under the Council-Manager form of government adopted by that city in 1921. He is President of the

City Planning Board and was chairman of the Zoning Commission. He is President of the Board of Trustees of Wilbraham Academy; a Trustee of the Chapman Technical High School of New London; a Trustee of the Manwaring Memorial Children's Hospital and of the Norwich State Hospital at Preston. He is a Republican. He is a member of the Second Congregational Church, Brainard Masonic Lodge and Pequot Lodge, I. O. O. F. He has been for many years a member of the American Society of Mechanical Engineers. He is treasurer of The Whiton Family Association and a member of its Publication Committee. His residence is at 836 Pequot Avenue, New London, Conn.

Children:

HELEN KING, born at New London November 4, 1888. A graduate of Smith College in 1910. Resides at home.

DOROTHY QUINCY, born April 20, 1891, married at New London, April 28, 1923, Allen Winchester Jackson of Cambridge, Mass., and has a son, Lucius E. Whiton Jackson, born at Cambridge December 30, 1925.

DAVID ERSKINE, born November 5, 1895, and died October 5, 1896.

WINIFRED GARDINER (or "Wynyfride"—See pp. 19-20), born August 22, 1899. Graduated from Smith College in 1921. Resides at home.

LUCIUS GAY, born August 23, 1903, died April 26, 1904.

JAMES BEALE, born June 20, 1906, died in July, 1906.

265 EDWIN CARLTON, son of Francis (203), was born at Viola, Minn., October 22, 1866, and married at Rochester, Minn., December 25, 1890, Abbie Minnie, daughter of Gilman and Melissa (Harriman) Robinson, who was born at Viola, April 14, 1867, and died October 12, 1898. He is a farmer and resides at Deerwood, Minn.

Children:

ARTHUR LOUIS (310).

IVA BELLE, born June 11, 1892, married Clair Lloyd Harvey April 7, 1915, and died at Riverside, Cal., August 1, 1921.

266 GEORGE CALVIN, son of Calvin (204), was born in Tolland, Conn., January 1, 1840, and married Mary Catherine, daughter of James Monroe and Catherine (Phelps) Griswold, at East Granby, Conn., in March, 1864, who was born May 18, 1845, and died September 29, 1929. He died at Hazardville, Conn., January 16, 1916.

Children:

CATHERINE PHELPS, born September 27, 1864, and married Francis F. Leary January 28, 1885, who was born at Scitico, Conn., December 5, 1856, and had children: Florence M., born at Scitico August 1, 1888, married Frederick C. Munyan, and resides at 126 West Alvord Street, Springfield, Mass.; Ethel M., born at Scitico February 12, 1892, married Joseph P. Long, and resides in Springfield; and George Francis, born at Scitico August 26, 1886, and married Catherine, daughter of Michael and Catherine Keating. He was educated at Amherst College, graduated in 1909, and at Boston University Law School, graduating in 1912, in which year he was admitted to the Massachusetts Bar. He is a member of the Tau Delta Fraternity. Their children are: Barbara, born October 16, 1918; George Whiton, born October 15, 1923, and Robert Keating, born May 20, 1925.

JENNIE ELEANOR, born April 30, 1877, at Enfield, Çonn., resides at Hazardville, and is a school teacher at Enfield, Conn.

267 AMMI PAULK, son of Calvin (204), was born at Tolland, Conn., May 22, 1854, and married (1st) Sarah Ida, daughter of George Edson and Sarah (Morley) Shepard, at Westfield, Mass., May 18, 1881, who was born December 20, 1858, and died August 4, 1897, and (2d) Laura Georgianna Classon, who survives him. He was a manufacturer of church organs and died at Plaistow, N. H., April 2, 1924.

Children:

EDSON ERASTUS, died in infancy.

CORA EMMA, died in infancy.

BERTHA E., born February 20, 1882, married September 28, 1929, Edmund Eugene Morand, and resides at 8 Cross Street, Westfield, Mass.

268 ERASTUS TAYLOR, son of Calvin (204), was born October 4, 1849, at Tolland, Conn., and married (1st) Ella, daughter of William B. and Elmira (Kirkland) Lewis, who was born at Fairhaven, Conn., January 25, 1851, and died at Pueblo, Col., February 29, 1916, and (2d) on June 7, 1917, Mrs. Jessie (Burdick) Gladwin, who died in 1929. He was a builder and founded the Whiton Mortuary Association, dying at Pueblo November 24, 1921.

Children:

LOTTIE, born in 1877 and died June 3, 1892, in Pueblo, Col.

MYRA ELEANOR, born May 30, 1882, in Brooklyn, N. Y., and married June 14, 1904, at Pueblo, Col., Scott R., son of Joseph and Caroline Peterson, and died June 29, 1929, at their home in Corning, Cal. Their children are: Eleanor Carolyn, born July 14, 1905; Scott Roscoe, born August 30, 1908, and Dorothy Whiton, born at Pueblo April 29, 1915.

EMMA, born at Brooklyn, N. Y., August 3, 1886, and married John Hector McDonald at San Jose, Cal., December 19, 1926, and resides at 769 Vincente Avenue, Berkeley, Cal.

269 JAMES MORRIS, son of James Morris (206), was born April 11, 1833, and married Mary, daughter of William and Mary (Crie) Bartlett, of Portland, Me., May 1, 1855, who was born in Portland January 28, 1834, and died in New York City September 27, 1917. Her father was the owner of a large fleet of sailing vessels. James Morris received the degree of A.B. from Yale College in 1853, and Ph.D. in 1861. He was the author of numerous books on Theological subjects and text books of Greek and Latin. He was the editor of *The Outlook;* and under his leadership the New York State Conference of Religion was founded. It has been said of Dr. Whiton that "he was one of the few constructive thinkers and builders of his time." He was in his early life principal of Williston Seminary at Easthampton, Mass., and later pastor of the Congregational Church at Lynn, Mass., 1865-75; the Congregational Church at Newark, N. J., 1879-85, and of a

REV. DR. JAMES M. WHITON (269)

(270)

Congregational Church in New York City, 1886-91. He died January 25, 1920.

Children:

JAMES M., died in May, 1862.

MARY BARTLETT, born in New Haven, Conn., August 17, 1857, and was for many years associated with Miss Lois A. Bangs as principals of National Cathedral School for Girls, Washington, D. C., 1900-1906, and then of Miss Bangs's and Miss Whiton's School in New York City. She is now retired and resides at 12 Arnold Avenue, Northampton, Mass.

JAMES B. (311).

HELEN ISABEL, died in October, 1923.

270 JOHN MILTON, son of James Morris (206), was born June 7, 1845, and married (1st) Mary E. Bond of Geneseo, N. Y., May 15, 1873, who died April 12, 1887, and (2d) Adeline P. Newton of Plainfield, N. J., September 15, 1897. He was in the insurance business in New York City for over forty years, and was for several terms President of the New York Board of Fire Underwriters. He was educated in Boston and Germany, and completed one year at Sheffield Scientific School (Yale University). He was a member of the Board of Governors of Muhlenberg Hospital, Plainfield, and President of the Plainfield City Common Council, and a Director of the Plainfield Library, and prominent in Congregational Church matters, having been superintendent of the Sunday School for over twenty-five years. He died at Plainfield May 28, 1927.

Children:

NELLA BOND, born February 22, 1874, married June 22, 1898, Leighton Calkins, a lawyer of New York City. Their children are: Wolcott, born June 12, 1899; Mary Bond, born March 1, 1902, and Dorothy Whiton, born August 28, 1904.

MARY KNOWLTON, born February 17, 1878, at Plainfield, married May 11, 1905, James A. Hutchinson of Lynn, Mass., who was born May 20, 1874, and now resides at 55 Valentine Street, West Newton, Mass. Their children are: James A., born January 25, 1906; John Whiton, born April 10, 1907, and Mary Whiton, born June 22, 1911, and died April 9, 1912.

271 LUCIUS A., son of Oren (207), spells his name Whiting, was born at Hanover, Mass., April 22, 1837, and married Lydia, daughter of John and Lydia J. (Mann) Poole, at Hanover November 28, 1855, and died there February 25, 1894.

Children:

IDA E., born December 12, 1858, and died August 9, 1863.

HENRY W., born December 17, 1862, and died at Connaut, Fla.

ANABEL, born at Hanover November 17, 1865, married Josiah W., son of Josiah Hinckley, at Boston November 13, 1883. She was Past President of Woman's Relief Corp and Past Noble Grand of Rebecca (I. O. O. F.) and resides in West Hanover. Their children are: Josiah, born November 24, 1884; Fannie Stuart, who married C. F. Robart; Chester F., and Esther W., who married Russell Osgood of Rockland, Mass.

272 EZRA J., probably son of Ezra J., who was the son of Ezra (138), was born in Hingham and married Josephine Hoanes, who died in Newton, Mass., in 1915. He died there about 1908.

Children:

FLORENCE, married Dudley Edwards, M.D., of Watertown, Mass.

JOSEPHINE, unmarried.

EFFIE, married ——— Pearson of Newton, Mass.

KITTY, who married ——— Hall.

FRANCIS HENRY (312).

273 WALLACE W., son of Bela H. (210), was born June 20, 1856, and married at East Weymouth, January 31, 1882, Virginia Whitney Burrell, who was born October 11, 1860, and resides at 30 Hillcrest Road, East Weymouth, Mass. He died there April 1, 1913.

Children:

FANNIE BURRELL, born May 22, 1883, and married William A. Hodges October 13, 1909.

WALLACE ASHTON, born March 22, 1886, and died in May, 1886.

273a HENRY EDSON HERSEY, son of Bela H. (210), was born in Hingham June 22, 1871, and married (1st) at Hingham June 10, 1896, Katherine Geddes, daughter of Nathaniel and Abby Brackett, who died July 21, 1903; married (2d) at Cohassett, Mass., November 21, 1906, Edith Bates, daughter of J. Wentworth and Sarah A. Earle. He is a salesman and lives at Hingham.

Children by Katherine:

MARGARET BRACKETT, born September 14, 1897.
NATHANIEL BRACKETT, born July 12, 1903.

Child by Edith:

ELINOR H., born November 27, 1913.

273b ELIJAH, son of Bela H. (210), was born at Hingham November 30, 1874, and married at Boston, Mass., August 9, 1905, Annie J., daughter of John and Mary (MacRae) MacKenzie, who was born at West Bay, Nova Scotia, March 10, 1872. He is a shoe worker and lives at East Weymouth, Mass.

Child:

KENNETH ELIJAH, born November 20, 1908.

274 FREDERIC, son of Erastus (211), was born June 25, 1870, and married (1st) Mary Snow Dillingham in 1898, who died June 26, 1903, and (2d) Edith, daughter of Harry and Mae Hunt, of Melrose, N. J., July 3, 1906. They reside at 418 Washington Street, Westfield, N. J.

Child by Mary:

HELEN, born 1900, died 1914.

Children by Edith:

HARRY HUNT, born in Melrose April 15, 1907.
PRISCILLA BURR, born in Melrose November 1, 1908, married Ralph J. Van Derwerken April 26, 1930.
JOHN CHADWICK, born in Melrose April 24, 1911.
NANCY BOSWORTH, born in Melrose September 29, 1917.

275 CHARLES FEARING, son of William (215), was born at Hingham August 20, 1844, and married October 26, 1870, Sarah F., daughter of John O. and Frances E.

(Batchelder) Lovett, who was born at Hingham January 22, 1845. He was a commission merchant, residing at Hingham, where he died May 21, 1915.

Children:

ELEANOR LOVETT, born May 28, 1872.
LUCY SOULE, born June 1, 1874.

276 EDWARD WINSLOW, son of Henry (218), was born in Boston July 10, 1864, and married Nina, daughter of Aaron C. and Elizabeth Rogers, at Holliston, Mass., who was born at Hyde Park, Mass., September 14, 1871. They reside at Hingham Center.

Children:

HENRY ROGERS, born August 27, 1897, married Olive Holmes.
WILSON W., born July 28, 1900, married Ruth Ripley.

277 HARRY F., son of Moses Lincoln (219), was born at Somerville, Mass., December 29, 1856, and married Mary K., daughter of Andrew and Mary Pettingill, of Newburyport, Mass., January 10, 1908. He is a railway clerk and resides there.

Children:

ELIZABETH COFFIN.
ERNEST FOSS.

278 CHAUNCEY GILBERT, son of Starkes (220), was born in Hingham February 17, 1872, and married Harriet Loring, daughter of William and Mehitable (Fuller) Cushing, October 12, 1898, who was born in Hingham September 7, 1871, and died in New York City September 1, 1926. He was a graduate of Massachusetts Institute of Technology, in 1894, and specialized in Marine Engineering and Naval Architecture. He was Marine Superintendent of the Hudson River Day Line in New York City, and resided at Jackson Heights, New York, where he died September 29, 1928, and is interred at Hingham.

CHAUNCEY GILBERT WHITON (278)

Child:

HELEN LINCOLN, who was born October 20, 1899, and resides at 172 Main Street, Hingham, and is the Librarian of the Public Library in Passaic, N. J.

279 DAVID THOMAS, son of Starkes (220), was born in Hingham March 18, 1875, and married October 28, 1903, at Hingham, Lottie Frances, daughter of Liba and Henrietta E. Studley, who was born in Hingham August 22, 1873. He is a graduate of Massachusetts Institute of Technology, receiving his degree in 1897. He served ten years in the Massachusetts State Militia, and two years in the Connecticut State Guard. He is the Superintendent of the New London Ship and Engine Company, and resides at 65 Lower Boulevard, New London, Conn.

Children:

THEODORE STUDLEY, born in Hingham November 18, 1904.

MARIAN PEIRCE, born in Quincy October 21, 1912.

280 HERBERT STARKES, son of Starkes (220), was born in Hingham August 4, 1879, and married Edith Harris, daughter of William Harris and Ella Russell (James) Wyer, at Nantucket, Mass., June 20, 1908, who was born at Nantucket September 12, 1882. He is a graduate of the Class of 1901, Harvard University, with the degree of B.S. He is a Mechanical Engineer and member of the American Society of Mechanical Engineers. He is the Assistant to the Chief Engineer of Byllesby and Company of Chicago, and resides at 1614 Colfax Street, Evanston, Ill.

Children:

DOROTHY STARKES, born September 17, 1910, at Minneapolis.

RUSSELL THOMAS, born at Minneapolis March 11, 1912, died there February 25, 1916.

ROBERT WYER, born at Evanston June 29, 1928.

281 WILLIAM E., son of Edward (222), was born January 1, 1856, and married Eleanor S. DeWolf October 12, 1883. Together with his younger brother Charles H., he purchased a farm on the shore of Lake Erie, near Conneaut, Ohio. Later he sold this farm and after the death of his uncle Edwin Whiton (142) he settled on the original Whiton homestead, where he remained until 1900, when he removed to Springfield, Ohio, and engaged in the wholesale produce business, and served as Township Superior. In 1905 he moved his family to North Girard, Penn., where he died January 13, 1925.

Son:

GLENVILLE W. (313).

282 CHARLES H., son of Edward (222), was born January 30, 1862, and married May B. Thompson of Conneaut, Penn. He was a farmer in Springfield Township, Penn., and active in local politics, serving as tax collector.

Children:

EDWIN, a farmer in East Springfield, Penn.
CORAL, married ——— Mook and lives in Cleveland, Ohio.

283 JOSEPH LINCOLN, son of Isaiah Gorham (223), was born in Quincy, Mass., October 18, 1844, and married Mary A., daughter of Caleb Lincoln and Mary S. Littlefield, at Quincy, who was born December 4, 1844. He was a Boston merchant and died at Quincy October 23, 1911.

Children:

HENRY LINCOLN (314).
ROSS KITTRIDGE (314a).
JOSEPH LINCOLN (315).

284 WALTER STOWELL, son of William Stowell (225), was born at East Weymouth, Mass., April 27, 1866. He is the proprietor of a hotel on Common Street, Hingham Center, and is unmarried.

WILLIAM E. WHITON (281)

ROYAL WHITON (285)

285 ROYAL, son of Royal (226), was born July 28, 1846, and married Ella C., daughter of Alvin A. and Eleanor (Woodbury) Rice, in Dorchester March 9, 1887. He was the Eastern Agent of the Atchison and Sante Fe Railway, then of the Central Vermont; then of the Ogdensburg and Lake Champlain Steamship Company. Later he became a building contractor. The club house of the Dorchester Woman's Club, of which his wife was a president was named Whiton Hall. He was a 32d degree Mason, retired from business in 1919 and died April 20, 1928. No children.

286 HENRY JACKSON, son of Royal (226), was born August 2, 1860, and married Lottie Augusta, daughter of Frederick H. and Sarah A. (Beckett) Dodge, February 20, 1895, at Jamaica Plains, Mass. He is an accountant and resides at 11 Warwick Road, Brookline, Mass.

287 ARTHUR ELBERT, son of Edward Everett (229), was born January 29, 1886, and married Etta M., daughter of L. Willard and Grace (Eaton) Flint, June 25, 1920, who was born March 17, 1896.

Child:

NORMAN ELBERT, born in Malden, Mass., September 7, 1923.

288 CHARLES EDWARD, son of Edward Everett (229), was born in Charlestown, Mass., October 3, 1874, and married Daisy L., daughter of August and Sarah (Wheellus) Shields, March 21, 1906, who was born in Atlanta, Ga., August 15, 1881. He graduated from Tufts College in 1896 with the degree of B.S. He served as First Lieutenant Signal Corps, U. S. A., during 1917-18. He is now Electrical Engineer for the Navy Department, residing at Alta Vista, Bethesda, Md. He has one (adopted) son, and step-son, William Ipark, born August 9, 1897, who resides in Brooklyn, N. Y.

289 EDWARD HUMPHREY, son of Loring Livingston (230), was born in Somerville, Mass., September 30, 1862, and married Emily, daughter of Horace and Azelia (Cutter) Woodman, in Somerville, October 4, 1897. He was a manufacturer of piano hammers and died in Somerville January 9, 1919.

Children:

ANNA GERTRUDE, born in Somerville March 12, 1899.

IRMA, born in Newton, Mass., June 9, 1900, and married Wesley Clyde, son of Joel Edward and Mary (McCann) Newcomb, on October 10, 1922. She was employed in the Civil Service department at the State House, Boston, from 1919 to 1921, and resides at 167 Central Street, Somerville, Mass.

TENTH GENERATION

290 ROSCOE BENJAMIN, son of Edgar Benjamin (232), spells his name Whitten, was born at East Boston February 5, 1876, and married Winnifred Marie, daughter of Robert Frederick and Mary A. (Yould) Rutherford, at Sydney, Nova Scotia, December 8, 1904, who was born at Truro, N. S., October 21, 1884. He is an architect, a graduate of the Massachusetts Institute of Technology.

Children:

RUSSELL RUTHERFORD (316).
GILBERT YOULD, born at Winthrop, Mass., July 25, 1909 .
MARY ELIZABETH, born at Chelsea, Mass., October 24, 1916.

291 HENRY GRANT, son of Henry Benjamin (233), was born at Troy, N. Y., December 21, 1868, and married Julia, daughter of Thomas and Maria A. (Finlay) Ratigan, at Troy October 27, 1887, who was born August 10, 1867. He was a pharmacist and served in the World War as Chief Inspector at Alliance, Ohio, in the Steel Works. He was connected with L. K. Liggett and Company in Troy, N. Y., where he died October 5, 1931.

Children:

SOPHIA, born December 13, 1888, and died October 18, 1890.
EDNA MARYLAND, born December 23, 1901, is unmarried and resides at 2539 Sixth Avenue, Troy.
HARRY FINLAY (317).
ARNOLD GRANT, born April 13, 1895, and died November 9, 1906.

292 ALPHA RAY, son of Alpha Mason (234), was born in Brockport, N. Y., December 31, 1890, and resides at 12 Fifth Avenue, New York City, and has a country place at Carmel, N. Y. He volunteered in 1917, and was commissioned lieutenant, and assigned in charge of a Company of Pioneer Infantry, serving in the Meuse-Argonne campaign in France. He also served in the 27th and 82d Divisions. He is a real estate operator in New York City.

292a CHARLES LOOMIS, son of Charles M. (234a) was born in Wellington, Ohio, July 17, 1875, married July 20, 1903, Cecil L. Curry, and resides at Wellington.

Children:

LOIS E., CHARLES WILLIAM, twins, born June 11, 1904.
PHYLLIS E., born July 27, 1910.

293 HARLEY BERT, son of Hezekiah J. (235), was born in Royalton Township, Ohio, May 19, 1900, and married June 28, 1922, Orphy Lutton.

Children:

VIVIAN MARIE, born September 3, 1923.
HARLEY BERT, JR., born August 30, 1925.
WESLEY WAYNE, born April 9, 1928.
AGNES ORPHY, born January 13, 1930.

293a ARTHUR EMERSON, son of George Edwin (236a), was born at Greenville, Mich., February 2, 1890, and married August 8, 1909, Anna Feichtenbiner, who was born October 22, 1889, at Ithaca, Mich. They live at 1020 May Street, Lansing, Mich.

Children:

DENNIS GEORGE, born May 30, 1910.
HELEN ALBERTA, born March 17, 1912, married at Bowling Green, Ohio, March 31, 1929, Nelson S. Dill.
RUSSELL EMERSON, born April 1, 1916.
ROBERT ARTHUR, born April 1, 1916, died in 1926.

294 JOHN STARR, son of Walter Starr (239), was born in Duluth, Minn., August 13, 1908, resides at 280 West Olive Street, Stillwater, Minn., and is a student at Carleton College, Northfield, Minn.

295 JESSE PAULMIER, son of Augustus Ward (241), adopted the name Whiton-Stuart, after his step-father, and was born in Jersey City, N. J., June 4, 1874, and married Mary, daughter of John R. and Josephine (Marshall) Ogden, in June, 1904. He was educated by private tutors and at Harvard University, and is in the real estate business in New York City. He is a member

of the Union Club of New York City, and the Essex Fox Hounds of New Jersey, and resides in New York City.

Children:

SYLVIA, born in New York City July 4, 1906, and married (1st) Eric Stow, son of Frederic Horace and Mary (Daly) Hatch, at Elkton, Md., September 4, 1922, and (2d) Lawrence, son of George E. Turnure, in New York City, September 4, 1929, and resides at 46 East 66th Street, New York City.

ROBERT WATSON, born December 16, 1909, and resides at 8 East 54th Street, New York City.

296 AUGUSTUS SHERRILL, son of Louis Claude (242), was born in New York City January 7, 1887, and married in the Collegiate Dutch Reformed Church October 15, 1910, Claire Henriette, daughter of Henri Louis and Marie Antoinette (Bernard) Bouché, of New York City, who was born February 11, 1889. He was educated at the Columbia University School of Architecture and the Ecole des Beaux Arts, Paris, France. For several years after his return to New York he was associated with leading firms of architects, and later, in an office of his own, specialized in country house architecture. In 1921 he organized and became President of the New York School of Interior Decoration. He is a member of the Delta Kappa Epsilon Fraternity, the Society of Beaux Arts Architects, the Architectural League of New York, the Art-in-Trade Club, and the Sons of the Revolution, and served two years in Sqaudron A, National Guard of New York. He resides at 1150 Fifth Avenue, New York City, and at Westport, Conn.

Child:

AUGUSTUS SHERRILL, born in New York City June 26, 1918.

297 LOUIS CLAUDE, son of Louis Claude (242), was born in Garden City, Long Island, May 5, 1891, and married in the Protestant Episcopal Church of the Holy

Trinity, Paris, France, May 27, 1920, Colette, daughter of Marcel and Irene (Fekete) Ritcher, of Paris, France, who was born in Paris November 25, 1896. He graduated from the Sheffield Scientific School of Yale University in 1912, receiving the degree of Ph.B. In 1913 he received the degree of M.A. from Columbia University, at which College he was an Instructor. He specialized in chemical engineering. He served as First Lieutenant in the Chemical Warfare Service, United States Army, in France, 1917-18, and after the armistice was connected with the Board for Determination of War Damages under General McKinsky. In 1924 he organized and became President of the Prat-Daniel Corporation of New York City, Engineers and Constructors of Machinery. He is a member of the Delta Kappa Epsilon Fraternity, the Engineers Club of New York, The American Oil Chemists Society and the American Society of Mechanical Engineers; and he has won recognition as a sculptor, in which art he is interested as an avocation. He resides at 308 East 79th Street, New York City and at Westport, Conn.

Children:

JACQUELINE, born in New York City July 12, 1924.
NADINE, born in New York City December 6, 1929.

298 HENRY DEVEREUX, son of Edward Nathan (243), was born at Piermont, N. Y., January 30, 1871, and married (1st) Frieda, daughter of Herman and Romalda (Berks) Frasch, of Cleveland, Ohio, October 15, 1902, and (2d) Gwendolen Harris, daughter of Edward Henry and Sallie (Whiton) Harris, at New York, October 14, 1922. He was President of the Union Sulphur Company and a member of the following clubs: New York Yacht, Downtown, Union, Nassau County, Seawanhaka Corinthian Yacht, Rockaway Hunting, Larchmont Yacht, and Piping Rock. He and Harrison Williams financed the cruise of the Arcturus for scientific research in the Sargasso Sea in 1925. Among other discoveries were two volcanoes on Albemarle Island,

HENRY DEVEREUX WHITON (298)

west of Ecuador, which were named Mounts Whiton and Williams. He resided at Glen Cove, Long Island, where he died in October, 1930. He had one son by his first wife:

HERMAN FRASCH, born April 6, 1904, graduated at Princeton University in 1926, and Harvard Law School. He is secretary of the Union Sulphur Company, and is prominent in yachting, and represented the United States with his yacht Frieda at the Olympic races in Holland in 1928. He is a member of the Seawanhaka Corinthian Yacht Club, and of the New York Yacht Club, and resides at 34 Park Avenue, New York City.

299 JOHN LIONEL, son of Edward Nathan (243), was born February 15, 1875, in Jersey City, N. Y., and married Mabel Cole and resides at Rivera, Los Angeles, Cal.

300 RUSSELL RUFUS, son of Arthur Sylvester (247), was born November 26, 1896, and married February 14, 1917, Muriel Winnie Sayles, and resides at Perry, Iowa.

Children:

ROLAND RUSSELL, born September 6, 1918.
SYLVIA ADELINE, born May 26, 1920.
LOYD ARTHUR, born November 20, 1922.
VIRGINIA MAE, born January 25, 1926.
DONALD WARD, born December 5, 1927.

301 GEORGE HUSTED, son of Arthur Sylvester (247), was born November 9, 1899, and married October 24, 1923, Helene Didely, and resides at Perry, Iowa.

Children:

JOHN HUSTED, born October 14, 1924.
WILLIAM KEITH, born February 27, 1927.

302 FRANK WARREN, son of Andrew (250), was born in Hartford, Conn., January 31, 1872, and married June 20, 1900, Elizabeth Sarah, daughter of Stephen and Nancy (Lanphere) Carter, at Christ Church, Hartford. He studied architecture and after ten years practice of that profession alone, formed a partnership with

Major John J. McMahon. They have designed numerous residences, a large number of school buildings, churches and public buildings, and are recognized as one of the leading firms of the State. In politics he is an ardent Republican, having served as a member of the Republican Town Committee, and having been elected as a member of the Court of Common Council of Hartford, the Board of Education, and as Alderman. As Alderman he was chairman of the important Committee of Railroads. He is a thirty-second degree Mason, and a member and high official in numerous lodges of the I. O. O. F.; Mystic Order of Samaritans, of which he is Supreme Monarch, and of the Knight Templars, and other Masonic bodies. He is a member of the Hartford Chamber of Commerce, The City Club of Hartford, The Republican Club of Hartford, The Putnam Phalanx, The Kiwanis Club, The Connecticut Society of Civil Engineers, The Connecticut Architectural Club, and is an Ex-President of the Whiton Family Association. In religion he is an Episcopalian, formerly a member of the Vestry of Christ Church, a member and secretary of the Cathedral Chapter, and chairman of the Committee on Buildings and Grounds in his Diocese. He is also a past President of the Laymen's Association. During the World War he was active on a number of War Committees. His wife is also active in the organizations of Christ Church Cathedral, an active member of the order of the Eastern Star and Amaranth White Shrine and a Past President and Treasurer of the Woman's Guild. He resides at Hartford, Conn., at 25 Keney Terrace.

Children:

STEPHEN CARTER (318).

WARREN CARTER, born May 8, 1912, and is a pupil at the Weaver High School, Hartford.

303 WALTER THAYER, son of Elisha Byles (251), was born in Leicester, Mass., June 26, 1890, and married Bertha, daughter of Charles B. and Annie E. True, at

Boylston, Mass., August 20, 1917, who was born at Shrewsbury, Mass., December 8, 1898. He was a sergeant in the World War, and from wounds was totally disabled. He lived in Phoenix, Arizona for three years in an effort to regain his health and resides at Grove Street, North Grafton, Mass.

Children:

MURIEL TRUE, born August 31, 1918, at Worcester.
WALTER THAYER, born January 21, 1927, at Worcester.

304 WALTER HUMISTON, son of Sylvester Gilbert (253), was born in Brooklyn, N. Y., July 2, 1881, and married Avice McIntosh, daughter of John and Jessie P. (Whitehead) Watts, who was born in San Francisco, Cal., October 8, 1880. He graduated at the College of Physicians and Surgeons of New York in 1904, and served as First Lieutenant in the Medical Corps, U. S. A., at the Base Hospital in Ardeche, and at Camp Covington, in Marseilles, France, in 1918-19. Later he gave up the practice of medicine and became active in farm organizations, and has been a lecturer of the New Jersey Grange since 1922, and resides at Neshanic Station, N. J. He is now (1932) President of The Whiton Family Association.

Children:

JAMES SYLVESTER, born in Brooklyn April 16, 1911.
JANET FRASER, born in Brooklyn December 20, 1914.
ISABEL ATWATER, born in Brooklyn November 26, 1917.

305 SYLVESTER GILBERT, son of Sylvester G. (253), was born in Brooklyn, N. Y., October 29, 1895, and married July 23, 1919, Mildred Augusta, daughter of John Banks and Florence Bruce (Auld) Holman, who was born in Brooklyn October 25, 1898, and resides at 689 East 19th Street, Brooklyn, N. Y. He enlisted in 1917 and served in France until May, 1919, receiving two citations, carrying the Croix de Guerre.

Children:

SYLVESTER GILBERT, born in Brooklyn August 20, 1921.
ELIZABETH BRUCE, born in Brooklyn January 19, 1925.
CHARLES ROBERT, born in Brooklyn, November 18, 1931.

306 CHARLES SKIDMORE, son of Sylvester G. (253), was born in Brooklyn, N. Y., March 12, 1899, and married November 4, 1918, Dorothy, daughter of Woolsey A. and Frances (Daly) Moran. They resided at Larchmont, N. Y., where he died May 9, 1927.

Children:

JOAN MARJORIE, born April 3, 1922.
MARY LAURENE, born August 5, 1926.

306a ALBERT ERNEST, son of Albert Franklin (255), was born in Willimantic, Conn., April 26, 1880, and married Florence Pearl, daughter of Frank H. and Annie L. Johnson, at Monson, Mass., November 30, 1918, who was born July 8, 1886. He is a stationary engineer and resides at 192 Albemarle Street, Springfield, Mass.

307 ARTHUR WESLEY, son of Arminious Wesley (258), was born September 24, 1876, in Mansfield, Conn., and married Ella, daughter of John E. and Eunice E. (Kegwin) Greene, June 29, 1904, at Willimantic, Conn., and resides at 10 Edgerton Street, East Hampton, Conn.

308 HARRY AUGUSTUS, son of Tudor (260), was born in Bloomfield, Conn., January 11, 1876, and married Emma Jane, daughter of Alfred Chesbro and Abigail Jane (Haskins) Case, at Bloomfield September 27, 1905, who was born there January 13, 1877. He is an architect, attached to the Supervising Architect's Office, Treasury Department, Washington, D. C., and resides at 4437 Holladay Street, Brentwood, Md.

Children:

ABIGAIL AUGUSTA, born August 12, 1906, at Waterbury, Conn.
HARRY AUGUSTUS, born February 1, 1908, at Washington, D. C.
TUDOR, born October 14, 1909, at Washington, D. C.
ALFRED CASE, born December 7, 1917, at Washington, D. C.

309 ERNEST LEANDER, son of Nelson (263), married Anne, daughter of Benjamin F. and Harriet (Fowler) Gates, at New London, Conn., October 15, 1894.

Children:

CHARLOTTE ANNA, born in New London, Conn., November 16, 1895, is a teacher and resides at 90 Mountain Road, West Hartford, Conn.

HOMER GATES, born in New London, April 6, 1897, died in infancy.

THEODORE ROBERT (318a).

ERNEST LEANDER (318b).

MARJORIE E., born February 8, 1911, at New London, Conn.

310 ARTHUR LOUIS, son of Edwin Carlton (265), was born at Viola, Minn., August 24, 1896. He graduated at the University of Minnesota, and was First Lieutenant in the 27th Squadron, First Pursuit Group, U. S. Air Service, and saw service at Chateau-Thierry and in the battle of the Marne. He was shot down behind the German lines and was a prisoner of war for four months at Laon, France, and at Karlsruhe and Landshut, Germany. He is the Department Sales Manager of the Chicago Mill and Lumber Co., and resides at 1810 Chicago Avenue, Evanston, Ill.

311 JAMES BARTLETT, son of James Morris (269), was born at New Haven, Conn., June 11, 1862, and married Eleanor, daughter of James K. and Eleanor (Banta) Howard, February 14, 1893, who was born in New York City February 4, 1867, and died April 16, 1918. He graduated from Williams College in 1884, where he was a member of the Chi Psi Fraternity. He is a Past Master of the Montauk Lodge, F. & A. M. 286, Brooklyn, and a member of the Crescent Athletic Club of Brooklyn, and the Arkwright Club of New York. He is engaged in the insurance business in New York City and resides at 119 Lincoln Place, Brooklyn.

Children:

ROBERT HOWARD (321).

JAMES BARTLETT (322).

312 FRANCIS HENRY, son of Ezra J. (272), was born in South Boston May 13, 1865, and married (1st) Nellie Pearl Green of Kansas City, Mo., and (2d) Lilly Kossman Burnham, at Jamaica Plains, Mass., June 14, 1898. He was a manufacturer and died at Malden July 20, 1925.

Children:

HELEN MARGARET, born in Kansas City, Mo., October 31, 1893.

LILLIAN ALBERTA, born at Wollaston, Mass., December 22, 1899.

LEWIS FRANCIS (323).

ROBERT HENRY, born in Jamaica Plains, Mass., April 25, 1906, and lives at 1099 Fellsway, Malden, Mass.

ALFRED K., born in Jamaica Plains, September 14, 1908, resides at 38 Lambert Street, Medford, Mass.

313 GLENVILLE WILLIAM, son of William E. (281), was born in Springfield Township, Erie County, Penn., December 25, 1890, and married Ethel, daughter of William Duvall and Parmelia (Boueltinghouse) Pratt, February 18, 1914, at North Girard, Penn., who was born November 10, 1890. During 1911-12 he was an assistant on the Pennsylvania State Highway Corps, and in 1918 Civil Service Clerk in the Quartermaster's Corps, Washington, D. C. He is now an insurance agent and resides at 1056 West Sixth Street, Erie, Penn.

Child:

WILLIAM PRATT, born May 23, 1921.

314 HENRY LINCOLN, son of Joseph Lincoln (283), was born in Boston, Mass., September 17, 1869, married Clara F. Reading at Malden, Mass., June 16, 1896, and died at Quincy, Mass., October 29, 1900.

Child:

RUTH, born May 8, 1898, married Samuel Ripley of Quincy, Mass., October 11, 1922. They have two children, Joan, born September 23, 1923, and Carol, born May 4, 1927.

314a ROSS KITTRIDGE, son of Joseph L. (283), was born November 25, 1879, and married Clara F., daughter of Walter Scott and Eliza Clark (Martin) Redding, at Malden, Mass., June 16, 1896, who was born in Boston December 26, 1866. He is a physician and resides at Concord, Mass.

315 JOSEPH LINCOLN, son of Joseph L. (283), was born in Quincy, Mass., February 28, 1873, and married Edith, daughter of Jesse P. and Minnie (Morton) Woodbury, at Francistown, N. H., October 3, 1895, who was born in Quincy February 5, 1874. He was Mayor of Quincy from 1917-21 and is Vice-President of the Hewitt Rubber Company of Boston. He resides at 29 Whitney Road, Quincy, Mass.

Children:

MARY, born October 19, 1901, and married October 25, 1922, Kenneth Edwards.

MINNIE MORTON, born December 26, 1905.

EDITH LOUISE, born October 11, 1908.

PUBLISHERS' NOTE

The "make-up" of this book (each generation beginning on the right hand page) leaves this page available for the following statements, which are in the nature of current advertising at the date of publication, rather than parts of a permanent record.

In the Foreword (Page 8) the care with which the proof sheets have been read with respect to typographical and similar errors, was mentioned.

In many cases only very brief particulars have been obtained. It is hoped that the publication of this genealogy may lead to increased interest in the Whiton Family Association and that more detailed information may be obtained from direct or collateral descendants in many of these cases.

Such additional details may be sent to the Association Secretary at any time and will be included in the next following report to the Annual Association meeting.

Eventually such additional information, and current information from the members of living generations, may justify the publication of a pamphlet supplement, or, in the future, a revised edition.

CRADLE ROLL

Just at the close of the 1932 annual meeting, following a vote instructing the Secretary to send the congratulations of the Association to the parents of children born during the year, the President suggested the establishment of a Cradle Roll. This was enthusiastically approved. It was an impromptu suggestion, not followed (at the late hour) by a definite vote; but the Secretary especially requests notice of all such happy events and will gladly record every such "Doctors Degree" conferred thus early upon new members of the Whiton Family.

COST OF PUBLICATION

The cost of preparing and publishing this Genealogy has very considerably exceeded the amount at first estimated and the guarantee fund then contributed. The sale of the entire edition of 400 copies at the original estimated price will probably not quite cover the cost. It has been necessary for the Whiton Family Association, Inc., to borrow a considerable sum to finance the publication.

Hitherto the Association income has been only the small sum obtained by voluntary contributions from those attending the annual meetings. A special Finance Committee was appointed at the 1932 meeting to consider this subject. After such consideration this Committee may recommend that an annual dues fee be substituted for contributions at the annual meetings, a portion of this income to be applied in liquidation of any debt which may remain after the books have been distributed; or it may devise and recommend some other plan.

Copies of this Genealogy may be obtained by writing to the Chairman of the Publication Committee, Lucius E. Whiton, New London, Conn.

ELEVENTH GENERATION

316 RUSSELL RUTHERFORD, son of Roscoe Benjamin (290), spells his name Whitten, was born at Sydney, Nova Scotia, January 22, 1906. He is a student of entomology at the Massachusetts Argricultural College, and a member of the Lambda Chi Alpha Fraternity, residing at 104 Ashland Street, Melrose Hills, Mass.

317 HARRY FINLAY, son of Henry Grant (291), was born in Troy, N. Y., May 21, 1892. He is a graduate of the Albany Law School, and was admitted to the Bar of the State of New York in 1918, and practices in Troy where he resides. He married in New York City, January 7, 1931, Katherine Marion, daughter of John P. and Bertha A. (Schotte-Grieme) Nelson.

318 STEPHEN CARTER, son of Frank Warren (302), was born in Hartford October 16, 1901, and married Dorothy Celeste Corder, June 7, 1925. He is a graduate of the American School of Osteopathy of Kirksville, Mo., and practices in Hartford, Conn., where he resides at 25 Keney Terrace.

318a THEODORE ROBERT, son of Ernest Leander (309), born in New London, Connecticut, November 7, 1900, and married April 23, 1924, Edna Louise, daughter of Mr. and Mrs. Max Ponedel of Waterford, Conn. He is a mechanical draughtsman with the Atwood Machine Co. of Stonington, Conn., and lives in New London.

Child:

THEODORE R., JR., born April 3, 1925.

318b ERNEST LEANDER, son of Ernest Leander (309), born in New London, Conn., November 9, 1901, married February 8, 1931, Marcella Frances, daughter of Mr. and Mrs. Ernest A. Harris of Columbus, Ohio. He is a traveling representative of the Arrow Hart & Hegeman Electric Co., and lives in Columbus, Ohio.

319 ROBERT HOWARD, son of James Bartlett (311), was born in Brooklyn, N. Y., February 5, 1894, and married Margaret, daughter of John H. and Clara Louise Low, at Cranford, N. J., October 17, 1924, who was born in Bayonne, N. J., January 27, 1903. He is a member of the New York Stock Exchange. He trained at the first Plattsburg camp and went to France as 2d Lieutenant of the 316th Infantry, 77th Division, returning at the end of the war a staff officer with the rank of captain and personal aide to General Alexander. He resides at 25 East 9th Street, New York City, and at Westport, Conn. They have a son born in August, 1932.

320 JAMES BARTLETT, son of James Bartlett (311), was born in Brooklyn, N. Y., November 3, 1896, and married Ethel Sutton. He volunteered at the declaration of war and served throughout, being assigned in charge of auto service at the Base Hospital on Staten Island, and was made sergeant.

321 LEWIS FRANCIS, son of Francis Henry (312), was born at Jamaica Plains, Mass., July 3, 1903, and married Edna, daughter of Curtis Andrew Jackson and Alexandrine (Bonin) Foster, at Fall River, Mass., March 4, 1904. He is an accountant and resides at 119 Brainard Road, Allston, Mass.

Appendix A

THE AMIDON FAMILY

A. 1. JULIA SOPHIA WHITON, daughter of Stephen (192), was born in Ashford, Conn., April 7, 1849, and died March 26, 1925. She was married November 11, 1868, at Ashford, to Gilbert Eliphalet, son of Horatio and Marcia (Strong) Amidon, who was born August 20, 1836, at Ashford and died November 27, 1918. He was a graduate of the New Britain Normal School, and a teacher and farmer. They had nine children all born in Ashford: 1. Charles Sanford, born November 9, 1869, and married (1st) Alice May, daughter of Lucien W. and Angeline (Clark) Holt, at East Willington November 19, 1894, who was born July 3, 1875, at Willington, and died April 1, 1919, and (2d) Nettie, daughter of George and Mary (Griggs) Copeland, on September 14, 1926, at Hampton, Conn., who was born at Mansfield, Conn., September 26, 1892. He is a manufacturer of portable saw-mills at East Willington. He had ten children, all by his first wife, and born in Willington: (a) Raymond Holt, born February 20, 1896, married Clara Maud, daughter of Frank and Emma (Plumley) Pearl, in Willimantic, Conn., January 22, 1921, who was born at South Windham, Conn., December 9, 1894. They have three children born in Willington, where they reside: Charles Malcomb, born November 10, 1921; Clarence Raymond, born July 12, 1923, and June Leone, born June 19, 1925. (b) Frank Rupert, born February 13, 1897, and resides in East Willington. (c) Mildred Julia, born May 9, 1899, graduated at the Willimantic Normal School, and married June 24, 1924, at East Willington, Frederick Maitland, son of William and Caroline (Loomis) Abell, who was born December 10, 1891, at Middletown, Conn. They have one child, Marshall Maitland, born April 8, 1927, at Plainfield, Conn., where they reside. (d) Doris Mabel, born July 21, 1902, is a graduate of the Baptist Institute for Religious Workers at Philadelphia, and is now doing editorial work for the American Baptist Foreign Missionary Society, and resides at 49 West 9th Street, New York City. (e) Lawrence Gilbert Lucien, born July 10, 1904, and resides at East Willington. (f) Charles Rudolph, born August 9, 1906, and resides at East Willington. (g) Alice Hazel, born June 12, 1908, and is training at the Hartford General Hospital. (h) Marjorie Angeline, born August 29, 1909, and died October 21, 1909. (i) Barbara Frances, born December 25, 1917. (j) Elsie Mae, born March 18, 1919. 2. Mary Louisa, born May 11, 1871, married April 26, 1892, at Ashford, John William, son of John and Martha (Taylor) Armitage, who was born January 28, 1869, and resides at Westford. He is engaged in lumber manufacturing in Ashford. They reside in Westford, and have two children, born in Stafford, Conn.: (a) Nathan Gilbert, born June 25, 1895, and married Lina Emma, daughter of Charles and Lena (Isham) Wheeler, at Scotland, Conn. They have one child: Martha Louisa, born February 20, 1928, at Ashford, and reside at Westford. He is engaged with his father in the lumbering business and in 1927-8 represented his town in the General Assembly. (b) Clara Martha, born December 12, 1899, is engaged in stock and poultry raising in Westford. 3. Gilbert Whiton, born August 23, 1872, and married at Godfrey, Ill., July 9, 1908, Catherine Frances, daughter of George and Ellen (Strong) Churchill, who was born August 23, 1868. He has a woodworking shop at Stafford Springs, where he resides. 4. Robert Strong, born June 8, 1875, married October 28, 1903, at Ashford, Josephine Electa, daughter of Lionel and Mary (Calhoun) Prentice, who was born June 30, 1876, at Torrington, Conn. He has a general store at Scotland. They have four children, the first born in Ashford and the others in Tolland, Conn.: (a) Howard Prentice, born December 15, 1905, married Esther, daughter of John and Anna (Anderson) Lawson, who was born September 30, 1905, at North Easton, Mass., where they reside. (b) Helen Constance, born July 7, 1908, and resides at Scotland, Conn. (c) Roberta, born December 14, 1911, and died November 16, 1913. (d) Richard Ross, born July 21, 1913. 5. Lillian, born March 11, 1877, graduated from the Willimantic Normal School, taught school for a number of years and resides at Westford. 6. Andrew Huntington, born March 11, 1879, and married April 3, 1907, at Tolland, Stella Alberta, daughter of Roger and Carrie (Beach) Clough, who was born November 16, 1879. He is engaged in dairy farming in Abington, where he resides, and had five children, the first two born in Stafford, and the others in Abington: (a) Stanley Clough, born January 24, 1908, and is an Inspector for the State Highway Department. (b) Norman Whiton, born October 1, 1909, and is engaged in sheep raising. (c) Ellsworth Sykes, born May 28, 1912, and died July 12, 1925. (d) Ruth Huntington, born September 10, 1914, and (e) Charlotte Beach, born October 16, 1920. 7. Harlan Page, born May 8, 1881, married August 16, 1918, at Thompson Conn., Grace Allen, daughter of Joseph and Addie (Allen) Cruff. They had three children, born at Thompson, where they reside: (a) Gilbert Allen, born September 18, 1919. (b) Julia Delight, born June 4, 1921, and (c) Leon Joseph, born March 4, 1924, and died December 30, 1928. 8. Abigail Delight, born July 22, 1884, graduated from the Willimantic Normal School, has taught school for a number of years and resides at Westford. 9. Henry Nathan, born December 7, 1887, is engaged in farming and lumbering in Ashford and resides at Westford.

THE AMIDON HOMESTEAD
Westford, Conn.

Appendix B

THE BACK FAMILY

B. 1. AMY, daughter of Elijah Whiton (28), was born at Ashford, Conn., August 16, 1773, and married January 30, 1798, Samuel, son of John and Sarah (Bliss) Moore, who was born at Union, Conn., June 9, 1771, and died there August 15, 1861. He was the grandson of James Moore, who emigrated from the North of Ireland in 1717-18, with other Scotch-Irish pioneers; Sarah Bliss was the daughter of Ichabod and Mehitable (Stebbins) Bliss of Brimfield, Mass., and granddaughter of Thomas and Hannah (Cadwell) Bliss and Thomas and Sarah (Strong) Stebbins. She was the great-granddaughter of Samuel and Mary (Leonard) Bliss; Joseph and Sarah (Dorchester) Stebbins; Thomas and Elizabeth (Stebbins) Cadwell, and of Ebenezer and Hannah (Clapp) Strong.

B. 2. SOPHIA, daughter of Amy (Whiton) (B. 1) and Samuel Moore, was born at Union, Conn., December 12, 1802, and married there January 27, 1835, Lucius Back, who was born at Hampton, Conn., May 26, 1803, and died at Holland, ~~Conn~~., September 18, 1879. He was the son of Judah, Jr., and Elizabeth (Abbe) Back, and grandson of Lieutenant Judah and Priscilla (Gates) Back of Hampton, Conn., and great-grandson of John and Elizabeth (Benjamin) Back of Preston, Conn. Elizabeth Benjamin was the daughter of John and Phoebe (Larrabee) Benjamin of Preston, and great-granddaughter of John and Abigail (Eddy) Benjamin, who settled in Cambridge, Mass., in 1632. Priscilla Gates was the daughter of Robert and Mary (Clark) Gates of Preston, granddaughter of Thomas and Margaret (Geer) Gates, and a descendant of Stephen Gates, who settled in Hingham, Mass., about 1638. Elizabeth Abbe was the daughter of the Rev. Joshua, Jr., and Trephena (Bass) Abbe, and granddaughter of Joshua and Mary (Ripley) Abbe, and Henry and Elizabeth (Church) Bass of Windham, Conn. She was a descendant of James Abbe who resided in Salem, Mass., in 1637, and of Governor William Bradford, William Backus, Lion Gardner, Thomas Bingham and Jonathan Rudd.

B. 3. ADNA BACK, son of Lucius and Sophia (Moore) Back (B. 2), was born in Holland, Mass., March 26, 1844, and married Mary Elizabeth Young at Warrenville, Conn., March 10, 1869. She was the daughter of Captain William Clark and Mehitable (Swift) Young, and a descendant of Captain Joseph and Margaret (Warren) Youngs, who settled in Salem, Mass., in 1635, and removed to Southold, L. I., about 1649, and of their grandson, Joseph Youngs, one of the first settlers of Hebron, Conn. She was the granddaughter of William Clark and Nancy (Crane) Young, and great-granddaughter of Eliphalet and Martha (Burnham) Youngs of Hebron, Conn. Nancy (Anna) Crane was born April 3, 1776, and was the daughter of Isaac and Eunice (Walcott) Crane of Windham, Conn., the great-granddaughter of Jonathan and Deborah (Griswold) Crane of Windham, Conn., and great-great-granddaughter of Benjamin and Mary (Backus) Crane of Wethersfield, Conn. Mehitable Swift was the daughter of Ira and Sarah (Robinson) Swift, and the granddaughter of Thomas, Jr., and Mehitable (Barrows) Swift, and great-granddaughter of John and Jerusha (Clark) Swift, and Thomas and Abigail (Crane) Barrows of Mansfield, Conn. Mary Elizabeth Back died at Northampton, Mass., June 30, 1889. Adna Back was in charge of one of the departments of the Nonotuck Silk Company at Florence, Mass., a member, treasurer and trustee of the Methodist Episcopal Church of Florence and superintendent of its Sunday school. He died at Northampton, Mass., December 20, 1887. Their children were: Mary Adella, born at Northampton June 17, 1871, and married Frank Manley Readio; Lucius Adna, born August 18, 1874, and died November 17, 1878; Ernest Adna (B. 4) and Vera Ethel, born February 24, 1882.

B. 4. ERNEST ADNA BACK, son of Adna Back (B. 3), was born at Northampton, Mass., October 7, 1880, and married Clara Winifred, daughter of Frederic Seymour and Harriet Wetmore (Chapell) Newcomb, at New London, Conn., September 27, 1919, who was born at New London February 5, 1884. He graduated from the normal and high schools of Northampton and at Massachusetts Agricultural College (B.S., 1904, and Ph.D., 1907). He is Chief Entomologist in charge of investigations of insects destructive to stored food and manufactured products, in the Bureau of Entomology, United States Department of Agriculture. He is the author of numerous papers on economic entomology, a member of various entomological societies, Cleveland Park Congregational Church, Phi Kappa Phi, and Alpha Sigma Phi fraternities, and of the Cosmos Club, and resides at 2936 Macomb Street, Washington, D. C. Their children are: David Newcomb, born in New London, Conn., September 30, 1920, and Richard Chapell, born in Washington, October 20, 1921.

Appendix C

THE CHISM FAMILY

C. 1. ANNE LUCINDA, daughter of Chauncey Whiton (125), was born July 29, 1836, and married Charles Chism, who was born at Westford, Conn., February 11, 1837, who served as a soldier in the 16th Regiment of Connecticut Volunteers in the Civil War. She died March 21, 1915. He died at Westford Hill April 8, 1931. They had three children: (a) Anna Lucinda, born February 19, 1869, at Westford, married May 20, 1890, William, son of Joseph Franklin and Sophronia (Robbins) Dawley, and resides at 51 Lincoln Avenue, Norwich, Conn. During the World War she was President of the Connecticut Branch of the King's Daughters, and later a Regent of the Faith Trumbull Chapter of the Daughters of the American Revolution. (b) Emily Josephine, born April 3, 1871, and resides at Westford. (c) James Whiton, born February 13, 1876, and married Dora Almira, daughter of Norman and Ellen (Pilcher) Somers, September 29, 1909, who died at Schenectady February 15, 1923, at their home. He died August 11, 1932, at the home of his sister, Mrs. Dawley, in Norwich, Conn.

C. 2. SARAH, daughter of Stephen Whiton (192), was born in Ashford, Conn., June 10, 1846, and married Marvin K. Chism, brother of Charles Chism (supra) at Ashford March 15, 1876, and died at Westford March 7, 1895. They had four children: (a) Frank Ellsworth, born August 29, 1877, resides at Abington, Conn., and married (1st) Margaret Meach, who died in Norwich, Conn., February 24, 1910, and (2d) Blanche Warren at Danielson, Conn., September 19, 1917, who died in Putnam, Conn., January 8, 1919, by whom he had a daughter, Olive Louise, and (3d) Mrs. Lillian (Ballard) Burgess at Pomfret, Conn., on May 1, 1926. (b) Louis Whiton, born June 15, 1879, married Florence, daughter of Isaac Hamilton and Mary (Hunter) Mallory, at Springfield, Mass., June 1, 1910, by whom he had a daughter Lois, born November 26, 1911. He resides at 18 Whittier Street, Springfield, Mass. (c)

Abigail Byles, born May 4, 1881, married Bert Winfred, son of Thomas Henry and Ada Ann Whitehouse of Abington, Conn., October 17, 1908, at Norwich, Conn., who was born in Ashford, Conn., November 25, 1874. They have two children: Karl Chism, born at Pomfret, Conn., August 24, 1910; and Dorothy, born at Pomfret July 22, 1912. (d) Julia Belle, born at Ashford, Conn., January 1, 1884, and married Louis Alva, son of Allen and Ellen (Pomeroy) Gowdy, at Abington, Conn., June 30, 1909, and resides at Hazardville, Conn.

THE CHISM HOMESTEAD
Westford, Conn.

Appendix D

THE INGERSOLL FAMILY

MARY WHITON, daughter of John (55), was born October 23, 1786, in Stockbridge, Mass., and married February 4, 1813, Henry Ingersoll, a physician, who removed to Ithaca, N. Y., and subsequently to Canton, Ill., where he died March 14, 1872. She died March 17, 1875. They had four children: (a) Henry, born October 31, 1815, who married at Lewiston, Ill., April 2, 1846, Evaline A. Dewey, who, it was said, was the first white child born in the United States west of the Illinois River. They had five children: (1) Charles Edward, born July 3, 1849, who married December 9, 1880, Alice Caroline Parlin, having three children: Winifred, born March 2, 1883; William Parlin, born February 2, 1885, and Charles Dewey, born January 14, 1887. (2) Ernest, born August 7, 1853, married June 22, 1881, Edith Munn, and had a son Max, born March 12, 1883. (3) Wyllys King, born August 8, 1856, studied at the New York Homeopathic Medical College, and is a physician in Philadelphia; married ——— Beck, and resides at 4004 Chestnut Street, West Philadelphia, Pa. (4) Eva Dewey, born March 17, 1859. (5) Sylvia Whiton, born October 1, 1862, and married November 22, 1893, Thomas T. Woodruff. Their children were: Thomas Tyson, born November 19, 1894; Henry Ingersoll, born February 6, 1896, and died February 18, 1896, and Wyllys Ingersoll, born May 7, 1897, and died July 23, 1897. (b) John Whiton was born December 24, 1817, and married June 6, 1841, Elizabeth Cook Sage, a sister of Henry W. Sage, at Ithaca, N. Y. They removed to Canton, Ill., where he died September 28, 1877. They had the following children: (1) Henry Sage, born September 1, 1842, at Canton, and married Ida M. Sayles at Einona, Mich., and had four children: Elizabeth Sayles, born September 26, 1874; Grace Louise, born May 8, 1878; Florence, born November 7, 1880, and Alma Henrietta, born July 14, 1887. (2) Ellen Amelia, born April 24, 1844, at Canton, studied medicine and became a practicing physician, skilled in her profession. She died in November, 1888. (3) Mary Elizabeth, born November 11, 1850, at Canton, and married Humphrey Bell at Canton April 29, 1875, and had three children: Edith Thornton, born February 14, 1878; Bertha Sage, born April 6, 1879, and Harold Ingersoll, born August 16, 1880. (c) Mary Griswold was born February 21, 1820, and died at Ithaca February 10, 1846. (d) Edward Payson, was born November 10, 1828, and married (1st) Ann Eliza Lord at Canton, who was born at Lyme, Conn., October 20, 1829, and died at Canton, December 15, 1861. They had two children: (1) Edward Arthur, born June 27, 1858, at Canton, and (2) John Lord, born May 13, 1860; and (2d) Emmaline Warren at Rushville, Ill., March 24, 1863, who was born at Winchester, Tenn., October 30, 1830, by whom he had three children: Warren, Harry, and Nellie Whiton.

CAROLINE E., daughter of Luther (105), and niece of Mary (supra), was born April 1, 1830, and married at Rochester, N. Y., Jared O'M. Ingersoll, M.D., who was born at Pittsfield, Mass., June 21, 1824, and died at Ithaca April 13, 1859. She died at San Diego, Cal., June 10, 1887. They had three children: (a) Mary Cooper, born May 22, 1851, and died May 3, 1857; (b) Frederick Augustus, born February 15, 1853, and died January 12, 1903, and (c) Albert Mills, born August 9, 1857, and married Laura Isabel Stevens, and resides at 908 F Street, San Diego, Cal.

Appendix E

THE RICHARDS FAMILY

HELEN DOROTHY, daughter of John Milton (122) was born July 8, 1814, and died in Meriden, N. H., March 10, 1860. She married in 1836, Professor Cyrus S. Richards, L.L.D., of Hartford, Vt. He was principal of Kimball Union Academy for over thirty-six years. Their children were: (a) Helen Morris, born in 1837, and married Rev. George P. Herrick, D.D., and died in 1920. He lived for over fifty years as a Missionary in Turkey. Their children were: (1) Frederick Morris, who resides in New York City; (2) George, deceased; (3) Marion Tyler, resides at Drew Seminary, Carmel, N. Y., and (4) Abbie, deceased. (b) Rev. Charles Herbert, born in Meriden, N. H., in 1839, and died in 1925. He graduated at Yale College in 1860 and the Union Theological Seminary in 1864, and married Marie Miner. Their children were: (1) Paul Stanley, born in 1870, married Mary Block and died in 1922; (2) Charles Miner, born in 1872 and died in 1877; (3) Helen Dorothy, who resides at 3900 Spuyten Duyvel Parkway, New York City; (4) Marie Louise, married Paul Terry Cherington and resides at 159 Park Avenue, Greenwich, Conn., having two children: Charles Richard, born in 1913, and Paul Whiton, born in 1918; (5) Mildred Whiton, born in 1890, and (6) Gladys Lyman, who married Murray Hoffman Stevens and resides at 15 Jacobus Place, New York City. (c) Abbie Louise, born in 1842, married Rev. Frank Porter Woodbury, D.D.; six children: (1) Claire, married William Holbrook and died in 1897, one child, Allison, died in infancy; (2) Alice, married Rossiter Howard, two children, Elizabeth and John Tasker, the latter born in 1911; (3) Frank, died in infancy; (4) Abbie, married John Langdon Hawes, two children, John Richards, born in 1903, and Frank Woodbury, born in 1905; (5) Mary, married Tasker Howard, M.D., two children, Anne and Tasker, the latter born in 1913; (6) Margaret, married George Burton Hotchkiss, had five children: George Burton, born in 1911, Barbara, Jean, Margaret Richards, born in 1922, and Mary. They reside at Hawthorne Place, Flushing, N. Y.

Appendix F

THE TUCKERMAN FAMILY

F. 1. SARAH, daughter of Elijah (28), was born October 26, 1764, at Ashford, Conn., and married Roger Ascham Crain, May 20, 1784, at Ashford and had children. (See Crain Genealogy.) One of their children was Abigail, born September 14, 1786, who married David Hopkins November 11, 1813, and died September 16, 1833, at Groton, N. Y. (See Descendants of James Hopkins and Jean Thompson of Voluntown, Conn.) Their children: Alfred, born December 26, 1815; Warner Whiton (F. 2); Nancy Jane, born August 15, 1818; Mary Abigail, born November 11, 1820; Harriet, born July 26, 1821; David, born November 24, 1822; Phebe Ann, born June 4, 1824; Charles Morrison, and Hannah, born October 30, 1829, all born at Groton, N. Y.

F. 2. WARNER WHITON HOPKINS, son of David Hopkins (F. 1), was born January 19, 1817, at Groton, N. Y., and married Lucy Ann Slater, daughter of Amos and Fanny (Seymour) Slater, February 2, 1847, at Cherry Valley, Ohio, who was born November 16, 1822, at Norwich, N. Y., and died at West Andover, Ohio, January 12, 1909. Warner was a County Surveyor of Ashtabula County, Ohio, and was an officer in the Quartermaster's Department in St. Louis and New York City during the Civil War. He died at West Andover, Ohio, February 27, 1895. Their children were: Mary Ellen (F. 3), Harriet Cornelia, born July 28, 1850, and died at West Andover, Ohio, March 26, 1876; Addison Warner, born June 6, 1852, married Isabel Aurelia Root, who lives at 47 McGovern Street, Ashtabula, Ohio. He was a well-known physician and surgeon and died March 5, 1927; Silas Gilbert, born November 9, 1853, married Ella Batholomew, who died August 13, 1906, and he resides at West Middlesex, Penn.; John Howard, born May 22, 1855, at West Andover, married Mary Rosalie Hyde and resides at Salem, Ohio; Margaret Lucy, born September 14, 1857, and married Rev. Levi Gaylord Kendall, and resides in De Leon Street, Tampa, Fla.

F. 3. MARY ELLEN, daughter of Warner Whiton Hopkins, was born at West Andover, Ohio, September 13, 1848, and married Louis Bryant Tuckerman, son of Jacob and Elizabeth (Ellinwood) Tuckerman, there February 15, 1875. He was born at Cleveland, Ohio, February 15, 1850, practiced as a physician and surgeon in Cleveland, and died there March 5, 1902. She resides at 1387 East 105th Street, Cleveland. Their children are: Jacob Edward, born August 23, 1876, and practices as a physician and surgeon at Austinburg, Ohio; M. Katherine Barton, resides at 1387 East 105th Street, Cleveland; William Colegrove, born May 29, 1878, practices as a physician and surgeon at the last address; Warner Hopkins, born May 29, 1878, at West Williamsfield, Ohio, married Florence McMilly, deceased, and practices as a physician and surgeon at 3120 Corydon Road, Cleveland; Louis Bryant, born September 26, 1879, at West Williamsfield, married Una Venable, and has a position with the Bureau of Standards at Washington, D. C., residing at 4605 Stanford Street, Chevy Chase, Maryland, and had an infant daughter born January 29, 1901, and died at Austinburg, Ohio, March 13, 1901; Lois Margaret, born February 11, 1885, at Cleveland, married Dr. L. E. Mook and resides at 3253 Ormond Road, Cleveland.

RECORDS OF WHITONS NOT PLACED

Oliver C. Whiton of Goshen, married Lavinia Pearcy (Percy?) October 22, 1920.

——— Whiton of Willington, married Eliza Clark of Mansfield by Rev. Henry Greenslit. No date. Rev. Henry Greenslit was located at Windham, Conn., 1839-1848.

Eaton Whiton from Willington admitted freeman at Hampton in 1842.

Louis C. (Lorin?) Whiton, son of Lorin and Lucinda, born January 5, 1851. Somers.

Walter U. Whiton, son of John B. (coffee-grinder), and Gertrude, born July 28, 1849. Norwich.

Sarah Whiton, daughter of John B. (æt. 41), and Gertrude (ae. 32), born August 1, 1851. Norwich.

David and Eleanor, twin children of Whitfield and Rachel Whiton, born March 18, 1783. Ashford.

In the old cemetery at Westford Hill is a stone with this inscription: "In memory of Mr. Whitfield and Mrs. Rachel Whiting. Mr. Whiting died Sept. 23d, 1822 ae 83 years. Mrs. Whiting died July 17, 1820 ae 75 Years." A child Nathaniel or (Nathan) aged (perhaps) 5 years lies near. Miss Chism says: "Rachel was Rachel Haile of Rhode Island, I think. There was a Hale Whiting who married Abigail Morey in 1793 and they had a son Nathaniel. Hale was probably the son of Whitfield. Whitfield also had a daughter Eleanor (see above) who married Benjamin Chapman, Jr., in 1805. Two of the grandsons of Benjamin Chapman, named Sharpe, were Presbyterian ministers out in Ohio, I think."

Query: Where does Whitfield Whiting (or Whiton) connect? He was born 1738/9.

A Copy of Original Massachusetts Muster Rolls, The Property of The Society of Colonial Wars in the State of New York

(Presented by LOUIS C. WHITON, a member.)

Co. D

A list of the Foot Company of solgers in Hanover in the County of Plymoth in New England under the command of Capt. Ezeckel Turner and Capt. Baniam Stetson, and Ensigne John Bailey.

Sergants: Seth Setson, Joseph Bates, Joseph Hoose, David Cortis.
Corporals: Samuel Hoose, Othnial Prat, Stephen Torey, Simeon Curtis.

John Studley
Ezeckel Palmer
Nathaniel Gill
Preble Hoose
William Curtis
Ruben Curtis
Cornilas Brigs
Jese Curtis
Jacob Baley, Junr.
Solmon Bates
Isaac Grove
Isaac Lambord
Talen Brooks
James Cornish
Addom Stetson
Luther Step
David Genckens
Thomas Palmer
John Baley
Abner Curtis
Nathaniel Joslyng
Joshua Simmons
Joseph Daniel
Beniam Stetson, Junior
Thomas Barstow
William Withrell Eals
Joseph Cane
Elahab Stedley
Beniam Stedley
Jacob Whiten
Ezeckel Turner, Junior
Josiah Tomas
Ezekel Curtis
John Love
Joshua Plmer
Seth Woodworth
Clamon Bates, Jun.
John Stetson
Beniam Taler
Nathaniel Stetson
Josiah Cornish
Elisha Plmer
Thomas Silvester
Josua Staples
Jeremiah Hatch
Isaac Hatch, Junr.
Thomas Wilcks
John Curtis, Junr.
David Hoose
Ebenezer Woodworth
Abiger Stetson
Thomas Whiten
John Bray
William Whiten
Thomas Calmon
Job Stetson
David Hoose, Junr.
Robert lenthen Eals
Beniam Cane
Lemuel Curtis
Addom Prouty
Eccobod Tomas
James Bates
Jeremiah Hatch, Junr.
Thomas Coock
James Silvester
Isaiah Wing
Lemuel Otis
Amos Woodworth
Thomas Joslyng, Junr.
Joseph Hose, Junr.
Joshua Staples, Junr.
Stephen Torey, Junr.
Joseph Ramsdel
Jese Teage
Nemiah Ramsdel
Charles Paley
Solveny Wing, Junr.

Jubel Monrow
Jabes Joslyng
Caleb Rogrs
Uriah Lambord
Joseph Bats, Junr.
Beniam Silvester, Junr.
Jacob Silvester
Thomas Torey
Jese Torey
Samuel Withrell, Junr.
John Torey
Beniam Turner
Solmon Bates, Junr.
Samuel Barstow, Junr.
Seth Bates
Thomas Hill
Amos Silvester
John Joslyng
Theophilus Withrell, Jr.
Seth Stetson, Junr.
Joseph Calmon

(Endorsed on the side.)

Joseph House of Hanover,
in the Joseph Bates
Joseph Stetson. Joseph House, Junr.
Ramsdell. Edmund Semeon
Lot. 9, 1750 in Hanover
in the County of Plumouth, Mass.

A List of the Willing Soldiers under ye command of Capt. Theophilus Cushing of Hingham, being the Second Foot Company in ye Town, Septr. ye 15, 1755.

Sargt. Joseph Stowers
Sargt. Robart Garnitt
Sargt. Jacob Sprague
Sargt. Sam'l Witon

Solomon Dunber
Nathaniel Stodder
Joseph Tower
Daniel Witon
Samuel Low, Junr.
Nehemiah Sprague
Thomas Garnitt
Isaac Witon, Junr.
Ephram Wilder
Solomon Witon
Solomon Loring, Junr.
Caleb Campbell
Pyam Cushing
Benj. Sharkey
Peter Tower, Jr. 3
Benj. Stowel
Thomas Wilder, Junr.
Jonathan Farrow
John Garnitt
Sam'l Tpwer
Stephen Garnitt, Junr.
John Jacob, Junr.
Isaier Tower
Enoch Stafford
Peter Hobart, Junr.
Jacob Witon
Mark Witon
Peleg Garnett
Nathaniel Garnitt, Junr.
Jabes Loring
David Garnitt, Junr.
Jonathan Dunbar
Benj. Dunbar
Sam'l Wilder
Joshua Witon
Isaier Stodderd
Jonathan Witon
Joshua Garnitt
Joseph Carrier
Noah Garnitt
William Garnitt
Jacob Sprague, Junr.

Cor. Sam'l Garnitt, Jun.
Cor. David Farrow
Cor. Abel Cushing
Cor. James Hek Lewies

Isaac Wilder, Junr.
James White
Elijah Whiton
Joseph Garnitt
Jonathan Anderson
Seth Dunbar
Elisha Whiton
Malichi Tower
Wil'm Prouley
James Stodderd
Abraham Witon
Job Loring
Theop's Wilder, Junr.
James Hazard
Robert Dunber, Junr.
George Lane French
Isac Smith, Junr.
Norman Garnitt
Benjamin Ward
Jacob Dunber
Elisha Garnett
Moffat Jacob
Elijah Whiton, Junr.
Enoch Witon
Nathaniel Garnett
Stephen Garnett
Benjamin Garnett
Isreal Lazael
James Day
Ebenezer Cushing
John Cushing
Elisha Cushing
Theophus Wilder
Isich Wilder
Edward Wilder
Edward Ward, Junr.
Jonathan French
Peter Tower, Sr.
Peter Tower, Junr.
Joshua Hovey, Junr.
Nehemiah Hazard

A Larom List of the Second Foot Company. The Command of Capt. Stephen Cushing of Hingham.

Capt. Stephen Cushing
Lt. Abel Cushing
Insi. Hezekiah Leavitt
Ser. Marthew Sprague
Ser. Enoch Whiton
Ser. Joshua Burr
Ser. Thomas Wilder
Corp. Ephram Wilder
Corp. John Hall
Corp. Benjamin Gernitt
Corp. Peter Jacob
Clerk Theophilus Cushing
Clerk Hezekiah Cushing
Drom. Jonathan Burr
Drom. Thomas Jones
Capt. Thomas Loring

Presarvit Holl
Peter Ripley
John Lazel
Henry Garnitt
James Day
Robert Dunber
Thomas Whiton
John Smith
Seth Cushing
Nathaniel Wilder
Mark Whiton
Luke Whiton
Josiah Sprague, Junr.
Ephram Sprague
Solomon Whiton
Noah Ripley
Samuel Goold
Peter Ripley, Junr.
Thomas Tower
David Garnitt
Daniel Beal
Joseph Stower

INDIAN AND COLONIAL WARS

Abraham (41)
Daniel (27)
Elijah (44)
Elisha (47)
Enoch (5)
Enoch (43)
Jacob (42)
James (2)
James (3)
James (7)
John (13)
Jonathan (46)
Joshua, p. 31
Samuel (26)
Solomon (34)
Stephen (40)
Thomas (18)
William (32)

also

John Shaw, p. 35

REVOLUTIONARY WAR

Abel (69)
Abijah (38)
Abraham (41)
Amasa (58)
Asa (74)
Barzillai (49)
Benjamin (67)
Comfort (35)
Daniel (56)
Ebenezer (54)
Elias (45)
Elias (73)
Elijah (44)
Elijah (61)
Elijah (77)
Elisha (47)
Enoch (43)
Ezekiel (68)
Ezra (78)
Hosea (27)
Isaac (39)
Israel (63)
Israel (82)
Jacob (42)
James (29)
James (51)
James (71)
John, p. 38
Jonathan (46)
Joseph, p. 43
Joseph (53)
Joseph (60)
Joseph (76)
Jotham (48)
Lemuel (33)
Levi (90)
Matthew (23)
Moses (79)
Nathan, Jr. (24), p. 37
Nathan (92)
Ozias (31), p. 44
Peleg (34), p. 46
Peter (38), p. 48
Samuel (33), p. 45
Samuel (65)
Solomon (34)
Solomon, Jr. (34), p. 46
Stephen (40)
Thomas (31)
Thomas (52)
Thomas (70)
Zachariah (57)
Zenas (59)

also

Nathan Bullock (10), p. 29
Peter Eastman (64), p. 71
Ammi Paulk (121), p. 105
Abijah Smith, Sr. (28), p. 42

WAR OF 1812

Abner (120)
Archelaus (128)
Elijah, Jr. (121)
Flavel (123)
Hosea (112)
Job Stowell (147)
Joseph (53)
Sylvanus (109)
Theophilus (111)
Thomas (100)
Walter (44)

also

Josiah Clark (221), p. 156
Abijah Smith, Jr. (28), p. 42

CIVIL WAR

Alpha, Lieut. (171)
George W. (166) Killed
Henry, Corporal (261)
Henry Benjamin, M.D. (233)
John, Sergeant (120)
John Chadwick, Colonel (212)
Lester, Lieut. (259*a*)
Loring Livingston (230)
Lyman Barnes, Major (227)
Nelson (263)
Porter, Corporal (259*b*)
Tudor (260)
Wilbur (194A)
William Henry (179)

also

Carlos A. Bombard (204)
Charles Chism (App. C.)
Penuel Eddy (119)
Warner W. Hopkins (App. F.)

WORLD WAR

Alpha Ray, Lieut. (292)
Arthur Louis, Lieut. (310)
Charles Edward, Lieut. (288)
Glenville William, Quartermaster's Corps (313)
Henry Grant, Chief Inspector of Ordinance (291)
James Bartlett (320)
Juliet (234)
Louis C., Lieut. (297)
Robert Howard (319)
Sylvester G. (305)
Walter Humiston, Lieut. (304)
Walter Thayer (303)

also

Herbert Kelly (60)
Walker Kelly (60)
John Franklin Merrill (253)

Augustus Sherrill (296) served two years in Squadron A, National Guard of New York.

David Thomas (279) served ten years in Massachusetts State Militia and two years in Connecticut State Guard, according to family records.

Starkes (142) served in Massachusetts Militia in 1805, according to a muster roll in possession of Hingham Historical Society.

James Weston Myers (180) Adjutant General of State of New York at the time of his death, April, 1929.

There are many other names of Whitons and Whitings in the Massachusetts and Connecticut Records and Muster Rolls, but they have not been included as they could not be identified.

References

Ancient Landmarks of Plymouth, Mass. Davis. 1899.
Ancient Wethersfield, Conn. Stiles. 1904.
Ancient Windsor. Stiles. 1892.
Antrim. John Milton Whiton.
Colonial Families of the U. S. Rhoades. 1920.
Connecticut Men in the Revolution. Published by the State.
Connecticut Revolutionary Sick Bills.
Connecticut State Records.
Converse Genealogy. Charles A. Converse. 1905.
Crane Genealogy. Ellery B. Crane. 1895.
Draper's Pensions.
Early History of Tolland. L. P. Tolland.
Genealogical Dictionary of First Settlers of New England. Savage. 1862.
Genealogical Register of First Settlers of New England. Farmer. 1829.
Historical Register of Officers of the Continental Army. Hertman. 1914.
Historical Sketch of the Town of Hanover. Barry. 1883.
History of Lancaster, Mass. Marvin. 1883.
History of the Town of Hingham. 1893.
History of Windham County, Conn. Larned. 1880.
Mayflower Descendants. Mayflower Society of Mass.
Niles Register and Family Records.
Old Houses of the Ancient Town of Norwich.
New York in the Revolution, and supplement. Published by the State. 1900.
Pioneers of Massachusetts. Pope. 1900.
Vital Records, Records of Deeds and Probate Proceedings in Boston, Hartford, Hingham, Lee, Middletown, Pittsfield and Plymouth. Also old Tombstones in Hingham, Great Barrington, Stockbridge, Middletown and Westford.

INDEX—Descendants

References are to pages

WHITEN

Benjamin 43
Jacob 219
Joseph 43
Nathaniel 43
Ozias 44
Thomas 43, 219
William 219

WHITING

Abby 123
Abel H. 151
Abigail 86, 96
Abigail (Morey) 218
Adelaide 113
Adoniram 85, 124
Albert 124, 151
Amasa 100
Anabel 184
Ann Eliza 100
Augusta 123
Avis 77
Benjamin 57, 86, 124
Betsy 114
Betty 77
Betsy C. 113
Caleb 77
Caroline 96, 123
Catherine 100
Charles 75
Cynthia 114
Daniel 66, 83, 95, 96
Edward 124
Eleanor 85
Elisha 85, 123
Eliza 96
Elizabeth Doten 85
Ella S. 112
Ellen 123
Ellis 86
Elmer 114
Emma 123
Ephraim 57, 86
Ephraim W. 112
Fanny 123
Frances 96, 111
Francis 66
Gardner 96
George 85, 123
George D. 114
Georgianna 123
Hale 218
Hannah 86
Hannah M. 113
Harriet 66, 124

WHITING

Henry 85, 123, 124
Henry W. 184
Ida E. 184
Iowa 123
Jairus 113
James 42
James Harvey 85
Joanna 38
John 86, 123
John B. 151
Joseph 85, 123
Joseph Jacob 100
Josiah 57, 86, 124
Josie 57
Judith 39
Laura A. 113
Leah 66
Leavitt 124
Levi 57, 85, 86
Lewis 96, 113, 151
Lucius A. 151, 184
Lucy M. 113
Lydia 124
Lyman 96
Marcia 113
Margaret 39
Martha 86
Martin 75
Mary.......... 39, 57, 76, 77, 114, 123
Mary R. 114
Mary W. 112
Nancy 86
Nathan 57, 85, 113, 123, 218
Nathaniel 218
Nelson 96
Olive 75, 85
Oren 113, 150
Oren T. 151
Pelham 123
Phoebe 96
Polly 123
Rachel 75, 218
Rebecca 86, 96
Samuel 38, 85
Sarah 66, 85
Sarah A. 112
Simeon 114
Sophia 66
Stephen 86
Sylvanus 77, 113
Thankful 75
Thomas 74, 75, 112
Thomas H. B. 113
Triphena 114

WHITING
Walter 114
Whitfield 218
William 77, 114
William P. 75, 112
Winslow 123
Zenas 65
Zenas Loring 66

WHITON
Abbie Harriet 154
Abbie Morris 108
Abbie R. Ripley 154
Abel 30, 43, 44, 74, 222
Abigail 23, 25, 28, 29, 40, 43, 46, 56, 63, 65, 72, 74, 83, 84, 97, 107, 109
Abigail Augusta 198
Abigail Bowker 99
Abigail W. 43
Abijah 32, 47, 48, 79, 80, 117, 156, 222
Abner 68, 104, 105, 222
Abraham 32, 41, 49, 50, 57, 222
Ada Bowker 139
Addie 171
Addie Keziah 132
Adelaide L. 122
Adelaide M. 127
Adeline 100, 116, 136
Adeline Francis 142
Adeline Osborn 136
Agnes 60
Agnes Lavina 92
Agnes Lillian 129
Agnes O. 192
Albert 83, 100, 119, 138, 158, 178
Albert C. 133
Albert Elbert 174
Albert Ernest 198
Albert F. 137
Albert Franklin 140, 174
Albert G. 95, 135
Albert Hersey 158
Albert L. 137
Albert T. 138
Alberta 135
Alden 83, 113
Alfred B. 137, 170
Alfred Case 198
Alfred K. 200
Alice 27, 30, 85, 171, 173
Alice Alena 177
Alice Lincoln 152
Alice Maria 161
Alice P. 174
Alice R. 99
Alida Ashmead 159
Almira 120, 126, 132

WHITON
Alpha 90, 128, 223
Alpha Mason 128, 161
Alpha Ray 162, 191, 223
Alpheus 27, 35
Althea Violet 169
Alvan 82, 121
Alvin George 163
Amanda 57, 93
Amasa 40, 64, 139, 170, 222
Ambrose 74
Amelia S. 83
Ammi 106
Ammi Paulk 147, 181
Amoret T. 131
Amos 57, 74, 76
Amy 42, 208
Amy Ann 105
Andrew 74, 96, 139, 170
Angeline S. 137
Angeline Bell 167
Ann 31, 99
Ann Eliza 100
Anna 37, 47, 69, 72, 80
Anna Easterbrook 119
Anna Eliza 92
Anna Gertrude 190
Anna L. 97
Anna Lincoln 152
Anna Louise 165
Anne 140
Anne Lucinda 110, 211
Annie 114
Annie Laurie 174
Annie Wilson 155
Andrew 74, 96, 140, 170
Anson 170
Anson V. 137
Antoinette 134, 156
Antoinette Jerusha 176
Antoinette Lord 167
Archelaus 73, 112, 223
Arminius Wesley 175
Arnold Grant 191
Artemus 90
Arthur 144
Arthur E. 189
Arthur Elbert 160
Arthur Emerson 164, 192
Arthur H. 176
Arthur Lee 130, 165
Arthur Louis 180, 199, 223
Arthur Lucas 130
Arthur Lyman 159
Arthur Parr 169
Arthur Sylvester 136, 169
Arthur Wesley 175, 198
Asa 44, 46, 77, 78, 114, 222
Asa Allen 114

WHITON
Asenath 73
Ashbel 101, 102, 139
Ashbel Henry 140
Augustus 102, 141
Augustus Sherrill 95, 132, 167, 193, 194, 223
Augustus Ward 133, 166
Avis 44
Awdry 19
Azariah 27, 35, 37
Barzillai 34, 55, 222
Bathsheba 27
Bela 78, 115
Bela H. 115, 151
Bela Herndon 115, 152
Belle 157, 162
Benjamin 23, 30, 43, 57, 72, 73, 76, 111, 117, 222
Benjamin Shurtleff 100, 138
Bertha 82
Bertha E. 174, 181
Bertha Julia 171
Bessie 177
Bessie Mabel 169
Bethea 38
Bethia 25, 27, 51
Betsy 46, 50, 80, 101
Betsy Ann 42
Betty 44, 77, 114
Beulah 45
Blossom 53, 82, 83
Boaz 42, 71
Bonnie Bell 165
Buchsa 45
Caleb 44, 54, 75, 76
Caleb L. 151
Calista 103
Calvin 47, 106, 147
Campbell 81, 120
Caroline 60, 100, 121
Caroline E. 95, 214
Caroline W. 94
Carrie Ettie 129
Carrie Winifred 159
Cassius 129
Catherine 60, 92
Catherine Bowker 138
Catherine Cushing 119
Catherine Delia 88
Catherine Louise 95
Catherine Phelps 181
Celia 44
Charles 64, 96, 99, 100, 108, 121, 129, 138, 159, 162
Charles Albin 108
Charles Alonzo 174
Charles B. 160
Charles Blossom 158

WHITON
Charles Chambers 126
Charles Davis 138
Charles Easterbrook 118
Charles Edward.... 160, 189, 223
Charles Fearing 154, 185
Charles H. 155, 157, 188
Charles L. 176
Charles Loomis 192
Charles Lyman 136, 169
Charles M. 126, 140, 162
Charles Robert 197
Charles S. 173
Charles Skidmore 198
Charles Washington 105
Charles William 192
Charlotte 52, 82, 104, 121
Charlotte Anna 199
Charlotte Bell 174
Charlotte Grosvenor 150
Charlotte Lincoln 151
Chauncey 72, 110
Chauncey Gilbert 156, 186
Chauncey Newton 110
Chester 102, 140
Chloe 50, 51, 80
Christiana 141
Christopher 82
Clara Abigail 170
Clarissa 61, 80, 84
Comfort 31, 46, 222
Cora E. 127
Cora Emma 181
Cora Phinney 165
Coral 188
Cornelius 27
Curtis Warren 129
Cynthia Mabel 168
Cynthia Marsh 95
Cynthia Stetson 112
Daniel 28, 31, 32, 37, 39, 40, 49, 63, 83, 222
Daniel Garfield 59, 92
daughter Alfred B. (248).. 170
daughter Thomas (52) 58
David 22, 24, 31, 32, 47, 48, 50, 67, 79, 80, 97, 110, 116, 154, 218
David Bruce 118
David Erskine 104, 144, 180
David Randall 80, 118
David Thomas...... 156, 187, 223
Davis 65, 99
Davis Jacob 100
Deborah 24, 30, 31, 32, 48, 49, 51, 77, 80
Deborah Kimball 119
Deliverence 42
Dennis G. 192

WHITON
Desire 28, 37, 80, 82, 83
Devereux 134
Dexter 99
Dexter Brigham 151
Diantha S. 137
Dolly 51, 71
Donald Ward 195
Doris Evelyn 163
Dorothy Elton 125
Dorothy Quincy 180
Dorothy Starkes 187
Eaton 218
Eben 115
Ebenezer...... 36, 38, 60, 93, 222
Ebenezer Gay 103, 143
Edgar Benjamin 161
Edmund 76
Edith 175
Edith Caroline 176
Edith Lavina 129
Edith Louise 201
Edith May 163
Edna Aurelia 144
Edna F. 94
Edna Maryland 191
Edna May 163
Edson Erastus 181
Edward 83, 118, 157
Edward Carlton 147
Edward Everett 121, 159
Edward Franklin 103, 144
Edward Humphrey...... 160, 190
Edward L. 176
Edward Nathan 134, 167
Edward Rufus 169
Edward Vernon 59, 92, 93, 130, 166
Edward Winslow.......... 155, 186
Edwin 98, 113, 118, 188
Edwin Carlton 180
Edwin Dwight 140
Edwin Martin 139
Edwin W. 136, 137
Effie 105, 184
Effie Amelia 158
Elbridge 84
Eleanor 218
Eleanor Lovett 186
Eleanor May 164
Eleanor Richmond 152
Eleazer.... 26, 34, 42, 56, 72, 84
Elias...... 33, 44, 52, 53, 76, 222
Elijah........ 29, 33, 35, 37, 40, 41, 52, 67, 68, 69, 70, 71, 77, 78, 82, 83, 84, 102, 103, 105, 106, 114, 120, 152, 185, 222
Elijah, Jr. 221, 223
Elijah Lincoln 115, 151

WHITON
Elinor H. 185
Elisha 27, 33, 35, 53, 54, 57, 221, 222
Elisha Byles 139, 171
Eliza 59
Eliza Porter 158
Eliza Rosebella 140
Elizabeth...... 24, 29, 32, 36, 38, 40, 47, 48, 52, 82, 97, 111, 112, 116, 121, 125, 133, 168
Elizabeth Angelina 140
Elizabeth Bruce 197
Elizabeth Coffin 186
Elizabeth Cordelia 176
Elizabeth Devina 119
Elizabeth Dorothy 106
Elizabeth Julia 148
Elizabeth Loring 153
Elizabeth Pierson 134
Ella Jean 165
Ella Matilda 176
Ellen 92, 120, 157
Ellen J. 141
Ellen L. 164
Ellen Lucretia 110
Elmer E. 175
Elva Luella 128
Emma 54, 55, 115, 182
Emma J. 97
Emily 93, 125, 141, 156
Emily A. 121
Emily E. 119
Emily L. 137
Emmeline J. 132
Enoch 22, 24, 25, 33, 51, 81, 82, 95, 221, 222
Enoch F. 90
Epaphroditus 58
Ephraim...... 38, 55, 57, 83, 122
Erastus 106, 115, 147, 152, 182
Ernest Foss 186
Ernest Leander.... 179, 199, 203
Esther 37, 142
Esther E. 109
Esther Rebecca 159
Ethel Cora 178
Ethel Grace 169
Eunia 111
Eunice 65
Eunice Dana 69
Eunice Julia 168
Evaline 88
Everett Bryant 160
Ezekiel 43, 73, 74, 222
Ezra 47, 76, 78, 79, 113, 115, 184, 222
Ezrah J. 115
Ezra Thomas 153

WHITON
Fannie 154
Fannie B. 184
Fannie Louise 168
Fidelia 80, 81
Flavel 58, 72, 108, 109, 223
Flaveline 109
Flavia Rodelia 109
Flora 113
Flora Daisy 148
Flora Estelle 178
Florena Ella 165
Florence Eugenia 134, 174, 184
Florinda C. 138
Forrest Nelson 179
Frances 94
Frances Howes 152
Frances Jeannette 88
Frances Sylvia 168
Francis 104, 146
Francis E. 94
Francis Henry 140, 175, 184, 200
Frank 127
Frank E. 164
Frank Earl 163
Frank H. 176
Frank Henry 108
Frank J. 163
Frank Louis 147
Frank Monroe 159
Frank Warren 170, 195
Franklin 83
Fred M. 127
Frederic 153, 185
Frederick 115
Frederick A. 135
Frederick Jeffrey 135, 168
Frederick Luther 95, 134
Galen 63, 96
George 63, 95, 97, 100, 104, 120, 121, 126, 138, 146, 163
George A. 114
George Brainard 137
George Calvin 147, 181
George D. 114
George Eby 125
George Edwin 127, 164
George Egbert 95
George F. 121, 160
George Francis 138
George Franklin 138
George H. 115
George Henry 154
George Husted 169, 175, 195
George Jackson 136, 168
George L. 83
George Leslie 125
George Morris 108

WHITON
George Rufus 168
George W. 126, 223
Geraldine Ellen 164, 165
Gertrude 218
Gilman 98
Gilman C. 137
Glenville William 188, 200, 223
Grace 33, 44, 46, 54, 125, 177
Grace Isabel 176
Grace Richards 150
Hamson S. 126
Hannah 23, 28, 35, 38, 42, 54, 69, 72, 97, 117, 120, 142
Hannah C. 98
Hannah Cady 103
Hannah M. 137
Hannah R. 151
Hannah Richmond 115
Hannah Stowell 81, 119
Harlan Eugene 140, 174
Harley Bert 163, 192
Harley Bert, Jr. 192
Harriet 59, 80, 99, 102, 116, 120, 141, 147
Harriet Augusta 140
Harriet E. 122
Harriet Ellen 177
Harriet Tryphena 110
Harry Augustus 198
Harry F. 186
Harry Finlay 203
Harry Hunt 185
Harry J. 163
Harry L. 137
Hattie Emeretta 129
Heber 67, 103
Helen 50, 108, 152, 185, 192
Helen Atwater 173
Helen Dorothy 107, 215
Helen E. 122
Helen G. 138
Helen Isabel 183
Helen King 180
Helen L. 187
Helen Margaret 200
Henry 63, 83, 88, 90, 102, 116, 120, 122, 139, 141, 143, 155, 177, 223
Henry Benjamin 125, 161, 223
Henry Chadwick 153
Henry Clay 132
Henry Devereux 167, 177, 194
Henry Dyer 159
Henry Edson Hersey 152, 185
Henry Grant 161, 191, 223
Henry Jackson 119, 159, 189
Henry Kirke 92, 130
Henry Lewis 155

WHITON
Henry Lincoln 188, 200
Henry Lyman 126
Henry Rogers 186
Herbert J. 122
Herbert Kenneth 116
Herbert Starkes.......... 156, 187
Herman Abner 105
Herman Frasch 195
Hezekiah J. 126, 162
Hiram 98, 119
Hiram B. 89, 126
Hiram L. 136
Homer 44
Homer Gates 199
Horace 72, 109
Horatio 75, 113
Hosea 40, 63,
64, 98, 99, 137, 222, 223
Huldah 29, 80
Ida Isabel 171
Ida May 127
Ida McKinley 105, 164
Inez 128
Irma 190
Irvin Lane 176
Isabel 144
Isaac...... 24, 32, 37, 48, 49, 222
Isabel Atwater 197
Isaiah 52, 81, 118
Isaiah Gorham 118, 157
Israel 32, 41, 48,
49, 70, 71, 81, 104, 222
Ithamar 84
Iva Belle 180
Jacob 30,
32, 37, 44, 50, 84, 98, 222
Jacqueline 194
Jael........... 25, 27, 30, 46, 65, 80
James 20, 21, 22,
23, 27, 29, 35, 36, 42, 44,
57, 72, 75, 83, 87, 119, 121
James Bartlett...... 183, 199, 204
James Beale 180
James Clinton 125, 161
James F. 89, 127
James Morris 106,
149, 150, 182, 183
James Pomeroy 159
James Sylvester 197
James W. 74
Jane 99
Jane Ann 89
Jane Rosetta 109
Jane Tirrell 116
Janet F. 197
Jared....... 72, 76, 111, 113, 151
Jay 127
Jedidah 27

WHITON
Jennie Eleanor 181
Jennie 94
Jenny Barnard 177
Jerusha 55
Jesse Paulmier 160
Joan M. 198
Joanna 25, 35, 38, 46,
51, 56, 67, 73, 82, 101, 111
Joanna E. 84
Job 27
Job Stowell 81, 119
Joel 111
John 22, 23, 24, 27,
31, 32, 36, 38, 61, 62, 72,
105, 108, 114, 127, 222, 223
John Bassett 88
John Chadwick 115,
153, 185, 223
John Edward 164
John Edgar 126
John Fuller 140, 173
John H. 67
John Husted 195
John L. 167
John Lewis 94, 131
John Lionel 195
John M. 89, 108
John Mandley.... 57, 89, 128, 163
John Milton 71,
106, 108, 150, 183
John P. 116, 155
John Starr 165, 191
John W. 155
Jonathan...... 22, 26, 33, 53, 222
Joseph.... 23, 28, 29, 36, 41, 43,
46, 57, 58, 67, 73, 77, 87,
93, 101, 111, 117, 222, 223
Joseph Eben 131, 165
Joseph Edward 129
Joseph Jacob 65
Joseph Leander 103, 144
Joseph Lincoln...... 158, 188, 201
Joseph Lucas 59,
90, 92, 129, 130
Joseph Merrill 111
Joseph Seward 93, 131
Josephine 184
Josephine M. 137
Joshua 31, 53, 222
Joshua S. 113
Josiah 57, 63, 97
Josiah B. 89, 127, 164
Josiah Wilder 120
Josie 57
Jotham 34, 54, 222
Judith 23, 39, 41, 74
Judith Amelia 104
Julia 63, 133, 143, 178

WHITON

Julia A. 97
Julia Ann Bowker 100
Julia Caroline 134
Julia Eliza 111
Julia Emmeline 94
Julia Frances 125
Julia Francis 125
Julia Marsh 136
Julia May 169
Julia Sophia 139, 205
Julian 126
Juliet 162, 223
Julius Royal 103, 142
Justus 76
Kenneth L. 185
Kesiah 28
Kimball 120
Kitty 184
Laban 50, 74
Lauder Kirke 130
Laura 154
Laura Edna 172
Laura Ernestine 160
Laura J. 90
Laurena 51
Lavinia 82, 121
Leah 26, 33, 51
Leah Stetson 82
Lemuel 30, 45, 46, 222
Lena Belle 178
Leonard 84, 96, 98, 122
Leonard A. 122
Leroy M. 137
Leslie S. 125
Leslie V. 125
Lester 141, 176, 223
Levi 57, 222
Lewis C. 115
Lewis E. 80
Lewis Francis 200, 204
Lillas 44
Lillian Alberta 200
Lillian Elizabeth 175
Lillian Eva 178
Lillian M. 129
Lillie Crocker 135
Lincoln B. 83, 121
Lizzie L. 155
Lizzie Thomas 158
Lloyd Garland 105
Lois 74
Lois E. 192
Lois Ellen 165
Loranus W. 137
Loretta 88
Lorin 218
Loring 82, 121
Loring Livingston 121, 160, 223

WHITON

Lorne Herman 105
Lottie 182
Louis C. 218, 223
Louis Claude 133, 166, 167, 193
Louise 96, 118, 130
Louise B. 132
Louise V. 174
Loyd Arthur 195
Lucinda............. 45, 48, 80, 117
Lucius C. 113
Lucius Erskine 145, 179
Lucius Gay 180
Lucius Heber 103, 142
Lucretia Atwood 101, 130
Lucy 44, 48, 55, 75, 101, 113, 114, 115, 118, 120
Lucy Ann 90
Lucy Barrell 111
Lucy Cornelia 171
Lucy Dorr 154
Lucy Emmeline 126
Lucy Soule 186
Lucy Stoddard 158
Lucy Wellington 150
Luke 222
Lusanne 137
Luther 48, 61, 73, 94, 106, 112
Lydia 24, 31, 32, 43, 50, 55, 60, 65, 78, 83, 84, 97, 99, 111, 117
Lydia A. 120
Lydia Almira 120, 159
Lydia G. 84
Lydia P. 76, 113
Lydia Ripley 116
Lyman 88, 126
Lyman Barnes...... 120, 159, 223
Lyman Charles 169
Mabel 173
Mabel Janet 174
Mabelle Georgie 164
Madison 118, 156
Madison Monroe 156
Mandley 127
Marah 42
Marcia 102, 106, 113
Marcia Gay 144
Marcy 27
Margaret 25, 28, 31, 39, 45, 53, 185
Maria 69, 98, 102, 106, 111, 147
Maria A. 94
Maria J. 170
Maria L. 155
Marian C. 153
Marian Pierce 187
Marie Rebecca 131
Marietta 146, 157

WHITON
Marilla 56, 84, 104
Marjorie 125
Marjorie Ann 166
Marjorie E. 199
Mark 222
Marshall Lincoln 158
Martha 29, 40, 41, 53, 63, 64, 67, 69, 81, 82, 115
Martha Davis 118
Martha Gorham 157
Martha L. 98
Marvin 101
Mary 16, 22, 24, 27, 31, 32, 33, 37, 39, 42, 43, 44, 45, 46, 48, 50, 52, 55, 57, 61, 74, 75, 79, 80, 82, 83, 97, 100, 101, 109, 126, 140, 141, 147, 201
Mary A. 97, 120, 136
Mary Alice 152
Mary Amanda 147
Mary Ann 88, 117
Mary B. 98
Mary Bartlett 183
Mary Chrystie 107
Mary Collier 99
Mary Cushing 170
Mary Cutler H. 102
Mary Dorothy 169
Mary Elizabeth.... 105, 150, 176
Mary Emily 108
Mary Farnham 170
Mary Fidelia 108
Mary Florence 165
Mary Francis 145
Mary Jane 126, 127
Mary Jewett 135
Mary Knowlton 183
Mary L. 97
Mary Laurence 198
Mary Lincoln 115, 139, 151, 157
Mary Louise 166
Mary Lord 134
Mary Matilda 110
Mary R. 116
Mary S. 89
Mary Sophia 94
Mary W. 76, 137
Mary Wing 82
Matilda 69, 72
Matilda W. 102
Matthew 22, 23, 24, 27, 32, 36
Maud M. 163
Mehitable.... 42, 63, 72, 83, 222
Mehitable Siser 120
Melia 31
Melzar 53, 57
Mercy 31, 35, 42

WHITON
Meriel 52, 55, 84, 97, 116
Merrill 143, 178
Mildred 152, 165, 173
Mildred A. 175
Milo James 88, 125
Minnie B. 164
Minnie Morton 201
Miriam Blagdon 150
Molly 37, 48
Morris 108
Morris Fearing 154
Moses.... 28, 47, 78, 79, 117, 222
Moses Lincoln 117, 155
Muriel True 197
Myra Eleanor 182
Nabby Fearing 116
Nadine 194
Nahum 97
Nancy 98
Nancy Bosworth 185
Nancy Maria 88
Nathan.......... 27, 37, 57, 97, 222
Nathan, Jr. 222
Nathan G. 137
Nathaniel.... 30, 43, 46, 137, 185
Nathaniel Starbuck 126
Nella B. 150, 183
Nellie 129
Nellie Adelia 147
Nellie Irene 168
Nellie K. 148
Nelson 144, 178, 223
Nettie Melissa 144
Nora 105
Norman Curtis 130
Norman Elbert 189
Nymphas 83
Olin Everett 141, 175
Olive 74, 78
Olive A. 139
Olive Marble 119
Oliver C. 218
Oliver Otis 140
Osborn 97
Otis 102
Otis Crosby 71
Ozias 44, 222
Pamela 111
Patience 38
Patty 53
Paul 176
Pearl M. 168
Peggy 48, 78
Peleg 46, 222
Perez 45, 65, 99
Perez S. 100
Persis 52, 58, 72, 99
Peter 32, 47, 48, 222

WHITON
Peter Lane 115, 153
Peter W. 84
Phoebe 37, 38, 51, 95
Philena 73
Philip 46
Phyllis E. 192
Piam A. 137
Piam C. 98, 137
Piam W. 137
Polly 51, 57, 64, 83
Porter 141, 176, 177, 223
Priscilla 38, 41, 44, 53, 64, 67, 152
Priscilla Burr 185
Prudence 64
Rachel 26, 47, 54, 80, 97, 156, 218
Rachel (Haile) 218
Ralph Abner 105
Ray A. 164
Rebecca 23, 29, 34, 43, 46, 50, 75
Rebecca Cleverly 119
Rena 105
Reuben 51
Rhoda 53, 80
Richard 111
Robert Arthur 192
Robert Henry 200
Robert Howard 199, 204
Robert Porter 177
Robert Watson 193
Robert Wyer 187
Roland Russell 195
Rose 105
Rosella Lenette 145
Ross Kittridge 188, 201
Roswell 72
Rowena 84
Roxana 84
Roy 162
Royal 81, 119, 158, 159, 189
Ruby 32
Ruby W. 174
Rufus 75
Rufus Henry 95, 136
Russell Emerson 192
Russell J. 121
Russell Rufus 169, 195
Russell Rutherford 203
Russell Thomas 187
Ruth 30, 36, 38, 42, 46, 76, 99, 111, 200
Ruth E. 164, 175
Sage 76
Sally Couch 89
Sally Craig 134
Salome 111
Samantha 59, 90, 93

WHITON
Samuel 23, 28, 36, 37, 39, 42, 45, 58, 61, 72, 74, 82, 222
Samuel James 110
Sarah Augusta 119
Sarah 25, 27, 30, 32, 37, 42, 43, 44, 47, 49, 53, 55, 58, 68, 73, 74, 76, 79, 82, 83, 114, 139, 211, 216, 218
Sarah Antoinette 126
Sarah C. 116
Sarah Henrietta 138
Sarah J. 159
Sarah Jane 156
Sarah Loomis 88
Sherman 58, 89
Shurleff 139
Sidney 74
Silas 97
Silence 31
Simeon 102, 141
Simeon D. 122
Solomon 20, 30, 45, 46, 222
Sophia 58, 62, 191
Sophia Stetson 112
Sophia Tuttle 161
Sophronia 102
Starkes 79, 117, 155, 223
Stephen 32, 41, 49, 67, 69, 84, 100, 101, 106, 120, 122, 139, 148, 222
Stephen Carter 196, 203
Stephen W. 122
Susa 50, 64
Susa G. 76
Susan 97
Susan Allen 119
Susan Cushing 115
Susan L. 115
Susan Lincoln 114
Susan M. 83
Susan Mary 95
Susanna 24, 27, 32, 55, 98
Sybil 41, 64, 69
Sylvanus 63, 97, 136, 223
Sylvester Gilbert 140, 172, 173, 174, 197
Sylvia 193
Sylvia Adeline 195
Tabitha 72
Tamar 54
Tamsen 52
Temperance 97
Terza 58
Thankful 31, 39, 45, 75
Theodore 80
Theodore P. 118
Theodore R., Jr. 203
Theodore Robert 199, 203

WHITON
Theodore Studley 187
Theophilus 64, 98, 223
Theophilus W. 98
Thomas 19, 21, 22, 25, 26, 27, 30, 33, 34, 36, 37, 38, 43, 58, 90, 116, 222, 223
Thomas Fearing 154
Thomas J. 116
Thomas Lowell 115, 153
Tower 42
Tryphena 44
Tudor........... 141, 177, 198, 223
Vernon Conger 130
Vernon E. 164
Victor Atwood 131
Vida Pearl 163
Virginia May 195
Vivian Marie 192
Vodicea 69
Wallace A. 184
Wallace W. 152, 184
Walter 42, 52, 83, 127, 223
Walter B. 122
Walter G. 127
Walter Grant 164
Walter Humiston 173, 197, 223
Walter Leslie 161
Walter U. 218
Walter Scott 127
Walter Starr 130, 165
Walter Stowell 158, 188
Walter Thayer 171, 196, 197, 223
Warren 61, 67
Warren Carter 196
Webster 139
Wesley Wayne 192
Whitfield 218
Wilbur 141
William 19, 30, 36, 44, 108, 116, 118, 147, 154, 156, 222, 223
William Augustus 80
William Chandler 80
William E. 157, 164, 188
William Franklin 154
William Henry 95, 134
William Ipark 189
William J. 164
William, Jr. 176
William Keith 195
William L. 137
William Loomis 89, 126
William P. 96, 112
William Pratt 200
William Stowell 119, 158
Will W. 128
Wilma Nell 164
Wilson......... 29, 42, 72, 79, 116

WHITON
Wilson W. 186
Winifred Gardiner 180
Winnie Bell 169
Winslow Lewis 100
Wynyfride 19, 20, 180
Zachariah 40, 63, 222
Zaccheus 27
Zenas L. 40, 98, 136, 222

WHITON-STUART
Jesse Paulmier 192
Robert Watson 192
Sylvia 192

WHITTEN
Abbie 87
Abraham 57, 86, 125
Alice 87
Amos 57, 86, 87, 125
Charles 86, 124
Charles N. 125
Chester H. 125
Cora 87
Edgar Benjamin 125, 161
Edward W. 124
Elisha Cobb 124
Francis L. 124
Gilbert Yould 190
Harriet E. 87
Horace C. 124
Isaac 87
Joseph B. 87
Lewis Holmes 124
Lucia Ann 87
Mary Elizabeth 190
Matthew 87
Melzar 57, 87
Nathan 87
Orrin B. 124
Polly 86
Priscilla 87
Roscoe Benjamin 161, 191
Rufus Robbins 124
Russell Rutherford 191, 203
Sally 86
Samuel A. 87
Samuel Marshall 87
William Melville 125

WHYTON
Matthew 23

WITON
Abraham 221
Daniel 221
Ebenezer 35, 40
Enoch 221

WITON
Isaac, Jr. 221
Jacob 221
James 35, 40
John 35, 40
Jonathan 221
Joseph 35, 40

WITON
Joshua 221
Mark 221
Nathan 37
Samuel 221
Solomon 221
Thomas 35, 40

INDEX—Collaterals

The collateral index appearing on the following pages contains the maiden names of Whiton wives, the married names of Whiton daughters, and the names of the descendants of Whiton daughters, so far as this information may be compiled from this book.

It is not complete as no information has been obtained about the children of many Whiton daughters, merely the fact of birth or marriage being given.

The Association Secretary will be glad at any time to receive such further information.

INDEX—Collaterals

(W) Signifies "born Whiton"—References are to pages

Abbe, Isabel (W) 144
Abell, Marshall M. 205
Mildred (Amidon) 205
Abbott, Leah (W) 51
Alden, Abigail 77
Ackley, Anna L. (W) 152
Lucy Ann (W) 90
Alderman, Bruce 164
Dortha Mae 164
Isalon Robert 164
Harry Lenons 164
Ida Leona 164
Minnie (W) 164
Allen, Agnes L. (W) 92
Hannah 142
Amidon, Abigail 207
Alice H. 206
Andrew H. 207
Barbara F. 206
Charles M. 205
Charles R. 206
Charles Sanford 205
Charlotte B. 207
Clarence R. 205
Doris M. 207
Ellsworth S. 206
Elsie M. 206
Frank R. 205
Gilbert A. 207
Gilbert W. 206
Harlan P. 207
Helen C. 206
Henry N. 207
Howard P. 206
Julia D. 207
Julia S. (W) 205
June L. 205
Lawrence G. L. 206
Leon J. 207
Lillian 206
Marjorie A. 206
Mary L. 206
Mildred J. 205
Norman W. 207
Raymond H. 205
Richard R. 206
Roberta 206
Robert S. 206
Ruth H. 207
Stanley C. 207
Anderson, Ann S. 144
Bert P. 143
Harriet M. 143
Anderson, Helen E. 143
Henry 143
Idella M. 143
Julia (W) 143
Kate 163
Mabelle L. 143
Margaret (Swett) 107
Martha 143
Mary E. 143
Andrews, Emma (W) 115
Helen V. (Woodworth) 109
Ardene (or -derne), Catherine 19
Armitage, Clara Martha 206
Martha L. 206
Mary (Amidon) 206
Nathan G. 206
Ashley, Caroline 67
Atwater, Isabel T. 172
Atwood, Esther (W) 37
Mary 130
Austin, Clarence J. 128
Clarice 128
Cora E. (W) 127
Gertrude A. 127
Janet A. 128
Mandley 127
Mary Electa 127
Axt, Emma 129
Axtell, Agnes May 92
Catherine (W) 92
Bacon, Ada B. (W) 139
Back, Adna 209
Clara Winifred (Newcomb) 210
Mary Elizabeth (Young).... 209
David Newcomb 210
Ernest A. 209, 210
Lucius A. 208, 209
Mary Adella 209
Richard Chapell 210
Sophia (Moore) 208
Vera Ethel 209
Bailey, Sarah (W) 83
Baker, Judith A. 122
Lucy D. (W) 154
Baldwin, Barbara M. 175
Edith (W) 175
Eleanor M. 175
Raymond John 175
Ballard, Agnes Anna 107
Clarence E. 107
Edward 107
Elizabeth D. (W) 106
Ettie E. 107

Ballard, Herbert E. 107
Kate 107
Ballou, Lina M. 146
Bancroft, Benjamin L. 147
Burdette W. 147
Edward A. 147
George F. 147
Lydia B. 155
Mary A. (W) 147
Mary W. 147
Minerva 147
Noah P. 147
Olin F. 147
Paul C. 147
Thomas W. 147
Barnard, Ellen A. 177
Helen C. 171
Jane W. 171
Mary F. (W) 170
Robert S. 171
Barnes, Abigail (W) 29
Hannah (W) 33, 81
Leah S. (W) 82
Barrell, Lucy 111
Barrows, Elizabeth 37
Barry, Adeline O. (W) 136
Bartlett, Elizabeth 86
Harriet 87
Loretta (W) 88
Mary 182
Barton, Mary 85
Nannie O. 61
Bates, Deborah (W) 31, 79
James 176
Jane 176
Lucy 113
Mary L. (W) 157, 176
Batholomew, Ella 216
Battles, Betty (W) 77
Mary 98
Bassett, Deborah 87
Beal, Abigail 55
Arabella G. 158
Caleb 30
Deborah (W) 77
Hannah S. (W) 119
John 21
Lydia (W) 32
Maria (W) 98
Mary 21, 25
Molly 73
Nathan 77
Priscilla (W) 44
Rebecca (W) 75
Sarah 34
Sarah (W) 55
Susan 114
Tryphena 44
Tryphena (W) 44
Beals, Maurine 173
Beck, —— (m. W. K. Ingersoll) 213
Bell, Bertha S. 214
Edith T. 214
Harold I. 214
Harriet Louise 166
Mary E. (Ingersoll) 214
Samantha 105
Beman, Caroline W. (W) 94
Katherine 94
Louise 94
Nathan S. 94
Benjamin, Frances L. 125
Benner, Lucy (W) 55
Bennett, Claire 140
Clarence 140
Cora 140
Elizabeth A. (W) 140
Forrest C. 140
Minnie A. 140
Roland A. 140
Berk, Terza (W) 58
Berry, Jael (W) 46
Sarah 43
Bevelheimer, Esther Marie 163
Ida M. (W) 163
Lois Martha 163
Ruth Irene 163
Bicknell, Temperance 97
Bidwell, Cordelia 141
Bingham, Electa R. 127
Birge, Esther E. (W) 109
Lucy M. 109
Black, Abigail 74
Blackmer, Jennie 102
Mary (Newton) 102
Blakely, Una (Rounds) 104
Blanchard, Clarissa (W) 84
Blancher, Mehitable 42
Bleekman, Alice (W) 94
Arthur 94
Bet 94
Clara 94
Ruth 94
Block, Mary 215
Blossom, Sarah 52
Susan A. (W) 119
Bombard, Carl C. 148, 223
Clara E. 147
Edna F. 147
Harriet (W) 147
Idella M. 148
Leora E. 148
Lillian M. 148
Milton W. 148
Ruth C. 148
Walter W. 148
Bond, Mary E. 183

Bonney, Thankful (W) 31
Bosworth, Arthur S. 146
Charles A. 146
Frank N. 146
George F. 146
Herbert A. 146
Lillia 146
Lina, M. B. 146
Lucy M. 146
Marietta (W) 146
Ruth A. 146
Bouché, Claire H. 193
Bowker, Abigail 99
Catherine 100
Lydia (W) 84
Mary 99
Brackett, Katherine 185
Bradford, Elizabeth 38
Lydia N. 124
Phoebe (W) 38
Bradley, Donald H. 177
Jennie B. (W) 177
Marrietta 126
Marshall J. 177
Mary Jane 126
Sally 89
Tudor W. 177
Brady, Charlotte B. (W) 174
Madeline 177
Brett, Harriet T. (W) 110
Mary Ann 109
Samuel 110
Brevillier, Bernice (Lathrop) 177
Bridge, Hannah K. 74
Briggs, Lucy 74
Lydia P. (W) 76
Phoebe E. 129
Brigham, Mary B. (W) 98
Brockway, Elizabeth A. 162
Bronsdon, Deborah (W) 119
Bronson, George 66
Sophia (W) 66
Brooks, Ann 75
Brown, Agnes (W) 60
Anne (Thompson) 88
Earl W. 89
Elizabeth (Eddy) 103
Julia A. B. (W) 100
Louise E. (June) 89
Nelson W. 89
Pearl S. 89
Perry 89
Philura 140
Sarah D. 137
Bryant, Mary D. (W) 169
Sally 121
Una (Venable) 217
Buchanan, Ethel (Gray) 127
Ida May 127
Buchanan, Ruth Gertrude 127
Buck, Hattie E. 177
Buddington, Lena A. 179
Lena B. (W) 178
Leon D. 179
Roy W. 179
Ruth S. 179
Bugbee, Mabel (Anderson) .. 143
Buland, Altha V. (W) 169
Bonnie Ruth 169
Robert A. 169
Wayne 169
Bullock, Huldah (W) 29
Nathan 222
Bump, Charlotte (W) 52
Lydia (W) 65
Burdick, Caroline E. 104
Ethel 105
Minnie 105
Burgess, Hannah (W) 86
Lillian (Ballard) 211
Nancy 123
Burnham, Lilly K. 200
Burr, Doris 104
Mabel 104
Priscilla 152
Burrell, Elizabeth (W) 111
Virginia 184
Burritt, Nellie 156
Bush, Alice 94
Emily 94
Maria A. (W) 94
Bushell, Mahala M. 105
Byington, Keziah 131
Byles, Abigail 139
Cady, —— 124
Olive 175
Calkins, Charlotte G. (W) 150
Dorothy W. 183
Grosvenor 150
Leighton 150
Mary B. 183
Mary W. 150
Maud 150
Nella B. (W) 150, 183
Raymond 150, 183
Wolcott 150, 183
Campbell, Mary 45
Mercy 49
Canton, Rebecca (W) 46
Carpenter, Ella M. 164
Carter, Elizabeth S. 195
Maud M. (W) 163
Cary, Bertha J. (W) 171
Caryl, Sarah H. (W) 138
Case, Emma J. 198
Caswell, Deborah 87
Chadwick, Eloise 164
Lydia (W) 78

Chaffee, Amy 104
Etta B. 171
Herman R. 110
Joanna 67
Martha 110
Rebecca (W) 43
Chamberlain, Patience (W) 38
Chandler, Eliza 142
Chapman, Anna (W) 92
Eleanor (Whiting) 218
Emma 178
Sarah (W) 68
Chappell, Annie L. (W) 174
Herbert Eugene 174
Reginald, H. W. 174
Cherington, Chas. R. 215
Mary (Richards) 215
Paul W. 215
Cherouny, Janet (Little) 133
Child, Julia 161
Chism, Abigail B. 212
Anne L. (W) 211
Anna Lucinda 211
Charles 223
Emily Josephine 211
Frank E. 211
James W. 211
Julia Belle 212
Lois 211
Louis W. 211
Olive L. 211
Sarah (W) 211
Choate, Grace R. (W) 150
Helen A. 150
Miriam F. 150
Chubbuck, Elizabeth (W) 112
Joanna (W) 57
Melia (W) 31
Church, Amanda (W) 59
Catherine 59
Frances 59
Helen 59
Joseph 59
Churchill, Annie (W) 114
Catherine F. 206
Martha (W) 86
Rebecca 38
Claffe, Agnes 128
Clapp, Betsy 77
Frances H. (W) 152
Clark, Eliza 218
Emma (W) 123
Mary (W) 82
Parmilla 156
Suzanne 62
Classon, Laura 181
Cleverly, Esther 119
Rebecca 81
Clough, Stella A. 207
Clute, Mary E. 125
Clyde, Irma (W) 190
Cobb, Christina 168
Jemima 43
Colby, Sarah J. (W) 156
Cole, Georgianna 119
Mabel 195
Collamore, Hannah 98
Margaret (W) 25, 31
Sarah 82
Collins, Barbara 107
Elizabeth (Paine) 107
Mary Ann (W) 88
Marjorie 107
Ruth (W) 42
Susan 88
Colson, Muriel (W) 55
Converse, Almeda 142
Bertha J. (W) 171
Cooke, Eliza (Anderson) 143
Cooley, Nancy 142
Cooper, Nancy 94
Copeland, Alice 110
May 110
May A. (Towne) 110
Nettie 205
Philip 110
Robert 110
Copethorn, Bertha 152
Corder, Dorothy C. 203
Corkendale, Almira (W) 126
Corthell, Lydia (W) 50
Cosgrove, Nancy E. 131
Sylvia M. 155
Cotton, Clara E. 162
Couch, Nancy E. 126
Sally 89
Craig, Susannah 127
Crain, Abigail 216
Anna (W) 72
Sarah (W) 216
Crane, Ann Eliza 100
Crocker, Bethiah 27
Hannah 40, 56
Crosby, Christina 160
Dorothy 70
Crose, Anna L. (W) 165
Cross, Emily E. (W) 119
Cruff, Grace A. 217
Cummings, Elizabeth (W) 29
Joseph 29
Curry, Cecil L. 192
Curtis, Alice 30
Alice (W) 30
Asa 30
Bethia 137
Cynthia 114
Hannah (W) 28
Jason 30

Curtis, Joseph 30
Sally 113
William 30
Cushing, Abby 124
Abel 79
Andrew J. 98
Brainard 98
Davis 98
Fanny W. 98
Hannah C. (W) 98
Harriet L. 186
Henry J. 98
Mary C. (W) 99
Mary W. 170
Sarah (W) 53
Sarah C. 98
Susanna (W) 55
Urban W. 98
William S. 98
Daggart, Edith (Lee) 104
Damas, Idella H. (Eddy) 104
Damon, Olive (W) 75
Anna E. (W) 119
Jael 39
Mary 137
Pyam 75
Dana, Eunice 69
Danforth, Lydia 110
Daniel, Catherine W. 60
Eliza (W) 59
Mary G. 59
Daniels, Judith (W) 74
Dart, Emma 109
Davis, Angeline B. (W) 167
George H. 84
Marilla (W) 84
Martha K. (Anderson) 143
Willard W. 84
Virginia A. 143
Dawley, Alberta (Roller) 136
Anna L. (Chism) 211
John W. 136
Dean, Winona 148
Delano, Susan 87
Wealthea 87
Deming, Elizabeth 176
Rachel (W) 97
Dennison, Amy 62
Augustus Seymour 62
Clara (Seymour) 62
Louise Seymour 62
Mary Sherrill 62
Densmore, Sarah A. P. 153
Depeau, Mabel J. (W) 174
Devereux, Mary 167
Devine, Mary 164
Dewey, Evalina A. 213
Theresa 157
DeWolf, Eleanor 188
Didely, Helene 195
Dillingham, Mary Snow 185
Dimick, Margaret (W) 53
Dimock, Amorette 92
Dixon, Rena (W) 105
Dodge, Carrie (Newton) 102
Lottie A. 189
Dorfler, Rose (W) 105
Dorman, Laura 124
Dorr, Lucy P. 116
Doten, Alice (W) 27
Joanna (W) 35
Mercy (W) 35
Rebecca 85
Downing, Ruth (W) 174
Drew, Gertrude 176
Harriet (W) 87
Drumond, Louise (Beman) .. 94
Dudley, Priscilla (W) 41
Dumpelberger, Olive (Gammack) 129
Dunbar, Hannah 33
Jael 30, 53
Keziah (W) 28
Mary (W) 52
Olive (W) 74
Duncan, Kate 107
Mary C. (W) 107
Dunham, Abigail 23
Eileen 164
Hannah (W) 38
Joanna 35
Merle 164
Ruth E. (W) 164
Duncklee, Laura E. 171
Dunworth, Abigail (W) 72
Matilda 72
Dweller, Deborah 77
Dwelley, Betsy B. 113
Elmira L. 113
Dyer, Hannah 117
Mary 97
Sarah F. 159
Earle, Edith 185
Easterbrook, Martha 118
Eastman, Peter 222
Tryphena 71
Eaton, Alberta L. 142
Aurelia L. 144
Esther (W) 142
Esther L. 142
Ivy G. 142
Lucius F. 142
Echem, Susan 121
Eddy, Elizabeth L. 103
Hannah C. (W) 103
Idella H. 104
Lillie M. 104
Minnie F. 103

Eddy, Penuel 223
Edwards, Florence (W) 184
Mary (W) 201
Elderkin, Gladys 143
Eldredge, Alberta (Osgood).. 163
Eldridge, Abiel 41
Abigail 41
Abigail (W) 41
Elijah 41
Hezekiah 41
Hosea 41
Micah 41
Stephen 41
Sybil 41
Ellery, Mildred (W) 173
Phyllis 173
Ellis, Nellie 87
Elton, Mary E. 125
Erlandson, Anna E. 143
Estes, Polly (W) 83
Evans, Alberta A. 135
Alfred R. 135
Bertie R. 135
Julia W. 135
Laura A. (Roller) 135
Leila A. 135
Everson, Patience 86
Fadden, Grace 46
Farnham, Alice 101
Frank 101
John R. 101
Mary 101
Mary (W) 101
Sylvester Gilbert 101
Farren, Lucy 119
Farrington, Emily 155
Farrow, Joanna (W) 25
Jonathan 23
Judith (W) 23
Leah (W) 26
Faulkner, Julia (Little) 125
Faxon, Hanna M. (W) 113
Sarah C. 150
Fearing, Anna C. 138
Chloe (W) 50
Hannah L. 139
Martha 53
Nabby 116
Nabby (W) 116
Olive 138
Patty (W) 53
Sarah G. 138
Feichtenbiner, Anna 192
Felch, Olive (W) 78
Ferres, Alice (W) 173
Laura Ann 173
Walter D. 173
Walter D., Jr. 173
Finney, Betsy 85
Finney, Elizabeth D. (W)...... 85
Experience 123
Ruth 85
Susan 124
Fisher, Jane (Bates) 176
Flemmons, Phebe R. 86
Fletcher, Gertrude (Austin).. 127
James A. 127
Flint, Etta M. 189
Frederick 101
Harriet 101
Joanna (W) 101
John L. 101
Lucy 58
Foote, Anna 92
Nellie F. (W) 148
Ford, Alpheus 80
Daniel 80
Deborah (W) 80
Desire (W) 80
Elizabeth 80
Emily 80
Horace 80
Ira 80
Mary 80
William 80
Foster, Alice L. (W) 152
Annie C. 168
Edna 204
Frances R. 152
Hannah W. 152
Harriet 141
Helen M. 152
Lewis W. 152
Mayone L. 152
Fountain, Effie (W) 105
Fowler, Lois Anita 88
May Palmer 88
Foy, Phoebe 140
Francis, Asenath 144
Frasch, Frieda 194
Frazier, Grace (Lee) 104
Freeman, Hariet (W) 59
Lydia P. (W) 113
French, Joanna (W) 111
Fuller, Jane S. 103
Jerusha H. 102, 139
Mary (W) 141
Minerva 68
Fulmer, Mollie A. 68
Gammack, Inez (W) 128
Olive May 129
Gardiner, Florinda C. (W) 138
Jeanette 173
Gardner, —— (W) 170
Catherine 96
Charles 97
Chloe (W) 51
Elizabeth 45, 112

Gardner, Hannah (W) 97
Jennie M. 156
Joanna 72
Judith (W) 74
Lois S. 112
Lydia 43
Martha 170
Mary 47
Mary (W) 100
Miriam 47
Susa (W) 64
Sybil 136
Garfield, Amanda 58
Garnet, Elizabeth 28
Garnett, Joanna M. 25
Lydia 32
Mary (W) 31
Rebecca 28
Sarah 30
Gates, Anne 199
Mary Agnes 161
Gauthier, Anna 148
Gawn, Annetta J. 129
Gay, Marcia 103
Gero, Doane R. 148
Elizabeth J. (W) 148
Irving W. 148
Karl Wm. 148
Marshall D. 148
Paul W. 148
Pauline May 148
Raymond Whiton 148
Robert I. 148
Robert M. 148
Roland E. 148
Stephen W. 148
William B. 148
Gibb, Ann 30
Gibbs, Abigail (W) 85
Polly 71
Gilbert, Mary 47
Gillette, Alice R. 156
Edwin C. 156
Frank W. 156
Lena 156
Mary P. 156
Rachel (W) 156
Gladwin, Jessie 182
Glen, Eva L. 148
Goddard, Sarah E. 114
Godfrey, Beulah 164
Goffe, Rebecca (W) 29
Goodell, Lillia (Bosworth) 146
Goodrich, Alice R. (W) 99
Goold, Mary L. 158
Gorham, Martha D. (W) 118
Gowdy, Julia B. (Chism) 212
Grafton, Ruth 35
Grant, Bertha 88
Grant, Hannah 161
Gray, Catherine (Church) 59
Ethel 127
Frances H. 59
Ida May (W) 127
Green, Greeley 102
Maria (W) 102
Nellie P. 200
Greene, Ella 198
Gregory, Mabel (Wander) 176
Griswold, Helen C. (Barnard) 171
Mary 61, 181
Groce, Catherine (W) 138
Mary L. (W) 139
Sarah (W) 66
Gross, Margaret (W) 28
Thankful (W) 39
Grubb, Lydia 129
Gulliford, Nora 108
Gunkle, Julia C. (W) 134
Haille, Rachel 218
Hall, Ann 24
Harry 147
Henry James 101
Kitty (W) 184
Laura 123
Lucy (W) 101
Maria (W) 147
Nathaniel 24
William Albert 101
William Henry 101
Hamlin, Clarissa (W) 80
Hammond, Lucy 124
Hankinson, Ruth E. (W) 175
Hanks, Mary 72
Hanna, Raymond, Mrs. 175
Haplinger, Lucile W. 62
Harding, Madeline F. 108
Mary 57
Wynyfride 19
Harlow, Alice (W) 87
Martha 86
Harrington, Lydia (W) 43
Harris, Agnes F. 134
Gwendolen 134, 194
Marcella 203
Ruth 134
Ruth E. (Parsons) 128
Sallie C. (W) 134
Hart, James B. 163
Maggie E. 67
Marie 163
Martha S. 109
Maud M. (W) 163
Hartshorn, Mary J. 108
Harvey, Iva B. (W) 180
Hatch, Lucy J. 151
Sylvia (W) 193

Hathorn, Anna M. (Leonard) 63
Judd W. 63
Hawes, Abbie (Woodbury) 215
Frank W. 215
John R. 215
Maria A. 137
Hayes, Chester S. 170
Clara A. (W) 170
Haynes, Persis (W) 99
Heath, Frances 108
Janet 133
Hebard, Martha L. (W) 98
Herrick, Abbie 215
Frederick M. 215
George 215
Helen M. (Richards) 215
Marion T. 215
Hersey, Effie A. (W) 158
Emma (W) 54
Martha G. (W) 158
Mary C. 151
Sarah (W) 32
Sarah A. 158
Sarah J. 159
Susan C. (W) 115
Hibbard, Rachel (W) 80
Hill, Harriet (W) 141
Lois (W) 74
Hinckley, Anabel (W) 184
Chester F. 184
Esther W. 184
Fannie S. 184
Josiah 184
Hitchcock, Julia (Keep) 69
Hixon, Louisa 127
Hoanes, Josephine 184
Hobart, Elizabeth 122
Jael (W) 25
Miriam F. (Choate) 150
Mehitable 83
Nancy 84
Susanna 118
Hodges, Fannie (W) 184
Hodgkins, Mary 67
Holbrook, Allison 215
Claire (Woodbury) 215
Holcomb, Agnes (Brown) 60
Holman, Mildred A. 197
Holmes, Abby 123
Almira 123
Betsy 57, 123
Ellen (W) 123
Grace 123
Lucia H. 124
Mary R. 124
Olive 186
Priscilla 86
Rebecca 35, 37
Holt, Alice May 205
Hopkins, Abigail (Crain) 216
Addison W. 216
Alfred 216
Charles M. 216
David 216
Ella (Bartholomew) 216
Florence (McMilly) 217
Hannah 216
Harriet 216
Harriet Cornelia 216
Isabel (Root) 216
John H. 216
Margaret 216
Mary Abilgail 216
Mary Ellen 216
Nancy Jane 216
Opal 163
Phoebe A. 216
Silas G. 216
Warner W. 216, 223
Horton, Abigail (W) 97
Hotchkiss, Barbara 215
George B. 215
Jean 215
Margaret R. 215
Margaret (Woodbury) 215
Mary 215
Hoxie, Louise V. (W) 174
Hough, Mary Cutler 102
Houghton, Augustus S. 62
Clara 62
Clarence Sherrill 62
E. Russell 62
Florence 62
Helene 62
Henry Seymour 62
Hezekiah 62
Louise (Seymour) 62
Margaret 62
Mary 62
Matthew H. 62
Robert Serviton 62
Sarah (Seymour) 62
Seymour P. 62
House, Maria (W) 111
Howard, Alice (Woodbury) 215
Anne 215
Eleanor 199
Elizabeth 215
John Tasker 215
Mary (Woodbury) 215
Mercy (W) 31
Tasker 215
Howe, Agnes 60
Catherine (W) 60
Mary A. 115
Howland, Betsy 85
Hubbard, Polly (W) 57
Hueston, Betsy 86

Humphrey, Gertrude L. 128
  Joanna (W) 82
  Mehitable (W) 83
Hunter, Elizabeth (W) 97
  Jessie 177
Huntington, Matilda (W) 102
  Sophronia 83
Husted, Matilda 136
Hutchinson, Clara (Houghton) 62
  Emmeline 124
  James A. 183
  John W. 183
  Mary K. (W) 183
  Mary W. 183
Hyde, Mary R. 216
Hyland, Abigail 119
Ide, Eunice 111
Ingersoll, Albert M. 214
  Alma H. 213
  Caroline E. (W) 214
  Charles D. 213
  Charles E. 213
  Edward A. 214
  Edward P. 214
  Ellen A. 213
  Elizabeth S. 213
  Ernest 213
  Eva Dewey 213
  Florence 213
  Frederick A. 214
  Grace L. 213
  Harry 214
  Henry 213
  Henry S. 213
  John W. 213
  John L. 214
  Mary (W) 213
  Mary C. 214
  Mary E. 214
  Mary G. 214
  Max 213
  Nellie W. 214
  Sylvia W. 213
  Warren 214
  William P. 213
  Winifred 213
  Wyllys K. 213
Ingalls, Lucy 86
Ingraham, Edna 94
  Edna F. 94
Ipark, William 189
Irving, Charlotte 124
Jackson, Bethiah (W) 27
  Deborah 76
  Dorothy Q. (W) 180
  Ella 169
  Lucius E. W. 180
  Mary (W) 27
Jacobs, Adeline (W) 100
  Bertha E. (W) 174
  Caroline (W) 100
  Erminia 138
  Helen M. (Foster) 152
  Lucy 100
  Lydia 64
Jewett, Abbie (W) 87
Johnson, Clarence J. 157
  Eliza (W) 96
  Ellen (W) 157
  Florence P. 198
  Howard 157
  Marietta (W) 157
  Merrill 157
  Nellie 157
  Stanley 157
  Stanley W. 157
  Theresa 157
Jones, Eliza Burnham 139
  Emma 115
  Ethel 105
  Mary 150
  Mary F. 152
Jordan, Baruch 22
  Desire 120
  Mary (W) 22
Joy, Mary (W) 80
Judd, Caroline (Leonard) 63
June, Dawn 89
  Edwin Mandley 89
  Henry O. 89
  John W. 89
  Mary S. (W) 89
  Milo James 89
  Louise E. 89
  Lyman 89
  Pearl 89
  Sally C. (W) 89
  William D. 89
Kahle, Edith M. (W) 163
  Frieda May 163
  Letha Vivian 163
Kappely, Frieda 130
Kasson, Mary V. 172
Keane, Lucinda (W) 80
Keating, Catherine 181
Keeney, Jane R. (W) 109
Keep, Elvira 69
  Jason S. 69
  Julia 69
  Juliana M. (Smith) 69
  Marcia 103
  Marcus 69
Kelleran, Ellen D. 116
Kelley, Annie (Walker) 68
  D. L. 68
  Herbert 68
  Walker 68

Kelly, Herbert 223
Walker 223
Kemp, Lucy M. (Bosworth) .. 146
Kendall, Margaret (Hopkins) 217
Kenzle, Mary (Lockett) 167
Kidder, Calvin P. 69
Clarence L. 69
Emma E. (Nichols) 69
Louise A. (Parsons) 69
Mary Louise 69
Kilborn, Lena (Gillette) 156
Kimmel, Sarah M. 128
King, Albert Hugh 163
Beth I. (Osgood) 163
Eleazer 23
Ellen (W) 92
Hannah (W) 23
Ivan E. 163
John 23
Mildred A. (W) 175
Phyllis Jean 163
Robert M. 163
Viola 179
Knapp, Flora D. (W) 148
Frederick W. 148
Knickerbocker, Isabella 126
Knowlton, Mary Elizabeth 149
Lackore, Donald E. 169
La Voune A. 169
Veoune 169
Winnie Belle (W) 169
Lane, Bessie A. 176
Lucy 113
Mary 136
Priscilla (W) 53
Lapham, Meriel (W) 52
Latham, Belle Janet 174
Lathrop, Antoinette (W) 176
Bernice C. 177
Carrie 147
Eleanor L. 176
Elizabeth L. 176
Emily B. 150
Ida L. 164
Robert H. 177
Latimer, Harriet E. 176
Lauder, Louise 130
Law, Mildred 134
Ruth L. (Harris) 134
Lawrence, Julia 125
Mary (W) 75
Lawson, Esther 206
Leary, Barbara 181
Catherine P. (W) 181
Ethel M. 181
Florence M. 181
George F. 181
George W. 181
Robert K. 181
Leavens, Almira (W) 120
Leavitt, Hannah (W) 33
Mary 158
Ledoyt, Judith A. (W) 104
Lee, Albert 104
Blanche C. 104
Caroline 104
Edith 104
Esther Pitkin 104
Grace 104
Harriet 104
Helen 179
Marilla (W) 104
William A. 104
Lenning, Edith Caroline 176
Grace I. (W) 176
Herbert Kenneth 176
Irvin Lane 176
Paul 176
William, Jr. 176
Leonard, Anna May 63
Caroline 63
Julia (W) 63
Lewis, Elizabeth (W) 47
Ella 182
Hannah (W) 54
Lillibridge, Martha 146
Mary E. (W) 105
Lincoln, Bethia (W) 25
Chloe (W) 50
Hannah S. 154
Levi 25
Lydia (W) 32, 78
Margaret (W) 31
Martha 78, 79
Mary 25, 114
Mary W. 157
Rachel C. 151
Salome (W) 111
Sarah 82
Littell, Elizabeth 103
Janet (Storrs) 103
Little, Carrie 133
Janet 133
Julia (W) 133
Julia 133
Robert F. 133
Littlefield, Abijah 80
Caroline 80
Hiram 80
Jael (W) 80
Joshua 80
Mary A. 188
William 80
Lockett, Antoinette (W) 167
Lombard, Caroline (Newton) 102
Long, Ethel M. (Leary) 181
Loomis, Mary E. 175
Sarah 37

Lord, Ann L. 214
Hannah (W) 142
Kate I. 142
Sarah P. 134
Loring, Bethia (W) 51
Charity 82
Desire 76, 151
Elizabeth B. 153
Judith (W) 39
Leah 65
Lydia 119
Sarah 65
Sophia S. (W) 112
Lothrop, Rebecca A. 158
Lovell, Lydia (W) 117
Prudence (W) 64
Ruth 113
Lovett, Sarah F. 186
Low, Margaret 204
Lucas, Molly 35
Lutton, Orphy 192
McAllister, Ann J. 170
McCarty, Ellen 127
McComber, Rhoda (W) 80
McConkey, Jack C. 165
Lois Ellen (W) 165
Phyllis Elaine 165
McConnellogue, Katherine 107
McCoy, Amoret T. (W) 131
McCracken, Angeline 140
McDonald, Emma (W) 182
McGown, Lucy S. (W) 158
McIntire, Ruth E. (W) 175
McKnight, Mary 108
McLain, Edna 89
Grace 89
Herman 89
Jane Ann (W) 89
Lewis 89
Lewis Dale 89
McLintock, Agnes (Harris) .. 134
McMilly, Florence 217
McMullen, Altha L. 169
Frances E. 169
Shirley A. (Winterton) 169
McQueston, Caroline 107
MacKenzie, Annie 185
Maitland, Mildred (Amidon) 205
Mallory, Florence 211
Mandigo, Mrs. Wm. J. (Woodworth) 109
Manley, Mary (W) 37
Mann, Abigail 84
Desire (W) 82
Hannah 112
Lucy B. (W) 111
Pamela (W) 111
Manter, Sarah 86
Marble, Bette 50
Marne, Susa 75
Marsh, Abigail (W) 84
Mary W. (W) 112
Sarah (W) 25
Marston, Katy (Miller) 131
Louise (Beman) 94
Martin, Anna E. 160
Juliana 101
Mason, Mary Jane 128
Sarah E. 175
Mathes, Addie (W) 171
Mathews, Maria (W) 106
Matthews, Alice 103
Matthewson, Mary (W) 97
Maze, Betty Louise 164
Ellen L. (W) 164
Virgil Clark 164
Meach, Margaret 211
Mead, Lucy (W) 120
Melcher, Abby R. (W) 154
Merrill, John Franklin.... 172, 223
Laura E. (W) 172
Mary W. 167
Mikell, Sarah J. 154
Miller, Carrie W. (W) 159
Frances M. 164
Hazel 131
Katy 131
Marie R. (W) 131
Miner, Marie 215
Misner, Pearl 105
Monroe, Sarah (W) 114
Moody, Elucia 146
Mook, Coral (W) 188
Lois M. (Tuckerman) 217
Moore, Amy (W) 208
Fanny (W) 123
Harriet J. 68
Lucinda 110
Sophia 207, 208
Moran, Dorothy 198
Morand, Bertha (W) 181
Morey, Abigail 218
Morgan, Dorothy 175
Morris, Abigail 106
Morse, Amy A. (W) 105
Morton, Betsy 85
Deborah 85
Mary (W) 57
Polly 85
Rebecca (W) 86
Sarah 85, 122
Moule, Agnes M. (Axtell) 92
M. Axtell 92
Richard H. 92
Munger, Carrie E. (W) 129
Munn, Edith 213
Munyan, Florence M. (Leary) 181
Murdock, Priscilla (W) 87

Murray, Emily (W) 93
Myers, Lillie C. (W) 135
Myrtle, Sylvia 165
Nash, Reverence 84
Susan M. 157
Nelson, Alice L. 165
Katherine 203
Newcomb, Anne 97
Clara W. 210
Newton, Adeline P. 183
Caroline 102
Carrie 102
Edwin Hall 102
Frank 102
Frederick H. 102
George 102
Hiram 102
Marcia (W) 102
Mary 102
Nellie 102
Nichols, Emma E. 69
Mary M. 114
Sage (W) 76
Nickerson, Hannah C. 86
Nims, Sophia (W) 58
Nixon, Ruth L. (Harris) 134
North, Mabel 90
Northway, Sylvia 95
Nottingham, Anna G. (Rathburn) 60
Oaks, Jane E. 146
Ogden, Mary 192
Olds, Katherine (Beman) 94
Opdyke, Agnes 150
Henry B. 150
Howard 150
Miriam B. (W) 150
Orcutt, Meribel 97
Orne, Maria E. 155
Osgood, Alberta Helen 163
Beth Irene 163
Esther (Hinckley) 184
Viola P. (W) 163
Otis, Betsy 101
Otterson, Hazel (Miller) 131
Page, Helen A. (W) 173
Paine, Elizabeth 107
Horace Whiton 107
Kate (Duncan) 107
Malcomb 108
Marian D. 107
Mary 98
Whiton 108
Palmer, Julia (Starbuck) 88
May 88
Sarah (Thayer) 36
Parker, Harriet 118
Parks, Laurena (W) 51
Parkhurst, Ethel (Burdick) 105
Parlin, Alice C. 213
Parmenter, Robie D. 125
Parr, Arthur D. 136
Burnham 136
Cynthia G. 136
Julia M. (W) 136
Rufus H. 136
Viola F. 169
Parsons, Calvin 69
Clarence L. 69
Elva L. (W) 128
Eunice D. (W) 69
Frank 128
Louise A. 69
Mary Louise 69
Oliver A. 69
Ruth L. 128
Pasco, Ann (Parsons) 69
Paulk, Ammi 222
Keziah 105
Paulmier, Jennie M. 166
Pearcy, Lavina 218
Peakes, Priscilla 44
Rachel 74
Pearl, Clara M. 205
Pearson, Effie (W) 184
Pierce, Hannah 23
Peirce, Mary A. (W) 117
Penniman, Ruth (W) 99
Pepin, Caroline (Thompson) 88
Percy, Lavina 218
Perkins, Catherine D. (W) 88
Perry, Tamar (W) 54
Peterson, Dorothy W. 182
Eleanor L. 182
Maria 83
Myra E. (W) 182
Scott R. 182
Pettingill, Mary K. 186
Pfaff, Hattie E. (W) 129
Phillips, Augustus S. 62
Lillian E. (W) 175
Louise 62
Lydia G. (W) 84
Margaret 62
Patty 150
Sarah (W) 85
Seymour 62
Phinney, Mary F. 130
Pitkin, Abigail (W) 109
Alfred N. 109
Charles W. 109
Emily 111
Harriet (Lee) 104
Sarah 104
Pitts, Anne 23
Deborah 23
Edmund 23
Planz, Mary G. (Daniel) 59

Planz, Wyatt Garfield 60
Platt, Frances J. (W) 88
Pomeroy, Miranda 177
Ponedel, Edna L. 203
Poole, Lydia 184
Powell, Gardiner W. 173
Jeannette A. 173
Mabel (W) 173
Whiton 173
Powers, Bert 94
Emily (Bush) 94
William 94
Pratt, Ethel 200
Lydia 43
Susan L. (W) 114
Mary Wing (W) 82
Prentice, Josephine E. 206
Preston, Saidie 62
Price, Helen (Thompson) 88
Prickett, Adeline 178
Prouty, Margaret (W) 39
Mary 122
Meriel 97
Rachel 96
Rainey, Harry A. 127
Mary E. (Austin) 127
Roger F. 127
Rowland K. 127
Ramsdell, Mary 44
Rand, Harriet (Anderson) .. 143
Frank P. 143
Randall, Rachel 80
Rasie, Cora M. (Bennett) 140
Lawrence 140
Rathburn, Anna G. 60
Catherine (Daniel) 60
Ratigan, Julia 191
Raymond, Phebe 65
Reading, Clara F. 200
Readio, Mary A. (Back) 209
Reager, Edna F. (Bombard) 148
Redding, Clara F. 201
Reed, Hannah (W) 117
Josephine 68
Rees, Almira 128
Remington, Rachel 117
Rich, Alice W. (Spencer) 141
Ella C. 189
Richard, Rachel (W) 26
Richards, Abbie L. 215
Charles H. 215
Charles Miner 215
Gladys L. 215
Helen D. 215
Helen D. (W) 215
Helen M. 215
Marie L. 215
Marie (Miner) 215
Mildred W. 215
Richards, Paul Stanley 215
Richardson, Esther C. 115
Rickard, Abigail 23
Ripley, Abigail **154**
Ann E. 100
Carol 200
Elizabeth 31
Eunice (W) 65
Joan 200
Mary 49
Ruth 186
Ruth (W) 200
Susanna (W) 98
Ritcher, Colette 194
Robart, Fannie (Hinckley) .. 184
Robbins, Martha 110
Mary G. 110
Mary M. (W) 110
Sally 86
Roberts, Ida I. (W) 171
Sarah (W) 37
Robinson, Abbie M. 180
Rogers, Dorothy E. (W) 125
Edna May (W) 164
Joslyn W. 125
Mary A. (W) 136
Nina 186
Peggy Marie 164
Priscilla (W) 64
Robert H., Jr. 163
Roice, Sally 126
Roller, Alberta (W) 135
Alberta Whiton 135
Laura A. 135
Leonidas 136
Root, Isabel A. 216
Rose, Rhoda 53
Rossiter, Lydia (W) 60
Rounds, Harriet (Lee) 104
Mabel 104
Una 104
Rowland, Almira (W) 132
Royce, Priscilla (W) 67
Russ, Priscilla 40
Russell, Mary (W) 109
Rutherford, Winnifred 191
Ruthven, Marian 103
Sabastian, Ludisa 67
Sage, Elizabeth C. 213
Sampson, Nancy (W) 86
Sanders, Bertha May 157
Sangster, Ida (W) 105
Saunders, Delia 102
Sophronia 102
Sophronia (W) 102
Stephen 102
Sayer, Mary (W) 22
Sayles, Ida M. 213
Muriel W. 195

Schubert, Elsie 129
Scott, Charlotte M. 153
Searles, Lucretia 72
Sears, Anne 124
Eleanor (Lathrop) 176
Ruth 124
Sarah 48
Seymour, Amelia 62
Augustus S. 61
Clara 62
Henry Cook 62
John Barton 62
Louise 62
Mary 62
Mary (Sherrill) 61
Minnie T. 62
Nellie 61
Polly (W) 64
Sarah 62
Seward, Abigail 57
Sewell, Florence E. (W) 174
Shafer, Martha B. 165
Shaw, Ann (W) 99
Betsy (W) 80
Diantha 80
Harriet (W) 80
Jane (W) 99
John 222
Lucretia 80
Lydia (W) 55
Martha (W) 64
Shepard, Sarah I. 181
Sheridan, Minnie (Bennett) .. 140
Sherman, Julia E. 128
Nancy M. (W) 88
Sherrill, Clarissa (W) 61
Mary 61
Shields, Daisy L. 189
Shipman, Mary F. (W) 145
Simmons, Agnes L. (W) 129
Catherine 130
George H. 130
Leah 33
Mary 102
Mary A. 130
Priscilla 130
Ruth L. 130
Sarah 99
Tamsen (W) 52
Simonds, Sophia 102
Simons, Ada E. 107
Dorothy B. (Swett) 107
Duncan F. 107
Virginius B. 107
Webster Littis 107
Simpson, Mildred 105
Skidmore, Ella F. 172
Slade, Minah Isabel 173
Slater, Lucy A. 216
Smith, Abijah 41, 222, 223
Bertha 107
Douglas 143
Elizabeth 140, 143
Elijah W. 42
Ellen 134
Emily (W) 125
Eunice (Stowell) 42
Hannah 42
Harriet (W) 120
Idella (Anderson) 143
Jane 34
Jeremiah 20
Judith 42
Judith (W) 41
Julianna M. 69
Kate (Ballard) 107
Katherine 107
Mabelle A. 143
Maria (W) 69
Martha 41
Matilda 102
Maxfield M. 143
Patty 41
Phoebe Foy 140
Polly 42
Sarah Ann 101
Stephen 42
Walton 107
William H. 42
Snow, Alice P. (W) 174
Snyder, Carrie 163
Somers, Dora A. 211
Souther, Sarah (W) 73
Speare, Augusta (W) 123
Spencer, Alice W. 141
Antoinette W. 141
Christiana 141
Ellen (W) 92
Mabelle (W) 164
Spicer, Mary (Walker) 68
Phoebe 37
Spielman, Ida E. 165
Sprague, Ann M. 153
Betsy (W) 50
Deborah (W) 51
Elizabeth (W) 32
Lucy (W) 115
Mary (W) 79
Mary L. (W) 115
Persis (W) 52
Susa (W) 50
Squire, Caroline LaB. 62
Dolly (W) 51
Polly (W) 51
Stacks, Alberta (Roller) 135
Standard, Emma E. 162
Starbuck, Alice 88
Dorothy Edyth 88

Starbuck, Evaline (W) 88
Grant N. 88
James 88
Julia 88
Minnie 88
Sarah 88
Theodore W. 88
Theodore Wilbur 88
Walter 88
William 88
William H. 88
Steel, Rhoda (W) 53
Stephens, Jane E. 124
Stetson, Cynthia E. 112
Leah 33
Lucy Ann (W) 78
Stevens, Alice (W) 171
Charles H. 171
Gladys (Richards) 215
Laura I. 214
Marian (Paine) 107
Stillman, Sarah L. (W) 88
Stillson, Elizabeth P. (W) 134
Henry W. 134
Stock, Mary 163
Stocker, Lucy M. (Birge) 109
Stoddard, Anna 98
Diantha 137
Grace M. 74
Hannah 97
Julia A. (W) 97
Lydia 111
Mary 111
Stodder, Abigail (W) 28
Ann 117
Anna 98
Desire 63
Grace (W) 24
Hannah 97
Jeremiah 43
Lois 54
Mary 120
Olive 73
Sarah 39
Stokely, David Allen 169
Julia M. (W) 169
Mountford S., Jr. 169
Richard Whiton 169
Stone, Mary E. 137
Storrs, Alice Mary 103
Arthur H. 103
Elizabeth S. 103
Harriet Grace 103
Harriet (W) 102
Janet 103
William Henry 102
William J. 103
Stowell, Apphia 42
Elijah 42
Stowell, Eunice 42
Florella 42
Hannah 81
Hannah (W) 42
Jason S. 42
Samuel 42
Selinda W. 42
Straffin, Sophia 123
Strong, Sarah (W) 58
Stuart, Jennie M. 166
Studley, Anna 44
Anne 76
Lottie F. 187
Sult, Valois 166
Sumner, Lauretta (Swett) 107
Sutherland, Annie 177
Sutton, Ethel 204
Sweet, Elizabeth A. 175
Swett, Barbara 107
Donald B. 107
Dorothy B. 107
Douglas McQ. 107
Douglas S. 107
Ettie 107
Elizabeth (Ballard) 107
Lauretta L. 107
Margaret A. 107
Mary E. 107
Swift, Abigail B. (W) 99
Taft, Myrnie (Washburn) 142
Tarbell, Lucy (W) 114
Taylor, Mary C. D. (W) 107
Rachel 48
Templeton, Laura V. 135
Thayer, Belle (W) 157
Beryl 157
Edward 157
Eugene 157
Jael (W) 27
Sarah 36
Thistle, Anna 114
Thomas, Helen 155
Lydia (W) 50
Thompson, Abbie (W) 108
Alice 88
Anne M. 88
Carolyn S. 88
Frances 108
Helen 88
Mary Ann (W) 88
May B. 188
Raymond 108
Virginia 108
Willys Duer, Jr. 108
Willys Duer, 3d 108
Thoyse, Idella 148
Tilson, Martha 27
Silence (W) 31
Tirrell, Lavinia (W) 82, 121

Tisdale, Alice 98
——(?) 99
Tomson, Mary (W) 50
Torrey, Sarah J. 113
Tower, Elizabeth (W) 24
Lydia (W) 24
Margaret (W) 28
Martha 28
Mary 31
Sarah 30
Towne, Mary G. (Robbins) .. 110
May Agnes 110
True, Bertha 196
Tuckerman, Jacob E. 217
Lois M. 217
Louis B. 217
Mary E. (Hopkins) 217
M. Katherine 217
Warner H. 217
William C. 217
Turner, Abigail (W) 56
Avis (W) 77
Bessie A. 140
Elizabeth D. (W) 119
Grace (W) 44
Jael (W) 65
Margaret (W) 28
Mary (W) 44, 55
Tuttle, Esther 142
Sophia 125
Van Derwerken, Priscilla (W) 185
Van Wagenen, Katherine 156
Venable, Una 217
Vinal (m. Ozias Whiton) 44
Vining, Abigail (W) 65
Vose, Lydia A. (W) 120
Wagner, Blanche G. 166
Walcott, Harriett (W) 99
Waldo, Ruth E. 142
Walker, Annie 68
Celia 68
Daniel 68
Frank 68
Frederick H. 58, 67
Harriet J. 68
Hartley 68
Hartley Reed 68
Harvey 67
Harvey S. 68
Joanna (W) 67
John 68
John M. 67
Josephine 58, 67
Laura W. 58, 67
Levi 67
Lucretia (W) 101
Lucy 146
Lyman 67
Mary B. 67
Walker, Milo 68
Minerva 68
Paulina 68
Philo 67
Timothy 68
Walsh, Nellie (Newton) 102
Wander, Ella M. (W) 176
Mabel 176
Ward, Caroline 132
Juliana V. 148
Warfield, Alice 101
Charles 101
George 101
Harriet (Flint) 101
John 101
Julia 101
Warner, Fidelia (W) 81
Warren, Blanche 211
Emmeline 214
Harriet 138
Mary (W) 83
Mehitable 24
Washburn, Adaline F. (W).. 142
Arthur 150
Blanche 142
Charles G. 150
Eugene 142
Florence Bell 142
Henry B. 150
James M. W. 150
Jennie 142
Mary 142
Mary E. (W) 150
Miriam 150
Myrnie A. 142
Philip B. 150
Polly (W) 86
Reginald 150
Robert M. 150
William 142
Wasmund, Pearl (Brown) 89
Waters, Abigail (W) 25
Sally 112
Sarah H. 115
Watkins, Angeline (W) 167
Anna 68
Armitage 167
Watson, Almedia 83
Lizzie 121
Lydia A. (W) 120
Wattles, Betsey Ann (W) 42
Caroline Swender 42
Chauncey Lathrop 42
Gurdon Wallace 42
James 42
Mason 42
Walter Tower 42
Watts, Avice McI. 197
Weaver, Della 89

Webster, Blanche C. (Lee) .. 104
Charlotte (W) 104
Welsh, Augustus S. 62
Nellie (Seymour) 61
William T. 62
Wellington, Pauline 124
Wescott, Eleanor 147
Weston, Harriet (Storrs) 103
Lillie C. (W) 135
Wheeden, Anne (Thompson) 88
Wheeler, Jerusha (W) 55
Lena E. 206
White, Antoinette (W) 156
Chloe 116
Cynthia S. (W) 112
Elizabeth (Lathrop) 176
Grace D. 169
Hannah 44
Judith (W) 23
Julia Ann 67
Laura 139
Lydia C. 124
Martha G. (W) 158
Whitehouse, Abigail (Chism) 212
Dorothy 212
Karl C. 212
Whiting, Betty (W) 77
Mary 51, 76, 77
Phoebe (W) 45
Thankful (W) 45, 75
Whitman, Elizabeth (W) 176
Theodore 176
Tirza 176
Whitmore, Betsy (W) 101
Harvey 101
Joseph 101
Sibel M. 58
Whitney, Emily (W) 156
Martha L. 115
Whittemore, Abigail (W) 107
Whittenback, Huldah (W) 80
Wickes, Frances J. (W) 88
Wiggan, Martha (W) 115
Wilbur, Nellie 88
Wilder, Abigail 76
Anna 47
Chloe 53
Isaac 22
Keziah 63
Lydia 120
Mary 52
Mary (W) 22
Olive M. (W) 119
Susanna 54
Susanna (W) 32
Wilkinson, Harriet 90
Wilkie, Ada (Parsons) 69
Williams, Christina 168
Emmeline J. (W) 132
Harriet Alida 174
Mildred (W) 173
Selinda 42
Wilson, Charlotte E. 168
Cora (W) 87
Cynthia (W) 168
Eunice M. 168
Fay P. 168
Fidelia 108
Louisa M. 168
Rebecca 28
Wing, Mary 38
Winsor, Mary 114
Winterton, Bessie M. (W) 169
Shirley Alice 169
Wood, Abigail 50
Mary B. 151
Wolfe, Elizabeth J. 163
Woodbury, Abbie 215
Abbie (Richards) 215
Alice 215
Claire 215
Edith 201
Frank 215
Margaret 215
Mary 215
Woodman, Emily 190
Woodruff, Henry I. 213
Mary (Farnham) 101
Sylvia (Ingersoll) 213
Thomas T. 213
Wyllys I. 213
Woodworth, Esther E. (W) .. 109
Flavel Whiton 109
Helen 109
Helen V. 109
Helen (W) 108
John 108
Woofindale, Ernestine 159
Wormell, Nora (W) 105
Wright, Eunice 63
Lavinia 90
Sally (W) 86
Wyckoff, Alice (W) 177
Dayton T. 177
Edith M. 177
Grace 177
Isabel 177
Wyer, Edith H. 187
Yates, Lauretta S. T. 107
Yeomans, Thankful 143
Young, Mary F. (W) 165
Youngs, Mary E. 209

THE "LOST TRIBES"

It may have been noticed that there are many sons whose names have not been numbered and about whom no (or very few) particulars, other than the fact or date of birth, have been obtained. Several are recorded as having married and "moved west" or "south" or elsewhere.

These sons may have become fathers of many Whitons about whom no information has been received. The early use of various spellings (Whiten, Whiting, Whitten) has also very likely resulted in the failure to obtain particulars about some descendants who should properly be included in a complete Whiton genealogy. Thus there are probably some "Lost Tribes" which should be invited back to the ancestral fold.

To facilitate this return the following index of the names of these sons of earlier generations (to the tenth) has been compiled, with an assignment of numbers according to a system which uses, first, the father's number; next a serial number preceded by the letter "L" (indicating "lost"), followed by lower case letters a, b, c, etc., for grandsons; by aa, bb, cc, etc., for great grandsons, and by aa1, aa2, aa3 (or bb1, bb2, bb3), etc. for more than one son of any grandson.

Some blank pages are bound in, following this index, for the entry of new information about any of these numbers or the regular numbers appearing throughout the book.

WHITON—Sons of Fourth Generation

Number	Name	Page
7-L 1	JOB	27
"-L 2	CORNELIUS	27
8-L 3	ZACCHEUS	27
"-L 4	ALPHEUS	27
10-L 5	JOSEPH	29
"-L 6	WILSON	29
11-L 7	ABEL	30
13-L 8	JOSHUA	31
15-L 9a	JOHN	32
"-L 9b	MATTHEW	32
18-L10	THOMAS	33

WHITON—Sons of Fifth Generation

Number	Name	Page
21-L11	ALPHEUS	35
"-L12	AZARIAH	35
23-L13a	JAMES	36
"-L14	JAMES	36
"-L15	ISAAC	37
"-L16	SAMUEL	37
"-L17	THOMAS	37
24-L18	NATHAN	37
"-L19	ELIJAH	37
"-L20	DANIEL	37
"-L21	SAMUEL	37
"-L22	JACOB	37

Number	Name	Page
25-L23	THOMAS	38
" -L24	JOHN	38
" -L25	EPHRAIM	38
30-L26a	NATHANIEL	43
31-L27a	OZIAS	44
" -L27b	JACOB	44
32-L28a	HOMER	44
33-L29	SAMUEL	45
" -L30	LEMUEL	45
" -L31	PEREZ	45
" -L32	BUCHSA (if a son?)	45
34-L33	ASA	46
" -L34	SOLOMON	46
" -L35	PELEG	46
35-L36	PHILIP	46
" -L37	NATHANIEL	46
" -L38	LEMUEL	46
" -L39	COMFORT	46
38-L40	PETER	48
" -L41	LUTHER	48
40-L42	ISAAC	49
41-L43	ABRAHAM	50
46-L44	JONATHAN	53
" -L45	JOSHUA	53
47-L46	CALEB	54

WHITON—Sons of Sixth Generation

Number	Name	Page
50-L47	JOSIAH (Whiting)	57
51-L48	SAMUEL	58
55-L49	WARREN	61
" -L50a	HENRY	63
56-L51	HOSEA	63
57-L52	CHARLES	64
59-L53	ZENAS LORING (Whiting)	66
" -L54	FRANCIS (Whiting)	66
" -L55	DANIEL (Whiting)	66
63-L56	OTIS CROSBY	71
64-L57	ELEAZER	72
66-L58	SAMUEL	72
" -L59	JARED	72
" -L60	JAMES	72
" -L61	JOHN	72
68-L62	EZEKIEL	74
69-L63	ABEL	74
" -L64	AMOS	74
" -L64a	SIDNEY	74
" -L65	EZEKIEL	74
" -L66	AMBROSE	74
" -L67	LABAN	74
" -L68	ANDREW	74
" -L69	SAMUEL	74
" -L69a	JAMES W.	74
70-L70	CHARLES	75
71-L71	JAMES	75
72-L72	JARED	76
73-L73	BENJAMIN	76

Number	Name	Page
73-L74	AMOS	76
74-L75	ASA	77
77-L76	BELA	78
81-L77	THEODORE	80
" -L78	LEWIS E.	80
83-L79	SAMUEL	82
" -L80	CHRISTOPHER	82
85-L81	BLOSSOM	83
" -L82	ALBERT	83
" -L83	WALTER	83
" -L84	HENRY	83
86-L85	FRANKLIN	83
" -L86	NYMPHAS	83
" -L87	EDWARD	83
87-L88	HENRY	83
88-L89	ELBRIDGE	84
" -L90	JACOB	84

WHITON—Sons of Seventh Generation

Number	Name		Page
90-L 91	LEVI	(Whiting)	85
91-L 92	JOSEPH	(Whiting)	85
" -L 93	JAMES HARVEY	(Whiting)	85
92-L 94	ADONIRAM	(Whiting)	86
" -L 95	LEVI	(Whiting)	86
" -L 96	STEPHEN	(Whiting)	86
93-L 97	EPHRAIM	(Whiting)	86
" -L 98	BENJAMIN	(Whiting)	86
94-L 99	ELLIS	(Whiting)	86
" -L100	JOHN	(Whiting)	86
" -L101	JOSIAH	(Whiting)	86
96-L102a	SAMUEL A.	(Whitten)	87
" -L102b	JOSEPH B.	(Whitten)	87
97-L103	MELZAR	(Whitten)	87
100-L104	ENOCH F.		90
107-L105	DANIEL	(Whiting)	96
" -L106	LYMAN	(Whiting)	96
108-L107	LEONARD		96
" -L108	ANDREW		96
" -L109	CHARLES		96
" -L110	WILLIAM P.		96
" -L111	DAVID		97
110-L112	OSBORN		97
" -L113	JOSIAH		97
" -L114	JACOB		98
112-L115	CHARLES		99
" -L116	DEXTER		99
113-L117	DAVIS		99
114-L118	PEREZ S.		100
" -L119	WINSLOW LEWIS		100
" -L120	DAVIS JACOB		100
115-L121	JOSEPH JACOB	(Whiting)	100
120-L122	ISRAEL		104
" -L123a	HERMAN ABNER		105
" -L123aa1	RALPH ABNER		105
" -L123aa2	LLOYD GARLAND		105
" -L123aa3	LORNE HERMAN		105

Number	Name		Page
120-L123b	CHARLES WASHINGTON		105
121-L124	LUTHER		106
122-L125a	CHARLES ALBIN		108
" -L125b	JOHN M.		108
" -L125c	FRANK HENRY		108
" -L125bb1	JOHN		108
" -L125bb2	WILLIAM		108
" -L125bb3	CHARLES		108
126-L126	JARED		111
127-L127	JOSEPH MERRILL		111
130-L128	EPHRAIM W.		112
131-L129	JAIRUS		113
" -L130	LEWIS		113
132-L131	ALDEN		113
133-L132	EZRA		113
" -L133	LUCIUS C.		113
134-L134	SYLVANUS	(Whiting?)	113
" -L135	NATHAN	(Whiting?)	113
" -L136	THOMAS H. B.	(Whiting?)	113
" -L137	GEORGE D.	(Whiting?)	114
" -L138	ELMER	(Whiting?)	114
135-L139	WILLIAM	(Whiting?)	114
" -L140	WALTER	(Whiting?)	114
136-L141a	GEORGE A.		114
" -L141b	JOHN		114
138-L142a	LEWIS C.		115
" -L142b	EZRA J.		115
" -L143	EBEN		115
140-L144	THOMAS J.		116
142-L145	JOSEPH		117
143-L146	WILLIAM		118
" -L147	EDWIN		118
144-L148	DAVID BRUCE		118
" -L149	THEODORE P.		118
145-L150	CHARLES EASTERBROOK		118
148-L151	HENRY		120
" -L152	KIMBALL		120
" -L153	GEORGE		120
149-L154	GEORGE		121
150-L155	STEPHEN		121
" -L156	ALVAN		121
152-L157	RUSSELL J.		121
153-L158	WALTER B.		122
154-L159	LEONARD A.		122
" -L160	HENRY		122
155-L161	SIMEON D.		122
" -L162	HERBERT J.		122

WHITON—Sons of Eighth Generation

Number	Name		Page
156-L163	HENRY	(Whiting)	123
" -L164	WINSLOW	(Whiting)	123
" -L165	PELHAM	(Whiting)	123
157-L166	IOWA	(Whiting)	123
" -L167	ELISHA	(Whiting)	123
" -L168	JOSEPH	(Whiting)	123
" -L169	JOHN	(Whiting)	123

Number	Name	Page
159-L170	NATHAN ....(Whiting)....	123
" -L171	ALBERT ....(Whiting)....	124
" -L172	EDWARD ....(Whiting)....	124
" -L173	ADONIRAM ....(Whiting)....	124
" -L174	LEAVITT ....(Whiting)....	124
160-L175	BENJAMIN ....(Whiting)....	124
" -L176	JOSIAH ....(Whiting)....	124
161-L177	FRANCIS L. ....(Whitten)....	124
" -L178	HORACE C. ....(Whitten)....	124
" -L179	ORRIN B. ....(Whitten)....	124
162-L180	CHARLES ....(Whitten)....	124
" -L181	LEWIS HOLMES ....(Whitten)....	124
" -L182	ABRAHAM ....(Whitten)....	124
" -L183	RUFUS ROBBINS ....(Whitten)....	124
" -L184	ELISHA COBB ....(Whitten)....	124
" -L185	EDWARD W. ....(Whitten)....	124
163-L186	CHESTER H. ....(Whitten)....	125
" -L187	CHARLES N.	125
" -L188	WILLIAM MELVILLE	125
164-L189aa	LESLIE V.	125
165-L190	JULIAN	126
164-L191	NATHANIEL STARBUCK	126
165-L192	HENRY LYMAN	126
172-L193	CASSIUS	129
173-L194a	JOSEPH LUCAS	130
" -L194b	NORMAN CURTIS	130
175-L195	VICTOR ATWOOD	131
184-L196	HIRAM L.	136
" -L197	EDWIN W.	136
" -L198	HARRY L.	137
" -L199	ALBERT F.	137
" -L200	WILLIAM L.	137
185-L201	NATHAN G.	137
" -L202	ANSON V.	137
186-L203	EDWIN W.	137
" -L204	PIAM A.	137
" -L205	LEROY M.	137
187-L206	GEORGE BRAINARD	137
188-L207	GEORGE FRANCIS	138
189-L208	GEORGE	138
190-L209	WEBSTER	139
" -L210	SHURLEFF	139
194-L211	EDWIN DWIGHT	140
" -L212	CHARLES M.	140
194a-L213	HENRY	141
" -L213a	(Not named)	141
" -L213b	(Not named)	141
" -L213c	WILBUR	141
203-L214	FRANK LOUIS	147
207-L215	LEWIS ....(Whiting)....	151
" -L216	OREN T.	151
" -L217	JOHN B. ....(Whiting)....	151
208-L218	CALEB L.	151
" -L219	JARED	151
213-L220	EZRA THOMAS	153
217-L221	JOHN W.	155
" -L222	CHARLES H.	155
223-L223	MARSHALL LINCOLN	158

Number	Name	Page
225-L224	CHARLES BLOSSOM	158
227-L225	ARTHUR LYMAN	159
228-L226	CHARLES	159
229-L227	EVERETT BRYANT	160

WHITON—Sons of Ninth Generation

Number	Name	Page
233-L228	WALTER LESLIE	161
236a-L229	RAY A.	164
249-L230	AMASA	170
255-L231	CHARLES ALONZO	174
277-L232	ERNEST FOSS	186
282-L233	EDWIN	188